The Smoke and the Sea

THE ISLES SERIES
BOOK ONE

KATIE CROSS

www.katiecrossbooks.com

To Kerri.

Your attention to detail, loyalty to my books, and intense scrutiny makes me a better writer everyday.

Your friendship is one of my greatest treasures. I hope this beautiful new story is worthy of your heart.

Thank you for everything.

The Isles

The Greater Isles:
(listed from greatest to smallest size)

Stenberg
Kapurnick
Narpurra
Siloam

The Lesser Isles

Caledon
Cmeaddon
Calsica
Krackalack

The Chain

This reference does not include the hundreds of smaller, arcane islands in the Chain, along the south to southeast of the general Isles. Because reliable archivists are few and far between, and the arcane wildness prohibits consistent life and trade, the Chain Islands are largely undocumented, unpopulated, and not subject to the same governing laws.

Chapter One

BRITT

I f the ship rocked any harder from side to side, Denerfen would *lose* it. And the last thing Britt needed was a wild, tiny dragon rampaging through a closed vessel with his little snout spraying steam.

"Do not," Britt sang between clenched teeth, "do it. You lock that attitude up and swallow it like smoke."

A hiss replied.

Denerfen, a butterfly-sized emerald dragul, hid in the pouch of her hood. In the layers of fabric, he could fold his delicate wings against his spine and disappear when Stenberg sailors passed by.

Like right now.

"Keep it together, Den," Britt muttered, then smiled as she glided past yet another sailor. Two weeks on this wretched ship, and she'd only seen sailors once a day. Three in the last ten minutes?

Something must be brewing.

She ignored the frisson of paranoia that predicted they might stop her. If they were concerned, the first two sailors would have flung her back to the main servant's hold. This sailor ignored Britt like the others, so she'd take her luck while she had it.

Fortunately, Stenberg sailors weren't interested in island social norms like smiling. Their rigid social system—tyrant, wealthy, soldat, sailor, or scum—prohibited the higher-status islanders from acknowledging the lower-status ones.

As the scent of the sailor passed, so did Denerfen's irritation.

"Thank you, little one," Britt crooned.

Denerfen huffed, and the liquid-hot air rippled along the back of her neck. Britt's fixed smile turned pained. By the sea god Norr, why did steam hurt so much? *Denerfen, you maniacal dragul!* she wanted to shout. *Stop burning me!*

Britt kept the smile plastered on as she continued down the hallway. Instinctively, her right hand slid into her dress. With delicate precision, she wrapped her fingers around a warm, coiled body.

Tesserdress, a female dragul who should have been in the prime of her life, yet her violet scales had turned to lavender the past week. Without more potion, they'd start to shed, signaling the beginning of the end.

Thankfully, Britt had enough Helandalenda potion for a few more weeks.

If Tesserdress died, the entire race of draguls would go with her. Not to mention Britt, all of her family, and probably her island's people. The Greater and Lesser Isles, too, considering the draguls' importance in export and trade. Only Malcolm, Britt's second-oldest brother and Tesserdress' bonded partner, could save the wee thing.

"We'll find Malcolm," Britt whispered. She wrapped her lips around the promise, as if boldness could make it true.

Withholding her scoff hurt as she swallowed the skeptical truth.

How will we find him? her cynical half demanded. *Malcolm was lost in Stenberg, a prisoner of war. As nephew of the General over Kapurnick island, he led the battle against Stenberg near Narpurra island. No Stenberg officer would allow him to live, certainly not His Glory. Malcolm is dead.*

Britt steeled herself. The mean-spirited voice might be true, but better sense could go hang with the rest of the Stenberg islanders. She wouldn't give up while there were draguls and brothers to save.

As she squared her shoulders and rounded the corner, a giant blur startled her.

Acting on instinct, Britt leaped back with a cry, just in time to avoid a collision. Two hands caught her shoulders, preventing her from tipping backward. A Stenberg sailor gripped her arms seconds after his instinct arrested her plummet.

Smoke curled in his eyes like loose clouds. His brooding intensity carried to the slash of lips, square jaw. Scars riddled the edge of his neck like the ends of coiled snake tails.

Whip scars.

For five seconds, Britt stared in mute silence.

Not *just* a sailor.

A soldat.

The highest and most trained of all Stenbergian sailor ranks, the soldats lived, breathed, and slept their profession. Torn from their families at age five, stripped of their names, and reformed into a machine through constant exposure to pain and endless hours of training with all weapons available, the soldats made their reputation and kept it through sheer brawn and ferocity.

Her heart lodged in her throat. She didn't know soldats were on board. She wouldn't have been so . . . careless.

From the back of her neck, Denerfen growled, releasing a hiss of smoke. He vanished into her hood with a squeak. The cool brush of his teeth on the sensitive skin near her spine followed, but she stopped Denerfen from biting her with a cry.

"Not now!"

The soldat's steely eyes narrowed.

Flush with horror, Britt dropped her gaze. Blessed mermaids, why had she spoken? She posed as a traveling servant in order to get on the ship, which made her presence here very suspect. Surely, a soldat wouldn't be too shy to interrogate.

In fact, the opposite.

Islanders rarely made eye contact with soldats, thanks to the soldat reputation for suspicion and ruthless questioning. Her survival hinged on him asking all the wrong things. Any soldat that discovered her family pedigree would take her prisoner and . . . well . . . the rest of that horrific thought didn't bear acknowledgement.

She sealed her lips and closed her eyes. A tremor of fear issued from her right pocket. Britt had to stop herself from setting a hand over Tesserdress's form and reassuring her with a whisper.

Four sailors in as many minutes, and one of them a soldat.

What did it mean?

"You said *not now*?" he asked, hands folded in front of him. His gaze darted around in a mixture of curiosity and suspicion. "Why?"

"Why not?" she immediately countered.

He glowered.

She forced herself to smile.

Her heart slammed in her chest as she held his stare. By the skies, but she'd provide her own rope for a hanging if she kept this up. Stenberg sailors made a game out of forcing servants into errors, then punishing them. She had no reason to believe soldats would behave differently. Eye contact could be an accident, but speaking? There was no escaping that punishment. She couldn't search for Malcolm if her back was shredded to skin bits, could she?

Stenbergians loved their whips.

Denerfen growled again. The percussive sound echoed in the tomb-like silence of the hall. She coughed, poorly hiding her dragul's noise two seconds too late. From the edge of her downturned vision, she noted how the soldat's head cocked to the side in inquisition. His hair, cut to pristine shortness along the sides, gave way to long strands on top. He kept it out of his face in a knotted queue, khaki-colored, like many in Stenberg. All of their thick mops had a reddish sheen.

He drawled, "Did I hear—"

"No."

"No?" Amusement laced his deep tone. "I didn't hear anything?"

Britt silently cursed her temper as she repeated, "No. I didn't hear anything. Perhaps your ears deceive you?"

"My ears? No. But perhaps your eyes . . ."

She squeezed them shut, her nose wrinkling.

He laughed.

Shock brought her gaze open again.

The soldat laughed?

Was it possible?

Legends of soldats ruthless ways and surly temperaments abounded, but none of them included the descriptors of *amused* or *curious* or *unfortunately handsome.* Thankfully, a commotion from down the hall drew his attention at the same moment Denerfen threatened to bite her again. Reaching back, she pretended to itch under her hair, but flicked the dragul deeper into her hood.

Denerfen tumbled over himself and harrumphed.

"Considering I haven't heard anything, I will be on my way," the soldat said before sliding past her, eyes trained ahead. His heavy tread thudded down the hall.

She stood there, frozen for several seconds, before finding the courage to spin around. What drew his attention and removed him so unexpectedly? The dank, narrow hallway, illuminated by arcane-infused, glowing stones that swayed in netted bags hanging from the ceiling, revealed nothing.

"I imagined him, Denerfen," she concluded with firmness. "No soldat could be that handsome, or that . . . normal. Come, my darlings. Let's return to our closet for the rest of the evening."

And, she silently added, *to prepare for the hard parts yet to come.*

Finding Malcolm.

On Stenberg.

Alone.

Chapter Two

HENRIK

An entire ship of jord floating back to the homeland, and only idiots to be found. Henrik ground his molars together.

Sailors scurried around the deck like lost rats. The waves, pitching higher with each passing moment, escorted a coming storm. Slaps of water rumbled against the hull, which hung low in the water. Too heavy.

Fools.

But desperate fools.

Somehow, that seemed forgivable.

Sea spray pitched in white bursts that speckled the sails as Henrik crossed to the side. He used his forearm to wipe the moisture from his forehead, then leaned onto the edge. The churn of the dark sea caught his stomach. Fear, that fever pitch of emotion, was his greatest enemy. He dedicated his life to controlling it.

On the sea, it returned.

His hands pressed against the side of the ship, near a line of neatly-tied knots anchored to the wall. He ignored the way the surging wind whistled through them with a piercing, eerie tune. Amidst the fog ahead, something solid sidled into view. A bank of clouds obscured it again.

He held his breath.

Was that—?

A sailor behind him bellowed, "Land-el!"

Land-el, the common phrase for sailors when they first approached land. Most considered it as sacred as a prayer, dedicated to the Stenberg sea god Norr. A scurry of voices echoed the same cry, rippling in a swell of shouts.

"Land-el!"

"Thank Norr," Ossian, captain of the ship, muttered as he passed behind him. "Can't wait to throw your ugly carcass overboard and never see you again. You smell as foul as the draguldung jord I'm carrying in my ship and you frighten my sailors."

Henrik grinned.

He'd miss Ossian.

A little.

Bells chimed in a flowing tinkle. The delicate song came from a sheet of miniature bells the sailors hung from a mast when land appeared. Prayers to the sea god for a safe landing, and an acknowledgment of their return.

Henrik fought not to roll his eyes.

Inky thunderheads chased the ship, racing closer with webs of lightning. The rocking of the boat, bucking up and down, lurched his stomach. He was grateful not to be near the bags of jord, thick with the tang of rot and refuse. They made him itch.

Henrik swallowed acid for the tenth time that day. Sailors would gape if an ironclad soldier vomited over the side, and the seasick reputation would follow him back into Stenberg. No soldier would be caught weaker than waves.

He shoved away from the side and headed toward the interior. He'd be in the way here. Besides, they were an hour from land. He'd be the first off this blasted ship, if he had anything to say about it.

Sailors ignored him, which he preferred. Two of the new sailors had never worked directly with a soldier until this leg of the journey. They tried to talk to him, but the other sailors stopped them.

As he descended the ladder—cautiously, because the ship rolled yet again—his mind edged to the woman in the hallway. A servant, surely. Why had she wandered that hall alone? He meant to ask, but something had lodged in his throat. He found himself saying something inane.

Had she really been a servant? Her eyes had been too healthy. She lacked the desperation of the lower workers, bound for Stenberg from Narpurra, who tended to send slaves instead of fruit in a pinch. Wealthy Stenberg islanders were too happy to take the forced labor, prior trade prohibitions notwithstanding.

Frowning, he strode toward his cabin, a thin room with a straw mattress on the floor and a round glass window that opened from within. The hints of fresh air had saved him from embarrassing himself many times. A bucket, which he kept strictly clean, filled the corner. On the opposite side stood his pack, perpetually put together and tidy.

Inside the cabin, he glanced around, the door closing behind him. Reluctantly, he thought of the woman again. What had prevented him from stopping her? Servants weren't allowed to roam, nor was it wise. Particularly a woman as young and pretty as her. He knew what stopped him. Her surprise, which morphed to mild irritation.

Irritation.

What servant had the courage to be blatantly irritated by a soldat?

She stirred a memory to life, reigniting the terror of a scream. *Selma!* the panicked recollection called. *Your mama's name is Selma!*

Her shrill voice faded with a sharp exhalation. Every day Henrik tugged on the memory. Every day he replayed it and set it aside. Almost thirty years after it happened, the recollection mattered. He never doubted its veracity. Today of all days, it might matter most.

After the soldats tore him away from his mother at five years old, he'd promised himself two things.

Never forget.

Find her.

Henrik blinked out of the mess with a shake of his head. A year-long campaign across islands securing their latest jord shipment, fulfilling yearly contracts with imports and exports, as well as surveying His Glory's holdings—or desired holdings—ended in one hour.

No more hopping ship to ship. No more writing letters and finding a worthy messenger. No more long dinners with windy captain Ossian or assessments of strategic risks for His Glory to peruse in case of further invasions.

Jord, Henrik, soldat Captain Oliver had said. *Stenberg needs jord like we need air. Without it, we'll starve. The workers are already hungry. They'll begin to die if you don't keep the steady supply. Our food grows lackluster. The mainland makes the pressure worse, what with the tempestuous relationship between His Glory and the Lordlady. Bring us jord to bury our seeds in, grow our plants, and keep our people alive.*

"I brought your jord," Henrik muttered.

Sort of.

The precious compost, rich in minerals, crumbled like black bread in his hands. It cost more than gems, minerals, or precious cloth. Some Stenberg islanders would give their children in exchange for several bags of the jord.

Many did.

Like his parents.

Or not, he immediately thought, recalling Selma's final scream in his boyhood. *Your mama's name is Selma!*

She must have shamed herself eternally for making a display, which meant she hadn't wanted to part with him. Other Stenberg mothers planned to give their sons to His Glory from birth and proudly turned them over to the training soldats. Not his.

It meant something.

It had to.

When the soldats darkened a doorstep, no one argued. Children disappeared. Their name and pedigree vanished. They huddled in half-frozen groups for weeks on end, tested to the limits of their endurance, and awaited death. Nothing as merciful as death had been granted to Henrik, nor his brother-in-arms, Einar.

Henrik hiked the pack onto his back. At the end of his year-long service, His Glory had promised Henrik two weeks. Two weeks of silence in a bungalow off the beach. Two weeks to dig his toes into firm sand and stand still. Two weeks where neither Captain Oliver nor Captain Arvid could require an accounting of every minute. Such freedom was a rare offer, and one he'd planned on every day since he left a year ago.

Two weeks to find his mother.

The door slammed behind him.

Chapter Three

BRITT

Agitated waves, which the Stenbergians called *frenzies*, rocked the ship as they pulled into port, drawing sailors to the bow and sails.

Wind whistled through Britt's partially-opened porthole, filling her ears with the sensation of stuffed cotton. She tucked farther into her hood, standing just inside the tiny locker where she hid, and sucked in a salty breath through her nose.

"Denerfen," she whispered, shoulders expanding, "it's time. Bite me. Go easy, eh? Nothing wild. We just need to get off the ship."

Weight shifted near her spine, preceding the cool caress of pearly teeth and the warm purl of a breath. She lifted her right cheek in an early wince, but the tension didn't prepare her for the sharp sting. Heat gathered in a spiral on her neck and rippled through her skin, down her arms. The languid crawl flowed over her scalp in a tingling cascade.

One breath at a time, her body disappeared. Denerfen plunged into her hood.

The moment her toes vanished, she darted into action. Thanks to a little bit of dragul venom—one of the rarest luxuries in the Isles—she had about fifteen minutes to navigate off the ship, dodge through a market, and run as far from the dock as she could manage before her body became visible again.

The empty hall led to the ascending ladder that climbed onto the deck. Freedom from her salty confines awaited, but it wouldn't be easy. Bangs and whistles and shouts from below meant the sailors planned to unload the jord quickly. Better to beat the storm.

Three steps from the ladder, the door flung open. She hid a gasp, pressed her back to the wall. Sailors poured down the ladder, shouting obscenities, cursing the land, the sky. One of the sailors brushed the edge of her sleeve as he strode away. She held her breath as he passed, blessedly not registering her presence.

Scampering, she raced up the ladder.

Chaos ruled on the main deck, but with orders to keep them occupied, no sailor interrupted her path. Britt scuttled out of the way of a man carrying ropes, another bellowing at a sailor tangled above, and dodged a lowering bag of cargo.

Less than a minute later, she slipped down the dock, barefoot, heart racing, breath thready. Arcane hummed in her veins with the viscous feeling of flowing, hot oil. She had twelve minutes before the chills set in. She'd need to find a place to hide before emerging.

Halfway to freedom, she almost leaped into the water from sheer surprise.

Striding ahead of her, wearing a familiar set of black leather gauntlets and shoulder armor, was the soldat from earlier. His high chin canvassed the area. As she slowed, he stopped in the middle of the dock and glanced back. His low-slung, hooded gaze glittered with questions, and his flared nostrils sent cold terror into her heart like a spike.

He sensed her.

Swallowing, Britt mimicked his frozen stance. Could soldats detect the effects of dragul venom? Wild rumors claimed that even a nescient soldat could smell the venom at work. She, a dragul keeper, never could. It seemed too ludicrous to believe that a soldat could do what a dragul-bonded keeper could not.

From behind her, a shout started, clearly aimed at the soldat.

"Aye! Where are you—"

Seeing the dangerous glare, the sailor shut up as quickly as he spoke. The foolish man turned and fled. For that moment, a flicker of uncertainty registered in the soldat's gaze. Britt grew roots to the dock as his attention returned to the spot where she stood.

He stared right *at* her.

Those incandescently blue eyes held onto hers. They must have, because his stare stirred the marrow of every bone in her body. His voice, stunned but soft, replayed in memory. This soldat, already so dangerous, had just become lethal.

Stenberg lingered in the distance. The smoky chimneys, cobblestone hills, splashing wharf, and smell of burnt oil beckoned with the slimmest margin of hope she'd ever encountered. To come this far, and fail because of a soldat?

Not happening.

An open pier led the way to firm ground. To freedom.

The soldat's locked muscles released as he half-spun away, angling his gaze farther to the right. His body twisted with the movement, and all her shock fled. Taking her final chance, Britt dodged around him and raced off.

He shouted, but the reverberations of his following feet didn't chase.

She didn't look back.

STENBERG.

What a depressing place.

Sealstone occupied most of her view. The strange rock was native to the island, composed of various gray hues speckled with black blotches, like the skin of the fat seals that lived on the south-western Chain Islands. The tyrant, His Glory, claimed that seal-stone prevented the arcane from being used against Stenberg.

No arcane in Stenberg, came the reports. *It doesn't work there.*

Walls, roads, towers formed an endless sea of stone buildings with little variation from wood or greenery. Stenberg simply didn't have much soil, like the rich islands of her home, Kapurnick. What little existed resembled sand instead of mulch, creating the necessity of importing jord.

Britt hurried past linens flapping above tables that lined the port road. Stenberg islanders stood beneath, bedraggled, sunstained, and coarse. They shouted at each other, or nothing, or the sea. As Britt raced away from the soldat, the ship, and all ties to who she used to be, she tried to escape.

Their cries followed at her heels, nipping like dogs.

"Goat legs!"

"Pouches."

"Don't forget your ale!"

Britt raced up the filthy hillside street, away from the crowded port and toward an outer ring of the famous Stenbergian market. When space grew between the stalls, and the crush of people faded, she slid into a narrow alley between two buildings, pressed her spine to the wall, and breathed deep.

That was close.

The uncomfortable prickling of venom had ebbed during her sprint, but tremors replaced the feeling. A precursor to the true emergence out of the venom. She shivered in languid waves, teeth rattling. Withdrawal was a harried experience, but it wouldn't be too difficult this time. Denerfen hadn't loaded much into his bite.

Britt clutched her arms over her chest and glanced down.

Her sandals appeared.

"Not yet!" she whispered. "Denerfen, it should have lasted longer!"

He grunted. His rough, warm tongue licked the back of her neck. She would have pet his scaly spine, but kept her arms locked against her chest. Soon, trembling would overtake her body and she'd be truly helpless as she re-emerged into sight.

The clack of wooden wheels crossed the paved road outside the alley, loud in her sensitive ears. Everything heightened as the venom faded. Panic threatened to consume her, but she forced it away. Downright dangerous for a Kapurnickkian dragul keeper to emerge from the venom in Stenberg, of all places.

Britt dropped to her bottom, pulled her knees into her chest, and yanked her hood over her face. Emerging was the most vulnerable state. The withdrawal of the invisibility created a short span of time with bone-deep weariness and shivers. The reversal occurred from the feet up. Instead of the warmth, ice slaked her veins. It tumbled through, worsening her chills. She clenched her jaw to keep it from rattling and tucked herself into a tighter ball.

Denerfen rubbed his neck along hers, snagging the snowy hairs curling near her spine. He'd track her changing smells. The nature of his sounds would alert her if danger appeared. Her eyes screwed shut.

"I-i-it's fine," she whispered to Tesserdress, though she couldn't reach down to touch her. "It'll . . . s-s-s-top soon."

The sound of approaching footsteps sent another shiver through her. Too weak to lift her head and check who might be there, and vaguely aware that she might be half visible, she didn't move.

One pair of footsteps passed by . . . and another one. The second stopped.

A shadow fell over her.

Denerfen hissed.

"Those are Kapurnickkian sandals," said a small, astonished voice in native Kapurnickkian.

The islanders who inhabited the hundreds of islands of the Greater and Lesser Isles spoke the same tongue, Elestrian. But the greater islands—Kapurnick, Stenberg, Siloam, and Narpurra—hosted home languages. They were spoken so rarely they'd started to die away.

In general, the population of the Isles possessed few physical similarities. Light hair, dark eyes, pale skin, broad shoulders, none of it held consistently to any tract of land. Only the manner of speaking.

Isle people held their language as an extension of soul and history. Chattering words, singsong flows, and sheer depth gave away heritage far more than visible attributes. Words were as sacred as jord, or blood, or soul. Napurra slew people who used their native words without permission.

Hope flooded her. If someone spoke native Kapurnickkian, they'd know about emerging. Britt wrenched her head to the side. A child peered at her, likely no older than nine or ten. She didn't know children's ages well at first glance. Her knees washed into legs, revealing the lower part of her linen skirt and bare ankles. Though her legs stopped knocking together, her arms rattled against her ribs.

The child hissed, summoning the second pair of feet.

"Philip," the first cried. "It's a Kapurnickkian dragul keeper!"

Britt attempted to speak as another body cast a shadow on her. Beyond them, a commotion rose from the marketplace. Bells tinkled and an angry man brayed like a donkey. Shouting voices gave way to thudding fists.

"It *is* a Kapurnickkian!" the second child breathed, only slightly taller than the first. Britt's waist appeared. The swirling cold ebbed from her lower half. "It's dragul venom. She's emerging."

"What's a Kapurnickkian doing here?"

"Don't know, but we gotta keep her safe. Stand there."

Her heart elevated. Sweet boys! As they scrambled to shield her from view, commotion increased. Other people sprinted past, pursued by shouts. The repeating clink of marching sailors came from farther away.

As the seconds ticked away, coolness curled away from her elbows, her arms. The roving release traveled up her neck, trailing warmth in its wake. The oldest boy turned, glancing over his shoulder to check on her, and issued a cry.

"She's done!"

Their wide eyes stared at her.

"What're you doing here?" the youngest whispered. He had rounded cheeks and a long neck, with a dark complexion. Her teeth stopped chattering as the venom dissipated. The feeling of a wrung rag permeated her body. A needle would be too heavy to lift right now.

"I'll tell you everything." She managed a weak smile. "But not here. Do you have somewhere I can hide?"

As the boys conferred, their heads bent together. Britt's spastic fits and spurts slowed, indicating a near completion. Only her arms trembled. Within a minute or two, the exhaustion would sweep out of her, and she'd recover entirely.

The taller one nodded.

"We know a place."

A minute later, Britt stole through the shadows in their wake. The nimble boys dodged past structures made of bamboo poles, thick white canvas, and doused fires. Behind the manicured market stalls hid an entire city of people. Shadowlands, they called it. Prior slaves, set free, but unable to afford passage home. Orphans. Hidden criminals. Not just Stenbergians, but Kapurnickkians, Caledonians, Narpurrans, and Calsicans.

A blur of languages wove a distinct tapestry she pretended not to notice. Realistically, she *shouldn't* be able to separate the individual words, nuance, and tone, but General Helsing taught her sacred and forbidden languages since she was a little girl.

Britt kept her hood on, attempting to track where she followed the two boys. By whose grace did she stumble on these helpers?

Not the Stenbergian god of the sea, Norr.

Surely not.

His Glory, supposedly the direct son of Norr and leader of the Stenberg islands, would as soon string her up by the end of a whip as send her aid. She *could* use Norr's temple to orient herself, however. It loomed higher than all buildings, set on the tallest hill, where it jutted into the air with impressive girth and height. The black-and-gray sealstone sprinkled the sides with shadow.

If the Stenbergians had perfected anything, stonework was it. Their bulwark structures dominated landscape and sky and impressed isles folk and mainlanders alike.

Glimmering gold paint created tiny sunbursts around open windows, dazzling in the sunshine. Servants risked their life to paint the exterior wall in criminal detail. Ivory drapes fluttered in the breeze brought by the storm, a symbol of His Glory's purity.

She turned her study away from the Temple. A crash of incoming thunder foretold greater surges, and her concern for shelter intensified. Stalls clattered under the bursts, and islanders called out as they pulled goods to higher, safer ground. Such a close sea would wreak mighty havoc on the market, even built around steep hills.

Within minutes of following the scampering boys, understanding her location proved to be futile. She kept track of His Glory's Temple, and that alone. The maze of tents, abandoned fire pits, and piles of discarded coal proved useless. The Shadowlands lived up to their prestige. When the boys veered left and set the Temple at their backs, she breathed more freely.

The trodden footpaths gave way to stone roads. Stenberg had so little growable soil on its rocky face that mud didn't slick the space between cracks. No growing things here. The Stenbergians would steal the jord in which a weed sprouted and slap it into their own planters, where they coaxed lackluster vegetables and fruits to grow. What little dirt existed beneath the hills of stonework was pale, bleached, and sandy.

"Where are we going?" she whispered.

"Somewhere safe," the youngest said over his shoulder.

Wind whipped past, nearly removing her hood. She bit back a retort of, *do you know what you're doing*? and kept a hand over her pocket instead. Tesserdress shuddered under her touch, sighing a pocket of sultry air onto Britt's thigh. In her hood, Denerfen would be fine. She felt him burrow deeper, underneath the safety of the fabric.

She wouldn't tell the boys about her bounty, though her emergence indicated at least one dragul. Kapurnickkian or not, if they knew she carried two venom-biters, the draguls' lives would be in danger. The boys scampered wordlessly, winding through a hidden world locked behind industry.

Miniature pig bones littered the ground as fat raindrops splatted the stone earth. Beyond the carefully-trod paths, the sound of wooden wagons and shouting merchants faded as Stenbergians scrambled for shelter.

Against a blast of wind, the older boy pointed to a structure at the edge of an enclosure. They stood just outside a stone fence, peering through a small hole. Wind blasted his loose shirt, but he didn't seem to notice. The dilapidated building had gaps between wooden boards and a questionable, sagging roof. Beyond it, through a rocky landscape, was another cottage, dark and abandoned.

"The cottage is empty, but I wouldn't recommend hiding in there, just in case." The oldest smiled with pride. "You'll be fine in the shed. I slept in it last night!"

Britt called over the gale, "Who lives here?"

He shrugged. "Don't go in the cottage," he shouted, "Stay in the garden. You'll be safe out there until morning."

She eyed the shed, the broiling sky, and the boy. With his eager brow raised, she managed a grateful smile.

"Thank you!"

She didn't have the heart to show her terror. The arrival of the rain escorted her inside. A shed would be preferable to the stinging raindrops assaulting her arms. They waved her through the hole, around a rock-strewn yard, and to the shed. The tall fence provided shelter from the road and surrounding houses. Not that anyone here would be outside in a building tempest of this magnitude.

The door to the shack groaned open. Surprisingly, a dry spot of ground existed in the exact middle, though rain collected around the edges. The younger boy scratched the side of his head where a clump of dirt tied up his nappy curls.

"Might get wet," he called over the thrumming rain, "but it's better than being in the street."

Oh, how true.

"It's exactly what I wanted. Thank you! What are your names?"

"Philip." The taller jabbed a thumb at the other. "Mace."

"How long have you been in Stenberg?"

"Always."

"But—"

"Mum is Kapurnickkian," Philip said. "She was enslaved, now she works, but they don't pay her much. The Stenbergians don't know about us. We can't afford to sail home, so we're stuck."

Her mouth dropped. Years ago, the slave trade had been active between Kapurnick, Stenberg, Siloam, Narpurra, and other islands, but agreements initiated by General Helsing from Kapurnick had stopped the selling of human life. Except for Narpurra, who seemed to leave no trace and boasted an underground market for slaves to this day.

With the treaty agreement between islands, enslaved people had become employed servants, but wages were poor. Too low to survive and save resources to cross the ocean and return home, though General Helsing had tried to help the native Kapurnickkians return.

A crescendo of thunder swelled over the island. Despite the thrumming rain, Britt thought she heard breakers on the ocean, crashing into Stenberg with the vengeance of a livid god. Perhaps she brought her own deities with requital and water.

Philip eyed the door. "Gotta go!"

He dashed into the maelstrom. Britt started after them, but they disappeared into the gray blur of rain sheets.

Shocked by the speed of their departure, Britt could only blink at first. Water sprayed onto her cheeks. The pants she wore beneath her dress clung to her ankles. A reverberating loneliness replaced her momentary friends. Twenty minutes on the island, and all her preconceptions had disappeared.

"I'm sorry, Tess," she whispered, though Tesserdress wouldn't hear her over the sky racket. "I thought . . ."

She didn't finish that.

She didn't know what she thought.

Britt spun on the spot. There wasn't room to step, anyway. Crates lined the back wall, as well as pickaxes for prying up stones, a giant basin for cement mixing, and a stack of warped boards. Stenbergians prized wood almost as much as jord.

Almost.

Despite the warmth of the Stenbergian isles, the chilly rain swamped her from the shoulders to toes. Her fingers felt cool when she reached into her hood. Denerfen hissed and recoiled from her touch.

Quickly, Britt withdrew them.

"Sorry. My hands are cold."

Denerfen huffed.

Tesserdress shuffled around Britt's pocket, scooted into a ball, then settled.

Britt set her hands on her hips as she studied her surroundings. As General Helsing's adopted daughter, luxury was a rarity. The General had Britt camping in the sand, forming her own huts, drinking rainwater she collected with woven fronds, and cutting fruit off high-reaching trees since she'd turned five. Not to mention her two rambunctious, stubborn older brothers, Pedr and Malcolm. She'd expected not to sleep at all her first night at Stenberg, but to roam until she had a general lay of the island. People always roamed at night, if you could find shadows to hide in.

The storm wiped the wisdom of that possibility out.

She settled her back against a crate, adjusted her cape and skirt and the pants underneath her skirt in such a manner that Denerfen, Tesserdress, and she could rest. From her bag, she withdrew a handful of thin glass flutes, stoppered with small bits of cork at the top. Three of the vials were supremely precious. A Kapurnickkian potion more legend than reality.

Tollybryck.

Each potion flute was a shade of orange, starting with a hue so pale it more closely resembled yellow. It progressed to marmalade and burnt sunshine. The infamous pirate Burning Beard had gifted them to her before departing Kapurnickkian shores a few months prior. Those vials she would use only in case of extreme life or death. They were healing potions.

The other?

Life for Tess.

A rag wrapped the first flute, as thick as her thumb and long as her hand. Inside, a rose-colored potion sloshed around. Helandalenda. The dragul-only fortifying potion would extend Tesserdress' miserable existence without Malcolm until Britt could find him. The trip to Stenberg had taken entirely too much time. Captain Ossian had a reputation for quick sailing, but with a load of jord on board, that meant plenty of precaution had been taken for safety.

The soldat proved that.

Britt settled Tesserdress on her tented skirt. While the dragul shifted around, purring and squeaking at Denerfen, who mosied down Britt's arm, Britt uncorked the Helandalenda. She touched the tip of her finger to the top, and withdrew it. A drop clung to her skin. Tesserdress hurried over, hastening with an eager chirp, and licked the potion free. Britt corked it, wrapped it, and set it carefully inside her bag.

"We have a few weeks, Tess." She traced the tip of her fingers down Tesserdress' neck and past her tiny wings. "We'll find him."

Britt slumped against the wall. Damp clothes, unknown island, rampaging storm, and no dinner in sight. Not ideal, but might have been worse. With her head leaning against a crate, and her draguls safely curled together on her lap, tussling lightly, she closed her eyes. The draguls settled. Tesserdress in her cozy pocket, Denerfen coiled around Britt's neck.

Sleep claimed her.

Chapter Four

HENRIK

Oliver, First Captain of His Glory's soldats, had been the only father figure Henrik had ever known.

Oliver held a wry sort of affection for most of his soldats, but Henrik had always been a silent favorite. The Captain didn't say much, but carried a legendary reputation for his grappling ability, for which many soldats gauged strength, professionalism, and power.

New soldats who entered the force always remarked on Oliver's tight-lipped strain. The fools made bets on when Oliver would smile, if ever. Anyone voting in favor of Oliver showing amusement lost.

Always.

They often disappeared, too.

Any old codger that survived to sixty-eight years of age as a soldat Captain deserved respect, even if his gruff style and obeisance to His Glory was irritating.

Henrik set a paper on top of Oliver's barren desk. Grids, numbers, words cluttered drawn boxes in gray ink. The jord measurements and reported numbers he'd scripted in green, to help them stand out for His Glory.

"As His Glory requested," he said. "The final shipment of jord is in the harbor and unloading is underway." He frowned, glancing outside. "Or it will be soon, once the sea settles. A gale's blowing in."

Oliver eyed the ledger of facts, weights, currency exchanged, and a few . . . interviews . . . conducted in His Glory's name. Lesser isles had a penchant of quantifying export freight short of promised contracts. The presence of a soldat dramatically decreased fraud in the isles, and thus, bloodshed when His Glory punished the smaller chains for lying.

War was expensive, and so was life.

Life required food.

Food required jord.

The chain of existence in the Isles never wavered.

Oliver barely blinked after surveying the reports. No *welcome home* or *well done soldat* or *congratulations on a productive year in the isles well accomplished.* Not that Henrik had expected any.

"Confirmed receipt," Oliver stated. "You're dismissed until the morning." He returned to his paperwork. Hints of stubble darkened his cheeks. The top of his head, clean shaved, had a blunt appearance as the storm whisked sunshine away.

"Sir?" Henrik asked.

Oliver lifted his gaze. "Yes?"

"At my final collection point for the jord in Kapurnick, rumors swirled about a battle between Captain Arvid and Kapurnickkian sailors, near Narpurra."

"Yes."

"Did something happen?"

The question was foolish, because Henrik already knew the answer. Kapurnick's infamous General Helsing defended the island nation of Narpurra against His Glory's Stenbergian sailors. Kapurnick stepped in to help Narpurra, of all places, which had gossipers wagging. Why would they bother? Narpurra's cutthroat and brutal reputation normally put them at odds against straight-laced Kapurnick, particularly General Helsing.

Rumors swirled, as they always did, never quite clear of the results.

Captain Oliver's nostrils flared slightly, then calmed. "Yes. Captain Arvid went to settle a dispute on Narpurra and Kapurnickkian sailors were there. A battle resulted."

"Is Captain Arvid okay?"

"Information is pending."

Henrik attempted to absorb that information without change of expression, but horror sank like a stone in his chest.

Pending meant lost at sea.

Dead.

The Second Captain of His Glory's soldats—gone. Only two Captains existed to oversee the soldats and overall military strategy. If something happened to Captain Arvid, which seemed unfathomable for such a large, talented man, that left Oliver standing alone in his leadership of thirty-three highly decorated and ambitious men.

Captain Arvid had been dependable. An admirable leader, acting from the frontlines. Obliging, when he could be, but stern with the task of caring for Stenberg and her trade. He had an affable exterior, and was a quiet observer of the world. He lacked Atticus' staunch reverence for His Glory, but that hadn't stopped Arvid from gaining the leadership position.

The devastating blow hit Henrik in the chest.

"Sir, I—"

"Search attempts are ongoing," Oliver said, speaking over Henrik's attempt to impart condolences. "I will update you if there is information that pertains to you. As it stands, we must assume that Captain Arvid is dead."

"Yes, sir."

Oliver eyed him. "Convenient that you should have returned from your reefer duty at the same time."

"Sir?"

Oliver rolled his eyes, a gesture more twitch than drama. "Assuming Captain Arvid isn't found, which appears most likely at this point, there will be a requirement for the Second Captain of His Glory's soldats. You and one other have been appointed the responsibility of reefer, which enables you for the position of Second Captain."

Such a realization wasn't new. Henrik went into his year-long reefer duties knowing it enabled a greater promotion. The reefer slot consisted of a one-year rotation on the seas, gathering the export bounty, delivering imports, and returning with jord. He hadn't dreamed such an opportunity would open this quickly.

"Yes, sir."

"It's between you and Harald." He shuffled through the paperwork, glancing idly at it. "The two of you will be up for consideration as soon as we confirm Captain Arvid is lost and have his memorial."

"But what about Hampus, sir?"

"Hampus died three months ago."

"Shite," he muttered. "Sir, I had no idea."

With the cold precision of a soldat Captain, he said, "I know. I'll relay your report to His Glory in the morning. You're dismissed. Report at first light." Oliver cast a wary eye to the window. "Or after the storm clears."

Henrik froze.

"At first light, sir?"

Oliver, sensing his undertone, lifted an eyebrow.

"Is there a problem, soldat?"

"At the beginning of the contract, His Glory promised a two week leave after the final jord delivery."

A muscle at the bend of Oliver' square jaw flexed, though his thin lips gave no hint of emotion. He lifted his chin ever-so-slightly, and lamplight cast a glow on the few shaven gray hairs. The five Captains in His Glory's service distinguished themselves by cropping their hair close. Henrik, in keeping with regular soldats, skimmed the sides short, and left the top long.

"You want two weeks of vacation?" Oliver asked with a care-fully controlled tone.

Henrik hid a surge of annoyance. The careful wording was a game designed to trap. *Desire* shouldn't enter the heart of a soldat, unless it revolved around bettering Stenberg's presence in the Isles.

"It was promised, Captain."

Oliver's lashes tightened around a locked and intense gaze. "The jord is in port on a ship."

"Yes, sir."

"There's a storm." Oliver tilted his head to the window. "A bad one. They'll be lucky to get the sailors off of the ship in time, never mind the hundreds of pounds of jord in the hulls."

"Sir?"

"Your jord isn't delivered until it's in His Glory's hands, and approved of for quality," Oliver snapped. "If that ship doesn't survive the swells and the jord isn't delivered, your mission isn't complete. If the foolish sailors managed to secure it in time, you might be in luck. If that's the case, you may have a two-day leave to get your cottage back in order. As far as I'm aware, your residence on the soldat grounds has not been disturbed. You should need only an hour, but I will give you two days."

Disbelief swelled, thick as the building storm. The five Captains that worked directly with His Glory every day, of which only two were soldats, should expect such a twist of terms. But not the soldats themselves. Promises were ironclad contracts. The Oliver of a year ago had supported the soldats directly. He wouldn't have changed meanings to deprive a soldat of something he'd earned. It spoke to turbulent waters.

Unable to help it, Henrik said, "Sir—"

"I know you aren't questioning me, soldat."

The hard words curved with implication and warning.

Henrik licked his bottom lip, fighting a surge of rage and helplessness. His life had never been his own to live. Not once. He grew up an asset of His Glory and that is how he would die. Trembling in the exposed cold as a child taught him the power of acceptance in the face of unfairness.

But sometimes, injustice rankled.

"Of course not, Captain. I would never question you."

Oliver tossed his eyes to the door. Understanding the implied command, Henrik lowered his chin and turned to leave.

Two days.

He had two days to dive into the Archives and search for Selma without drawing attention to his search, which was all but impossible.

Captain Oliver called after him.

"Soldat?"

Henrik paused in the doorway.

"His Glory has declared the start of a cleansing. Last night, he did an induction ceremony in the Temple and called the storm to begin the ritual. This will be a twenty day run of ritualistic cleansing in preparation for potential hostilities from the mainland. You know what that means."

Henrik closed his eyes in disbelief.

This had to be a joke.

A terrible, dirty prank.

Perhaps he'd overestimated the sea god. Norr didn't care about justice. Or Henrik had underestimated the troubles in Stenberg. Having been gone for a year, he felt blind. Their struggles might be great, indeed, for His Glory to call for a cleansing.

"Understood, Captain." Henrik paused, considered the wisdom in his surfacing question, and decided to ask despite the risk of irritating Oliver further. "Is something wrong, sir?"

Oliver blew a steady breath through his nose. One might call it a stabilizer, but it was thoughtful.

"Many things are wrong. Pressure comes from the mainland."

"Over what?"

"Doesn't matter," he barked. "We need more jord—more than Kapurnick is sending. Their shipments have been less and less year over year. Either they're holding back, the draguls are dying, or they've formed an alliance with the mainland, who is taking our jord. His Glory . . ."

Commotion outside the office stalled his response. Oliver's gaze narrowed. He cut short the conversation with a slice of his hand.

"Report in the morning, soldat, or at first storm clearing. Leave."

Three men strode past two soldat guards and into Oliver's office. The other Captains of His Glory. Two of them were sailors. The final one, Ingemar, was a voted islander representative and reputed to be the right hand of His Glory. Serious lines creased his expression.

Henrik studied them as they jostled by with careless regard, all of them grim-faced and hollow-cheeked. They stood like three giant cranes about to do battle, all beady eyes and pecking beaks as they clustered around Oliver's desk. One of them, the Third Captain of His Glory, appeared pale as he clutched a letter.

An update on Captain Arvid, no doubt.

Understanding when it was time to be invisible, Henrik slipped into the hallway without another word. He carried his frustration with him, the way all soldats had been trained for since capture.

You take that emotion.

You bury it deep.

You open it on the battlefield.

The door shut as he departed.

HENRIK BENT his head to the wind, welcoming the fighting elements. Pushing against something helped ease the urge to shout. He was soldat. He maintained control at all times.

Life had deserted the previously bustling market by the time he headed to his boarded up home in the soldat's quarters, along the north edge of what locals called the Quarter, where sailors and soldats lived. Sailors resided in the blue-ceilinged barracks that were little more than cobbled together rooms. Soldats, thanks to their higher rank and lifelong service, received private cottages with stone fences in a separately maintained portion of the Quarter. Modest, but quiet, which is what most of them desired.

His would be cold, dusty, and filled with miniature pig carcasses after a year, but he wouldn't be on a rolling, pitching ship filled with heavy jord and stinking sailors.

A cleansing, he thought, shaking his head.

What were the odds?

During a cleansing, any islander with a history of spilled blood or political resistance was not allowed to approach any building in which His Glory might be found. The Temple, the Armory, the Library, and the Archives.

Not only had Henrik lost his two weeks of downtime, but also the ability to search for his lost mother. The Sisters of Stenberg, women sworn to a lifetime of internal purity and service to His Glory, ran the Library and the Archives. During a cleansing, they refused male entrants, allowing only women and scholars to enter. He'd never pass as a scholar, though the idea had merit.

Shite luck.

Lightning streaked the sky as Henrik wound through the low court of the Quarter, held in by a perimeter of stone, and watched over by a constant guard. Henrik nodded to the old man in the wings, a building with a wide window and a floor that dropped out beneath the guard to allow quick access to a descending ladder.

Old Man, they called him. No one knew his real name, and no soldat cared enough to find out.

Seeing Henrik, Old Man looked surprised for a moment, then nodded. Grateful to avoid conversation, Henrik nodded in return and pushed on. After not seeing Old Man for a year, he was surprised to find he hadn't changed. Same scraggly white beard and splotchy cheeks. He wore a linen vest and a kerchief tied around his neck, which he sneezed into constantly.

By the time Henrik reached his cottage on the very edge of the soldat section of the Quarter, rain saturated him. The driving force prickled against his skin like descending needles. After two thuds of his fist and a firm jolt of his shoulder, he shoved against his cottage door. The amalgamation of wooden boards opened into exactly what he expected.

Silence.

Dust.

Darkness.

All his candles and lanterns had been packed away in case of storm or fire. He dropped his sopping wet pack and headed to the shed. He wanted warmth, dry clothes, a full meal, and a long sleep. After that, he'd figure out what to do next. Or how to let go of his old plan in order to develop a new one.

After twenty-seven years of dreaming he'd find Selma, this might be a sign from the gods to release her. To forget her, though her rampaging scream forbade it. *Your mama's name is Selma!*

The thought disappeared as quickly as it came. It wouldn't be the first time he questioned his allegiance to the woman in the last several decades. Often, the temptation to ignore Selma overwhelmed him, but it fizzled out.

Midstep toward the top crate in his shed, Henrik stopped.

If the storm hadn't bellowed overhead so loudly, the woman sleeping on the floor might have heard him approach. As it stood, he had a breath of a pause to comprehend the strange sight before her eyes fluttered open.

A woman.

In his shed.

That might not be totally unusual. The formerly enslaved had an entire city hidden in the catacomb streets behind the stone walls of the Quarter, except this woman wasn't a Shadowland local.

It was *her*.

The woman from the ship.

Two seconds passed between her eyes fluttering open and

Henrik registering his familiarity. In that span of time, which passed like an eternity, he formed one wild conclusion: the woman stalked him.

Instinct kicked in.

By the time he saw the whites of her eyes, he recalled his earlier suspicions. Her casual wandering on the ship, despite her lack of an official servant's outfit. Not to mention the odd noise that issued from her—or was it her clothing?—and the equally surreal understanding that someone he couldn't see sprinted past him on the dock. He'd felt their presence.

Their previous stop had been Kapurnick's main island for the final load of jord, and only Kapurnickkian dragul keepers could entirely disappear.

Circumstances painted a clear picture.

Henrik locked a hand around her wrist, yanked her off the wet floor, tossed her onto his shoulder, and strode halfway across his gravel-filled yard before her shock fully formed. He'd set her down in the house, calmly ask her what in the—

An elbow to his jaw waylaid the budding plan.

Henrik absorbed the blow, but not the shock. He stumbled to the left, momentarily disoriented, and gripped harder. The wildcat didn't shriek, but grunted. Instead of throwing her cape off and slithering out of his hands the way any self-respecting woman might attempt to do, she drove an elbow into the other side of his neck.

He shouted.

Before she could make another move, he whirled her spine to his chest and attempted to gain control by wrapping his arms around her. She lifted a foot to stomp on his toes, but a hiss and a flash of steam caught his attention.

Dazed, he stared at the base of her neck.

Was that a . . .

. . . dragul?

He sucked in a breath as an elbow found his sternum. A petite, but frenzied, roar bellowed from beneath her wet layer of hair. So, she had been suspicious. Not a servant, but a *high* Kapurnickkian. Kapurnickkians loved their dragul keepers.

Elation that his instincts had proven correct, and curiosity over this discovery, cost him another point of pride. Her heel slammed into his toes. He would have shouted, but his irritation was too powerful. If other soldats found out that this slip of a woman caused him pain, he'd be packed onto a ship, his throat slit, and dropped into the sea.

Instead of squeezing an arm around her neck and forcing compliance, Henrik plucked the writhing dragul off her neck and shoved her forward. The woman whirled around, one hand flying to her hood. Her eyes widened as she found it empty. She comprehended the writhing bounty pinched between his fingers with a livid gasp.

An emerald dragul.

She stilled.

Henrik held the dragul by its wing base to avoid stressing the little creature. Interesting thing, with its bitty talons and snarling mouth. The tiny muscles strained for freedom against Henrik's grip, and sharp teeth threatened to bite his wrist. No matter how it struggled, the dragul made no progress.

"Let him go," she insisted through the sheets of pouring rain. "He's done nothing wrong."

Her powerful voice, resonant in ways it hadn't been before, carried equal parts passion and terror. Bold woman. A bundle of questions, this one.

She didn't bother looking at Henrik. Her studious gaze locked on the dragul with maternal anxiety. Definitely bonded, then. He couldn't imagine any other reason for her to have a dragul off the main Kapurnickkian island. Sensing his failure to free himself, the dragul, almost too petite to comprehend, hung limp in Henrik's grip. Rain sluiced down the wings.

"If you want him to live, you won't move unless I tell you to," Henrik called over the rain.

Rage flashed in her eyes.

"Agreed. Release him."

He chortled. "Nice try. A dragul is no good without his bonded. If you want the dragul to survive the night, you'll turn around, walk inside my cottage, and sit down on the floor. If you give me any problems, he'll die."

Her eyes flashed with fire.

She said nothing.

"I have questions," he continued. "You'll answer them."

Her chin lifted. "Then what?"

Henrik eyed the dragul, her, and the dragul again. A deep-seated knowing stirred within. The premonition before deeper intuition. His gut told him something significant happened here. Perhaps Norr smiled on him when His Glory did not.

Henrik drawled, "We'll see how I feel. Impress me with your answers, and I'm inclined to think you'll live."

Chapter Five

BRITT

Britt had experienced loathing before, but nothing as deep as what she felt in the musty cottage of a soldat.

The soldat.

What were the odds?

Her breath was shallow and fast as she advanced into his living space ahead of him. Wisely, Denerfen stopped struggling and waited, his body limp. To the soldat's credit, he held Denerfen with care. He could have snapped Denerfen's neck, tossed his body into the alley, and had his way with Britt before dropping her into the sea.

Rumors abounded that the cunning soldats had done worse. The fact that he moved her out of the rain was a win, at this point. This cottage would be more comfortable than the shed. Her eyes skimmed the soulless interior, cluttered with little more than dust and stone.

She pressed her spine to a wall, sat down, and drew her knees to her chest. Having something against her bolstered a false and momentary sense of safety. Thanks to General Helsing, she'd long ago learned to take her wins as she found them.

Denerfen is still alive and we're out of the rain, she thought.

Her optimism ended there.

Britt's hand snaked into her cloak pocket, where Tesserdress stirred. She chirped, but settled at Britt's touch. Heat remained in her scales, which was good. She'd be thirsty, and tired, after all this movement and noise. Britt asked too much of her in her weakened state. A dragul, thrust into a pocket for hours on end.

Unheard of.

When the soldat didn't immediately follow her into the house, panic flared. She stood, then shuffled back into the rain to see his gray, broad form retreating to the shed. A cry gummed up her throat.

Before she could fling herself across the yard, he returned with a crate under one arm, Denerfen hanging miserably from the other hand. Relief flowed through her as the soldat stomped through puddles and into the house. A scowl appeared on his face as he closed the door, eyed her, and moved to a table.

Denerfen gave a pathetic mewl as he passed by. She swallowed her rising ire. Not only had Deneferfen met danger and captivity, but now the soldat knew too much. He knew she was Kapurnickkian, a dragul keeper, and snuck onto his island without registering with the port authority.

The clatter of the soldat dropping a lid, ruffling through the crate, and emerging with a candle echoed in the barren space. A coated match lit the candle. Light bounced onto the table in puddles of butter yellow. The soldat set Denerfen near it, but sent her a dirty look of warning. She glowered.

Rotten scoundrel.

He ignored her.

Aided by what little light the candle provided, Britt assessed the dim interior with a wary eye. Stone, like everything in Stenberg. Mortar pasted the smoky sealstone rocks into walls. Windows interrupted the walls with high, horizontal panes that admitted fresh air and light when opened, but didn't shuck the suffocation. All of Stenberg pressed too close, as if Stenbergians strove to control the sea with their walls.

Sound, though. The interior was militaristic at best. Little more than furniture to interrupt the sealstone, without a single decoration or personal effect visible. Had he been gone for a very long time?

Or did soldats live such boring lives?

She assumed the latter.

Minutes of tinkering later, the soldat set four candles on the table, shedding light onto two chairs, an elevated platform along the far wall that, at some point, might have held a mattress. No wonder crates packed the shed.

The soldat snapped two fingers and pointed down.

"Sit."

He commanded her into the chair across from him, but didn't sit himself. Britt clutched the chair in obvious defiance.

He canted an eyebrow. "You won't sit?"

"Not if you command it."

"Fine." He waved a hand. "Stand."

She sat.

He paused, schooled his expression into something halfway patient, and continued to rummage. Britt set her hands on the table and met her dragul's eyes. Denerfen hopped to his feet, a moment away from pouncing in her direction, when the soldat pinched his tail.

"Ah, ah," he tsked. "Not yet."

Britt growled.

Denerfen whirled around to bite the fingers, but the soldat anticipated him and grasped the base of his wings again. With a pathetic mewl, Denerfen wilted in defeat a second time. He must be colder than she thought. Britt tried to gather calm and project it through her mannerisms, but her blood boiled with the urge to wrap her fingers around the soldat's neck.

He tossed her a hard towel.

"Dry off."

Further irritated with the command, but openly trembling, she wrapped the fabric around her shoulders. Thrumming rain continued overhead. A leak sprouted near the far corner, trickling down the stones.

Maybe not as sound as she thought.

The man lowered Denerfen into a bowl padded with a rag, but kept the dragul close. He lifted the half-full crate to the floor, sat on the closest chair, and stared at her.

"So," he drawled, "we meet again."

Britt hid a wince. Her chin elevated. "Lovely to see you, soldat. You have a name, I presume?"

"I do."

She paused, hoping pressure would motivate an answer. It didn't. The soldat studied Denerfen, who cozied into the rag, but glared at the soldat. His mewls of frustration as he snuggled deeper into the blanket, hissing sleepily, would have been amusing if she wasn't so distressed. Denerfen yawned, his petite jaws closing like a baby alligator. Loading and injecting venom exhausted him, and he clearly hadn't slept well in the shed.

The soldat nodded toward Denerfen. "It's a handsome dragul, and impetuous. More . . . assertive . . . than other draguls I've met."

She blinked. "I'm sorry?"

A hint of amusement appeared in his lazuli eyes. Tall tales whispered to her by Malcolm at night, when they were children, said that Stenbergians had pure black eyes and drank blood when the moon went dark. The resulting nightmares kept her up beyond her bedtime, wondering if it was true. Malcolm's tall tales were wrong.

This soldat didn't have pure black eyes, but those of thunderclouds.

Unfettered sky.

Faygel flowers on the Kapurnick volcano slopes.

"The other draguls," the soldat insisted. "They were far more frightened, hiding behind their bonded. Until this firecracker tried to steam me when I grabbed you, I thought the rumors of their protectiveness were lies."

Britt's attention narrowed.

The other draguls.

He bluffed.

No doubt he acted so confident to trick her into spilling details. He thought her a fool? Well, two could play this game. He could draw all the assumptions he wanted. If she never confirmed details, suspicion would always bother him.

"Do soldats obsess over unconfirmed rumors?" she asked with a saccharine smile.

He frowned.

She could almost feel the power in the conversation slide her way, so she pressed her advantage. "You must have met the blue and purple dragul," she said lightly.

The soldat tilted his head to the side. "Mm . . . no. Yellow. Golden, really, because of the orange underbelly."

Her heart jumped into her throat. Blessed mermaids! Had he *actually* met Bamerbam? The infamous, tetchy golden dragul of legends?

A stroke of pain followed her astonishment. They had lost Bamerbam to old age a few months ago, which was only part of the reason that brought her to Stenberg in search of Malcolm. Losing Bamerbam had been hard enough. If the draguls lost Tesserdress as well? Bamerbam had lived to the ripe age of fifty-five, which was ancient for a dragul. Tess recently turned five, reaching reproductive maturity.

"Yellow," Britt said to buy herself another moment. "She was yellow, not golden."

Britt must have done a terrible job concealing her surprise, because the soldat stretched his legs, stacked his hands behind his head, and gave the impression of an uncoiling cat.

"It was a cranky dragul, all right," he mused, hiding a yawn. "Hiding in the hood of her bonded. Wise old man. Had stories to tell for days and days. Is it true that the opposite genders bond? Your little dragul is male?"

Britt's thready heart threatened to fly away in panic. He not only knew Bamerbam, but her bonded man, Yolf. Other details, too. Did this soldat try to earn her trust, or set her on guard? Her lips pinched together. She'd mentally prepared for almost every inevitability and deprivation as she headed for Stenberg, but not *this*.

Not a soldat, in his home, with Denerfen captured from her cape, and information about draguls open to someone outside the Kapurnickkian islands.

Shock unseated her, and Britt swam in the heady and dangerous waters of uncertainty for a breath too long. Sensing his opportunity, the soldat leaned close, forearms braced to the table, and stared at her with eyes too soulful for such chiseled intensity.

"I know who you are, Kapurnickkian."

Grateful to set aside the complicated subject of the dragul, Britt mimicked his posture. The only way to surprise him would be to act the same. Project arrogant certainty. Lean into his power in the conversation, thus lull him into a mistake.

"Britt. My name is Britt."

Just a hint of shock lightened his gaze.

"I'm a dragul keeper from the Kapurnickkian isles. Stenberg islanders call us *tamers*, but that's the wrong word. We don't tame draguls, we keep them. Care for them."

She resisted the temptation to add, *and I'm the niece to General Helsing*, just to see his reaction.

The soldat blinked.

She smiled.

A silence several beats too long passed between them. In it, she heard Denerfen's rapid breaths, felt his intense scrutiny. Draguls could sense or feed off of their bonded's emotions, but wouldn't understand such rapid back-and-forth language or the elaborate nuance of conversation.

Regardless of how this played out, at least she'd bested the soldat at his own game for control. The soldat strove to recover. He asked, "And why is a dragul keeper traveling to Stenberg?"

"What is your name?"

The instant rebuttal earned a grunt. Studying her, he eventually said, "Henrik."

"Henrik. Huh."

He frowned. "What?"

"You don't look like a Henrik."

"What do I look like?"

Amused with his disgruntled reply, she said, "Oh, maybe a . . . Shad?"

His nose wrinkled.

She fought to maintain an even expression. A line formed between his eyes when he looked annoyed. "It's beside the point," he muttered. "What are you doing *here*?"

"I'm going to lie to you, whatever I say next, Henrik. Truly. Would you like me to keep the lie simple, or elaborate?"

He paused for a beat, clearly ascertaining whether she was serious, before he waved a hand.

"By all means. Make the tale and lie as elaborate as you desire. You're only wasting time. Until I receive the truth, the dragul is mine. Based on what I know of the desperate predicament of the draguls in Kapurnick, I have an idea that every single minute is precious."

Britt clenched her jaw. Surely, he bluffed a second time. He couldn't *know* about the desperate and dire straits of their draguls or else His Glory would have long ago demanded meetings with General Helsing to reassure him that jord production wasn't in jeopardy.

The infuriating soldat bargained off a correct assumption, and wasn't that the worst luck? Falling from her high shelf of self-satisfaction at her own prowess was a hard leap to the dregs of annoyance. She dominated the conversation one minute, plummeted the next.

Tesserdress sensed her distress and stirred. Her position beneath the table prevented Henrik from seeing her, which might be the only advantage Britt had. Beyond Denerfen's venom, but to use it twice in one day?

She mentally shuddered.

Her gaze lowered to Denerfen. His eyes had closed. If the twitching lids meant anything, he longed to open them again, but couldn't. Seeing her dragul so depleted, a swamping exhaustion swept Britt.

Had she truly started the day on the ship, escaped this infernal soldat twice, avoided sailors to scuttle through the market, fled pursuit and trouble with the young boys, snoozed in a shed, and ended it by a conversation with the same soldat *at his home*?

Britt covered her face with a hand. "Sweet sea turtles," she muttered.

"What?"

Momentarily forgetting his presence, she startled at the sound of Henrik's voice. Irritated, she released a raspberry.

"Nothing."

"Did you just swear by turtles?"

"Er . . ."

His right eyebrow lifted.

All tolerance fled. Britt set her elbows on the table, leaned forward and said, "Yes! Yes I did. I swore by turtles. We have a lot of them in Kapurnick. If that's an insult, forgive me. It's something we do in the Kapurnickkian language. If it's wrong, it's wrong."

He punctuated each word that followed with a finger tap. "Why are you here?"

She said nothing.

"You must not care about your dragul."

The challenge didn't irritate her the way he clearly meant. The approval or disapproval of a Stenberg soldat wasn't high on her priority list.

"Your assumptions will get you in trouble," she replied.

Something negative must have happened to Henrik in the intervening time when she bumped into him on the ship, because he appeared as weary as her. He rubbed a hand over his face.

"Then we're at an impasse. I won't let you go anywhere until I know why you're here, and you won't tell me why. Tomorrow morning, I'll take the dragul with me to report to His Glory. I'm sure he'll be *very* interested in your story."

A slow, gradual understanding dawned on Britt, trickling like a warm summer stream. Was it possible that this soldat didn't know all the horrifying dominoes toppling for months now?

"You don't know," she whispered.

"Know what?"

"Where have you been for the last year?"

His back tightened like someone pulled a marionette string through it.

"Why?"

Britt shook her head. "It's impossible that you know about the dragul, and yet . . ." Her eyes widened as final understanding clicked into place. "You're the traveling soldat. The one that goes around, enforces the collection of jord. What is it . . . sweeper?"

"Reefer."

"Right, my apologies. Is that you? It must be! You picked up the jord. We rode the same ship to here from Kapurnick."

Clearly discomfited, Henrik set his hands on the table in front of him.

"Why are you asking?"

She chuckled, but it had no power. "You have no idea what His Glory has been doing, do you? The attacks on outlying Lesser Isles? Forcing people into ships against their will and whisking them away?"

"There have been skirmishes over violated contracts," he said slowly, recalling the rare update he received months ago. "I've heard about them from reports but . . ."

She laughed outright, breaking the strange heaviness in the air. His astonishment weighed almost as great as her concern.

"There have been violated contracts, all right, and it's from the Stenberg side of things. Slaves taken. Jord stolen. Ships scuttled."

"That's not right."

Britt's jaw locked. His denial, clouded by a very real uncertainty, was the only saving grace. If he hadn't set Denerfen so close to him, she would have risked snatching him out of the bowl and escaping into the storm. Had he been any Stenberg islander *but* a soldat, she might have had a chance.

Against him?

None.

Their second impasse fell. For a long pause, neither spoke. Henrik stood, shoving his chair back.

"We're done. If you haven't decided to tell me the truth by the morning, I'm taking your dragul to my captain and telling your story."

He reached into the crate, withdrew a woolen blanket, and tossed it her way. She'd stopped shivering beneath the towel, but the cold hadn't dissipated. Henrik snuffed the candles with a pinch of his fingers, gathered Denerfen, and retreated to the far side of the room. Laying on his side on the mattress-less platform, he put Denerfen so she couldn't see him and settled with a sigh.

Disheartened, Britt unwound the blanket, pulled it around her, crawled under the table, and stared at the wall. Tesserdress stirred in her pocket, so she carefully withdrew her. Tess's wobbly gait pitched left and right, as if they were still on the ship. She crawled along Britt's arm, closer to her warmth. Burrowing into the crook of Britt's bent elbow, Tesserdress settled with a sigh.

Britt ran her fingertips along Tesserdress's spine and fell into thought.

Henrik didn't strike her as depraved or desperate, so she assumed they'd survive the night. She'd tell him the details in the morning. She'd also find water and a little food. Like her, the draguls would be famished by then.

What more could she do?

With a sigh, Britt dropped into a surface sleep.

Chapter Six

HENRIK

A worn path guided Henrik through cobblestone streets, down the water-strewn road, and toward the Captain's Quarters.

The routine and obvious expectation soothed Henrik, though the luster of returning to Stenberg didn't shine as brightly once he walked the streets. He'd forgotten that it smelled like wet dung after the rain. At least it offered predictability. His stomach, no longer subject to the pitching sea, reminded him to eat. His appetite had been low for weeks.

Hunger felt good.

The storm cleared in the night, revealing a fresh horizon and bluebird sky scrubbed clean. Fluffy white clouds drifted with lazy, stacked splendor. Slate edges gave them texture as they passed, chasing the tail end of frothing storm clouds to the south. The Chain Islands would be subject to the same brutality soon.

His right hand curled into his pocket, delicately assessing the dragul. The tiny creature hadn't been pleased to be stuffed inside, but Henrik overcame his resistance easily enough. Another few twists and turns and they'd be far enough from Britt's scent, and deep enough into the island, to ensure the dragul couldn't escape and return on his own.

With Britt nearby and a dragul for leverage, Henrik slept in snatches. He needn't have worried. Britt didn't attempt to harm him or rescue her dragul. Her light, wispy breaths filled the silence within moments of her lying down. Fatigue worked against her.

This morning, Britt hadn't stirred when he prepared to leave. Not even a subtle nudge of her shoulder with his toe stirred her from the depths. At least he could say that he tried.

Henrik turned to the left. The looming shapes of His Glory's Temple, the Archives, the residence where His Glory lived, and the Compendium, cast few shadows. The Compendium was little more than several buildings clustered together, housing His Glory and the islanders who served him directly. Servant huts, sailor stations, and a market, dedicated solely to His Glory, where the best of everything arrived directly from the ships. Those lucky enough to live in and work through the Compendium enjoyed a higher quality of life, though they couldn't leave.

Enslaved, in a very real way.

He thought of what Britt said the night before, about Stenberg and enslaved islanders and broken contracts and scuttled boats. The uncomfortable subject made him squirm. Mistaken, surely. Stenberg had no reason to create enemies.

A bracing breath prepared Henrik to return to the Captain's Quarters. Undoubtedly, news of Captain Arvid had arrived last night with the three other Captains. Not likely to be good, either. Henrik didn't want to hear the report, but he couldn't wait another moment. Though he'd just spoken to Oliver yesterday, it felt like lifetimes had passed.

As Henrik climbed a set of forty stairs leading to the third floor, he almost smiled recalling the surprise in Britt's eyes when he mentioned the dragul he met during his tour of the Kapurnickkian isles.

She hadn't believed him. Not that he could blame her. By all accounts, he shouldn't have seen that dragul. The keeper had been remiss to introduce him to . . . Bamerbam, was it?

Yet the Kapurnickkian man had, because people in the outer isles were far kinder than Stenberg islanders. Kinder, or less paranoid. The nefarious shadow of His Glory's politics and the constant threat of mainland interference didn't have as strong of a grip out there. Henrik lacked experience with the mainland, but he knew many of the hundreds of Chain Islands, each known for a different type of arcane. Few islanders managed to navigate *all* of them, though the challenge of it thrilled him.

His reefer year exposed him to more of His Glory's workings and power, as Captain Oliver desired, but also a different life. Lesser Isles people collected coconuts, glimmering sand that yielded sparkling glass, massive fish the size of boats, and other resources.

Beyond that?

They didn't fear much.

For the past twelve months, he struggled to understand the disparity of lives. What existed without the threat of reprisal or outside attack? Could one just . . . be? As a soldat, he had no time for peace.

Henrik ducked into a familiar office on the left. Years of foot traffic left grooves in the stone floor, guiding him to the exact spot. He stopped inside the doorway. The square room split in half, with two doorways opposite each other. Captain Oliver's office on the left, Captain Arvid's office on the right.

A young soldat stood, hands at his side. He bent at the hips and straightened.

"Soldat," the young man said.

"Greetings."

"Are you Henrik?"

"I am."

"Good. I've been waiting for you."

"Oh?"

The boy could hardly be a man. He had thin cheeks, freshly-shaven hair on the sides of his head, and a tense stubbornness in his jaw. Baby soldat, they called boys like him. He was probably eighteen, a year from release, and testing here at the Captain's Quarters. He motioned toward Captain Oliver's office, where the door stood open and a desk perched inside, empty.

"The Captain isn't here, sir."

"I see that."

"He won't return for the rest of the day."

Acting intentionally stupid, because information was always easier to glean when he acted as if he didn't have the upper hand, Henrik said, "Fine, I'll report to Captain Arvid."

The baby soldat's face dropped. A serious edge claimed his voice. "Sir . . . Captain Arvid is gone."

"Gone?"

"Dead. Confirmation arrived last night. He died in a battle against Narpurra and Stenberg. Captain Oliver is meeting with the other Captains and His Glory to work through the details now."

The boy jerked a thumb over his left shoulder, gesturing to Arvid's room at the opposite corner, also dark, empty, and deserted. So the mysterious letter that arrived as Henrik departed was, indeed, final notice.

Henrik didn't have to work hard to summon outrage.

"An insult," he managed.

"I agree, soldat. Captain Oliver wanted me to relay that he won't have an assignment for you until after this is settled. He said you can have today off, but he wants you to report back tomorrow. He also requests that you double-check your jord shipment, as the numbers are lower than expected."

Henrik frowned. "It unloaded well?"

"Yes."

"No problems?"

"No, sir. But Captain Oliver was insistent that you double-check your jord shipment. He made me swear to tell you twice."

"And you have."

The baby soldat nodded, as if a great weight lifted from his shoulders. He passed Henrik an envelope. Within lay ten sheets of folded paper with the same sentence and paragraph structure. The top line said, *Location of jord reception.*

Ten different Kapurnickkian island names appeared on the ten alternating pages in a compilation of his latest and final jord acquisition. At the bottom, an ink seal of approval stamped each page, given by the local port authority.

Henrik perused the sheets, curious. Nothing seemed out of order at cursory glance. The report mimicked what he told Oliver yesterday, and provided in his own paperwork. His Glory required double reports around jord to protect their precious trade agreements. He housed all of them, along with other giant trails of paperwork, in the Archives, which were attached to the Library.

"I'm sure His Glory is celebrating yet another shipment of jord, particularly at the onset of a cleansing," the baby soldat said. "We can initiate another round of planting to prepare for the upcoming dry season."

Henrik couldn't help but wonder if *this* sailor knew his mother.

"What's your name?" Henrik asked.

"My name?"

With a stroke of amusement, Henrik asked, "You don't know it?"

"I do, sir," he stammered. "I just . . . no one in this office has ever asked. My name is Brodin."

"How long have you been in the Captain's Quarters, Brodin?"

"Nine months."

"Do you like it?"

"I do."

"Would you tell me if you didn't?"

The edges of Brodin's lip twitched.

"No, soldat."

Henrik chuckled, and cast another glance at the numbers. At first blush, all seemed fine. He couldn't shake the sense that something was off. What? He wasn't sure. Though he remembered the numbers easily enough, and they seemed comparable, they weren't exact.

"Is Ossian still in port?" he asked.

"No, soldat. His ship has already departed again. They left as soon as the storm lifted, in the wee hours of the morning."

"To where?"

"To Calsica."

Calsica was a small island off the northwest Stenberg shore, in a cluster of other islands with a similar reputation for skullduggery and thieving. Ossian probably fled the cleansing before the port authority closed the docks.

But why?

Something didn't quite fit. If suspicion had a smell, it would be rotten fish, and the ghastly perfume would flow thick through Henrik's nostrils right now.

"I thought Ossian planned to stay?"

"The port authority didn't say why the captain left, soldat."

Shaking the strangely fast departure off, Henrik tucked the papers under his arms. "I'll return with these tomorrow, so the Archives can have them."

"Yes, soldat."

"The mainland has been causing some problems, haven't they?"

While Brodin droned on and on about *unsubstantiated missing shipments* and *complaints about delayed cargo,* Henrik realized that the dragul in his pocket had become unnaturally still. He might have thought the creature escaped. A touch reassured him.

"That's what we hear, anyway," Brodin finished. "As Captain Oliver is always the first to hear the news, I'd say what you hear on the streets is probably a lie, or doesn't have all the information."

"Highlights the importance of this office, doesn't it? It means something that you're part of it, Brodin."

"Thank you, soldat."

Henrik paused halfway through the door, squinting as he

leaned back inside. "Are the other soldats busy during the cleansing?"

"Only a few. Captain Oliver called them back when Captain Arvid went missing two weeks ago. All should be returning."

"How many are here?"

"None on assignment, ten with His Glory, and twenty-two on the island, including Captain Oliver. You make it twenty-three, soldat, which means a full contingent."

"It's been awhile since that happened."

Brodin brightened, his eyebrows elevated. "Since all the soldats have returned, rumor has it they're starting the grappling tournament a week early."

Henrik ignored it.

Brodin plowed on. "Soldat Einar has been saying that when you return with your final jord shipment, you'll try to uphold your current grappling title *and* break Captain Oliver's."

The query in Brodin's tone wasn't an accident.

Henrik ignored it, too.

"Thank you, Brodin. Have a good day."

Henrik left an astonished baby soldat in his wake. Undoubtedly, Brodin never had a soldat ask his name or wish him well. The well wishing was more strategic than kind. Soldats referenced brute force tactics too often. A year in the Lesser Isles convinced Henrik that there was a different way to approach the same problems. The islanders out *there* opted for persuasion and kindness first when dealing with other people. A working reminder of the power of gentleness.

One could never have friends in too many places.

Henrik returned to the tropical sunshine, a delightful sensation on his skin after the ravaging winds. When the dragul attempted to bite his knuckle, he removed his hand. It would be harder for the little creature to weasel out of his pocket while he walked.

Despite his annoyance with Britt, he didn't want the dragul to meet harm.

THE CRACK of a whip split the air.

Henrik strode past the whipping stand, placed artfully across from the peaceful Archives and Library. Close enough to His Glory that the daily punishments were visible, but the screams too distant to distract from his daily prayer time to Norr. Flecks of gore marbled the cobblestones outside the Archives daily during a cleansing.

A disfigured man with visible ribs and a bony spine hung on the stock, wrists tied to the posts. The thunderous roar of a crowd shouted as the whipmaster lay into the pathetic, shriveled man. He passed out and slumped over. Bloody stripes slashed his back, oozing a dark crimson.

Poor chap.

Must have stolen something, else His Glory wouldn't dole out punishment to *cleanse Stenberg of all unholiness in the face of Norr's desired blessings* or other such rubbish.

A creaky wagon packed with blue-and-green-leafed plants rattled by. Burlap bags, triple-layered, wrapped their roots with precious jord. Two brawny men pulled the wagon in place of mules, while three surrounded each side to protect the cargo. Animals ate too much and required more jord, necessitating more hard labor than most islands.

The harvest timing wasn't accidental, either. Henrik's new shipment of mineral rich jord would pave the way for more food. Over the years, they'd built up enough protected planters to maintain Stenberg's population, but they required new shipments brought in yearly. The fertilizer kept Stenbergians' teeth in their heads and their children from dying. Without it, they'd have almost no sustainable access to plants.

The dragul shuddered in his pocket as they passed the

amassed crowd, drawing Henrik's attention to his pressing conundrum.

Britt.

Since he didn't have a chance to tell Captain Oliver about the woman or the dragul, what now? Only a fool would hold onto this information and resource, particularly with Arvid's death and with Captain Oliver's high emotions roiling against Kapurnick. Not to mention the hostility towards the mainland, for that matter.

It left one option.

Henrik departed from the holy side of Stenberg and angled toward the Quarter. A squat stone building with a trailing, dirty stream of smoke piping out of the chimney awaited. The Old Pub, aptly named for the ease of memory and because soldats lacked imagination. The smoke was a signal, for no island lacked heat on a pristine day.

It meant that soldats grappled within.

Perfect.

Henrik stepped inside the Old Pub, a gathering place for soldats when assignments ran scarce. Historically, it didn't happen often, so the rare chance to pull together after his reefer year was most welcome.

The dim place appeared as shabby as ever. Chiseled stone mugs lined the cupboards, drawing his eye to the rock-and-mortar walls, scattered tables, canted windows, and a thin, crackling fireplace that burned coal dredged from the depths of Cmeaddon island.

All furniture had been shoved to the side, creating a berth in the middle of the room. A dozen soldats littered the periphery, calling bets and jeering. Six soldats formed a circle within the chaos. Two grappled inside a chalk ring, wearing pants cut off at the knee. Their bodies smashed into each other with grunts and groans that led to the sweeping of one off his bare feet.

"Alas!" shouted a deep voice. "What bounty has the sea brought us?"

The raucous energy in the room stilled. Anticipating the welcome, Henrik lifted a hand and smiled.

"Land-el, ugly scalliwags! Your beloved Henrik has returned."

Slaps on the shoulder, whoops of welcome, and a chorus of cheers escorted Henrik further into the Old Pub. Fellow soldats pounded him on the back, demanded answers, teased him for his plush lifestyle, and faded to their activities within minutes.

A fist slammed into his shoulder.

"Been a year, beloved!" cried Timmer, an old soldat who refused to die, and whom the Captains couldn't get rid of, despite trying. "You're looking more handsome than ever. Roguish twinkle in those blue eyes. Find yourself a lady?"

Henrik planted a hand on Timmer's face and shoved him away. Timmer swung. Henrik dodged the hasty fist, ducked a follow-up uppercut, and swept his leg under Timmer's shins. Timmer stumbled to his backside, laughing until he turned bright red.

"The grappling king returns," Timmer shouted, a hand on his abdomen as he quelled his wheezy amusement. "He smells of jord!"

Laughter rippled through the room as Henrik reached out a hand and yanked Timmer to his feet. He smacked the dust off his clothes with a grin.

"Good to see you again, Timmer. Where's Einar?"

"Outside."

Attention on Henrik fizzled when one of the grappling soldats broke through the white-chalk square hastily drawn on the floor. A chorus of groans followed as the match completed, canceled because he crossed the line. Amidst the hushed chaos, a familiar smile crossed the pub floor. Tanned skin, sparkling white teeth with a slightly crooked top, and long arms.

Einar.

Henrik grinned and drawled, "My brother."

They met in a hug with the force of clashing gods. Einar

pounded him on the back, laughing, streaming queries, concerns, pulling away to study him, and then laughing again.

"What is your hideous mug doing here?" Einar demanded.

"Returned last night."

Einar shook his head, clucking. "One year as a reefer. Amazing how time flies. How was your tour of the world, future soldat Captain?"

Henrik shoved him off.

"Shut up."

With a twitch of fingers, Einar motioned for two meads. They retreated to a far table, settling underneath an awning that blocked the streaming sun. Waves broke on the beach, hissing.

Einar sent an appraising study. "How are you? You look . . . good. Wasn't sure what safety concerns you'd meet, particularly as you rounded up the jord."

"Nothing too concerning."

Einar sobered. "Looks like you broke away from Kapurnick before the issues escalated in Narpurra with Captain Arvid?"

"Happened on the same day, I think. We departed before word made it from Narpurra to Kapurnick. The messenger drakes were flying to Kapurnick with updates as I set sail here."

The arm-sized messenger dragons ferried notes between islands. Fierce, when compared to the bitty draguls, and surly as a simmering volcano. They had a special affection for Kapurnick's emerald mountains and verdant moss, and often settled there instead of Stenberg. Finding one to send a message was often a lost cause.

Einar whistled. "A stroke of good luck, brother."

Henrik nodded once.

"You might have only missed the news arriving by hours," Einar mused. "Bet they would have taken the ship and kept *you* prisoner, instead of us taking one of them."

"We took a prisoner?"

"A Major." Einar shrugged. "Not sure his name. M-something.

Doesn't matter. His Glory shipped him to the Unseen island. The man's a goner."

Einar nodded to the bartender who set down two stone mugs of watered mead and had a sip. Soldats rarely imbibed more than weakened mead, and only for the medicinal effect of the honey, but Henrik would be glad for the familiar taste. The cheap ale consumed on ships left a bitter aftershock. Henrik pulled his mug, curling his fingers around the warm stone as he absorbed Einar's information.

"What do you know about Captain Arvid?" Henrik asked. "Do you believe he's dead?"

Under his breath, Einar said, "I haven't heard much. What we know comes from captains, like Ossian. Neither Oliver nor the other three Captains have said anything."

"Not even Ingemar?"

"Not yet."

"His Glory must know because Ingemar arrived to Captain Oliver's office the other night. If Ingemar knows, His Glory knows."

Einar shrugged. "Captain Oliver, too. They haven't said."

The implication left a gaping hole in the conversation.

"If Arvid is dead, it's His Glory's fault," Einar muttered. A sinister thread hummed bright under his words. "There was no reason to start that fight on Narpurran shores, and now we've lost our Second Captain. The only one we liked."

Henrik swallowed a rising lump that tasted like uncertainty. "I hear His Glory has been . . . aggressive."

"Stupidly so."

Confirmation stunned him. For Britt to claim that Stenberg made problems was one thing, but for Einar to confirm it something else.

"Why?"

"No idea."

"Really?"

Einar nodded once, had a sip of mead. "Breaking treaties is the least of it, with the mainland peeking in." He made eye contact with Henrik long enough to impart a warning, then muttered, "All we have left is Captain Oliver, and he's shite."

Alarm bells clanged in Henrik's mind.

Shite?

"What happened?" Henrik asked.

Einar's attention flickered over Henrik's shoulder, focused on something for a pause, and diverted.

"Later."

The single word, flicked free, set tension crawling up Henrik's spine. With a far less bleak affect, Einar leaned back and grinned. "So," he drawled. "Are you glad to be home?"

The words *glad to be home* stalled in Henrik's mind. Stenberg hadn't ever felt like home. That notion existed in literature for children. Comfort bled out of them as stolen souls, the empty place stoked into fires hungry for battle and competition.

Home?

What a word.

What a question.

Stupidly, he hadn't prepared for the obvious query and didn't know what to say. *Was* he glad to return?

Not really.

The dismal stone island, the recently fickle leadership, and now the weight of Captain Oliver wanting Henrik as a Second Captain, was a lackluster welcome. He missed glittering sand and tropical, azure waters like the outer chain or Caledon island. At least those islands were interesting, with a mix of arcane and culture. His Glory pounded the arcane out of Stenberg ages ago.

Norr's son guides these islands, His Glory said. *We do not require the arcane. It does not work on our sealstone shores.*

"Yeah," Henrik said distantly, "of course I'm glad to return."

Einar chortled.

"How's Agnes?" Henrik asked to keep the focus off of him. The tactic worked, as he knew it would. Affection softened the edges of Einar's expression.

"She's good. Canny woman. Too smart to be with an oaf like me."

"About time you recognize it. You're not going to legalize the relationship, are you?"

"No." Einar's sober tone mimicked the way he traced the tip of a finger around the top of his mug. "No, I wouldn't do that to her. She wants to. She would have months ago."

Henrik made a noise in his throat, then sprawled his legs out, an elbow propped on the chair handle. He regarded the grappling match. Two soldats squared off, locked into an evenly matched confrontation. A deep longing to join them rose from suppressed corners. It had been too long since his last grapple. Two months ago, he accepted invitations from Ossian's sailors to wrestle. He proceeded to scrub the deck with their teeth until Ossian called a halt and cursed him to the sea god for three days.

"So?" Einar drawled. "How was your time in the Lesser Isles? I missed your first and second deliveries here because of assignments."

Henrik shrugged. "Don't worry about it. We unloaded in the morning and took off by the evening."

Einar laughed. "A year cut off from Stenberg, with the sea spray in your face, gathering jord for your people. Sounds idyllic to me."

"I hate sea spray," Henrik muttered.

Einar laughed harder, a hand on his stomach, but Henrik struggled to share the levity. Britt. The dragul. His conversation with Brodin. Einar's edge when speaking about Oliver. Nothing stacked up. Henrik drew in a breath, attempting to tell his story, but he didn't know where to start. He trusted Einar with his life, but too many other soldats surrounded them. He couldn't speak about the dragul here.

"How is Stenberg?" Henrik asked instead. Whatever Einar said first would be the better reflection of real updates.

"Fine."

"Oh?"

He spoke too evenly when he said, "Threats from the mainland, of course, but aren't there always?"

No, Henrik thought. *Not always.*

Henrik casually returned his hand to his pocket to confirm the dragul hadn't skittered off. The creature growled, nipping the tip of his finger. Henrik had a sip of mead, but the hint of honey tasted like ash.

"What kind of threats?" Henrik asked.

"I don't know."

"His Glory is normally too happy to pontificate over the mainland's ill temper."

Einar snorted, said, "Exactly," and pawed a hand through the air, ready to dismiss the topic. That was Einar. Quickly bored, unless he had a weapon.

Crescendos arose from the grappling ring. One had the other pinned. Muscular forearms held a black-haired soldat, Vilhelm, in check, refusing to grant freedom. After an impressive struggle, Vilhelm's eyes rolled back. His flailing ceased, arms went slack. The victor, a soldat Henrik didn't know, jumped to his feet. Guffaws rang out.

Einar tilted his head toward the ring. "His name is Vilhelm. Entered official service from the training camp the month you left as reefer. The bastid is an arrogant piece of work, but a solid grappler. He thinks he can beat you."

Amusement trickled through Henrik at the thought. While Vilhelm had good form—based on the few glimpses Henrik managed to see—the man wasn't ready for advanced grappling yet. Einar gave him a quizzical expression.

"Weren't you supposed to get two weeks off?"

Henrik nodded.

"Will you?"

He shook his head.

Einar paused, exhaled sharply, as the realization sank into understanding. Only Einar knew Henrik's motivation to find

Selma, and his plan to accept the two weeks and search. Irritation streaked Einar's response.

"Sorry, brother. That's . . . unfortunate. Demmed frustrating, too. After a year on the Isles, you earned those two weeks. And . . . "

Einar trailed off.

"Thanks."

"That's the problem, isn't it?" Einar hissed. "Soldats get nothing. No vacation. No payment. We're enslaved to His Glory, only held with different chains, and demmed for it." He shook his head. "It was bearable with Arvid around. Even a few years ago, when Oliver, the bastid, didn't fade all power to His Glory so easily. Oliver stopped caring about us, and now we can't even take a day off."

While Einar stewed in his fury and new grapplers entered the ring, Henrik's focus returned to the dragul, plagued by new worries after Einar's melodramatic speech. According to information gleaned during his time at the lesser Kapurnickkian isles, the draguls were a fragile race. The old man, Yolf, mumbled something about a sickness, but followed it up with a hasty, *everything is fine.*

This male dragul was a prime bargaining chip, yet he couldn't help wondering what might happen to the dragul if Captain Oliver found out?

As his bonded person, would Britt suffer if Oliver took him away? Vague details about the power of a dragul bonding filtered through Henrik's mind, but he couldn't put a certain finger on any of them.

Across the room, Timmer shouted, "Henrik! You next?"

"Next time," Henrik called.

Groans littered the room. Einar smirked, and had a sip of mead. "You're too out of practice to hold your crown as reigning grappling champion, Henrik?"

"I will defeat all of you in my sleep."

"Glad to see you haven't lost all your piss and vinegar." Einar grinned, held up his mead in salute. "The annual grappling tournament is in a few days. We held it off in anticipation of your arrival."

"I'm honored."

Einar chuckled outright. "You're going down, old man."

"You're the same age as me, bastid."

"But in sheer talent and raw charm," Einar retorted with impressive bravado, "I'm twice your age."

Chortling, the conversation broke from these brittle shards, steering to soldat gossip and updates on Agnes. Henrik mentally tucked away his concerns for the dragul, rising frustration with returning to Stenberg, and all that lay unknown.

At this moment, he couldn't change anything. He forced himself to relax and soak in Einar's welcome camaraderie. He'd missed his brother-in-arms.

A slow-growing plan formed in the back of his mind. Cogitating ideas had solidified into streams of thought. One that kept his hope to find Selma moving forward, while dealing with the butterfly-sized complication in his pocket.

HOURS LATER, Henrik strode down the cobblestone road that wound through the Quarters, toward the tucked-away soldat village. Two burlap bags dangled at his side: one full of food, the other contained clothes.

Both would be the keys to his success.

Old Man sat on his perch and nodded as he rose the portcullis to allow Henrik inside. Regret motivated Henrik to move faster. The sun spirited quickly toward the afternoon. He shouldn't have spent that much time with Einar while Britt waited in his cottage, but he couldn't help himself.

Separating a dragul and its bonded keeper was no meager problem.

Granted, Britt had spunk in spades. She didn't lack internal fire to fight her own battles, and a few hours wouldn't kill either of them. Hopefully, in the intervening time, she hadn't done something stupid.

He braced himself.

As his cottage came into view, he slowed. Britt might be his only chance to find Selma, if there was anything of her to find. The possibility that Selma existed in records wasn't unfounded. His Glory loved written praise to his holy name, and records were a natural result. But what if not?

What if Henrik remembered wrong?

Soldats didn't wander into the Archives every day, asking for census records. The Sisters of Stenberg might even track what he searched through and inform Oliver. Weirder things had happened, though he couldn't fathom that an archivist cared.

Not that it mattered, thanks to the confounded cleansing.

A trembling snout poked out of the fabric and into the air, sniffing. Ah, the dragul smelled his bonded. Henrik braced himself again, recalling Britt's quick wit and stolid determination to not betray herself. Her impressive courage was equally irritating.

The door flew open.

Fury awaited.

Britt's sparkling eyes and half-bared teeth brought to mind a wild banshee from the Corsican isles. Her clothes had dried into creased folds. Her pallor spoke to deepest stress, perhaps sickness.

Tears glimmered in her eyes when she wrenched out, "Where. Is. My. Dragul?"

Henrik gently extracted Denerfen.

"I come with a peace offering, and a proposal," he said. "Hear me out, and then you can decide if you stay or go."

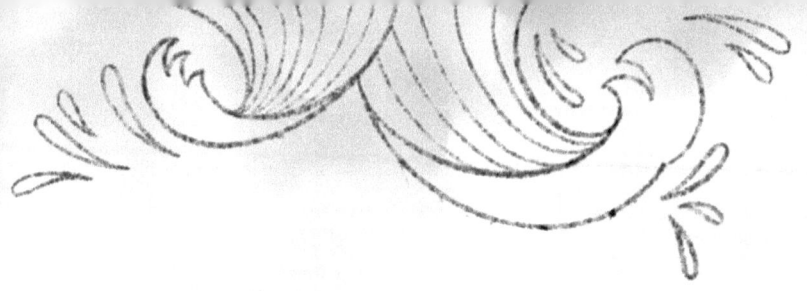

Chapter Seven

BRITT

Only twice before had Britt truly contemplated murder. Once when beset upon by a traveling merchant on the docks late in the night. With the aid of a hearty board and a wallop to his head, she'd taken care of that drunk miscreant before his hands found their mark.

The second time occurred when learning how to spar with Malcolm. He forced her to contemplate the value of a life—including her own—while he taught her ways to kill an attacker.

Today, Henrik made her rethink the intricacies and cost of ulti-mate punishment.

All day.

She woke to an empty house and damp stone walls. Gasping, she shot upright. Denerfen, and by extension, Henrik, was nowhere in sight. Panic propelled her into the cobblestone road outside the cottage, but not a soul lingered there. The empty neighborhood, punctuated by the lonely call of swooping gulls, rang.

"Denerfen," she whispered.

In four years, they'd never been separated out of sight for more than an hour or two, and only by necessity.

Fear whisked her back into the cottage. She couldn't afford to be seen, and there was more than one dragul in her care. Tesserdress curled on the blanket beneath the table and staved off a petite yawn. While Denerfen approached the world with brash energy, Tesserdress maintained a long suffering that defied her impatient dragul race.

A second bolt of terror slipped through Britt like crackled lightning.

Oh, no.

Had Henrik seen Tess?

If so, he left without waking her or Tesserdress, which meant . . . something. She didn't enjoy the idea that he might know. If he did, at least he hadn't taken both draguls. Tesserdress drew Britt back to the moment with a little cry. Britt picked her up and rubbed her cheek against Tesserdress' seeking face.

"It'll be fine, Tess. Henrik won't hurt Denerfen. He knows about draguls, remember? He met Bamerbam, and that's rare enough. He knows how precious you are. Let's give you some potion before the nasty soldat returns."

One forced, steady breath at a time, the abject horror of separating from her bonded dragul faded into the gut-clenching reality of her nightmare. She plucked the potion flute from her bag, popped the cork.

As she worked, alarm winnowed to reality. Presumably, Henrik took Denerfen to his Captain to force her hand. She might have revealed something akin to the truth after waking up, but he left without giving her a chance. If that had been his plan all along, she credited his intelligence.

She would have done the same.

Tesserdress lapped the drop of potion from her fingertip with a coo. Britt replaced the stopper, carefully setting it aside. Tesserdress ambled onto the table, sniffing around, wings held upright.

Head in her hands, Britt forced herself to strategize a plan for Denerfen *and* Malcolm's release. The picturesque, if boring, neighborhood provided an almost perfectly silent backdrop.

"It'll be fine, Tess." Britt absently traced a finger down Tesserdress' supple neck. The lady dragul shivered with a skim of energy and explored the rim of a candle plate. It clinked as Tesserdress pressed on it with her snout, then leaped away with a squawk.

Chuckling, Britt righted the swaying candle. Sweet baby dragul. Not all of them had such a lovely temperament. Certainly *not* Bamerbam, which made her lips curl in a smile. Trust Henrik to encounter the most difficult dragul.

Fitting.

Britt scooped Tesserdress up, set her on the table, and rummaged in the crate for a bowl. A wall spigot dripped water into a metal bucket. She plunged a chipped ceramic cup inside, filled it to the top, and carried it to Tesserdress. The dragul drank in fits and spurts before sitting with a sigh.

The urge to find the two orphan boys who'd helped her and learn more about the Stenberg Shadowlands was a tempting thought, but not her mission. Reporting *any* information to General Helsing would be welcome, and she'd need something to convince General Helsing not to shove her onto an island prison for several years for taking two draguls away.

If Britt left the cottage, Henrik and Denerfen could return while she was out. Henrik might assume she'd given up on her bonded dragul, and then what? Toss Denerfen out? Drown him? The thought filled her with a ferocity and rage previously unknown.

She would never abandon a dragul.

Ribbons of unease stirred in her belly, all because proximity underlined the power of the dragul bond. When separated, withdrawal inevitably resulted. Eventually, death for the dragul. A year of illness for the person.

Blessed mermaids. How did Malcolm tolerate so many days away from Tesserdress?

Like the mystery of their venom, the draguls were a puzzle imbued with unknown arcane. Somehow, breath and venom and the arcane tied the dragul bond together, but no one knew *how* exactly.

Her worried stare fell on Tesserdress. That lack of understanding over the dragul bond was precisely the reason she needed to find Malcolm immediately. Britt scrounged through the crate, and the soldat's pack, while she mumbled to herself.

No food.

Tesserdress ignored the other candleholders to sniff at the air, wings wide, tail coiled. Her little nostrils flared open and closed, eyes half-lidded, tongue scenting the air.

"A plan," Britt murmured as she paced, hands on her hips. "We can ambush Henrik when he returns, and knock him unconscious. I'll grab Denerfen and we'll leave. You'll already be in my pocket."

Tesserdress sneezed.

"You're right. It's a terrible idea. Not really a plan at all, if you think about it. Perhaps, with an average sailor, I could get away with it. But a soldat? We need a different scheme. A clever one."

Britt's stomach growled. She put a quelling hand on top.

"Food, too."

A shuffle of movement caught her attention. Bright yellow canaries fluttered by the windows, landing on the shed. Britt straightened.

"Hold on," she murmured.

The shed held crates.

Crates held things.

Presumably.

Weapons, perhaps? Opportunities to do . . . something? Considering Henrik had just returned home from a trip, it was unlikely to hold food. Worth snooping, however. Britt picked Tesserdress off the table and set her on her shoulder. The dragul curled into a contented knot, head held up.

"If he's going to leave us alone," Britt muttered, "he can bloody well tolerate a little privacy invasion. Let's go snoop in the shed."

EXPLORATIONS of the shed uncovered stashed clothing, Stenbergian leaflets on warfare, business papers, and sundries for the cottage.

Britt lugged stuff into the house and set the array on the table. Henrik didn't keep much. Two plates. Another bucket. More stiff towels. Blankets, a musty pillow fluffed with bird down, and a pile of clothes similar to yesterday's attire. Brown breeches, a gray shirt, and shoes with hearty soles. Old gauntlets, too. Worn on the inside edge, but in fair shape.

Nothing wild, but soldats loved to blend in.

The average Stenbergian sailor was an outlandish person with a penchant for attention, but like most things Stenbergian, the soldats were quite boring. Easier to blend in, and singular of focus.

Hours whittled away while she sorted, folded, refolded, dreamed about food, and coaxed Tesserdress into sips of water. Tesserdress fluttered around the cottage, toying with tiny bones not yet swept up and napping on a pillow. Footsteps hurried by twice, freezing Britt in her tracks. They slipped away as quickly, no wiser to her presence.

The cost of being away from Denerfen deepened. Exhaustion came readily. Anxiety spiked high. The intensity caught her by surprise.

"Blessed mermaids, Tess." She placed an affectionate hand over Tesserdress' wings. "How have you survived so long away from Malcolm?"

Midday came and went.

Britt walked the length of the room, alternating between daydreams of slamming her fist into Henrik's jaw and snuggling Denerfen. For all she knew, Henrik might have tossed Denerfen to his Captain.

The thought didn't serve.

When a heavy tread approached outside, she froze. The noise increased, instead of retreating. Hastily, she scooped up Tess and set her in her pocket. The steps stopped at the same moment a ray of light cut into the room. Britt threw open the door.

Henrik's broad figure interrupted the streaming sunshine, casting him in a halo. She barely restrained herself from scratching his eyes out. She set her hands on her hips and demanded Denerfen through clenched teeth, alive with righteous fury.

"Where. Is. My. Dragul?"

Henrik withdrew Denerfen from his pocket, extending him. Relief weakened her as Denerfen roared, wings spread wide, and hopped to her hand. The sound was little more than a hiccup and a hiss.

"I come with a peace offering, and a proposal," Henrik said. His wary gaze met hers. "Hear me out, and then you can decide if you stay or go."

Denerfen butted against her neck, cooing as he curled near her ear. His twitching wings rustled her hair. He nuzzled behind her, hiding in the drape of her tresses. She felt Denerfen's glare as he hissed in Henrik's direction.

"What kind of proposal?" she demanded, rapidly blinking away the tears in her eyes.

"Inside?"

Considering that she stood in his cottage, and he could have demanded instead of asked, she reluctantly stepped inside. He followed her, closing the door behind him. His left hand spread to the side in a gesture of peace.

"We have no reason to trust each other. You're hiding something from me, while sneaking onto Stenberg, and I'm a soldat for an island that's more powerful than yours."

She scoffed. Kapurnick was by *far* more powerful, but semantics would muddy the water. Britt folded her arms and glared. Denerfen purring against her neck didn't remove the haunting anxiety of the last several hours. She'd be loath to do anything he asked of her.

He carried two burlap bags to the table. One bulky with textiles, the other heavy with food. He set them on the table, his movements slow and careful. Her mouth watered at the smell of yeast and mingling cinnamon.

"I think we might be of use to each other, Britt."

Her name from his voice sent a zing from the crown of her head to her toes. "By taking what doesn't belong to us?" she snapped.

"I need something, and so do you."

"What do you need?"

Henrik braced his hands on the back of a chair and blew out a long breath. "I need help finding my birth mother."

A world of shock and curiosity passed by. Did he say . . . he couldn't . . . that is . . . a flash of something in his eyes arrested Britt as much as his statement.

Was that vulnerability?

It had to be.

His steady stare anchored her into the moment instead of spiraling into wild questions. With a breathy whisper, she managed to choke out, "Your mother?"

His jaw clenched, the sole indication of discomfort amongst the unfailing soldat exterior. "Her name is Selma. That's all I know."

"But . . . you must have . . . you were separated?" she asked, then regretted it. *Obviously* they were separated. Not only had he said as much, but his profession strongly implied it. She never heard of a soldat that kept his birth parents, but shock kept her mind from working correctly. Isles-wide tall tales whispered many supposed truths about soldats, but meeting one had overturned most assumptions. Particularly the frightening ones that Malcolm had whispered in the night while trying to terrorize her.

This blew all the rest out of the water.

If he thought her dumb, he gave no indication.

"When I was five."

"So young?"

"Yes."

"How do you remember her name?"

Another dent in his armor manifested through a frown. A chink right near the heart, like a full-grown dragon hiding heartscales.

"Selma screamed her name when they tore me away from her," he stated, his voice frosty. "She shouted and made a scene, one that I was certain not to forget. While doing it, she told me to find her."

"It's . . . impressive that you remember," she murmured, for lack of anything else. Her heart cracked at the image he painted. A small child, wrenched from his mother's arms, sobbing. Her throat thickened. She cleared it and said, "Five is . . . so young."

He didn't elaborate, but fathoms lay behind the silence. Feeling faint, Britt sat on the edge of the stone bed platform along the wall. Denerfen crossed her spine and nibbled on the bottom of her right ear. She reached up, rubbed his silky scales without thinking. The unconscious touch, and his heated breath, restored some of her difficult emotions from earlier.

Blinking away her surprise, she opted for tactical facts. "You never saw her again?"

"No."

"Your father?"

"No idea."

"Any other memories?"

He hesitated, brow furrowed. His simple, "No," was a loaded cannon. She'd dig into that later. A soldat didn't hesitate for fun.

"How am I supposed to help you find Selma?"

Seeming relieved for an outlet to his plan, he quickly said, "His Glory's Archives."

She pushed to her feet.

"What?"

He paced, one hand at his side, the other curled around his mouth. Grooves ridged his brow.

"The Archives have census records for the greater Stenbergian isles. Someone with her name should be listed there, as they don't typically take soldats from outer islands."

"Is Selma an unusual name?"

"No, and yes. It's not pure-blooded Stenbergian, if that's what you're asking."

"You have pure-blood names?"

Lips pinched, he stated, "Yes."

"I apologize if the question was rude. I didn't know."

He cut a hand through the air. "Regardless, Selma is likely to be from Stenberg, because a half-blood child cannot become a soldat. You have to be a pure-blood, unless you show beyond exceptional promise and a deal is made. Even then, you have to be at least half-Stenbergian."

"What does that have to do with the Archives?"

"Nothing," he growled. "You asked."

"Sure, but you can't go into the Archives?"

"No."

"Why?"

"Two reasons." He spread his fingers in a V. "First, my Captain can't know that I'm searching for Selma. It's not only frowned upon and punishable, but some soldats have died for launching a quest into their past. It's a threat to our focus on supporting Stenberg, and His Glory doesn't allow it."

Britt bit the inside of her cheek, awash with horror.

Blessed mermaids!

What a monster.

He continued, oblivious. "The soldats try to scrub memories of our family out of us as children. Some boys find it easier to forget. The soldats take them as young as four, but those don't survive as long as the five-year-olds."

Britt closed her eyes.

Those don't survive as long as the five-year-olds.

At this rate, she might vomit. She didn't bother asking if *survive* was the same as *live*. Of course it was. Stenberg islanders had always been obsessed with control over pain and fear. It partly explained their fixation on public flogging and torture by whip. Soldats too weak probably died in the training process.

"Second, His Glory has called for another cleansing. As a soldat, and someone who has spilled blood, I can't approach any buildings or areas near where His Glory dwells. It would be unclean."

"How terrible for you to go anywhere near the *obviously* pure man that forced you to do those deeds."

With an irritated eye roll, he ignored her sarcasm and finished his explanation with a rudimentary attempt to explain with his hands.

"The Archives are right next to the Temple and attached to the Library. His Glory is rumored to go there often to study history and make decisions, which is why it's blocked off."

"Which means you want me to go into the Archives and search for Selma."

"Yes."

He stopped moving. The intensity of his expression had taken on new weight. Gone were the breaths of vulnerability and hints of the little boy he once was. The soldat had returned, and she felt relief. This version of Henrik fulfilled her expectations. The idea that a bigger, more heartfelt shade of the domineering soldat existed stirred up flurries in her stomach. In the end, Henrik sought his mother.

Any islander could appreciate—fight for—that result.

"In return," he said slowly, "I'll give you the space to do what you came for, no questions asked."

Her head whirled in response.

No questions asked.

He offered something beyond her wildest expectations. To His Glory, the elusive and poorly-known leader of the greater Stenberg islands and their smaller chains, this offer would be akin to treason.

Henrik took an enormous risk.

He also offered just what she required.

The Archives.

Her plan to find Malcolm on Stenberg consisted solely of arriving at the island capital, finding a place to sleep, and reassessing for a new plan each day until she learned more about where he was taken. Desperation to reunite Tesserdress and Malcolm had propelled Britt to the wild plan, but it was better than their eldest brother, Pedr, could manage with his strange situation.

It was all she had.

"How often are the Archives updated?" she asked.

"Daily, as the ships come in. Mostly from the port authority, but once a month the census people check in. His Glory demands records of all port activity, shipments, invoices, etc. The port authority is the most active archivist, with imports, exports, trade contracts, wharf reports, ship manifests, etc. We calculate our return on investment from other islands, and the traffic that war and other events bring."

His casual statements made the hair on the back of her neck rise. *Our return on investment.* What an interesting way of looking at the world. Did the lens of domination lend such a calculated tone, or was that just the soldat's?

Deciding that Henrik's morality had nothing to do with her being here, she forced her mind back to the present.

In a way, Henrik offered everything she could have asked for. If His Glory truly had an obsession with such paperwork, finding Selma or Malcolm might be as simple as searching ship manifests, sailor reports, or others she didn't know existed. If she could gain access to them, any paper trail might lead her to her brother.

Or access to the Archives might *not* provide a realistic solution. What if Malcolm was far from here? What if they didn't list prisoners of war or report them or keep them? For all she knew,

Malcolm wallowed on some distant island outside her reach. She'd never heard of a local prison on Stenberg.

Dozens of questions rushed into her mind. She carefully calculated them, kept a watchful eye on Henrik's increasingly tense shoulders, and thought through the next few sentences of her response. Her decision might save all the draguls, or break them.

By extension, herself.

Her isles.

She met his glower. "The offer is bold. I can appreciate what sort of position this puts you in, and the necessity of secrecy on both our parts."

His forearms loosened, fingers relaxed. The deadly hold on his hips waned ever-so-slightly, though Henrik looked far from comfortable.

"Correct."

"If I do this, you cannot ever touch my dragul again."

"I swear it."

His immediate promise reassured her.

Questions brewed in his stormy stare. This was the crux of the agreement, and would determine just how much he wanted to know more about Selma. If he hungered for a connection with his mother again, he'd take the risk. The thought simultaneously melted her heart and cracked it again.

"Do you plan to harm anyone while here?" he asked.

She gasped, mouth open.

"Of course not!"

"How am I supposed to know?"

Irritated by the question, she snapped, "You think I'm capable?"

"Yes."

She frowned. Somewhere in that response was a compliment, but she wasn't overly interested in it at the moment.

"I swear it," she retorted, with as much truth as she could infuse in the words. "I'm not here to hurt anyone, but to . . . to save. That is all I will say."

Henrik's gaze dropped to her shoulder, where a hint of Denerfen's tail curled around her collarbone. The dragul had stopped purring to drop into a lazy sleep. No doubt his rest had been as fitful as her own. The time apart would have drained him.

Henrik studied her. "Agreed. I won't ask you why you're here as long as you aren't harming anyone, and you will conduct an honest and thorough search for Selma." The aspect of vulnerability appeared for another brief flash. "I think anyone can appreciate that sort of exchange."

She nodded once, then cast her gaze around.

"Where will I sleep?"

He nodded to the elevated stone section of the wall where he slept the night before. "I'll drag the mattress out of . . ."

He paused.

In her puttering, she'd already brought the mattress in from the shed and fluffed it up. Dust motes lingered in the air for almost an hour afterward, but her constant movements dispelled them. Seeing the plates, cups, utensils, a cushion, and folded clothes for the first time, he spun in a circle.

"I was stressed," she muttered. "You took Denerfen!"

He lifted a hand, stopping her assault of words. "It's fine. Thank you."

Surprised at his kind words, she asked, "Where can I buy food?"

Gruffly, he muttered, "I'm happy to share."

"*Happy* to share?"

Henrik waved a hand at the bags. "I bought enough for a couple of days. With any luck, both of us will be finished by then."

Hunger and relief made her lightheaded, and a bit giddy. Motivated by the stirring in her pocket, as if Tesserdress could sense that they'd just taken a step toward finding Malcolm, Britt opened her hands.

"When can I start?"

Chapter Eight

HENRIK

After Britt fed her dragul and herself, and delicately placed extra food in her pocket to eat later, she emerged from the cottage wearing an ivory linen dress. An empty linen bag hung at her side. The fabric shifted in a breeze that lifted her hair off her neck, revealing the hidden dragul under her wavy locks. The ends had a slight curl. He hated that he noticed. The slope of her nose, and the hint of a shy smile, almost enticed him to return the smile.

Almost.

In a word, she was charming, even in boring regalia. Kapurnickkians were known for bold dress and elaborate colors, with men and women wearing pants under skirts and long tunics or dresses, depending on the weather. Stenberg residents were far less extravagant than other islanders, which likely contributed to his less-than-exciting return to Stenberg.

Henrik extended a veil. A bone comb at the end would secure it into her hair, and allow her to cover her face. With a silent question in her eyes, she accepted. From his other hand, he extended a pair of ivory slippers.

"You have to wear the veil in the Archives during a cleansing, just in case His Glory shows up."

"Does he show up often?"

"Enough that the Sisters of Stenberg prepare for it. You don't want to be there without one if he does."

Her insatiable curiosity reared its head. "Oh?" she intoned with deepening interest and that prolific curiosity. "What horrible and grotesque things might happen?"

"Tossed to the whipping post, probably."

Lightly, she quipped, "Stenberg islanders love pain?"

"Just the soldats."

Her smile turned into a question. "Why is that?"

He shrugged. No one had ever asked before.

She plucked the comb from his hands to study it.

"Don't wear it now," he added, a hand upheld. "Wait until you're at the door. When we arrive at the Archives, remove your shoes and put on the slippers. There will be cubbies outside for your shoes."

"Why all the fuss?"

"The Sisters of Stenberg sanitize every surface during a cleansing, including the floors."

"It's a literal and metaphorical cleansing."

"Sure."

She studied the shoes, gaze tapered. Her hands wriggled back and forth when she held up the slippers.

"Hence these?"

"Again, you don't want to be the one bringing in sand—"

"Or not wearing a veil," she finished. "Got it. His Glory requires this?"

Henrik nodded.

If the obsessiveness of the clothing made her want to run away screaming, she gave no indication. Without any further questions, she accepted the slippers, too. Her willingness to blindly accept a move forward seemed foolhardy. If he didn't understand each nuance of a task he was assigned, he usually resisted.

"I'll walk you to the Archives today," he said, "but you'll be free to go on your own after."

Britt nodded, appearing relieved. He didn't relish the idea of strolling around Stenberg with her. Soldats drew attention wherever they went outside the Quarters. If he spent too much time with any female, tongues would wag. He might have to answer for her presence in the Archives *and* his life.

If all went according to plan, she'd find Selma, complete her task, and they'd part ways forever before questions surfaced and tongues wagged.

"What about Denerfen?" she asked.

"I'm sorry?"

A hint of color graced the top of her cheeks. "My dragul, Denerfen." With a bit more sauce she added, "Forgive me for not introducing you properly earlier. His name is Denerfen."

He hid a smile. "Can Denerfen understand me?"

"Yes . . . and no. He understands me because I use the same phrases, but he won't comprehend conversation."

"Like miniature pigs, you mean? You can train them to respond to commands. Come. Sit. Fetch."

Fire ignited in her eyes.

He wrestled back a wicked smile to ask, "What do you normally do with him, anyway?"

"I take him everywhere."

"Everywhere?"

"Mmm, but it's not a big deal in Kapurnick. Our islanders expect it, and dragul keepers are well-known. Stenberg is an altogether different world. I'm not leaving Denerfen with you."

Henrik held up two hands. "Fine. Take him."

"Can I wear my cloak?" she asked, brightening. "He always hides in the hood. Makes everything easier."

"What do you do when it's hot?"

"Wear him on my shoulder."

"Everywhere?"

"It doesn't matter on my island!"

He fought his rising exasperation. Conversations with her derailed like lightning. "No, you can't wear a cloak or take him into the Archives with you. At least, not visibly. It would draw attention and not be safe."

Challenge tightened her voice. "I won't go without him."

He pointed to the linen wrist bag in her hands. "I figured. That small pouch is big enough to carry him in it, and let it hang from your wrist. Women use them here. It won't be out of place."

Still wary, she studied the drawstring pouch with a series of questions in her eyes, then surprise. Finally, she said, "Thank you. That was . . . rather thoughtful. Give me just a minute to get him settled, and then I'll come back out and be ready to go."

Something in her specificity, and the subtle command for him to stay out here, piqued his interest. Would it really require privacy for her to put her dragul in a pouch? Deciding it wasn't worth the fight, and there was nothing wayward for her in his cottage, he brooked no argument.

Less than five minutes later, she returned. The pouch hung from her right wrist. Denerfen occupied more room than he thought. She grasped the veil and slippers in the other hand. A wide smile crossed her lips.

"I'm ready to go!"

HENRIK KEPT her by his side as they strode through the soldat's village and the Quarter, not sure what to expect. He'd never walked alone with a woman that he could recall. Not without an order to compel it. The realization hung like a heavy, and lonely, weight.

Britt massaged her bottom lip with her teeth, attention darting from stall to stall. Distant thoughts clouded her deep perusal. He wanted to inquire what frightened her most about Stenberg, but sometimes stating a fear made it bigger. She had enough to think about, although she didn't *seem* all that nervous.

"These Archives are run by the Sisters of Stenberg, you said?" she inquired in a clear voice.

He stepped around a puddle coated with sand.

"Yes."

She paused.

He realized, too late, she expected him to elaborate.

"And," she drawled, spinning her hand in a circle. "Who are they?"

"Women."

She snorted. "Well spotted."

"Women who don't legalize a relationship with any partner. They want to serve Stenberg and earn food and lodging in the meantime. Most of them would be in the Shadowlands if they didn't, or were raised as scholars."

"His Glory doesn't allow women to sail?"

He scoffed. "No."

She scowled.

Though he couldn't fathom why he cared what she thought, he said, "Stenbergians, particularly His Glory, see women as improvers. Men are brutes, for the most part. Women, though, have artistic strength and creativity our minds don't comprehend. His Glory tries to highlight them."

Her voice remained strangely still as she said, "Improvers?"

Frustration built with surprising speed. Soldats were trained for patience, so why did her every response irritate him? He struggled to know what to say. Did the shock in her voice reflect outrage, or true curiosity? He refused to look at her and find out. She made it too difficult to look away again. A woman of her beauty had no business in—

The thought stalled his feet.

Oh, no.

He paused in the middle of the cobblestone road, arrested by a sinking feeling. If *he* noticed her beauty, other Stenbergians would also.

Sailors, too.

He didn't like that.

A few paces ahead, Britt stopped and called over her shoulder, "Something wrong?"

Henrik managed to shake his head. "No," he bit out.

Mechanically, he forced himself to take one step, then another. Each one bore him closer to her and the disaster he brought upon himself. Britt wasn't stunning by the isles standards of exotic and wild features—smoky eyes, coy smile, wide hips, thick arms. Britt didn't command obedience because of her appearance either, but she had a far more powerful ease that imparted elegance.

He didn't like thinking about her beauty, which flowed deeper than prettiness, nor about the ragged edge of women's roles in Stenberg. But if *he* had noticed, others might as well. He'd have to keep her safe. Somehow.

Britt eyed him.

"Are you sure that nothing is wrong?" she drawled.

There.

Irritated *again*.

"It's just . . . I didn't think about the ramifications of working together."

"Like what?"

"How to keep you safe from Stenberg sailors, for one," he muttered, running a hand over his head. "Or what it would mean for you to be seen with me. You're a beautiful woman, I'm a soldat, and we're together in public."

A fanciful eyebrow danced higher. Why did she have to look so delighted with everything? "Not to mention that I'm sleeping in your cottage," she sang, poorly suppressing a chuckle.

"There are . . . implications."

With a flutter of eyelashes, she said, "Don't tell me that soldats don't take lovers, Henrik." Her voice lowered to a sultry whisper. "You'll never convince me of *that*."

He scowled.

She laughed.

Like a butterfly, she wandered up the cobblestone road

without him. Did she know where she was going? As she headed toward the wrong juncture in the road, he grabbed her above the elbow and tugged.

"This way."

Unbothered, she followed. He released his hand, hating the soft caress of her skin, too. He was too happy to let go.

Britt hummed under her breath as they strolled up the street. Eyes peered on them from everywhere. On this mainland isle, people were accustomed to spotting soldats, particularly with the Quarters so near. But a soldat walking with a woman drew gossipers from the shadows like rats to discarded food. Their glittering malevolence and wicked tongues seemed to lie in wait.

"Is it unusual for a soldat to be seen with a woman?" she asked.

"No."

"Just you?"

"Yes."

"Hmm . . . care to share why?"

Coldly, he said, "No."

"You might have a tendency to willingly head toward militaristic and uncomprehending deprivation," she said, "like basic shelter, warmth, and ease, but you'll never convince me that all soldats agree to live without the benefits of a lover. Don't soldats highly value their progeny?"

He ground his teeth together.

"Yes."

"Hmm . . ."

He let her drift on that unstated question, because he didn't know where to take the conversation next. Norr's breath, how far away were the Archives, anyway? When the double doors popped into view, he released a gentle exhale.

Finally.

He nodded ahead to indicate his change in subject. "The Archives. Don't underestimate anything. The Sisters of Stenberg are rumored to be the eyes and the ears of His Glory, and they pay attention."

Bemused, she asked, "To what end?"

"Searching for Selma as *my* mother will draw atten—"

"Oh, no," she cried a little too loudly, "I will search for my sister without you, silly soldat. Thank you for the offer."

She pushed against his arm with a coy smile, winked, and only a moment passed before he realized her game. She leaned closer, as if she planned to whisper, though her voice remained level.

"It's a cleansing. We must respect His Glory's dictates. You cannot go inside. Thank you for your protection, but it's not required here."

Did the churning in his gut have more to do with her adept pivot and on-the-spot thinking, or her ability to understand things so quickly he almost couldn't keep up? The twinkle in her eye hid a laugh.

He loathed that, too.

Britt stopped walking almost exactly fifty paces away from the building, which was the precise distance that custom required him to stop. Did she know more about Stenberg than he assumed? She must.

Which would be fair, because he knew about the draguls. But her knowledge of Stenberg went on the list of *things he didn't like about Britt being here.* The sudden tension in her shoulders clued him in. He followed her gaze to the left. She stared at the blood spattered whipping post.

"Cleansing," he said.

She spoke so softly he almost didn't hear. "Which includes whipping?"

"Only islanders that don't abide by His Glory's dictates. Thiefs." He hesitated, the words *crippled, maimed, unable to work,* on the tip of his tongue. Perhaps the man whipped yesterday hadn't been a criminal, but simply helpless. His Glory didn't look kindly on them, either.

"In public?" she asked.

"Where else?"

Her pressed lips uttered no response.

"You'll be fine," he said, affecting a casual stance. "I'll return in two hours—"

She waved a hand. "Don't worry about it."

"Britt—"

"I might require more than two hours."

"Don't."

"What if I don't find my sister?"

Sister.

Right.

"You can return tomorrow."

With a bite in her voice that made it clear she didn't appreciate orders, she asked, "What's the caution?"

Reality, he wanted to snap. Sailors patrolled the island and supposedly kept the market safe, but he'd trust them as much as he'd trust a toddler. He tucked those thoughts into the box with other unstated things, begging for release.

Did all Kapurnickkians breeze their way through other islands? It made no sense. She hadn't worked out a tactical plan, asked no queries about the layout of the room, the number of workers, the main objective. He hadn't even told her the hours to the Archives—

"The caution is—"

"—that you don't know if other lover-deprived Stenbergians could control themselves around me, a young and available female?"

His lips sealed, thoroughly livid now. Did she have no idea what an island full of sailors and other desperate islanders might do to a bright beam of sunshine like her? She must be jesting. She lived on an island. Kapurnick had sailors, too. This had to be part of her act.

"Two hours," he repeated.

Her gaze skipped over the whipping post as she capitulated with a shrug.

"Maybe. Ta!"

As she spun on her heels and headed for the main doors, she released a breezy wave. Half a minute later, she'd removed her shoes, shelved them, put on her slippers, and the doors closed behind her.

ONCE BRITT ENTERED the Archives and he mentally set her aside, it didn't take long to return to his cottage, sit at the table, and identify the problem in his jord paperwork.

The shipment amount that he reported wasn't the same as what the port authority captured. Henrik was missing twenty bags of jord that came into the port authority's hands. With already low numbers shipped, he couldn't afford a mistake.

He stared at the disparate columns with a steep frown. They weren't off by much, but enough. Set against the backdrop of six hundred and seventy-nine total bags of jord during his reefer year, to be accurate, the lost twenty didn't seem like much.

And yet . . .

Captain Ossian was the obvious first suspect. Had the ship captain stolen twenty bags of jord and whisked away to the islands with all haste? The option was a possibility, but didn't fit what he knew of Ossian. The captain might be a salty crustacean, but he wasn't dishonorable. Men like Ossian clutched honor like gold.

Had Henrik's other shipments reported less?

He hadn't compared notes this deeply on the other two jord shipments. Perhaps he *should* have. A niggling suspicion occupied the back of his mind. Twenty bags of jord here and there would add up to an enormous sum over the course of his year on the isles. The precious resource was hoarded to the quarter-bag by farmers.

"Captain Ossian," he said under his breath. "You are a thief, or you have one on board."

Henrik swept the paperwork up and stacked it out of sight, where water wouldn't mark the ink and he could mull on it. He grabbed his dagger, tucked it inside his pants, pulled his shirt over it, and slipped outside.

"WE'RE HOLDING a memorial for Arvid later this week." Oliver's hard stare bore into Henrik's head. "We expect you to be there."

"Yes, sir."

The Captain bent over his desk like a sea eagle, arms splayed to the side, teeth clenched. "They didn't find his body," he said quietly, and with a shake of his head. "Not a sign."

"Drowned?"

"Had to be."

After a pause, Henrik said, "Rumor says we took a hostage. A Major, at that."

"Yes."

"Can you question him?"

"Already did, before we left him at the Unseen island to battle for his life. Fitting end, if you ask me."

"No luck?"

Another head shake.

"Captain Arvid will be missed," Henrik concluded.

Oliver shifted his jaw from side to side in deepening deliberation before he straightened up. "His Glory wants to move forward with Arvid's replacement within the next month. He has confirmed that the position of Second Captain is between you and Harald. Interviews will commence . . . soon."

Shock stalled his words.

"Next month?"

"Yes," Oliver snapped. "You've proven capable except for an obvious issue with your jord reports." He braced his palms on top of the desk, forearms flexing like ham hocks. "Do I need to lecture you on the importance of details, soldat? You can *count*, can't you?"

The jibe didn't bother him.

"Yes, sir."

"Then fix it."

"I've noted the discrepancy. When the cleansing finishes, I'll go into the Archives to pull my other jord reports and ensure this was an isolated incident. I already visited with the port authority on my way over here. He's going to stall Ossian as soon as he returns so I can speak with him."

Far from mollified, Oliver said, "Where do you think the twenty bags are?"

"I have ideas."

"And?"

"I'll find the culprit."

Henrik wouldn't throw Ossian into suspicion without hard evidence, though Oliver clearly wanted more information. Losing a contract with His Glory's soldats would be the end of Ossian's illustrious career, and his life. He'd lose any other work and become a pirate, or die trying.

Oliver eyed Henrik, head tilted to the side, before he said, "It's your *job* to presume and deliver when jord is on the line. You realize that, soldat?"

"Yes, sir."

"His Glory won't settle for less."

"I hope not. I'll get to the bottom of it."

"Fine, because you're needed, Henrik." Oliver eyed him with a tension that manifested only in his eyes. He glanced down, shook his head ever-so-slightly. "Between you and me, you're a better fit than Harald. He's a good soldat, but he doesn't command the same respect as you. Other soldats will follow you, and we need that right now. More than ever."

More than ever carried the weight of fathoms in it.

"Thank you, sir."

"Not to mention that certain . . . perks . . . come with leadership."

Henrik tilted his head.

"Perks, sir?"

Drawing a deep breath, Oliver said, "Access, Henrik. As one of his five Captains, you have unfettered access to all His Glory has to offer. Whatever you desire to know, is yours. Whatever you want to see, you shall. Do you understand?"

Henrik's heart kicked up with a disbelieving hiss.

"That is very generous, sir."

Oliver scowled. "Don't toy with me, Henrik."

"I would never."

"Think about it." Oliver tapped his forefinger on the side of his temple. "All right? *Whatever* you want. His Glory is good to his Captains, particularly the First and Second. He leans on his soldats."

A moment of suspicion crept over Henrik with a creeping terror. Could Oliver know about Selma?

Impossible.

Yet . . .

"Sir, I—"

Oliver held up a hand. "No. No questions allowed. You'll receive commensurate pay, will work directly with His Glory, seal the name Henrik in history books yet again, and, of course, protect Stenberg from enemies without. There's little that His Glory with-holds from those he keeps dearest. All your closest-held desires."

All your closest-held desires.

A trap.

This had to be a trap. It wouldn't be beyond the soldat leader-ship to conduct a sneaky test, try to whittle out whether or not a soldat had closely held desires. They shouldn't. A soldat was a weapon of the island, and had no dreams beyond procuring safety for His Glory and Stenberg at large.

Before he could formulate a response, Oliver jabbed a finger at the door.

"Get out of here. Oh, and soldat? Keep things down at the upcoming grappling tournament. I won't be there."

"But—"

Oliver held up a staying hand. "I know it's tradition for me to start the grappling tournament by throwing the first punch, but you'll have to deal with it. I don't want the Old Pub getting out of hand like it did last year, or I'll cut mead rations for every bastid in the group." After a moment's deliberation, he added, "And if you can help it, win. His Glory is already inclined to choose you, but I'd like to firm up your worthiness as a candidate."

With that, he turned his back and dismissed Henrik without another word.

Chapter Nine

BRITT

When Britt stepped into the Archives, a new world unfolded.

His Glory commanded the best of everything, so white stone walls flowed in lazy grandeur, brilliant even through her veil. A line of windows too high for a person to reach without climbing spilled sunshine. A smooth exterior ensured no one could scale it. A protection from wayward, drunk sailors, no doubt.

She paused to take in the whispering women and floating dust motes.

In a word?

Lovely.

The first floor had the shape of a sprawling octagon, lined with wooden shelves and leaflets. Most islands bound their pages into books with leather covers to protect the words within, but Stenberg islanders created flimsy, short-form leaflets for their words. They opted to protect the Archives itself, instead of individual leaflets.

A tiny representation of their cosmic political strata. Forget the individual, think big.

Two women with flowing linen garb and undulating white

veils crossed her path. Sisters of Stenberg, presumably. Britt resisted the desire to remove the comb tugging on her hair. Her scalp would hurt within an hour, no matter how she adjusted it. The silky veil ended around her collarbone, frustrating her. Hope for Tesserdress and Malcolm lay on a razor-thin line.

She'd deal.

Lurking in the corner stood an older woman with a twist of lips that reminded Britt of someone sucking on a sour melon. She reeked of perturbation with her pursed bow lips and exaggerated sighs. Britt tried hard not to look at her.

A different woman hurried toward Britt. Her pearl-colored dress, simple as a prayer, hung to her wrists and ankles. The neckline scooped across her shoulders, stretching to either side with the sole decoration of a strip of bright blue lace.

"May I assist you?"

The hallowed silence permeating the room magnified through her folded hands and reserved expression. She couldn't be much older than eighteen, though her judgmental disapproval added years.

Britt smiled. "No, thank you."

The woman blinked.

"I'm sorry?"

"I don't need help."

"What are you here for?"

Silent panic assaulted Britt. She'd been so focused on getting here she hadn't planned out her next step. Eh. Such was life in the isles. *If it's not a hurricane,* General Helsing always said, *it's a typhoon.* A not-so-funny way of reminding Britt that she controlled nothing, certainly not Stenberg, Henrik, or Malcolm.

She said the first thing that came to mind. "What's your name?"

The woman reared back.

"My name?"

"Yes."

The pause bought Britt a moment to recover. *Why* had she come again?

Right.

Henrik. Malcolm.

Selma.

"My name is Raquel."

Like the name Henrik, Raquel was as Stenbergian as a woman could embody. From what little Britt had studied of Stenbergian history, at least four of ten famous women were called Raquel, earning acclaim for perfectly boring deeds in honor of unswerving loyalty to His Glory. In Stenberg, women didn't get the luxury of adventure.

"A lovely name."

Raquel lifted her brow, clearly immune to the compliment. "Again," she drawled, "how can I help you?"

Britt formed a circle with her thumb and forefinger. As she began to lift it upward, in the typical Kapurnickkian greeting, she stopped. Her fingers relaxed as she pretended to fan her face, preventing Raquel from seeing the giveaway motion.

Britt smiled, her lips tense. "Sorry. Hot in here today."

Suspicion lined Raquel's tone.

"Is it?"

Well, this wasn't going at *all* the way Britt hoped. She'd have to plow her way through.

"I'm Bri—"

Stopping mid sentence left a ringing vowel in the air. If she were any more foolish, she'd take herself to the depths of the sea and stop swimming. She couldn't tell this purely Stenbergian woman her name. If somehow it was discovered that she snuck around the island, and they tried to track Britt's movements around Stenberg, she'd lead them right to her.

Raquel's other brow rose slowly.

"Brih, did you say?"

"Forgive me!" Britt fanned her eyes, nose scrunched. "Almost had a sneeze. My name is Bridgette. That's it."

"Bridgette?"

"No, Bridge is fine."

"You want me to call you Bridge?"

"Sure."

Britt widened her tight smile. The look she received in exchange was anything but pleasant. Suspicion deepened with every second. Raquel folded her hands again, rearranging them so the bottom now rested on top.

"Bridge, how may I help you in His Glory's Archives? This is a sacred space that we take quite seriously." She motioned to Britt's slippers, then her robe. "We appreciate you taking care to support him with the cleansing as he strives to support Stenberg in our fights with the mainland."

Britt forced her sober expression to remain.

"Long live His Glory."

To Raquel's credit, the pinched intensity gave way ever-so-slightly. *Noted,* Britt thought. She could placate the Sisters of Stenberg with unswerving servitude to His Glory. Sometimes, the worst of tyrannical leaders made it only too easy to thwart them.

"I came here today for . . . ship manifests, Raquel. Do you happen to know where I can find any?"

Ship manifests sounded legitimate enough. It provided a starting point, anyway.

"You're here for ship manifests?"

Raquel's emphasis was utterly unmeasurable. What did it mean? Whether Britt shouldn't have been requesting ship manifests, or something in her physical appearance led Raquel to suspicion, she couldn't ascertain. The request had been made, and she couldn't withdraw it.

Britt lifted her chin ever-so-slightly. "Yes. I'd like to look at the ship manifests for all the ships that came into Stenberg in the last . . . three weeks. I'm looking for my sister," she tacked on.

Malcolm had been apprehended by Stenberg sailors just over two weeks ago, but that would be putting too fine and obvious a point. If she requested too large of a time gap, she'd waste precious minutes searching more than required. Henrik, Selma, Malcolm, and Tesserdress relied on her ability to navigate a simple search.

Then again, the mistake was hers.

This was *Stenberg.*

Nothing was simple.

Raquel made a noise in her throat and glanced over her shoulder at another woman in the same muted, bland clothes. Britt quelled the urge to race free. If she left now, they'd consider her nothing more than a weird patron. The longer she stayed and gabbed her fat mouth with details they didn't need, she'd give herself away.

The glowering woman from the far corner wandered over. She had a severe expression, no eyebrows, and sunken cheeks. Shadows created bags under her eyes. Britt wanted to curl up and take a nap for her.

"High Matron," Raquel said in an annoyingly unreadable tone, "this is . . . Bridge. She has requested to see the ship manifests for any ship that came into port over the last three weeks. She searches for her sister."

Did they train these women to be impossible to read? Did Britt imagine a pique in Raquel's tone when she said *for any ship*? It might have been wiser to be more specific, but she didn't want to say Kapurnick and create an association.

She didn't imagine the lour leveled at her. The High Matron, whatever purpose she served, graced Britt with undisguised suspicion and distrust.

For all Henrik's preparations in his life and the unswerving loyalty to find his lost birth mother, he couldn't have warned Britt about the High Matron's hostility before she crossed the threshold?

Then again, he likely didn't know.

Thankfully, Denerfen and Tesserdress remained calm in her wrist bag, possibly smelling Britt's tension. Denerfen had a habit of twitching through intense situations. Keeping him from giving himself away had always been a feat of willpower.

"You're looking for the ship manifests?" the High Matron murmured. "Your sister would be listed on the passenger manifest, assuming she arrived via ship?"

"True! I'd like to see those too, please."

"I'm afraid we cannot allow that."

"Why not?"

"His Glory's policy."

"I'm asking on behalf of Henrik. He's a soldat," she added.

"A soldat is looking for your sister?"

Britt smiled, her stomach in a fluttering panic.

"Yes."

The High Matron's infernal high-handedness lowered dramatically. Her lips drooped, then pursed. The sudden flash of reluctance disappeared almost as quickly as it came. Ah. Soldats *did* wield the power she anticipated.

Noted, she thought a second time.

"I've never had a soldat request a ship manifest in search of someone else's sister," the High Matron said. The drawling tone, combined with eyes the width of a slash, set Britt on edge.

Britt smiled with all her teeth. "Would you like to ask him yourself? He personally escorted me here and is waiting outside. I'm sure he'd love to explain himself to a Sister of Stenberg."

Hesitation replaced the bold inquiry. After several elongated beats, the matron dropped her inquisition with a prim, "I don't think that will be necessary," but didn't remove her glare.

"Henrik just returned from a year serving His Glory in the outer isles." Britt kept her breezy smile firmly in place. "If you like, I'm sure you could discuss this with his Captain?"

The question could backfire in magnificent ways. Britt didn't know the Captain's name, nor whether that threat had power. Fortunately, the High Matron didn't appear inclined to pick a fight with soldat leadership.

Raquel backed away and left Britt firmly in the dragon's

talons. The High Matron lifted a hand and curled two fingers and made a bold elevation of her upper lip. She made no effort to hide her disgust.

"Come, please."

THEY WAFTED through the first floor, which wasn't very big. Other sisters bedecked with veils and slippers shuffled through leaflets and ignored the dragon matron. Their murmurs resembled the dry rustle of turning pages.

The High Matron led Britt to the corner of the room, where a staircase wound higher. Questions gummed up Britt's throat as they ascended.

Why the garb? What did a High Matron do? How many women worked in the Archives? She couldn't fathom what His Glory found cleaner about women than men, but had a feeling it had something to do with violence. His Glory only sent male soldats and sailors to defend their lands, investments, or jord. Other island chains allowed women to fight or lead their warriors, but not Stenberg.

If Stenbergians truly believed women couldn't be violent, they wouldn't last a day on the mainland. Stenberg also didn't invest in or allow use of the arcane or potions. In a word?

Boring.

The stairs led past a second floor. Artifacts, paperwork, chairs, tables, magnifying glasses, and fountain pens littered the area. Four walls created a square wider than the floor below, though the outside of the building didn't mimic the interior.

Odd.

Also, Stenberg. They might hide things in the walls.

The High Matron persisted toward a third floor, where the air held an indefinable stillness. About half the size of the first floor, the walls loomed close. Aged wooden boards framed the inside. The lack of chipped stones and the freshness of the rug meant it had been erected later.

The High Matron stopped in front of a waist high cabinet. When she tugged on a brushed nickel handle, it rolled toward her. She swept a hand over the collection inside. Cluttered papers, with jagged edges and various stages of yellow coloring, packed together.

"The latest ship manifests, sorted by day, over the last year." She tugged open a second drawer to the right. "This is all passenger manifests."

"Between the two of them, it includes everything?"

"All imports and visitor logs."

Britt felt her stomach drop. She hadn't expected so *much* paperwork. Was the wharf really so busy? She hadn't been paying attention when she darted past Henrik and raced through the market before her venom faded, though it was possible. Ships constantly freckled the waters.

How could she find Malcolm in all this?

Was he an *import*?

A visitor?

It seemed unlikely that even Stenbergians would consider a prisoner of war an import, but one never knew with islanders. She'd heard of stranger things.

"Naval ships, too?" she asked.

The High Matron frowned. "No. They are in the third drawer to the right. In the event that you don't find what Henrik wants there, sometimes they are misfiled as a merchant acquisition." She patted the folders beneath her hand, in the fourth and final drawer of the cabinet. "Which are here. We close in two hours."

Two hours.

Henrik would get his wish after all.

Britt swung around to face the drawers. "This is quite helpful, thank you."

The Matron wafted the other direction, descending the stairs so smoothly Britt couldn't look away. Thanks to General Helsing's demands, Britt had sailed through her fair share of decorum lessons. Not that they were hard, as decorum was little more than rules around presentation, but Britt never had a tutor that truly floated, like the High Matron. A woman with that intensity was wasted in a rote place like the Archives.

After confirming she was alone, Britt lowered the pouch off her wrist and peered inside. Denerfen curled around a sleeping Tesserdress. They yawned together.

"Tess?" she whispered.

The sleepy female opened her eyes, peeped a noise, and closed them again. A tiny bald spot behind one of her ears drew Britt's attention. Her heart rose into her throat. "I'm working on it," she whispered. "I'll find him, I promise."

Denerfen wrapped one wing over the top of Tesserdress. She snuggled in, hidden beneath. Britt settled them on top of the second drawer. Determination cleared her irritation against the High Matron.

Against all odds, she would uncover both of their lost family members.

Chapter Ten

HENRIK

The last two hours had been agony.

Between worrying that she'd find nothing, she'd find something, or would never return, Henrik's composure nearly crumbled to ash the moment a breath of wind skittered by.

The wicked swirl of his thoughts spun constantly around this plan. Idiocy lined everything about his pursuit of Selma. His past was a lost cause. He had never heard of a soldat attempting to find his family, nor reuniting. Most of them remained satisfied with not knowing, or if they weren't, never spoke of it. Other soldats came from orphanages or the Shadowlands and proved scrappier than most because they lacked ties, not because they had family to begin with.

He'd given Britt the dragul, so why wouldn't she flee? Any self-respecting islander would take their advantage and throw away the rest.

Because, whispered his instinct, *this* is *to her advantage.*

The thought led to others that distracted him away from fear of Selma being eternally lost. Whatever Britt sought on Stenberg, she must assume she'd find it in the Archives. She'd agreed too quickly for it to not provide benefit. Britt cradled fire while sneaking around Stenberg, searching.

With that thought, a familiar visage appeared in the Archives doorway. Britt's neutral expression and bland smile utterly confounded him. In the very small amount of time he'd known her, she flouted all emotions on her face. Something terrible must have happened.

After taking a painstaking amount of time with her slipper removal, she managed to drag out donning her shoes, removing her veil, balancing the bag on her wrist, tucking her slippers into a hidden pocket, and sedately crossing the fifty steps between them.

When she joined his side, his nerves frayed. "Take you long enough?" he sniped.

The scorn she leveled at him did the job of reprimanding him without words.

"Sorry," he mumbled. "I just . . . I've been worried."

"About me?"

"Well . . . yes."

"Darling," she trilled. "A soldat with a soul. Who knew?"

His insecurities bled away as she smiled at him. That irrational surge of frustration swelled again, this time more confounding than ever, for he leveled it at himself.

Britt strode in the correct direction toward the soldat Quarter. Fists doubled at his side, he followed. Breaths restored his internal equilibrium. With as neutral a voice as he could manage—he had a feeling that he didn't execute it all that well—he asked, "What did you find?"

"Nothing."

"I'm sorry?"

"Nothing so far. For all your island conquering and alliances, Stenbergians are rather unorganized. Have you noticed?"

"No."

"Not surprising. We're all blind to the truth before our eyes. Myself included," she added, as if making a great concession.

Henrik tightened his fingers until the bones threatened to crack. Clearly, he'd have to find a different approach to speaking with her, as common sense didn't shout loud enough.

"Britt, please explain to me what you did or did not find."

Using her name had a surprising effect. Her perpetual smile widened. "I will, thank you for asking so nicely. I can tell that doing so is hard for you. I found ship manifests, census records, a few women that didn't really like me, and a lot of obstacles."

"Obstacles?"

"Namely, my inexperience with the Archives."

"What were you doing for the last two hours if you have nothing to show for it but an idea of what they offer?"

Somewhere in the back of his mind, he regretted the harsh question. Too intense, too revealing. If she dove to the end of his thought, she'd comprehend how much he cared. Caring was dangerous. Yet, he couldn't take it back. Admittedly, he wouldn't. Britt could handle a little more fear for her daily life.

The saucy look she shot him made it clear she didn't appreciate his demand. Henrik backed off, but only in his head. The question lingered as they strolled past a grocer stall. An apple flew toward him from within. He caught it, waved a hand to the grocer as thanks for the gift.

"For your beautiful lady!" the man called.

Britt blew him a kiss, and the man laughed until his belly quaked. Henrik schooled the ever-building fires of his righteous indignation. Did she have to command attention everywhere? Particularly *that* sort of attention?

She illuminated as she spun to face Henrik, setting a hand on his arm. "Is that a Stenbergian apple?"

The heat of her warm palm distracted him.

"What?"

"Is that a Stenbergian apple?" she repeated, more slowly this time. "Shiny. Purple. Slightly firm, but not egregiously so, with a stem out the top. You know? They grow on vines, from the jord."

He lifted the little fruit, tinted with swirls of lightest blue around the edge of the royal purple rind. The entire thing fit easily in his palm, no more than a few bites big, with white spots along the top.

"This?"

"No, the *other* fruit he chucked at you."

"What do *you* think this is?"

"Looks like an apple to me," she reasoned. "But I've never eaten one from Stenberg before. They're so . . . quaint."

"You've never eaten an apple?"

"Not from here! Can I try it?"

He withheld it to his other side. "After you give me more details about the Archives. You're dodging an answer. Why? Bad news? We can't find Selma? If there are census records, there must be a trail."

She rolled her eyes. "You. Are. So. Emotional."

He stopped in his tracks.

"What?"

Her hands propped on her hips. "I'm not taking it back. You're the most emotional man I've ever met."

"Emotional!" he thundered. "I've been called many things, but nev—"

She smiled so prettily he balked into silence.

"Point made," she sang, twirling a finger toward him. "And no, I'm not avoiding talking about what I found or didn't find. I'm . . . soaking in the details and thinking about how to tell you what I observed. You flung me to the barracudas, thank you very much. I don't want to bore you with dumb trivialities."

The broader explanation nearly distracted him from the fact that she'd called him emotional. Not a soul in his life had ever applied such a descriptor to him or anyone he knew. Yes, he had emotions. Of course he did. Only fools discounted the truth. He *controlled* said emotions, however.

"Dumb trivialities?" he repeated.

She made a grabby motion with her hand.

With a warning glare that should have frightened her, but clearly didn't, he dropped the apple in her open palm. She studied it, flicked a piece of dirt off the edge, giggled to herself, then bit it with her eyes closed. Her dark lashes splayed, highlighting her elegant cheeks. Her lazy chewing, the way she sucked the juice out of the apple, and then feathered her eyes open would have leveled a lesser man.

Norr's breath.

Did this woman have seduction, or innocence, down to an art? She either knew exactly what she was doing or she simply lived her life through the lens of enjoying every little thing. Confounding, either way.

"Delicious!" she cried. Her expression lowered as she tossed her gaze to the right, then the left, then to him again. Her thumb jerked to the side.

"Are you ready to go, or did you want to stand here all day?"

BRITT UNRAVELED a tale that should have bored Henrik, but her cadence, emphasis on details like *disapproving frown* and *petite face* and *why do so many Stenbergians wear ivory?* prevented it. She wound them together, holding his attention, as he couldn't recall anyone doing before. She was his only path to Selma, which meant he had to accept her strange way of storytelling instead of recitation of facts, observations, and obvious next steps in her action plan. He accepted it, and . . . enjoyed it.

In her unraveling report of locating cached census records and struggling through ship manifests and unfiled import lists, he lost the sense that she hid something from him and began to understand the biggest obstacle they'd face.

Somewhere in her unholy amount of words existed a simple line of fact: policy. His Glory loved layers of security created by standardized practices, particularly with a place as valuable as the Archives.

That was Henrik's enemy.

She paused for her first breath, so he took his opportunity to speak. "Unfortunately, I won't be able to change any of those details. The policy is the policy."

"I know."

He sent her a questioning glance.

She finished a delicate bite of apple and said, "I never asked you to fix the problem. I was just telling you what it was." She pointed a finger to herself. "Perfectly capable, thank you."

Stupidly, he'd expected complaints. Groans. Dramatic demands that he make it easier. His experience with women had limited bounds.

Very limited.

"Well . . . great."

He capitulated with a hand, and she continued her exposition. At the end, exhaustion swept through him. This journey to find Selma had only begun, and was already riddled with obstacles. Buried in the layers of his mind had been a hope that she'd float out of the Archives and into his hands.

Foolish.

No, capricious.

Two things he'd never had the luxury of being.

Britt plucked seeds out of the fruit's core and flicked them away. "That was that. I'll return in the morning, and plan to focus on the census. Any idea when Selma might have been born?"

He grimaced. "Not really."

Britt waved a hand, smiled at a little girl as she passed, and trailed next to his left arm as they turned toward the Quarters. Most people walked slightly behind a soldat. Britt showed no such compunction.

"The second floor had more people on it than the third floor," she said. "Hopefully, in the morning, it'll be simpler."

"Hopefully," he echoed.

She stopped in the middle of the road, head cocked to the side. "Have you been in the Archives before?"

"No."

"Why not?"

"Why?" he countered as quickly.

She set a hand on her hip, considered, and shrugged. "Sure. Why would you have been inside? You're a soldat. Who needs to pursue academics when you're mastering weapons?"

He left the metaphorical question behind, surprised at her lack of judgment. Soldats were anything but uneducated simpletons. The training Captain required as much mental work from his trainees as physical. Grueling hours of philosophical, algebraic, and literary homework tightened his schedule as a young man, along with brutal physical training.

Besides, every fool that lived in the isles perfected some sort of weapon, so she wasn't being flippant.

"Is going berserk a real thing?" she asked.

"What?"

"You know . . . the phrase? *Don't let a soldat go berserk.*" She fluffed a hand in the air. If he held her wrists, would her mouth stop working? "Islanders say it all the time at our wharf, from all over the Isles. It's rooted in truth, isn't it?"

"Yes."

"Is it real?"

He ran his tongue over his teeth, loath to answer. "It's . . . real. *Going berserk* is a state of mind in battles where all senses are heightened and you're making fast decisions to keep yourself alive. It's . . ." He paused, casting for a comparison. "Like when a painter stops eating and drinking because they're consumed by their art?"

She quirked an eyebrow.

"Same thing."

Except it's not, her silence seemed to say. He wouldn't normally entertain such a question, but considering the path to Selma relied on her cooperation . . .

"Interesting," she said. "Have you *gone berserk*?"

"No. I hope I never have to."

"Ever seen it?"

"Once."

"What happened?"

"He died," he said flatly.

She kept silent.

Henrik ground his molars together as he walked.

"So," she said in a long-suffering tone that made his fury rise. As if *she* had been the patient one these last twenty minutes of getting to the point. "I did manage to gather some interesting documents and place them somewhere safe within the Archives. They'll receive my attention first tomorrow. Do you know when it opens?"

"Sunrise."

"Perfect!"

When they returned to the cottage, she squeaked, headed toward the bag of food on the table, and carefully set the handbag down. Denerfen's head peeked out, sniffing toward a small loaf of sourdough. His wings folded onto his spine.

Henrik sank onto a chair and put his head in his palms, grateful for a few moments without her chattering voice.

It didn't last long.

Britt sat on the chair next to him. He ignored her. When her warm palm landed on his shoulder and remained, he didn't brush it away. He should have.

"We'll figure it out, Henrik. I promise. We'll find Selma. It'll take me a little time to get my bearings in the Archives, but I will. I promise. I'm on your side."

Before he could correct her—he didn't require comfort, just silence—she departed, swift as gossamer.

Here, gone.

Denerfen's long neck rooted through the white bag as she withdrew pitas and cheese and dried grapes and golden apple rings. The dragul stood on the table, front legs elevated, sniffing as she plunked a piece of hard yellow cheese in front of him.

Henrik stood.

He had to get out of here and away from Britt. Take some deep breaths, prepare himself for an evening full of her incessant chatter. Maybe she'd fall asleep quickly. Outside of Einar, he'd never heard the words, *I'm on your side*, and had no reason to believe he ever would again.

Oh, how he loathed them.

THE NEXT MORNING, Henrik awoke before he opened his eyes.

He fully expected that Britt wouldn't be there. If she had any sense of self-preservation, she would have stolen away in the night. Whatever information she sought on Stenberg, she likely found while in the Archives yesterday. The promise of *I'm on your side* might be a loosely given placation to someone she viewed as a captor.

One could hardly call him a captor, considering she had her dragul, he fed her, she slept on his mattress while he slept under the table, and she could leave at any time. Besides, she came here on her own. She probably said encouraging phrases to everyone. That was the only thing that made sense.

He rubbed the heel of his hand into his eyes to wake up. They opened to the underside of the table. Sunshine wasn't the only thing illuminating his cottage. Off to the side, Britt's legs shuffled around, giving him immediate pause. He couldn't see her from the waist up, but he could hear her. Of course. Britt trilled under her breath, her hips shimmying in a dance that rotated them in wide circles.

He turned onto his side.

"Sorry to wake you," she chirped in a not-sorry tune. "I wanted to arrive at the Archives early today and keep searching, but didn't want to go hungry. I've set out some food for breakfast, if you want to join. You *do* eat breakfast, don't you?"

He groaned and closed his eyes.

"No."

"Really?"

"Yes."

She mumbled something about grumpy soldats while a clatter of dishes, a squawk of her dragul, and the hush of her sandals brought him further out of sleep. Denerfen flew in circles overhead, zipping around the cottage and shooting smoke. Every now and then, he'd land on her shoulder, then push off again with a squawk.

Maybe it would have been preferable if she *had* left in the night.

"Oh, a letter came for you this morning." She tapped a finger on a small piece of paper, folded into an upright triangle on the table. "Looks official, with a wax seal." She whistled low. "You must be important. Anyway, I'm heading out."

Was it his sleepy state, or did she seem oddly comfortable navigating Stenberg? He'd expected light paranoia and moderate suspicion of Stenberg's less-than-safe markets, through which she had to walk to find the Archives.

She paused in the doorway. "Did you need anything while I'm out?"

Her question amused him deeply. "If I did, how would you buy it?"

"Trade." She scoffed, as if it should have been obvious. "You act as if this was the first time I've ever snuck onto Stenberg. Ta!"

The sun vanished.

Almost a full minute passed before Henrik gathered his brain and made sense of what she said. She'd been to Stenberg before?

Scratch that.

She'd *snuck onto* Stenberg before?

Stenberg was an open island, though mostly at the market. To venture into buildings or other places, known guests had to fill out a form. Which, as he considered her comments on their Archives, seemed a bit ironic. Visitors had to prove that they had a reasonable reason to stay on the island. His Glory welcomed anyone to the wharf market for purchasing, however.

Kapurnickkians, in general, remained far from Stenberg unless an invitation was granted. Surely, that's what she meant. She snuck onto Stenberg as a Kapurnickkian without invitation.

Ignoring the temptation of food, he rolled out from underneath the table, dressed in short pants and an old shirt, and forced himself outside. Worrying about Britt wasn't efficient. She'd be far safer from wandering sailors at the Archives, and he could avoid explaining her presence.

Henrik shook his head. Only a fool would hope for simplicity when Britt was involved. He may not know her well, but he knew *that*. One glance at the upright message drew his mind elsewhere entirely. He knew that wax seal.

The port authority.

Ossian was back.

CAPTAIN OSSIAN LOOKED like a man that the sea had gobbled up, chewed around, and spit back out. Decades of sea spray and sunshine and disease pockmarked his ruddy face. He had eyes sharp as flints, whittled to tapered lines, in the happiest of circumstances. Nothing made him smile except the smell of sea foam, jord, and the jangle of coins in his pocket.

He wasn't smiling now.

His salt-and-pepper sideburns bristled when Henrik entered the port authority's office. Ossian's impressive ship perched atop the splashing water in the outer bay. Smaller dories had ferried him and a few other sailors in. All of them waited, chained to posts, for the captain to be set free.

Henrik sat across from Ossian. To the port authority, Henrik said, "Remove his irons."

Without question, the port authority—a reedy, silent type of man around soldats—hopped up, removed Ossian's irons, and shuffled to the other side of the room with the clink of shivering chains.

"Out," Henrik commanded. "And remove the irons from his crew. Tell them to take an hour at the Iron's Brew Pub. The soldats will pay for one pint of grog for each man, and I approved the charge. The pub is expecting them."

With a sigh as his only form of rebellion, the port authority obeyed. Ossian studied Henrik as the door closed.

"My apologies," Henrik said. "I didn't tell him to put you in irons, or your crew. The disrespect was not intended."

Ossian leaned back ever-so-slightly, but his attention remained outside. He didn't say a word to Henrik until the port authority had released his men. Once free, they scowled at the grimy, sea-rubbed windows, gave a rude gesture with their arms, and filtered across the street to the seedy tavern.

Once inside, Ossian barked, "I didn't steal it."

Henrik hid a smile.

"Where is the jord, Ossian?"

"I swear I didn't steal it."

"I believe you."

Ossian paused, assessed. After a nervous twitch of his nose, he said, "While we were unloading, two men came to the port and took the twenty bags. They weren't even sneaking around about it. Just took them. We protested, naturally."

"And?"

He shrugged. "They didn't care."

Irritation filled Henrik like a cresting wave. "You didn't think to stop them? Do you let any bastid take whatever jord they want?"

Ossian recoiled, as if Henrik struck him. "Now!" he cried. "There's no reason to be insulting. You may have been on my ship for the last several months, but that doesn't make us friends."

"I never presumed."

"They were soldats," Ossian hissed, planting both hands on the edge of the table and gripping it. "I wasn't about to stop them and neither were my men."

Henrik's breath stopped in his chest.

"Soldats?" he repeated.

Ossian nodded once. He wound a hand over his head in a swirl. "With the hair, the body type, the surly glare they teach all of you. Soldats. I spoke with them myself, and they said that His Glory sent them for it. I asked how many, and they said twenty, but to count the jord on the register anyway."

"Why?"

"I tried to ask, but they threatened to take my teeth."

Take my teeth meant they'd remove his position as captain, through both literally knocking out his teeth and scuttling his ship. Most captains flecked their teeth with gold, a privilege only for captains. The tradition spanned all islands.

"Did you press it?"

"Not even for you," Ossian replied with his usual unflinching honesty. "They had weapons and my boys wanted to live. We let them go. Figured you'd come around if it was important enough."

"Is that why you reported your manifests to the port authority and then hauled off so quick?"

Ossian said nothing.

"You also noted the twenty bag discrepancy on the paperwork," Henrik said. "Why?"

Another shrug. Ossian tilted his head back, nose in the air. "Didn't seem fair to you. After so many trips together . . . you're decent," Ossian grumbled. "A bastid and a problem, but decent. Other soldats aren't."

Henrik leaned his elbows onto his knees, parsing through what he could. Two soldats? Twenty bags of jord? A threat to remove his captain's status?

Nothing made sense.

"Where did they take the jord?"

"Shite if I know." Ossian grunted. "They had a wagon, took it into the market. They're rolling in it with miniature pigs, I hope."

Henrik stood, the chair rattling behind him as he moved to the window and stared out. Up until the point Ossian said *soldats*, he hadn't been entirely certain this whole affair was worth the trouble. Having involved his comrades, however . . .

"How much could soldats get for a bag of jord on the black market, Ossian?"

"Not sure, but at least a month's salary." Hastily, he added, "A sailor's month salary, not you. You're not . . ."

He trailed off.

Paid, Henrik wanted to finish for him. *We're not paid, simply taken care of and given license to kill those who threaten without as much questioning as others.*

A raw deal.

"Thank you, Ossian." Henrik spun around to face him. "Good luck with your next haul."

Ossian paused. "That's it?"

"What more do you want?"

"You're not going to detain me?"

"Should I?"

Astonishment dropped Ossian's chin. "You believe me?"

"I believe two men you thought were soldats took it," he countered.

After months on the seas with Ossian, Henrik didn't think the man would lie. Not to his face. The opportunity for Ossian to take advantage of Henrik had been ripe for too long. Why on the last run, on Stenberg, and for only twenty bags?

It didn't follow.

Ossian swallowed. "I'm telling the truth," he insisted.

Against his instinct, Henrik admitted, "I know."

Further stymied, Ossian turned to go. As he spun, he stopped. "One of them, the soldat I spoke with? He had a really gruff voice.

Gravelly. Broad shoulders, too. Not the kind of man to mess with. He had the soldat brand. I saw them when they turned and strode away with the jord."

The *soldat brand* was the sign of whip scars along the back, curling across the top of the neck in wretched stripes. Ossian shrugged and vanished before Henrik changed his mind.

Henrik stared at the doorway where Ossian disappeared, lost in thought.

Chapter Eleven

BRITT

The Archives smelled as musty as the vegetables Henrik purchased. Stenberg vegetables tasted like sand, with little vitality and no soul. It was the jord. They needed more jord, and better jord. Kapurnick sent less and less, with less quality, too.

Britt wound up the stairs to the third floor and planted herself in front of the same shelf. With steely determination, she dove into Captain's logs and trained her eyes to find Malcolm's name. A pattern emerged on the page. Many merchant captains kept records in the same manner in order to please His Glory and stay in the port authority's good graces, so the columns became easy to anticipate.

When no archive patrons appeared after half an hour, Britt let both draguls prowl beneath her skirts. They instinctively stayed in the shadows, clinging to the inside of her underdress when a noise sounded, and tumbling quietly together when silence rang.

An hour later, she returned the Captain's logs from the past three weeks.

Not a single clue.

Bundling both draguls into the handbag, she made her way down the stairs. The crick in her neck faded. She'd spent who-knew-how-long on Malcolm. Time to search for Selma. Not only out of obligation to Henrik for giving her food and a place to sleep, but she couldn't stand the panicked desperation in his eyes.

Britt peeled off the stairs and onto the second floor, welcomed by the scent of oily ink. She navigated around tall shelves and toward the far edge of the room, where the placard read *Census Records*.

"Quick math, Den," she murmured. "Henrik said he's thirty-something, which means he's not exactly sure how old. Let's assume thirty-five. Most women in Stenberg, arguably, have their first child sometime in their twenties. Let's assume she was exactly twenty when she gave birth to Henrik, with a five year differential on either side. That puts her birth census record at anywhere from fifty to sixty years ago."

Her fingers bobbled along the edges of thin leaflets. Scads of them stuffed each shelf in a vertical, horizontal, and disorganized array. No arcane to liven this place up. The libraries on the mainland had arcane-infused shelves that automatically organized and coded books based on title.

Off to the side, two Sisters of Stenberg marched up the stairs in a sedate rhythm. Unnerving, their stiff shoulders and necks. Almost too late, Britt replaced her veil.

Close call.

A male figure ascended amidst a gaggle of women. Two things immediately distinguished him as different. First, short-cropped hair brushed with silver. Second, a uniformly unnatural confidence. Britt's heart dropped into her stomach. Her palms turned clammy. Blessed mermaids, but that bastid His Glory had arrived.

To the *Archives*.

She gripped the top of her pouch, hissed, "Not a sound!" and placed the draguls in her skirt pocket. It bulged, but she'd risk it.

Whispers accompanied an influx of Sisters of Stenberg, who surrounded His Glory like maniacal chicks. His Glory glided with liquid grace off of the stairs. Sisters of Stenberg ballooned with him, an artery chugging blood. Despite the infusion of life, hardly any sound accompanied the party.

The anticlimactic result of standing this close to His Glory was a dropping disappointment.

After years of building up his existence as Norr's son, Britt expected sunbeams to shoot out of his fingertips, or soft flute music to play in his presence. At the very least, an odd sense of attachment or euphoria on his face. Stenbergians believed him to be the penultimate example of a man. The son of their sea god.

He seemed fairly normal.

Bland, like his island.

Dark, assessing eyes. A patrician face and boxy chin, with an utterly normal set of shoulders. Nothing spoke brutal strength or fearlessness, the way his political methods suggested. His hair complimented the five Captains that helped run Stenberg, cropped near the head. She'd seen no other Stenbergian with a similar hairstyle.

Not an accident.

Just as only soldats were allowed to crop their hair along the side of their heads and leave the top long, wearing it in braids or wrapped buns.

One might call His Glory handsome. Not worthy of the sun comparison that the Stenbergians claimed, but not grotesque.

Nothing like Henrik.

She escorted the thought out.

Why had His Glory come to the Archives today of all days? It meant something. A shiver of paranoia wondered if she had called him here. No, because life didn't work like that. For however much the Stenbergians thought of His Glory as the literal son of Norr, he was only a man.

Breathless, Britt slipped to the end of the bookshelf and pressed her spine to the back. No matter what happened today, His Glory could *not* question her. She'd never make it through without betraying something. He may not appear as terrifying as he acted, but his political prowess and brutality remained unmatched.

Heart thumping, she peered around the edge shelf, then cursed under her breath. He moved closer.

Unlikely that His Glory would recognize her as Britt, niece of General Helsing, despite the uncanny resemblance. He might see something he recognized, but little else.

Still.

She couldn't risk it.

His beatific expression while he spoke with several Sisters of Stenberg nauseated her, not to mention their clucking approval. On deeper study, a lesser number of the Sisters of Stenberg didn't appear eager to fawn over him, adopting a general cool hauteur instead.

Didn't all Stenbergians blindly adore him? She overturned all sorts of false beliefs while here. His Glory strode toward the wall where Britt attempted to hide. The shelves held no backing, making it impossible to slide down the aisle and spirit away unnoticed. She chewed on her bottom lip and glanced from side to side. No obvious escape path lay apparent.

She'd walked herself into a corner.

Unless . . .

His Glory approached, speaking with a rise and fall of emotion and curiosity, " . . . the Archives are of utmost importance in Stenberg, sister . . ."

Throwing caution to the wind, she reached for the closest leaflet she could find, plucked it from the shelf, and threw the cover open. She pressed her right shoulder to the bookshelf, giving His Glory her back, and angled away from the approaching feet.

" . . . grateful for all the work that any willing citizen gives, even in the heart and soul of the Archives, which sometimes must be rather quiet . . ."

His Glory paused.

Britt held very still, eyes glued to the page. The leaflet could have been about the most gruesome deaths and she pretended utmost fascination. Attempts to loosen her grip so she didn't crush the papers met with failure.

The draguls shifted. Sensing a building protest in Denerfen, she reached one hand beneath the pamphlet and pressed it to her bulging pocket.

The rippling stopped.

Her heart nearly stalled when His Glory paused behind her. The pungent, saccharine smell of imported Caledon flowers preceded him. Stenberg didn't bother with flowers. With what soil would they grow? All was reserved for edible plant life. She breathed through her mouth.

The silence stretched to eternity.

Every muscle in Britt's body wanted to whirl around, paste on her charming smile, and woo her way out of the situation, but that would be a fool's errand. The deck was stacked too high against her. Her plan relied on utter incredulity.

A clearing of the throat followed. She didn't let her breath hitch or change. Seconds later, a loud and maternal, "Ahem!"

Britt turned a page.

A hard *tap-tap-tap* landed on her shoulder.

Britt whipped around, wide-eyed, as if startled. Her lips opened. She clutched the leaflet to her chest with an indrawn breath. His Glory blinked at her from barely a handspan away. Did the creepy man have to stand so close? She surveyed him, the Sister of Stenberg at his side, and His Glory again.

With a whimper, Britt dropped to the floor.

The Stenbergian supplicant position on her knees, hands folded to her chest, came easily enough. *That* much about the Stenbergian custom she had learned . . . mostly from shows in Kapurnickkian brothels that teased Stenberg culture.

"Patron," the fierce matron hissed, "you are in the presence of—"

Britt risked a glance up, touched her ear with one hand, shook her head, then dropped her gaze again. Surprisingly, His Glory wasn't her biggest issue right now. This new Matron Sister of Stenberg was. She studied Britt with great intent.

"Sister," His Glory said gently, and his voice had a cadence like a rippling brook. "This is a misunderstanding. Don't you see? The dear woman offers no insult. She is deaf."

The dear woman floated in a pained way.

Too sweet.

Sickly, almost.

Britt breathed fast from where she knelt on the floor. She trained her focus on His Glory's sandals, perfectly manicured. A rope-like sash closed the ebony robes that he wore, underlain by a pristine white shirt. The ensemble cast his dark skin into greater depth.

He understood far more rapidly than she expected. The Matron's tension dissipated. To say the woman relaxed would be a lie.

"I see."

The Matron lowered her hand, waved it. Catching the movement and the purpose, Britt cautiously lifted her head. She swallowed hard and mouthed, "Sorry," while touching her earlobe again.

In Kapurnick, the deaf used motion to speak intent, but each had their own style. There was no widely accepted communication method, and she prayed the same was true here.

His Glory smiled.

"All is forgiven," he said slowly. She studied his lips, thankful to avoid his eyes, and managed a relieved smile. Her hands steepled in gratitude.

His Glory spun to face the Matron. "Do you ask the patrons why they come?" His hand swept toward Britt. "Why would a deaf woman be in the Archives?"

"Has she less right?" the Matron rebutted.

He smiled in a long suffering way. The lowering of his lips suggested hidden displeasure.

"No, of course not. I meant to imply that it might be fascinating to hear more about her life on the island. Can you imagine never hearing the blessings that my father grants? Norr provides music from the flutes, the sea, even the gulls. To be cut off from such grace . . ."

And the crack of whip, the cry of orphans, the spattered blood of sailors, Britt silently added.

The Sister of Stenberg said nothing.

His Glory's pontification continued. "This woman was clearly found wanting in my father's eyes, which is a pity. She, or her parents, have crossed Norr in some unforgivable sense, hence her punishment. I do wonder . . . is she cleansed enough to be present here in the Archives? Has she violated my edict?"

The matron stiffened.

Britt kept her breathing stable by sheer willpower.

No, she thought. *No, no, no.*

His voice carried a naive question Britt couldn't peg. Contrived? It had to be. His Glory was known as one of the most ruthless men in the isles. He didn't ask questions, he simply punished.

"No, Your Glory," the Matron murmured, "we do not ask the patrons why they attend the Archives. We ask what they seek only to be of assistance. Our order does not feel the intrusion is justified."

"During a cleansing, surely?"

"No, Your Glory."

"Are the Sisters of Stenberg open to change?"

With greater steel, she said, "As you are aware, our laws have been established since the initiation of our order two hundred years ago. We have not, and we shall not, waver. Knowledge is for all."

The strength in the Matron's voice hinted at deeper intrigues. Did His Glory put pressure on the Sisters of Stenberg to change existing edicts? Is that why several of them didn't flutter over him? The Matron's firm tone didn't waver.

"We feel that no changes are required regarding access to

information. All may receive it, and we are not open to changing stipulations. Our bylaws are clear."

"Captain Arvid died in a recent confrontation, Matron." His syrupy tone gained fervor. No, that was anger. The edges shook. "A Captain of my father's army was murdered by the Kapurnickkian sailors, and I can't help but wonder . . . are we not cleansed enough? Would my father have brought this punishment upon us if we were clean?"

The air turned stale.

"I would never presume to understand your father's desires, Your Glory."

"No," he murmured, silky as a lover's caress. "No, you would not, Sister. You have no compunction for such a treasonous act."

After a tight pause, His Glory said, "You have not answered my question, Sister. Do we allow the unclean to live amongst us to our detriment? Is it possible that a woman of such innocent eyes could dirty the purity that is my father's favorite island?"

The Matron swallowed hard. Britt imagined the ground slipping away from the Matron. Crumbling stone that would drop Britt firmly in the lap of the whipping block. The Matron clearly had no trust for Britt, but also didn't want her to suffer.

Or, perhaps, didn't want His Glory to *win*.

"Are any of us pure in Norr's eyes, Your Glory?"

The counter question remained surprisingly unruffled for the steep challenge infusing it. A dramatic pause unrolled.

"Only I," he spoke with the softest breath. "Only I, Sister."

"As such," she said with a touch more reverence than before, "May we ask for your assistance around a potential security issue we have come across, Your Glory? We understand that such work might be beneath Norr's son, but as the Archives maintain the blessing of the sea god through the upholding of our edicts . . ."

"Of course, Sister."

The matron and His Glory seemed content to stand there, discussing the state of security in the Archives, while her ankles lost feeling and her calves prickled. Britt's skirt rustled, accompanied by a tinny squeak of protest. Panic streaked through her in a brilliant bloom, quick as lightning. Why did draguls always have the worst timing?

No, Denerfen! she wanted to scream. *Not now!*

He hissed, a yawn-like sound of protest. A fold of her dress might be pushing on him, or he needed more air.

His Glory paused, head canted to the right.

"What was that sound?"

"Your Glory?"

"A squeak. Did you hear it?"

"I did not."

"Do we have a problem with miniature pigs?"

"Not that I have seen."

The edge of his robes swayed. He spoke so near to Britt she thought he might be breathing down her neck.

"Disturbing."

"I heard nothing, Your Glory."

A figure appeared behind His Glory and the Matron, drawing their attention. "Forgive me, Your Glory, Matron. The room is prepared."

"Ah!" His Glory's voice expanded with excitement. He straightened. "Thank you very much. What was your name again?"

"Raquel."

Britt's blood turned to slush. Sweet sea turtles! She tucked her chin farther into her chest and squeezed her eyes.

Don't touch me, she silently pleaded. *Don't touch me.*

A hand lay on her shoulder. Reluctantly, Britt lifted her head. Attempts to remove her wariness were futile, but His Glory didn't seem to notice. If anything, the light in his eyes grew. He *liked* her alarm.

The bastid.

He smiled with a wooden note. This close fatigue tugged at the corner of his eyes as he stared at her. His lips hadn't moved.

Finally, he asked, "Your name?"

She kept her focus on his lips, appeared confused, and then brightened. She held up her left hand. With her right finger, she drew E-L-L-A on her palm.

"Ella?"

She nodded.

"Good day to you, Ella." His broad hand squeezed her shoulder. She imagined slime squelching between his fingers. "My father wishes you well, and grants forgiveness for past sins that created your condition. I bless you with grace." He closed his eyes, breathed on his palm, and set it on top of her head. "Be healed, child of the sea."

As he strode away, he said, "A deaf woman in the Archives? I've never seen it before. My father has revealed that he is pleased . . . for now. He has also revealed that, during a cleansing, he may not allow other conditions to sully his house, such as muteness, deafness, blindness, or maiming. The sins of those, you know . . . one can't be too careful . . . Captain Ingemar and I will discuss this today. I'm sure he will agree . . ."

Sister Raquel shrank against the shelves to allow His Glory passage. She maintained the same casual diffidence as the other Sisters of Stenberg, but scrutinized Britt. Britt stood, coughing to cover the sound of Denerfen and Tesserdress's protests. Her ankles and toes prickled as blood rushed into them again.

His Glory was out of earshot when Raquel quietly said, "You met His Glory and pretended to be deaf and changed your name."

Britt sighed, then asked, "Can you blame me?"

Raquel said, "I wish you well on your search," with the same tonal diffidence as before. She departed, joining other congregants, leaving Britt alone with the leaflet and her own fears. Once the room emptied, she rubbed a hand over her face. Denerfen wriggled, so she deftly extracted him, eyes darting around, and pushed him into her other pocket. Lumpy, but they needed a little space.

He settled, his little nose barely peeking out to sniff.

"Close call," she muttered, and reached to replace the leaflet.

She stopped.

The title, written in mulberry ink and blocky letters so rigid she could have stacked them on top of each other and created a wall, caught her eye.

Births in Stenberg (Main)

Her breath caught. She flipped through the first couple of pages, determined the date was all wrong, and reached for the leaflet next to it. Several pamphlets later, she found one, then five, in the date range.

"The Archives are closing," a Sister of Stenberg called through cupped hands. "The Archives are shutting down early for His Glory's purposes. Leave immediately."

Britt spun around, checked the area to ensure no one watched, and shoved the leaflets down the front of her dress. Held in place by the tension of her brassiere, she returned to the main area.

As she floated down the stairs, smiling to all the Sisters of Stenberg who did not smile back, she kept her chin high. Surely, Norr would have her put to death for the slight. Obtaining the records was as easy as sailing out of the Archives, removing her slippers, and putting on her shoes.

Not a soul stopped her.

Chapter Twelve

HENRIK

T he uneasy feeling that he was being watched never left Henrik.

Not at his cottage.

The market.

At the Old Pub while he listened to soldats swill around with the usual grumbles, complaints, queries about the upcoming grappling tournament.

Outside the Archives.

Although they had no prearranged agreement to meet up, he waited for Britt in the shelter of a market stall across from the Archives. The owner, a man named Gustav, had helped him outfit a ship at the last minute a few years ago. They'd been lukewarm acquaintances ever since, which was as friendly as most soldats managed.

The hot sun drove Henrik into the shadows as he waited. More importantly, he kept an ear tuned to the street chatter. It kept his mind off the annoying fact that he couldn't follow Britt inside.

Bells tolled overhead, near the Temple in the Compendium. The *clang-clang-clang* was comforting and anxiety inducing. He suppressed a sigh, which turned to raised hackles when a familiar entourage of soldats appeared at the far side of the Archives, near an exit door inaccessible to patrons.

His Glory's soldats.

They lined the street in a chain, leading to a walled garden just outside the Archives. Behind them marched His Glory's four Captains. Behind Captain Ingemar, Captain Arvid's glaring absence couldn't be understated. His Glory would be inside, but the Captains couldn't go within and maintain the power of the cleansing. They waited in the garden for the supposed power of sacrifice.

Norr's breath, this couldn't be worse.

His Glory in the Archives while Britt scoured records for his mother and who-knew-what-else. Had one of these soldats taken his jord? Ossian described a gruff, broad-shouldered man with a whipped neck, which described all of them. Henrik settled his prickling nerves by sheer force of training. His Glory's presence in the Archives didn't mean danger for Britt.

Necessarily.

"Another meeting." Gustav scoffed. "So many meetings. For months now, we see this. Another meeting, another cleansing, threats from the mainland." He dropped his fuzzy eyebrows into an animalistic scowl. "They meet, but nothing changes. You see? Nothing will happen. Another couple of weeks pass and—" he spread his fingers in mimicry of an explosion, "—poof! Another cleansing. His Glory cleanses anything. Blood runs in the streets. The crippled run away. Sailors jeer in the roads. He'll cleanse us to madness."

Britt appeared. She swapped slippers for sandals and headed down the walking path, her veil nowhere in sight.

Gustav whistled. "A beauty," he sang. "Have you seen her before? I haven't, and this island isn't that big."

Acid built in the back of Henrik's throat. He didn't like the lusty sing-song of Gustav's voice. Not at all. Just like the merchant that tossed her an apple. He had to do something about it. Though reluctant to commit to it, there was one option that would protect her more than most. These mostly-harmless comments would only grow as her presence became more well known.

Bastids.

Henrik tilted his head, popping his neck until the bones cracked in a line. He rolled his gaze to the sweaty little merchant, one hand tucked into the palm of the other, knuckles crackling. "She's here with me, Gustav."

Gustav's eyes widened. He held up two hands in capitulation and slunk back to the recesses of his stall. *Five minutes,* Henrik thought. *Five minutes until he disappears into the alley and tells everyone that Henrik the soldat escorted a woman and claimed her.*

Shite, but this would complicate everything.

He had no recourse.

Before Henrik stepped out of the shadows, Gustav had already disappeared into the filthy back alleys. Britt noticed Henrik right away, sweeping his thoughts in a different direction. Her quick smile reminded him of smoke in a bottle. Something unreadable lined it, making it thick and tempestuous. The power of her bright grin hit like a kick to the stomach. That eternal annoyance with her arose, but tapered into relief that she emerged at all.

"Ta!" Tension lined her eyes despite the bright greeting. Or was it a farewell? She used it indiscriminately, and wasn't that a Kapurnickkian? Unpredictable. Perplexion followed her warm words. "Why are you here?"

He grasped her elbow, spun on his heel, and steered them to a different route.

"I'd ask you how your day was," she muttered, trotting to keep up, "but I can already tell you're in a foul mood."

He steered down an alley away from the wharf. Seedy types congregated here, but he'd take the risk. They wouldn't bother him in daylight.

"Can you slow down?" she gasped. "I can't . . . keep up if you're sprinting like . . . hellhounds are . . . at your heels."

Embarrassed by his own force of emotion, Henrik slowed to

match her stride. After several minutes, she asked, "Something wrong?"

"No."

"This is you at your most charming?"

Her drollness hid a streak of irritation. "It gets better."

To his surprise, she broke the tension with a laugh. It eased him ever-so-slightly. They wound through Stenberg and to the Quarters without another word. She seemed to understand the need for prudence and didn't jabber his ear off, like yesterday.

The feeling of being followed crept over him again. With a gentle squeeze of her elbow, he said under his breath, "Act like something is wrong with your sandal, then stop to fix it."

Without missing a beat, she looked down. "Hold on, please. I need to fix something."

Like a queen, she lowered, fiddled with her sandal, and pretended frustration. How she understood the need to buy time, he'd guess later. Henrik turned his position, as if to help, but surveyed halfway behind his back. Nothing abnormal caught his eye. Another casual glance revealed no greater suspicion.

She straightened with a smile.

"Thank you."

They resumed. He didn't take her elbow, but placed his arm over her shoulders and pulled her close. Her breath hitched, but she didn't withdraw. They completed the rest of their walk in utter silence. At his cottage, he planted a hand on her back and motioned her inside first. Her half-smile remained firmly in place until she stepped within.

Concern replaced it.

After securing the door, he strode to the window and studied the neighborhood. She waited while he stood there, breathing, senses attuned for unnatural movement. After ten minutes, he gave up and peeled away.

Britt sat at the table. Her pouch had disappeared, but Denerfen stood near a loaf of bread, peering through slotted, distrustful eyes. A wisp of smoke steamed into the air. The tiny winged devil still didn't like him.

"Something wrong?"

"Everything is wrong," he muttered.

Her lack of immediate demand calmed his rankled nerves. Was it possible that he imagined his paranoia? Unlikely. Soldats didn't imagine anything, but that didn't mean he needed to tell her about it, either.

"Stay here, and don't leave."

He ducked outside.

HE SPENT an hour observing the neighborhood, spoke to Timmer who lived next door, and ascertained nothing out of place. Henrik returned to find Britt sitting in the midst of a multitude of leaflets. A flutter of wings below the table settled, and the cottage felt too quiet. The dragul had been flying around again, no doubt.

"What do you think?" She beamed, drawing his attention higher. "I found these census records today. They closed early, so I brought them with me to study."

Her wobbly finish meant she hid something, but he didn't have the wherewithal to ask what. His entire focus turned to the records that she'd taken *from the Archives.* His Glory had killed people for less.

Misreading what must be a surly frown, she said, "There are more leaflets, of course. I thought you could help me skim through them. If they get to close early and without warning, then we have to make up for lost time," she added with a testy little sniff.

As she extracted the leaflets she'd taken from the Archives from her bodice, he couldn't stop the cold thought from spinning through his mind.

She's broken the cleansing.

Any Stenberg islander who found out she'd taken records out of the Archives would lose their brains over the insult. As a Kapurnickkian, she wouldn't understand the cultural importance of the holy policy. Whether by unwillingness or sheer ignorance, didn't matter. They'd strap her to the whipping block and splay her skin open.

If their next still-undefined confrontation against the mainland went awry, His Glory would blame it all on her and the ill luck she brought. She'd be whipped, executed. He shouldn't care what happened to her or that dragul. Her mistakes, her business.

But he did.

He wouldn't find Selma without her and . . . it wasn't right. His irate temper worsened. Britt's bold elation died a swift death when she caught sight of his expression. Her smile lowered.

"What's wrong, Henrik?"

He licked his lips, locked in an internal debate. First of all, how dare she say his name? The lyrical note sent a pit into his stomach. Second of all, did he risk revealing the weight of what she'd brought upon them? It might distract her, and she was the only path to Selma. Not to mention his abject curiosity.

One of those leaflets might reveal his lifelong desire.

"Nothing," he said more gruffly than he meant. "Just . . . don't get caught. Taking records out of the Archives is . . ."

". . . punishable by death?"

He blinked, stunned by her lighthearted approach. "You already know?"

She drummed her fingertips on top of the files. "No, but I assumed so based on how much color drained out of your face when I produced them." She shoved a pile toward him. "I'll take the risk. And, at any rate, it's too late to worry about that. I have a question, if you don't mind?"

"That's a reasonable request."

"Don't sound so surprised." She smiled with coy amusement.

"I'm a rather reasonable person, if you got to know me. Anyway, these are written in old Stenberg, which I only know a little. Can you translate?"

She tapped on several columns, which he translated. She wrote down his translations on a scrap of paper produced from who-knew-where. From what he saw, she already had them correct, but had written them off to the side in a slanted, uncertain script. She didn't dally over questions or small talk, but waved a hand.

"That's all."

"That's it?"

"Of my questions," she clarified. "You can help me look through them, if you like. It would help the process go faster."

He carefully opened one of the leaflets, aware that she'd produced obvious proof of working toward their mutual goal. He shouldn't have been surprised. While he didn't know her well, she didn't seem like the type to lack integrity.

"This is what's inside the Archives?" he asked. "These leaflets?"

"*Infiniti langi.*"

"Which means?"

"Forever in old Kapurnickkian." She gave a little smile. "I've never seen so many of them. Why doesn't Stenberg bind them into books?"

"I don't know." He stood. "I stopped for a few more supplies and bought a . . . treat . . . for lack of a better word." He waved to the frukit on the table. She reached for it, avoiding the prickly edges that could slice open fingers, and tipped it onto its side. Self consciously, he added, "You liked the apple so much . . ."

Her eyes illuminated. "You like frukit?"

"I have a bit of a sweet tooth."

"Well, frukit is *very* sweet."

"I know."

"Ah ha!" She wagged a playful finger in his direction. "I knew there must be a weak spot in you somewhere, soldat. You're a young boy that loves his mother and a strapping man that loves sweet treats. It's frukit, is it?"

He didn't bother correcting her on many points.

"Stenberg special."

"I'll take it, thank you!"

"You haven't tried an apple, but you've had frukit? Lots of islands produce apples, but only Stenberg produces frukit."

She grinned from behind the pale, lumpy glob, inhaling deeply through her nose. "Told you already. This isn't my first time here. Mmm . . . smells like a sweet lemon. And, no. General Helsing isn't amenable to the exports from Stenberg when we have," her voice dropped to a militaristic mimicry, *"so robust a system ourselves and from other, more willing, islands."*

He cleared his throat, rubbing his hands together in a poor attempt to alleviate a sudden flow of curiosity. Did she often use mockery for her leadership? He couldn't comprehend the idea.

"There's something else I need to mention," he said.

Britt stretched her arms above her head in unabashed languor, using one hand to tug on another wrist.

"Hmm?"

He cleared his throat. "I realized outside the Archives today that we need to take another step to ensure your safety."

"Such as?"

He squinted as she held up a glass and poured water from the pitcher into it. She didn't look right at him, which bought him time to think.

"You've been spotted with me a couple of times."

"Naturally."

"Entering my cottage, too."

"Yes?"

"Well . . . it . . . means something in Stenberg."

She sipped the water, then spun to face him. Demmed lustrous eyes. She mocked him. Her amusement bled into her smile again.

"Do tell."

"On Stenberg, it means you're either my wife or my mistress.

Soldats only legalize their relationships if the union is approved by the two soldat Captains, and done with the intent to breed future soldats."

Britt studied him so boldly, and frankly, that it took a moment for him to realize he'd surprised her.

"You don't want that?" she asked.

"I'd never ask my child to endure this life," he immediately replied, and the intensity revealed too much.

Her previous amusement faded. "I see that."

"I'd think you'd be safer if I outright stated that you were . . . under my protection. I did as much," he hedged, thinking of nasty Gustav, "but I believe it would be wise to introduce you to the soldats. Before rumors spread. If we control the gossip, so to speak, it would be easier."

That wry grin returned.

"Let me guess. You don't want a wife?"

"I don't want to dishonor you as a mistress," he added. "I know how they feel about that sort of thing in Kapurnick."

"True," she cooed. "The old-timers are quite modest about relationships on my islands. You," she said quietly "are a bundle of surprises, soldat. I never knew the lot of you had feelings. I thought they beat them out of you with a whip?"

"Surprise, surprise."

She tilted her chin. "If you want to claim me as your mistress, feel free. Once I've finished my own . . . mission . . . and helped you find Selma, then I'll leave Stenberg. I don't plan to return in any bold fashion."

In any bold fashion hung on an invisible coat peg.

"Your islanders can think whatever they want of me," she continued. "My only concern is whether it will be harmful to your reputation."

"It won't."

She chewed on her bottom lip. "How very kind of Stenberg to shame the female and not the male. I accept the challenge. I am your declared mistress, Henrik." She winked. "Don't get too excited. You haven't earned the benefits yet."

Before she could turn him inside out with her gentle insinuation, he plowed into the rest. Like battle, sparring with Britt was easier when he could get it over with.

"So about meeting the other soldats, then?"

He fought not to cringe. Shite, but he never thought he'd have a reason to say these words. If she had any sense of self-preservation, she'd race from the room right now. Britt's neck straightened with renewed and growing interest. Of course, the dangerous circumstances excited her.

His old friend, irritation, swelled.

She shrugged. "Sounds like fun."

"You're kidding."

"I'm not."

"You're okay to meet other soldats?"

"Do I have a reason not to be?"

"They can be real bastids," he admitted, "but most aren't harmful. Not when you're with me."

Her courage gathered like a candle drawing power. "Could be an adventure. Won't be any more frightening than meeting you the first time. I won't have to hide as much."

But she still hid *something* and her eyes made that clear. No matter how much he pictured her in his head, or worried over how things went in the Archives, he couldn't forget that she had a goal, too. None of this was personal.

He'd be a fool to make it so.

"Tomorrow, after Captain Arvid's honor ceremony, the soldats are gathering for a grappling tournament. We'll meet at the Old Pub, and some of the other women will be there. That's the best possible place and time."

If possible, the vein of interest in her eyes deepened. "I look forward to it." She jabbed a finger at the pile of leaflets on the table. "Now, get to work, Henrik. We have your mother to find."

With a sparkle in her eye, she added, "I mean, my *sister*."

THE NEXT DAY, clouds blocked the sun as thirty soldats lined the wharf, brilliant azure bands tied around their upper left arms. Their shirts cut low in the back, revealing proud scar marks. A soldat honor. A calm sea stretched from the wharf to the horizon, interrupted by ripples of silver waves.

At the end of a stony pier, long dashed by crashing seas, two sailors released a raft. Coal and driftwood piled high, tugged by a small canoe steered by a soldat named Fritz. Silence was their only companion as Fritz rowed through the breakers, cleared the raft, and released it to the sea.

A soldat shouted in old Stenbergian from the pier.

"*Arae*!"

From land, an arrow magnified with a blaze of flames. As fire consumed the burning tip, it sprang free with a *twang*. The flaming arrow coursed over the sea, arced low, and embedded into the nest.

Henrik held his breath and counted.

Ten . . .

Eleven . . .

Boom.

An explosion of flames roared to life. Captain Oliver wouldn't know, nor approve, but Fritz, in charge of soldat honor ceremonies, used a Kapurnickkian potion to aid the blaze on the water-logged fire raft. Usually, a body would burn beneath the flames.

The rush of heat whispered across the beach as the soldats, one at a time, held a clenched fist high in the air. Captain Oliver, stolid and unrelenting at the end of the wharf, watched with a muted gaze. His hands hung at his sides, fingers slightly curled. Sapphire smoke billowed from the center of the raft, breezing out to sea.

In absence of Captain Arvid's body, the soldats initiated the same honor ceremony with smoke and the sea. Blue for mourning. Fire for ferocity. The conflagration would chew through the wooden raft and deposit the bones into the sea, returning the soldat to Norr's arms with honor and respect.

As the raft drifted into a current, Oliver did not raise his arm. The other soldats lowered theirs, one at a time, starting at the front. The quiet ripple effect made no sound, only the crackling fire snapped in the distance amid the hushed waves.

Before the last soldat lowered his arm and the ritual five minutes of silence could be observed, Oliver spun on his heel. He thudded down the wharf, stepped up the beach, and headed toward a mass of people waiting in the distance.

Collective, shocked silence followed the bold disrespect.

No soldat uttered a word as Captain Oliver strode up the cobblestone wharf street and vanished into the silent onlookers. Uncertainly, a couple of soldats peeled away, a few steps at a time with lurching hesitation. Finding no one to stop them, they drifted toward the Old Pub in uncaring silence.

Only ten remained, counting down the minutes-long tribute as the firestorm drifted away from the pier. When the time passed, Henrik let out a long breath. A black plume of smoke drifted in swirls.

On his right, Einar stood like a statue. His assessing eyes studied the spot from which Oliver had disappeared. They tapered, jaw tightening. The flare of his nostrils and taut neck spoke to a savage energy. Deep fury lay manifest.

Einar's words from earlier resurfaced, skimming Henrik's thoughts like oil on water. *That's the problem, isn't it?* Einar had said. *Oliver, the bastid.*

The sense that something stirred beneath the surface became a reality as Henrik glimpsed the ten remaining soldats. Those still here to honor Arvid, and those not.

On Henrik's left, Harald quietly said, "You and I are contenders for a Captain's position, Henrik." He had a rolling, firm voice, with concrete words and a certainty that would prove any leader. As one of the most nondescript men Henrik had ever met, Harald had a habit of disappearing everywhere. He had fairness down to an art, as he contemplated the relationship between justice and mercy with ruthless fervor. Harald would be a good Captain.

"So I hear," Henrik replied.

Harald's gaze flickered to the street where Oliver departed. The swilling crowd didn't move any closer. They knew better than to intrude on a soldat's moment of honor, but noise rose from them in a whispering hum.

A moment of reflection preceded Harald's scornful reply.

"You can have the position of Captain. I don't want it."

Einar called so all ten could hear, "Oliver is playing a dangerous game, Henrik. We," he tilted his head toward the others, "won't be part of it. You're going to have to decide where you stand, and you'll have to do it soon."

HENRIK HAD FOUGHT DERVISHES off of Krackalack island, sailed through the heart of a sea typhoon, and survived seven days without food, and four without water. Soldat leaders packed his life with an abundance of frightening prospects to control his fear response and lock into the moment. He'd glared most terrors into submission.

Then he met Britt.

A whole new host of monsters manifested, namely taking Britt to meet Einar and the other soldats. Equally as harrowing as wild dervishes en masse, though not quite as physically dangerous.

The problem was Britt's wide, curious smile and bright energy. She drew attention just by entering a space, and no situation cowed her natural inquisitiveness. Shite, but the woman made staying low-key a problem.

Apart from her insistence that the dragul accompany her to the grappling event, Henrik had no reason to believe they wouldn't slide through this evening with relative ease, though it would upset his profoundly controlled routine.

They still had to hide his ugly anxiety around keeping Selma their shared secret, and Britt safe, of course. Britt's ferocity in pursuit of Selma gave him relief and confusion. After spending hours in the Archives earlier today, Britt produced more obvious proof of her search for leaflets that winnowed the search by geographical area. Stenberg wasn't that big, so she'd land on something—or nothing—soon. She must have done something else in the Archives, but gave no clue as to what.

He could tell a liar by their eyes.

Britt was no liar.

His fears almost convinced him that this whole idea was a phenomenal mistake. If Captain Oliver found out he chased Selma through Britt, removal from the soldats would be the response. If they didn't kill him, they'd demote him to sailor. Horrifying, either way. Most soldats in that situation would take their own lives from the burden of shame.

He swam from the dark depths and glanced over when Britt tugged on his elbow.

"Are you with me, lover?" she chirped.

He shook his head, blithely ignoring her joking endearment.

"Lost in thought."

"You often are. I'm ready to go. You can't see Denerfen, can you?"

Beyond her lovely neck and into the sandy blonde tresses of hair that tumbled around her shoulders, Denerfen peered out with slotted eyes. After a quick shopping trip to the market, Britt wore a dress that appeared soft, and light. The bold sapphire reminded him of the sea, mingling with her complexion and full eyelashes in a lovely way. A hint of wild lingered in her free tresses.

Denerfen withdrew behind her neck.

"No," Henrik said.

"Good. Anything I should know about your friends?"

A landslide of things would provide ample warning. Never joke about sailors being better than soldats on the sea, nor challenge a soldat to an arm fight. If she smiled too long at one of them, he might think her interested, and some soldats would go out of their way to prove a woman unfaithful, just in case. He couldn't bring himself to say those.

"You'll be fine."

The lame response brought little more than a tilt of her head.

"Okay. What about affection?"

He stiffened. "What about it?"

"Do soldats display affection with their mistresses?"

"Ah . . . I'm not . . . that is . . ."

"Got it. We'll figure that out as we go," she said with a dismissive wave. "But don't swim for the horizon if I grab your hand, all right? I'm as invested as you, so I'll do what we need to do to convince them that I'm your mistress."

"Not many soldats show affection. Einar, perhaps, but he's a rare case. In most things," he added drily.

"Have you seen a woman before, Henrik?"

He glared.

She didn't back down.

He didn't deign that with a response.

"Let's start with something less frightening," she said. "Are you grappling tonight?"

"Yes."

"When?"

"After the trainees and baby soldats."

At *baby soldats*, her nose wrinkled, but she didn't ask. Her grappling question sent a thrill through him. He yearned for the comfort of a predictable, hard challenge based on physical strength, and grappling provided that in spades.

Yet, he didn't want to grapple.

Captain Arvid's honor ceremony had driven to light a clear,

though unstated divide into the soldats. Those ten who stayed, and the twelve who left. Ten other soldats served His Glory directly and didn't count in this equation. Einar's charge to choose sides had followed Henrik all day, winnowing each thought to the same question.

What happened over the last year?

Thanks to Britt's presence and the search for Selma, he hadn't dallied at the wharf for more details, and most soldats scattered with the pressure of islanders watching from the cobblestone road.

Oliver's pressure to win the grappling and convince His Glory of Henrik's ability to lead certainly didn't help.

Pressure from within.

Pressure from without.

At some point, breakage must occur. For soldats, the simmering *something* switched to a low boil. He had a feeling that tonight had meaning that eluded him.

Britt eyed him, oblivious to his internal meandering.

"You're grappling in *that* outfit?" she asked.

"No."

Heightened expectations appeared in her eyes. She lifted her brow.

"I only need short pants." He gestured to his thigh. "They're beneath these."

"Undressing in public." She grinned wickedly. "Can't wait."

Henrik tugged her out of the cottage and into the street. Across the way, two soldats wound down the cobblestones. As they steered under the open portcullis and toward the Old Pub, his stomach twisted in a knot. He didn't realize how tight he held onto her arm until she wriggled.

"I can't feel my fingers, Henrik," she hissed.

"Sorry."

She smiled with a fixed sentiment. After only a few days with her, he understood her brightness for what it was. A ruse. She hid, like he did, but differently. Henrik made no secret of his isolationist tendencies and willingness to avoid social situations. He had a feeling she longed for the same removal, but earned it through an alternate presentation.

They approached the brightly lit building minutes later. Voices shouted within, and laughter rolled without. The baby soldats grappling, a precursor to the soldats diving in, must have already started. Voices screamed like wildfire, rising and falling in the chorus. Suddenly, he couldn't tell her everything that she needed to know fast enough.

"Most soldats don't legalize their relationship," he blurted out under his breath, "because they don't want the responsibility, but they do want the companionship. The mistress is sometimes referred to as a *secusos,* but they're different things entirely, in case it comes up."

"Secusos," she murmured. "Does it mean *second heart*?"

"Yes. It's from old Stenbergian. A secusos is not a wife, but they're more than a mistress. The title protects the women, at least from society."

"How?"

"If a soldat shames himself or fails an assignment, she won't bear his shame by being legally tied to him. If their relationship is legalized, their children will also bear the shame. It's . . . ostracizing."

"I forget how seriously Stenberg takes itself. All right, the women aren't wives but aren't mistresses. I am the mistress, but not the secusos."

"Correct."

The assignment didn't seem to bother her. She took it in stride, her focus wide and roaming. They only had a few steps left before he couldn't speak without the risk of being overheard.

"What's our story?" she asked.

"Story?"

"You know, how did we meet?"

"Why do you need to know that?"

"The women are going to ask."

He scoffed. "They're Stenbergian. They don't care about romantic drivel. They care about safety, Stenberg, and shelter, in that order."

She didn't hide her eye roll, which amused him. "Women are women, Henrik. Doesn't matter what island they come from."

"I don't care. Make something up."

"Fine. I'll tell them that we were on a ship together and we met there. We've . . . joined together, for lack of a better term, since. It'll work because it's true."

He shrugged.

As they crossed the cobblestone street, the interior warmth illuminated their path. Distant roars of the ocean, and sparkling stars, cut a familiar scene. Laughter and elevated conversation covered the noise of the sea spray as they closed in on the front door.

"Good luck," he said.

She scoffed. "I make my own luck."

A familiar body popped out of the building. Einar spread his arms, smiled wide, and said, "Henrik, my brother! It's about time you showed your ugly face. Get inside. Soldats and glory await."

Chapter Thirteen

BRITT

A room of men awaited.

No.

Soldats.

An entire pub space teeming with the most elite sailors in the Stenbergian isles standing less than a few steps away. Their elaborate braids, long hair, and natural swagger gave them away. General Helsing would have words for Britt right now, and they wouldn't be flattering.

She'd left Tesserdress at the cottage—she'd be safest there, sleeping. Tess's mellow personality meant she'd remain in the same spot, unbothered. Denerfen, on the other hand . . . While she didn't want to bring him with her, she had little recourse. The impetuous dragul couldn't be trusted alone on Stenberg.

Britt steeled herself for the evening.

She smiled, her lips fixed, and hoped she didn't look intimidated. Henrik's hand pressed to the small of her back as he pulled her closer to his side. The minute shadow of protection sent a cold rush through her stomach, but didn't aid her frazzled mind. Such defensiveness was obligation, not desire.

Henrik gifted an approaching soldat with a sincere smile that said more than words. "Einar. Good to see you, brother. Ready to lose?"

Einar slapped a hand on Henrik's shoulder. "I will only ever lose to you, Henrik. That's a promise. Alas, I am not fighting tonight." A defiant sort of sparkle filled Einar's eyes. "I'm just hoping that *you* can win."

Einar defied most soldats with brilliantly blonde hair tied into a knot at the top of his head. Darker undertones sprouted from the roots, and his green eyes reminded her of the spongy carpet of Kapurnickkian mountain moss. His casual stance and ready smile was a near-perfect antithesis to Henrik's thoughtful intensity.

Einar reminded Britt of someone who laughed at the world, while Henrik contemplated it too deeply to find the hilarity.

Perfect dichotomies.

"You aren't grappling tonight?" Henrik asked.

Something dark flickered through Einar's eyes before he covered it up with a grin. "Nah. Not tonight. You're full enough."

Henrik lifted an eyebrow. "What do you mean?"

"Stacked you five high."

"Five?" Henrik retorted. "I have five grapples?"

Einar's neck remained taut as he nodded. His focus didn't waver from Henrik's momentarily astonished expression. The surprise bled away as quickly as it surfaced. Britt kept her aggregating questions to herself. Apparently, five grapples was more than usual.

"There are five soldats that want to challenge your title, but there are only two that might tire you out. Tonight is really about you and Vilhelm, which is the final fight. You remember watching him the other day?"

Einar met Henrik's questioning stare, and an unspoken something passed between them. "You and Vilhelm," Einar repeated firmly. "That's it." More sprightly, Einar added, "If you win all five, you'll defeat Captain Oliver's title of four grapples."

Henrik frowned.

Britt cleared her throat. With a start, Henrik's palm landed between Britt's shoulder blades.

"Einar, this is Britt."

Britt broadened her smile, infusing it with sincerity. Any person that could extract a smile from Henrik deserved her time. Einar blinked, glanced to Henrik, then Britt again.

"I'm sorry?" he said.

Henrik's smile tightened. "I'll explain later."

"A pleasure," she said, arm extended.

Einar gathered his shock, shook his head to clear it, and accepted her hand. Instead of grasping her hand, he pressed a quick kiss to the top of her fingers. With sparkling eyes, he said, "Any woman worthy of Henrik's attention is someone to take notice of. Forgive my surprise." His studious gaze flickered briefly to Henrik. "I had not heard your name before. It's good to meet you, Britt. I look forward to getting to know you better."

"I feel the same."

Einar gripped her hand more firmly, tucked her arm under his, spun on his heel, and called over his shoulder.

"Prepare yourself, you bastid. The fights are starting soon. I'll take care of Britt. Agnes will kill me if I don't introduce Britt right now."

Einar peeled her away. Britt caught a perplexed glance on Henrik's face before a swarm of soldat's separated them. Clearly, Henrik trusted Einar, which said quite a bit. Just as clearly, it seemed that Henrik had never brought a woman to a grappling event before.

How droll.

Einar swept her along the edge of the Old Pub, which carried a new vivacity thanks to the voracious occupants. Two separate groups congregated on either side, almost equally matched. The open windows and shifting sea air prevented it from becoming a broiling heat miasma. If they'd been in Kapurnick, arcane-infused stones might sing different types of music, or the stoneware mugs move on their own to new owners.

Stenberg.

So *boring*.

In the midst of at least twenty gathered men, a broad circle was drawn within an open square. Chalk lines, sketched on the ground, smudged in places where feet had clearly trod. A ring of men surrounded the square, preventing anyone from casually stepping inside.

"While it may not seem like it, there are women here, too," Einar said with a quick smile thrown over his shoulder.

"Oh?"

"Not many," he amended. "Soldat grappling is . . . a bit much for most."

She silently filed that tidbit away for later. How could a group of brute force men not draw women of equal power and strength?

Einar waved aside two burly soldats who split apart, allowing her through. She had a feeling they wouldn't have budged if Einar's wide shoulders hadn't been the one barreling toward them.

"You'll probably enjoy sitting with them better than us," Einar said, but his voice had a searching note. "Unless, of course, you're a woman that loves to gamble?"

Did he tease?

Or genuinely inquire?

She assumed the latter.

"I'm not opposed to a little gamble," she said. "If it's Henrik we're talking about. I can't fathom the man that would beat him."

Her sincerity rang in every word. Einar laughed. A rising ruckus elevated from the middle of the room, nearly washing the sound out. A cacophony of cheers erupted as two half-naked men entered the square, slapped each other on the cheek with three quick taps, and crouched. Einar slid her behind a waist-high stone partition that separated the inside from the outside.

She followed reluctantly. She did love a worthy risk.

Within three steps, the scenery changed utterly. Instead of a mass of teeming, sweaty bodies that smelled like overheated men, a floral scent filled her nose. Fresh air, a moving breeze, and the roaring ocean followed.

Still gripping her hand, Einar led her onto a wide veranda. The glorious space sprawled onto a sandy beach that belied the Old Pub's ramshackle appearance. She hadn't realized it sat so close to the ocean. Foamy waves hurled themselves at the sand bar, slurping. Behind them, the high, stony rills and cobblestone streets of Stenberg cast long shadows.

Women freckled seats and tables outside. Two pub workers distributed drinks amongst the women. At a quick glance, these women were prime Stenberg islanders. Broad cheeks, elegant profiles, and a shared motif of high island fashion.

Since a rather young age, General Helsing taught Britt to fear nothing. She actively explored unknown islands, put herself into situations she had to figure out through sheer cleverness, and understood that no one or anything was better than another.

Yet, everything about these women set alarm bells tolling. These were not women to trifle with. Powerful through the shoulders, they held themselves with firm confidence and attitude that, like their male counterparts, lacked no toil.

She'd *really* rather gamble with the men.

Einar pulled Britt forward. "Ladies, this is Britt. Britt, these are the highest quality of Stenberg citizens. Forgive my bias, but Agnes is the greatest of these."

A woman with auburn hair beamed. She had a charming gap in between her upper teeth. Agnes, presumably.

All eyes turned to Britt. She cranked her smile to full strength and met each curious stare. None of them spoke, but their deepening curiosity said enough.

The women varied as much as the men, from short and plump to tall and willowy. Few similarities existed, except a general ambiance of affluence. A certain privileged status came to a woman who caught a soldat's attention.

Einar released Britt's hand. In the gesture, she thought she heard a moment of tension tightening his voice ever-so-subtly.

"Make her welcome while the fights continue, will you?" His voice lowered to a teasing and conspiratorial whisper. "She came with Henrik."

He may as well have slapped her.

Curious stares widened. Two gaped. Another gasped. Littered whispers of "Henrik?" "Did he say Henrik?" "*Our* Henrik?" tore through the group.

The feeling of a closing ring surrounded Britt. Curiosity morphed to fascination. Einar, chortling, abandoned her to the swelling tones of a worsening fight. The woman with overt auburn in her hair hurried forward.

"Britt, I'm Agnes. Welcome to the ladies' lair."

WHETHER HENRIK UNDERSTATED his position in the soldat society, or he simply didn't care, Britt realized his popularity within five minutes of Einar's departure.

The purrs of the women's cat-like prying clued her in first. They closed in on her like predators, eyes gleaming with renewed interest. She staved off feelings of utter panic by matching their smiles. These women had a hardness about them, not unlike the soldats. To be the lover or wife of a soldat would require an entirely different *sort* of person.

Give her sharks, dervishes, or hissing camels any day.

But this?

"So," a woman drawled. She hadn't moved any closer, standing like a shadowed goddess from a few steps away. When she spoke up, other lips closed. "You're here with Henrik?"

"I am."

"But . . . how?" cried another, laughing. "Henrik?"

Their inability to believe it confirmed many suspicions.

Perhaps the ladies' lair would be more beneficial than she expected.

Bless Agnes, she put an arm around her shoulder and held on. "We love Henrik," Agnes said, her brown eyes kind, but firm. "He's sort of the . . . silent, quiet type. We just didn't expect him to bring a woman to the tournament, that's all."

"He never has," piped up another.

Murmured agreements.

"I'm Monika," said the luscious woman a few steps away. Her hourglass hips swayed as she studied Britt, lush lashes lowered, scrutinizing Britt with a cutting intensity. "We're a bit protective of him. He's never spoken of an interest in a relationship."

"He's like a brother to us," called a woman at the back. "And to our men." She held onto a silver goblet, filled with deep ruby wine, and lifted it higher, as if in salute. Britt noted the affection. Whoever Henrik was to these women, they cared.

A flicker of amusement lingered in Monika's gaze, but it lacked warmth. She slunk back to the couch where she'd laid before. Like Einar, Agnes grabbed Britt's hand and pulled her along.

Deciding it was too soon to tell the difference between friend and foe, and being on her guard would make everything worse, Britt allowed Agnes to lead her to a scrolled couch with her back to the sea. When Britt sat, seven women converged, their eyes glittering, drinks already half empty.

Inside, soldats packed more tightly than ever around the fighting ring, which thudded a musical rhythm from groans and thrown fists. A quick peek revealed no signs of Henrik. The separation of soldats and women must be intentional.

"Tell us about you and Henrik," Agnes asked with a guppy-like intensity that washed Britt's concerns to the side. She was a harmless young woman that wanted a romance story. Smugness slipped through Britt.

Ha!

Stenberg women *did* want to know the romantic story behind them meeting. Islanders were islanders everywhere.

Monika waited with an equally intense stare, but her lingering curiosity spoke to darker reasons. Several women clustered near Monika in an informal semicircle. Her position over the others was clear. In this group, Monika was the shark. The matriarchal power. Others flickered their eyes to her first, before agreeing to Agnes' request for a tale. To which soldat did Monika belong?

Britt said in a surprisingly clear voice, "Henrik and I met on a ship during his return voyage."

Agnes' smiled wider with starry-eyed excitement. A suppressed shiver, and dreamy sigh, completed the innocent vixen ensemble. Somehow, with what little Britt knew about Einar, Agnes seemed just right.

"Henrik's been the reefer for the last year," said a woman with a glimmering blue necklace and matching eyes. "Was that how you met him?"

Britt nodded, withholding the timeline. No need for them to know she and Henrik had been acquainted for only a few days.

Two women cooed.

Most glared, eyes slitted. One of Monika's hands lowered to her abdomen, which had an obvious swell. She was pregnant. Henrik's explanation about wives and their *secusos* rippled through her head in a reminder. Implications about Monika and her soldat existed because of her pregnancy. Britt didn't have the mental capacity to figure them out right now, so she made a note and moved on.

"So," coaxed a different woman with lips lined black. "What happened?"

"What happened?" Britt asked.

"On the boat!" the woman cried, waving a hand. "How did you meet him? What did he say? My soldat says Henrik is always focused, always thinking. I've never heard him say more than a few words."

"Was he a jerk?" asked another.

"Did he save you from someone?"

Britt softened into her most genuine smile. "No. He wasn't a jerk."

Technically, she silently added.

Sensing what they really wanted, and an opportunity to learn more, she added, "He took me by surprise. I can't recall the exact particulars of our first exchange, except that he didn't act the way I expected from a soldat."

Agnes sighed. "The good ones always do that."

"Soldats are as predictable as the tide. Mine included," Monika added with a smirk. "But it's why I like him so much."

With a raised glass, Agnes murmured, "Here's to the good ones," as if to dispel tension.

A woman with frizzy black hair and a wide smile handed Britt a goblet. Britt smiled her gratitude, and sipped a too-sweet dessert wine. Gems speckled the goblet in a gaudy display more humorous than serious.

Ladies' lair, indeed.

"Are all of you here with soldats?" Britt asked, eyeing the bushy-haired woman that imparted the wine.

"All of us," she replied.

"You have to be," Monika said with a smirk. "We don't accept anyone else at the ladies' lair."

"There's not many of us left," a third commented. Sparkling earrings dripped to the tops of thin shoulders. "Women willing to be with soldats are dropping like flies. Captain Oliver works our men to the bone," she added in a bitter mutter.

Monika sent the woman a cryptic look. "The soldats have been busy with increasing threats from the mainland," she said in sharp reprimand. "It's not easy being part of their world, but they're a necessary force on the Isles. We will love and support our soldats *and their commanders.*"

Her tone rang with authority.

Agnes tilted her head, scratching her hairline with a thumb, and whispered to Britt from behind her hand.

"Some of us get tired of waiting."

Stony expressions aimed at Monika stated the same, though no one said it directly.

A woman in a turquoise dress stood. She pointed to each woman, introducing them and stating a male name after. Britt didn't attempt to remember the individuals. With any luck, she'd never see them again after tonight. The woman, whose name Britt didn't catch, finished with a falsely breezy, "And you met Monika. Vilhelm is her soldat."

Vilhelm.

The soldat sparring against Henrik, who had some level of importance? Britt struggled to keep up.

A thunder of bellows and guffaws and slapping hands exploded from within. Celebrating men jumped up and down, laughing. Others frowned, spitting off to the side, muttering to themselves.

"Looks like Toby won," Agnes called with a chuckle and shook her head. "Not that anyone is surprised."

"That finishes up the recruits and ushers in the soldats," said Edith, the woman with the long earrings to her shoulders. Her lithe neck turned to regard the inner workings of the pub with a frown. "Only five grapples tonight, all of them with Henrik."

Britt almost choked on her wine.

Edith nodded. "Apparently, there's some subterranean bet going around. Did you hear they stacked him five fights high? They're the only grapplers that aren't recruits. It's strange. I've never heard of it happening before."

Agnes sipped from her glass, eyes fluttering in brief assessment to Britt.

"Vilhelm won the last competition a few months ago." Monika grinned with satisfaction. "I think we all remember that defeat. A precursor for tonight, I believe, when Henrik loses his attempt at Captain Oliver's beloved title."

Chirps of agreement followed from the women that half-surrounded Monika, poised like birds ready to fly. Whatever silent competition the women attempted to conduct on behalf of their men, Britt didn't desire to comprehend.

Agnes asked, "Does Vilhelm still plan to fight Henrik?"

The air on the veranda changed. Agnes' question had such an obvious answer. Hadn't Monika said as much? Agnes must have wanted something else besides the truth. A test, perhaps. Several women cast sidelong glances at each other. Two murmured from behind the couches, as if only Agnes would have the courage to break deep ice *and* walk on it.

Monika smiled with all her teeth. "No, he plans to *win* against Henrik."

Agnes had another sip.

Britt accepted the threat for what it was. At that moment, a pair of eyes snagged hers from the broiling miasma inside.

Henrik.

He sought her through the crowd. With an elevated brow, he asked a silent question. *Are you all right?* Heat coiled into a knot in her belly. She smiled. It was easy to infuse it with warmth. For all his many frustrations, Henrik was a good man. Two men shoved Henrik from behind, removing him from sight. The chorus changed from cheering to a taunting chant. The bold refrain set her hair on end. It sounded like a premonition.

Monika set her other hand on her pregnant belly. "I've known Henrik for years now. He's quiet, but universally respected. I admit that I'm surprised to meet a woman that caught his attention while he's up for a promotion. For a very *big* promotion."

"I'm aware."

Britt cursed her quick response. The hasty reply left her wide open because she hadn't known. He had a big promotion coming up? Henrik extrapolated next to nothing, and who was she to ask, anyway? But she couldn't fathom looking like an idiot in front of this woman.

Amusement glittered in Monika's black eyes. "You're aware that His Glory wants Henrik to fill the role of Second Captain?"

Britt bit her tongue.

Blessed mermaids! Second Captain? The position was only a few steps below His Glory. The First Captain, Oliver, and Ingemar, the Fifth Captain but right hand to His Glory, were the only spots between Henrik and a ridiculous amount of power.

No *wonder* he entertained such paranoia around finding Selma.

"Are you legally bound to Vilhelm?" Britt asked instead.

Monika rolled into the topic change with no fanfare. "I am." She gestured around, encompassing all the women. "I'm the only one. There's another wife, but she rarely comes to these events." Her lips compressed. "Bit too . . . strong willed."

Agnes stiffened.

"Anyway," Monika drawled, "back to Henrik and you. These soldats are interesting men, Britt. Unique, when you pit them against the isles at large, but oddly similar when you set them against each other. They think differently than most, which is expected, considering their lives and lines of work. Henrik?" She clucked her tongue against the top of her mouth. "He is altogether something else."

"Agreed," Agnes said quickly.

"In a good way?" Britt inquired.

Monika shrugged. "He sees the world through a broader lens than most soldats. Where they are focused on one or two possible solutions, typically physical, he thinks bigger. Finds many. It's why he's always the lord of the grappling ring. Can you blame His Glory for keeping him close?"

When Britt gave no response, Monika regarded her with an open and deep study. Her appearance of skepticism retreated every time Britt attempted to peg it down.

Denerfen nuzzled the back of Britt's neck in a chilling reminder of his presence. The more stressed she became, the more likely he'd bite her. She regulated her heart rate and attempted to project calm. Her smell changed when she endured great anxiety, and Denerfen tracked it.

"How long have you known Henrik?" Monika asked.

"Feels like forever," she immediately returned.

"And yet, it's not."

Monika waited, the air charged. Each woman listened in, eyes honed. Feeling as if she responded to a silent challenge, Britt fearlessly said, "Less than a month."

Three women hooted. Another jaw dropped. Britt's low, fixed smile remained. She bit the inside of her cheek to quell the details. She owed Monika nothing, and wouldn't set a precedent of explaining herself. Something about these women set her teeth on edge, and she wouldn't bow to it.

Not ever.

"Are you in love?" Monika asked.

Britt nearly swallowed her tongue.

"Love?"

Quietly, Agnes said, "She just arrived at the ladies' lair, Monika. Give her a day or two to breathe and take it in."

"I think I'll take a walk on the beach." Britt stood, set aside her goblet. The wine, so cloyingly sweet, burned her throat. "It's stuffy over here."

A smirk appeared in Monika's gaze.

Britt left it at her back.

THE SEA BREEZE rustled Britt's hair as she gratefully stepped away from the Old Pub, drawing a pleasant hiss from Denerfen. He leaned into it, nearly toppling off her shoulder, as he peeked around her neck. Britt stopped at the edge of the water and braced into the wind as it whispered by.

"That was rough," she breathed.

Denerfen agreed with a head butt to her jaw.

After a moment of solitude, Agnes made little sound as she stepped through the sand behind Britt, stopping shy of the tide. Britt curled her toes into the rushing water. Long moments passed in silence. Denerfen inched out of sight around her neck, breathing softly under the opposite earlobe to Agnes.

"I'm sure you noticed," Agnes said carefully, "that Monika carries a lot of weight amongst some women in the ladies' lair."

"I did."

"Her husband, Vilhelm, is young." Agnes lifted her chin into the wind. "Quite young. He joined the soldats just after Henrik left for his reefer year. Twenty one. She is twenty nine."

The designation of time was no accident.

Just after Henrik left.

Agnes continued with a succinct tone. "Monika has . . . taken Vilhelm under her metaphorical wing, I suppose you could say. They have a legalized relationship, but there's no real affection. The two of them have societal aspirations, and the match is useful to both of them."

Not unusual in the isles, where advantage worked longer hours than love when it came to legalizing relationships, but strange in this circumstance.

"She's using him," Britt said.

A hint of a smile graced Agnes's full cheeks. "You could call it that. *I* call it that."

Britt hid a chuckle.

"One might say," Agnes mused, "that Monika has more experience than Vilhelm in the world of soldats and politics, and she took a liking to him. Her first soldat, a man named Evert, died a year ago."

The clanging bells that Monika created rang with terrific cacophony now.

"Oh?"

Agnes laughed with fire. "Monika is a power seeker, as much as any soldat Captain or other Captain, but she's a woman. We aren't given many avenues to express initiative in Stenberg. The soldats give her status. When Evert died, she lost that status. She reclaimed it through Vilhelm."

"And his child?"

"If it's a boy, she'll give it to the soldats at five years old. The paperwork has already been signed."

A part of Britt's heart curled away.

How awful.

"What does she want that this life affords?" Britt asked.

"Who knows?"

"Vilhelm," Britt repeated, running the syllables over her tongue.

"Vilhelm and Monika are a sign that . . . things . . . are at work in the Stenberg navy. Politics. Unease."

"Amongst the soldats?"

"Amongst everyone." Agnes sighed with a chord of regret. Not quite fear, but not far off. "His Glory, the soldats, the sailors. There's restlessness."

"Because of the mainland?"

"Yes."

"What is the mainland doing?"

Agnes shrugged. "We don't get details. His Glory simply says they're making false demands and accusations."

Britt almost laughed. She highly doubted any of that was true, but the unsettling words set the air on edge. She tilted her head to the moonlight, grateful that her thoughts cleared away from the heavy wine and deep perfumes.

"Do you fear Norr?" she asked.

A flash of a smile split Agnes lips.

"Do you?"

"No." Britt turned away. "I don't fear the Stenberg sea god. Outside of Stenberg, no one believes in him."

Agnes pointed to the foam pooling around her feet in the sand. "That's brave, considering you stand in the water."

"I don't fear him."

A bold statement that Agnes didn't join or deflect.

"How did you meet Einar?"

Agnes' smile wreathed her face, brightening her eyes. "An accident, actually. I was purchasing a scarf at the market. A stall owner tried to swindle me. Einar stepped in, the man backed down, and I got the scarf for free for my trouble."

Britt chuckled. "A perfect love story."

"I saw him," Agnes whispered, "and I knew my life had changed."

Agnes' patrician profile stood proudly in the moonlight. Set against the other Stenberg women in their fine regalia, she'd appeared diminutive, as if she made herself small in order to fit a piece of the mold.

Out here, something else appeared.

Ferocity.

Determination.

The same fire that Einar also attempted to hide through his cocky grin, but couldn't quite. It burned too brightly. Britt realized all at once that she'd fallen into the oldest trap in the book. Under-estimating the sweet woman. The kind one.

Oh, yes.

Agnes deserved a soldat all right.

Agnes met her intent gaze, and a hint of a smile appeared on the sun-softened cheek, full as an apple. The rustle of Agnes' auburn hair was particularly gentle in the moonlight, glowing from the strands that surrounded her profile.

"Monika," Agnes whispered, sobering, "is an octopus in its lair, and I don't mean the ladies' lair. You're new, so consider it a warning. You pick your place by whom you associate with. Once chosen, grace is not extended."

Warning Britt was a calculated risk on Agnes' part. If Monika wielded such power, and the fact that half a dozen women rushed to span Monika in a circle the moment Britt stepped onto the sand to take a breather confirmed it, then nothing stopped Britt from going right to Monika, telling her about the warning, and gaining a place amongst her acolytes.

A game existed here.

Oh, yes, it did.

Britt returned the tentative smile with a broad one of her own.

"Agnes," she whispered, "I think we shall be great friends indeed."

FOR BEING A LITTLE THING, Agnes had moxie.

She shoved Britt through the crowd of chanting, thumping, jeering soldats. Arms thick as tree limbs surrounded them, but Agnes elbowed fearlessly through the crowd. Seeing her, the soldats allowed them ample room to pass. Apparently, Henrik and Einar's reputation sufficed.

The hard press of bodies sent Denerfen into spikes. His claws dug occasionally into Britt's neck, and breathy, petrified protests filled her ears. The growing din drowned out his noisy distress from anyone but herself, and her jaw tightened with his heightened anxiety. She couldn't speak to help his fears, so she sank into steady breaths and hoped he shared her calm.

With spectators ringing the room, Britt expected copious ale and sloppy drunkenness, but found only a vague smell of mead. None of the anticipated messiness manifested, reducing the ambiance to sheer brawn and raw talent. Everything felt far more intense without the blur alcohol provided.

Agnes brought Britt forward, to the powdered white ring, and touched a familiar pair of shoulders. Einar glanced over and smiled wide, wrapped an arm around Agnes, and pulled her close. He pressed a kiss to her forehead, earning a smile tinted with pure adoration. His protective nature was immediately apparent.

"There she is," he murmured. With a knowing grin over Agnes petite head, he said a languid, "Ah ha. Lady Henrik arrives. Are you ready for the fights? They just finished resetting the circle."

"Can I watch?"

"Of course. Stand here with me. I'll explain."

Agnes whispered something in his ear, squeezed Britt's hand, and vanished. Britt attempted to hide her awkwardness as she stood next to Einar. She wished Agnes hadn't deserted her. Where could she possibly go? To say Agnes fit in with Monika and the ladies' lair would be a bald lie.

Men hemmed in on every side of Britt. With Einar standing close, nearly all of them ignored her. Her breath hitched as Henrik stepped into the square wearing a pair of tight, cut-off pants. Great god of the sea, his thighs bulged beneath the material. His arms tightened as he flexed, rippling across his chest. The man was raw brutality packed into sinew and frame. He cracked his head to one side, then the other. Concentration filled his eyes.

She pitied Vilhelm.

Another soldat, twice as thick as Henrik, stood opposite him. Henrik smirked, tilted his head. They slapped each others cheeks three times in mutual camaraderie, and split to opposite sides of the circle. The display of pure, animalistic force made her stomach tumble.

Finally, she met Henrik as a soldat.

A dynamo.

Henrik in this concentrated form put the idea of going *berserk* into an entirely different light.

With a shout from someone outside the ring, the grappling began. The shuffling exchange of bets passed around in murmurs and staccato words.

"Henrik is our best grappler," Einar called over the raucous encouragement. "He's strong, but it's his speed that stops most men. Tonight is different. Normally, a bunch of different fights are set up, and winners work through the flow. This time, five different soldats wanted to spar with him and only him. He accepted every demmed one of them, the arrogant bastid."

Dizziness swept her at the thought. Trust a soldat to never pass up a chance for advancement.

"But . . . why?" she asked.

"Those soldats feel they have something to prove."

Those rang through her mind. Somehow, it felt significant. A placeholder. A line splitter. Something to signify an *us* and *them*. Nearly as important as the flicker of irritation in his eyes. Einar shook his head, clearing it.

"In this match, he's grappling Ebba, who is above Henrik's usual size." Einar grinned like a happy child. "Which makes it more fun."

"You grapple by size?"

"Usually. Except Henrik has been gone for a year and said he's open to whoever, which means he's defending his title. Soldats will take any opportunity to beat the trophy out of him. He has to accept any size in order to keep his standing."

The ridiculousness of it wasn't lost on her, but she bit the comment back. For soldats, it appeared to be a point of pride, and she wasn't here to trounce on their culture.

"Do these soldats think he's weakened because of his year away?" she asked.

Einar grinned. "Nah. No soldat would let that happen, but they are hoping he's out of touch. His odds of taking it all the way are shite, but that's Henrik. He's best under pressure."

A glaze of teeth brushed the back of her neck. Britt reached up, as if scratching her neck. Denerfen nuzzled, then nipped, her fingertips. She stroked a reassuring finger down his spine, and some of the prickling scales calmed. She hid a wince when he stepped on a hair and ripped it free. Bumbling baby dragul! Her eyes watered.

"No soldat has kept the title of best grappler after a year as the reefer," said a confident voice behind her, to no one in particular. "If Ebba doesn't win, Nils will."

Einar snorted, folded his arms over his chest.

"You're on!"

Henrik and Ebba transitioned from tentative testing with jerky, forward movements and minute advancement to a full tangle. Arms, legs, bodies, thuds, grunts. She sought to keep her eyes on roving appendages as the match unfolded. The music of the crowd flowed with the intensity between both men.

As a girl, Pedr taught Britt to wrestle her way out of predicaments, mostly if someone attempted to subdue her or swing a fist. She sparred with Malcolm as a child, in the sand, during cooler evenings. In the summer, he would chase her through the surf, waves crashing their ankles, until he grabbed her under the arms, dragged her into the waves, and tossed her in.

The memories were a sublime reminder of *why* she stood here. Yet, as she watched Henrik tackle the giant soldat and win the match, she couldn't help but forget Malcolm.

This was Henrik.

The match ended with Henrik yanking Ebba off the ground and slapping his cheek with a bright smile. The defeated soldat grinned through a bloody nose as he exited the circle within a square. Boos and cheers rang simultaneously.

A second soldat with a hooded gaze and honed features entered the grappling space, his eyes dark as a midnight sea. Muscles rippled through powerful arms, with skin black as night. His fierce expression gave him a hungry appearance. He was all the more terrifying for his similarity to Henrik.

The grappling began.

"This is Nils," Einar said, as an aside. "He's been a soldat for twelve years. He's good friends with Henrik. Fierce as the gods, but shite with a knife."

She couldn't fathom a world where one was described by prowess with a weapon. She winced as Nils brought Henrik to the ground by sheer persuasion of muscle. Henrik, seeming no worse for wear, moved with intentional but patient intent. This match had less of a back-and-forth intensity than Ebba's and more of brutal power. It moved an inch at a time, instead of winging around, dancing.

"How does he win?" She winced as Nils' back contorted at a strange angle while he attempted to wriggle behind Henrik.

"Pin the shoulder blades to the circle for two seconds."

In a move so fast she reared back, Henrik hooked an arm around Nils back, lifted him off the floor with both arms, and flung his own body weight on top. Both slammed to the ground. Henrik jerked his body forward, smothering Nils upper limbs, until a soldat outside the square slammed a hand.

Shouting commenced.

The match ended.

Einar tilted his head back and laughed. He reached behind him with a hand. The grumpy soldat behind her left shoulder slapped something into it. Before she could see, it disappeared into a pocket.

Her attention locked to Henrik again. He panted as he gained his feet, but smiled. Sweat coated him in a sheen as he reached a hand down, muttering something. Nils, with a pained grimace, accepted the help.

"Figured that," Einar cried, speaking to a nearby soldat on his left, who scowled. "You had bets on Nils? Shite. No one bets against my brother."

The soldat responded with a rude gesture, and Einar roared with laughter.

His words echoed in Britt's mind. *My brother.* She listened to the prattling bets, but couldn't tear her eyes off Henrik as he stalked around, wiping sweat free, accepting a cup of water. His muscles rolled. Face twitched as he rearranged his concentration. Thus far, fatigue showed no signs.

"Three on a black eye with the next grapple," the soldat countered with a bellow. "And two on blood loss from the face."

"I'll take that!" Einar cried.

Three of what? she wanted to ask, but the commotion had grown too loud. No wonder Agnes departed.

Another contender stepped closer to the square as Nils faded out. After Einar calmed, still shaking his head, she asked, "Is Vilhelm the final fight?"

"Yes."

"Is he as good as Henrik?"

Einar's eyes tapered as he pondered the question. "Vilhelm wants it," he said with a lift of one shoulder. "Whether he's as fast? Remains to be seen."

"Wants what?"

"Respect. He's had a hard time transitioning out of training." With flat lips, he added, "He needs it. Soldats aren't fond of his arrogance. He came out of training ready to be a hero, and he thinks he is. He's sidled up to Captain Oliver and tried to become a favorite, too."

"He can't be the first."

Einar scoffed. "There's an art to arrogance. We're not interested in soldats that get it wrong."

Get it wrong.

What a clear delineation. Britt couldn't help but wonder if Monika had been Vilhelm's attempt to get something right, or if she'd started Vilhelm's problem in *getting it wrong*. Probably the latter.

Further study of the room revealed details she'd missed while focused solely on Henrik, such as an obvious gap in the middle of the crowd. Less than half of the soldats stood on this side, the rest on the other. An obvious separation existed once she sought it. The tense stares might be from gambling, but . . . maybe not.

She jerked a thumb to the grappling square.

"*This* will buy respect for Vilhelm?"

"If he beats Henrik? Yes. It's something to build off of, anyway. For some soldats, it would be redemptive. Amongst . . . other things."

Other things hinted at desperation. She could almost taste Vilhelm's desire to belong. Couldn't imagine what it must be like, ripped from family at five years old, shoved into impossible situations, and forced to perform. To survive the hellish lifestyle and training that created these warriors would be winnowing enough, but pride and culture had its own breeding ground.

She felt for Vilhelm.

Even as she hated him.

The surge of protectiveness on Henrik's behalf caught her by surprise. She had a hard time buttoning it up. Should she? If Einar saw her care about Henrik, it would help their mutual purpose.

Some time later, another thud.

A third takedown.

Henrik visibly recovered by crouching to take a deep breath. The losing soldat ignored his offer for help and stalked out, muttering. Several livid soldats followed, and she shuddered. Weren't they supposed to be one in purpose? Could the soldats exist without mutual support from within? Other soldats scurried along the edges, trailing crushed white rock to reform the slightly marred circle.

Henrik drank deeply from a mug of water, doused himself with the rest, and shook out his arms as a fourth competitor entered the ring. Scuff marks created reddened spots over his cheeks, slashes across his back, a bruise to the side of an eye. So far, Henrik kept his back to her. Intentional? It seemed likely. She didn't mind. The unparalleled opportunity to fade into the background and watch who Henrik *truly* was tempted her too greatly.

Denerfen gave a little cry. She reached for him again, and his nip was unmistakably pained. Her emotions heightened too much around Henrik's fate in the ring. Deep breaths didn't quell her racing heart.

A little longer, she silently begged.

The fourth opponent asked more of Henrik, requiring him to grapple for longer than the first, second, and third combined. The crowd of soldats settled in with hushed breath, painstakingly analyzing every move. She winced, watching each strategic and intentional move. As he raced into a hold, the opponent anticipated it. Henrik's speed didn't have the same zest and zing.

"He's tiring." Einar clucked under his breath. "See his eyes? They're drooping. He's dancing on his feet to keep his energy high, but he's wasting it. He needs to focus."

"Think he can do it?"

"Yes."

"Will he?" she challenged.

Einar pursed his lips as he thought. Fresh bets, exchanges, and the smell of weak ale perfused the air, mingling with sweat and dirt and a hint of rabid hope. Soldats didn't receive wages for their work, so what would they gamble?

She didn't want to ask.

"Henrik'll win this round. Eventually," Einar tacked on. "But it might cost him the win against Vilhelm."

"Which is more important?"

"Depends."

"On?"

Lightly, he said, "Henrik's priorities."

The comment stayed with her in the minutes after Einar's response, while she attempted to put her attention to the grappling and understand it. Something *else* moved in the Old Pub background, swirling in the air between soldats. The same things that compelled an obvious separation and tension, perhaps.

All blurred to moving bodies and desperate faith.

Their entire profession, their lives, even the safety of their island nation, rested on a band of proven men that, from childhood, put their bodies through the rigor of pain and suffering in order to accomplish lofty goals. At some point, that breakdown would be a problem.

A big one.

Where did broken soldats go?

Who carried the lost?

The finalizing fight broke her concentration. The split in the room broke into deeper sides, betrayed with mutual groans or triumph. When Henrik's opponent took a hit, the majority moaned. When Henrik struggled, the soldats behind Britt echoed the pained refrain.

Tension built.

She had no idea why.

A cool brush against the back of her neck sent panic shivering through her. Affecting a tired yawn, she pretended to rub at a sore spot along her neck. She gripped her neck with three fingers, and probed for Denerfen with the other two. His rough tongue licked along her knuckle, and his nose nudged her finger bone in a precursor warning.

The absolute last complication she needed at this moment was invisibility.

Britt breathed deep, attempting to send waves of calm through her body. Tension bunched her shoulders, screwing her neck into a tight knot. No wonder Henrik warned her. A resounding *thud* drew her attention forward. The opponent's giant body sprawled on the floor, arms wide. He panted heaving breaths.

Groans and cheers swelled. Henrik, palms pressed to his bent knees, panted on the side of the ring. Sweat and blood poured off Henrik's shoulders. Streaks bubbled from a cut above his eyebrow that chugged over his left eye.

Britt gulped down her rising dread. If they didn't leave soon, Denerfen would bite her. He'd betray her secrets in front of a contingent of soldats. She could scuttle away, pull Denerfen from her neck, and shove him into a pocket, but then she'd miss the culminating fight.

The thrumming undertone meant this fight *mattered*, though she didn't understand why.

Henrik lifted his head and looked right at her. As he did, a hush fell over the congregants. Bodies split this way and that at her back. The pressure of a moving crowd swelled, pressing into her from behind. She had it wrong.

Henrik didn't look at *her*.

Someone else approached.

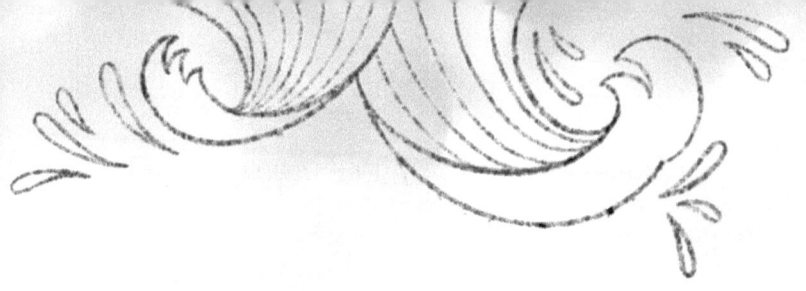

Chapter Fourteen

HENRIK

Soldats ringed Britt in a thrumming cluster. Strain lined their faces, underlying rigid arms and jerky movements. The crackling tension hit a fever pitch now that Vilhelm entered the room, and Britt stood at the cusp.

Henrik didn't like it.

Not one bit.

None of them would intentionally hurt Britt, but in a crowd this size their overpowering presence and sheer force might push her into the square. They could press too close, knock her over, trample Denerfen, any number of things.

He *really* didn't like it.

Britt didn't strike him as the type of woman to blanch at the brutality of grappling, so her quick note of fear probably had more to do with Denerfen than her own safety. He didn't understand why she held some innate trust in him.

Not a lot, but enough.

As Vilhelm shoved through the crowd, the chaos swelled to a deafening surge. Britt had a look of overwhelm, not quite panic, as she struggled against the inevitable swell. Maybe he should have warned her. Einar shoved his body between her and a soldat named Tonio with a shout, preventing her from falling, but it didn't quell the sudden aggression in the room.

Henrik started forward, ready to yank her into the relative safety of the ring, though no one would welcome a woman entering the sacred circle.

Who cared?

They could jump off a cliff. If she—

A split formed in the crowd, right down the middle. Taking advantage of the relative calm, Einar clasped an arm around Britt's elbow and spirited her away. She stumbled, broke eye contact with Henrik, and righted herself as Henrik tore his focus away.

Vilhelm birthed free from the parted soldats with a ferocious scowl, his upper lip curled into a half-snarl.

Norr's breath.

Was Vilhelm a child? Yes, but a large one.

Vilhelm strode arrogantly into the square. Soldats peeled from side to side, making way. Vilhelm's nickname *killer* had whispered through a few conversations before the grappling started. It failed to frighten him.

Puffed up with youth and folly, Vilhelm eyed Henrik.

"Will you fight?"

He had a tight voice, like a man barely restrained. Young, eager. Ready to prove all those years of torturous training with the freedom they unleash on new recruits. Like jumping into deep water the first time. He thought he was ready, but almost drowned. Henrik had been just like that not too many years ago.

Vilhelm's question held more than the promise of the biggest match of the year. The match was an opportunity for Henrik to keep his position, less an opportunity for Vilhelm to make a name for himself, though it could provide that. If Henrik won five levels of competition, with the youngest, freshest, and toughest at the end, he'd keep his soldat position of honor and break Oliver's record of four.

And for what? whispered a deep question.

One he'd never asked before. There was no answer. Soldat pride was all, though soldat pride never once filled a hungry belly.

He couldn't deny the ringing silence in his mind after the question. The subcurrent that flowed beneath it. Clearly, Vilhelm represented something else to the soldats, because half the room thundered at the sight of him. The rest lay silent, including Einar.

Henrik knew only that he wanted to grapple against Vilhelm, because soldat was all. Stenberg was all. He had something to prove.

That was it.

Henrik inclined his head once.

"I'll fight."

Henrik turned his back to Vilhelm, grabbed an offered towel and glass of water. He chugged, drenched himself with it, and wiped the blood free. Einar materialized at his side.

"You have to win, Henrik."

"Or what?"

"Prove you're more powerful than Oliver *and* prove you're more powerful than Vilhelm." Einar gripped Henrik on the shoulder and leaned in, so close only Henrik could hear. "Do this, and then I can tell you everything. I'll explain all of it. Tonight, we have to undermine Vilhelm's power in the sight of the other soldats. All right?"

The vague and mysterious promise dissipated out in the growing calls, demands for a fight, and foot stamping. As quickly as he came, Einar vanished. The floor trembled with demanding stomps.

Henrik spun around, ignoring his groaning body. He didn't acknowledge the pain yet, because that came later. A box hummed deep in his gut. The box of agonies. The box of pain. It formed the moment Selma screamed for him and his life, as he'd known it, funneled into that box. Henrik shoved all of it. Down, down deep. Adjacent to Selma.

To questions.

The soldats long trained him to stave it off. Later, the pain would barrel over him in an agonizing pulse, when the requirement of proving oneself didn't demand her due. But not now. Right now, he grappled.

Vilhelm met his gaze as Henrik clenched his bruised knuckles, probably one broken. He ignored that, too.

Time to focus on the grapple.

VILHELM HAD ALL the predictable energy of youth, coupled with speed, tenacity, and fresh motivation. His desire to prove himself would eventually become a weakness. Vilhelm would put winning over strategy and reveal his shortcomings through frustration.

The match began slowly, with testing strikes. A reach, flash of legs, thwarted takedown, and lilting rise and fall of men in the background. Henrik set aside thoughts of Britt, of honor, of the dark box in the gut and honed into instinct, bone, and sinew. He danced into the fight like a ribbon, fluttering from here to there, delighting in the pressured movements and light intricacy. It was the closest to *berserk* he recalled being.

He flirted with the inner power.

Vilhelm revealed himself, as Henrik hoped, through impatience. Prolonged time without total domination set Vilhelm on edge. His eagerness longed to win right *now*. Winning wasn't enough, but takeover. He planned to crush Henrik and show a conquering, indefatigable spirit within minutes of arrival.

Big dreams, big plummets.

Henrik played into the fatigue, keeping each movement low and intentional. Certainty made Vilhelm lazy. Henrik's moment to strike came after a failed takedown. Vilhelm pranced forward, attempting to lock Henrik's legs and pull him onto his back.

Henrik's spine hit the floor, and he rolled, resetting the two-count timer kept by three different soldats around the circle. With a shove from his hips, he regained his feet, and swiped a leg before Vilhelm fully recovered himself.

Vilhelm flailed, attempting to compensate for Henrik's burst of unexpected speed. The moment of imbalance drove Henrik off the ground, an arm around Vilhelm's upper body. He lifted, slammed. Immediately, Vilhelm attempted to roll onto his arm, ripping his shoulder blades off the ground.

Dirt puffed around him, staining his tawny skin and thick curls.

The timer reset.

Thighs pressed to the ground, Henrik threw his weight on top of Vilhelm. Their hands grappled, but he smothered Vilhelm's chest, pinning both blades.

One.

Two.

Two of the three soldats slammed their hands to the ground.

"Complete!" one roared. "Henrik for five!"

Vilhelm, flat on his back, wheezed a breath and shoved Henrik off. For all that energy, it ended simple and quickly. Henrik's experience trumped Vilhelm's desire. Uproars exploded. Arguments broke out between soldats, and several feet almost crossed the sacred circle. Einar shoved bodies off of Britt, who tried to duck away from the rabid onslaught pushing forward.

Seeing her inevitable peril, Henrik crossed the square in two strides, grabbed her by the waist, and twirled her into his arms. With a gasp, her feet dangled just above the floor, her chest pressed to his. Her eyes, wide as saucers, were a breath away. The rise and fall of her rib cage expanded against his bare chest. Heat and dust and sweat radiated from him.

Chaos continued, breaking into brawls.

Thudding fists.

Shouts.

Einar dodged a blow, landing his own.

Henrik whispered, "I'm going to lower you, but stand on my feet. Don't touch the ground. The soldats consider the circle sacred, and only for fighters."

"Denerfen," she breathed, "he's going to bite me. He's scared." Her eyes widened. "What do I—"

In three quick steps, he slipped to the other side of the circle, set her on a discarded table in the corner, and covered her with his body. The broad plane of his body blocked her from view.

"Grab him. Quick."

Hastily, she obeyed, gently extracting the dragul from her neck and sliding him into the pocket of her dress. He thrashed, hissing, blaring tiny sprouts of fire and steam that would have been amusing in any other circumstance. Carefully, she tucked him into her pocket, navigating flailing wings.

Relief crossed her features as she set a hand outside her pocket to settle the squirming.

"Thank you."

He set a bent finger under her chin and tilted it higher, surveyed her. His arms shook. A little too gruffly, he asked, "Anyone hurt you?"

Her hair swayed as she shook her head. "No. Einar protected me. And one other, the one that stood by him, he helped too. Just now."

The gods, but he wanted to kiss her. Seal the violence with her warm lips. De-escalate his raging blood, frothing questions. There was so much . . . A shout from behind stopped his lowering head.

Anarchy.

The room had split into two sides. Einar and a handful of others against the rest. Shite, but hadn't Oliver told him to keep control? It wasn't unusual for fights to break out after bets went awry, but this?

He held up a finger and growled.

"Don't. Move."

A surprisingly agreeable nod replied.

Henrik whirled around. With a thunderous roar, he shouted, "Silence!"

The bedlam settled. Panting shoulders, heaving breaths, and glazed eyes stared at him, shocked by the forceful command. Einar shoved a soldat off him with a sneer and peeled himself away. When one soldat attempted to lunge for another one, Henrik intercepted the swing and shoved him into the wall. The wild soldat crashed into a chair. As he rose to retaliate, Henrik raised a fist. The fool slithered back to his seat.

"Control yourselves," he barked. "We're honorable soldats, not drunk fools upset about a fight. Clear out, every bastid in here. If I hear of another problem happening tonight, I'll take you to Oliver myself."

Grumbling ensued, turning into a parting of hostilities. Reluctantly, the soldats veered away from each other. On one side, Einar and his men. The same group that stayed behind for Arvid's memorial. On the other, the rest. Vilhelm stood in the midst of them, one eye bubbling from a hit.

He panted. "It's not over, Henrik."

Henrik scoffed. "Yes it is, boy. Get out of here, and take your fools with you, if that's what this has become. You had your chance, you lost it. You're impatient, arrogant, and overconfident. Learn, or you'll fail again."

Hissing, Vilhelm spun on his heels. The rest of them filtered out with him, casting wary glances back.

Henrik stood in the middle of the square, seething. His boiling blood lowered gradually. Einar stepped forward. Henrik didn't understand the relief in his gaze as Einar clasped him in a hug.

"Later, brother," Einar whispered. "You've earned it."

Chapter Fifteen

BRITT

T he night passed in erratic bursts.

In the predawn hours, when Britt studied Henrik, she saw echoes of a vulnerable little boy in his weary features. A quick frown, worried lips. Anglerfish might have been a more apt description, considering the deliriously messy state of his face. Bruising everywhere. As if the swelling wasn't grotesque enough—his lip, his eye, and faintly along his jaw—the groans that accompanied every movement were worse.

Sighing, Britt stood.

"I suppose," she whispered to Denerfen and Tesserdress, "it's a good sign he's sleeping? He might be in a death spiral, with all that body slamming."

The thought of his half-naked body made her breathless, but compassion soon followed. He'd been pulverized through each fight. Denerfen blew smoke in Henrik's direction, thumping his tail on the table.

She giggled.

Tesserdress, perched on her other shoulder, gave a drawn sigh. She slumped down Britt's neck. Britt fought a wave of anxiety. Though Tesserdress had her potion this morning, color change hinted across her scales in a sweeping reminder. She refused to romp and play with Denerfen after Britt and Henrik returned.

A robust night faded outside, washing the blue-black dome into a brilliant pink and yellow visible through the windows. A breeze twined through the open cottage door, shuffling strands of her hair. Distant market sounds steadily rose with sleepy tones. Not even Stenberg wanted to let go of the beautiful sunrise and launch into the day.

With her hair masking Tesserdress from sight, Britt leaned against the doorframe. She stared out at the distant seascape, visible above the sloping angle of Stenberg. While her mind wandered over Malcolm, and the Archives, and Henrik's search for his lost mother, a moan drew her back to the cottage. She spun, not surprised to see Henrik blinking one eye awake. The other had swollen shut.

He jerked upright.

Britt slipped Tesserdress off her shoulder, deftly tucking her into her pocket. "Calm down, soldat!" she cried as Henrik almost vaulted off of the bed. "My goodness. No one is here to kill you. Just yourself, and you're doing a fine job of it."

Henrik flinched when she put a quelling hand on his shoulder, though no visible wound displayed there. He jerked away from her touch and lowered back to the mattress with a grimace. His hand probed his face, lips first, then puffy eye. He couldn't open the left, but the right fluttered without restraint. As he probed the excoriated skin, she grabbed his wrist.

"Ah, ah," she sang. "No you don't. It took me a considerable amount of time to put salve on that wound without waking you up. I won't have you marring my work now. You're alive," she said with a forced lightheartedness. "That's saying something."

He mumbled unintelligibly.

She reached for a glass of water. "Here. Try a small drink. I can't imagine you have a great taste in your mouth. You'll be lucky if you kept any of your teeth."

He sent her a wry look coated with something like disdain,

maybe exasperation, but obeyed. She helped him sit and take his next sip. He winced, then painstakingly finished the entire glass.

"Better?"

With great hesitation, he nodded. She pressed him back down. "Rest," she insisted. "You're not going to improve by sitting up."

He licked his lips. His words were only slightly muffled and thick when he asked, "What did you put in it?"

Britt chuckled. "You noticed, eh? Just a little tincture."

"Kapurnickkian?"

"Yes."

"Yours?"

"Mm hmm." The tincture, Jollymolly, was bright green, smelled salty, and had a faint sheen to it, like a glow. The briny scent wasn't unpleasant and it had a habit of inducing sleep. "Are you in pain?"

Henrik's reply took so long she realized he was having a hard time keeping his thoughts aggregated.

Eventually, he nodded.

Relief that he'd woken up led to equal parts relief that he managed to speak *and* swallow. What was the cost of last night's outpouring of energy?

Was it worth it?

Britt retreated from the bed, holding out a hand to Denerfen, who perched at the edge of the table, exploring an amalgamation of fruits she'd bargained for at the market. Ten in all, with various forms of color, lumpiness, and texture. She'd only tried one. A purple-rinded fruit with a soft interior that reminded her of the melons that grew wild in Kapurnick mountains.

Reaching for the closest piece, Britt sliced into half of the purple rind, separating a bright orange segment from a round, black seed in the center. The cool, squishy interior should help Henrik's teeth.

She cast a quick look over her shoulder to check on him. Stubbornly, Henrik glowered, now sitting, his feet firm on the ground. Exasperated, she put a hand on her hip and whirled.

"Really? You can't just lay down?"

"No."

He kept one hand cupped around his swollen cheek. With a roll of her eyes, Britt held up the sliced fruit.

"You want it?"

He mumbled something, but held out his other hand. She sashayed closer. "Agnes stopped by early this morning with some tea that she said should help a headache. Einar has already checked on you twice. He left a note for you, too. You have . . . quite a friendship with him."

In fact, this had been the first stirring of life around Henrik and any potential friends. Quite a late show, in her opinion. Still, Agnes' and Einar's offerings meant *something*. Something sad, in Britt's estimation, that those two were the only ones who checked on him.

"Thanks," he grumbled.

Britt set her other hand on her hip. Henrik lifted his gaze, dropped it again. It was an oddly revealing, sympathetic gesture, as if he couldn't quite bring himself to meet her eyes. He said nothing.

"Congratulations," she offered, but it felt pitiful. "I mean . . . it was quite the accomplishment."

He mumbled something that sounded like *grappling is different*, but didn't speak with enough volume to induce her curiosity. A don't-get-near-me warning radiated off him, and she had no desire to act against it.

Actually, that was false. A too-large part of her wanted to sit at his side and coax his head into her lap. Those soft and gentle hairs at the top of his head needed a good stroking, and he could use soothing.

At least, that's what *she'd* want.

It's what her older brother, Pedr, had done when she was sick as a child. His soothing touch, the baritone of his rumbling voice, had been all the center she needed to get through the seasonal illnesses that plagued their emerald mountains. General Helsing had always been too busy.

Then again, a battle-hardened soldat might be offended at the suggestion of nurturing. Deep thoughts appeared to stall Henrik, and she couldn't hazard a guess as to what they might be. His attention flickered to the pita bread on the table, the inner pockets stuffed with soft, white cheese and herbs.

"Have you been to the Archives already?" he asked.

"No, because it's early yet. Barely dawn. Why would I when you're half dying on the bed, anyway?"

Henrik matched her frown with an equally confused glower. The shadows and swollen distortion made it hard not to notice. Perhaps he didn't try to look mean, but he achieved it. A slight sheen above his right eyebrow—a salve that Agnes brought by with her tea, as if this sort of thing happened every day—glimmered.

He didn't answer her question. She had the feeling he didn't know *how* to answer her question.

"Are you feeling well enough to stand on your own?" she asked.

"I'm fine," he said, a bit too tightly.

Tetchy devil.

"Well . . ." She tilted her head from side to side with an indecisive bite of her bottom lip. "Let's not go that far."

A flicker of what might have been amusement created a grimace. He was hard to read when his face resembled a beaten boar.

Britt lowered her hand to the tabletop, and Denerfen stepped onto her palm. He scampered up her arm, winding in a fast, zipping motion until he perched on her shoulder, safely tucked under the curtain of her hair. When his tail swished back and forth along her shoulders, she felt rightness and relief.

Ah, sweet dragul.

Henrik tracked Denerfen's scampering body to the top of her arm with a contemplative gleam that left as quickly as it came.

Fleeting, whatever it was. Henrik carefully tipped his head toward the door.

"I'm fine. You can go to the Archives, search for . . . whatever."

She opened her mouth to protest, but he cut her off.

"Go, Britt."

"But—"

His voice resembled graveled stones sliding downhill. "I don't need you. I need to speak with Einar. Show myself to the other soldats."

"Why?"

"Because," he ground out, wincing. "It's one thing to win the fight. It's another thing to have to recover for days. It removes the . . ."

"Pride?" she offered, unable to hide her scathing judgment.

These fools!

He hissed, "Yes. There's little victory in it if I'm hiding in my cottage afterward. They'll call me an old man and question the title. I have to prove it, all right? It's probably why Einar stopped by twice already."

Her cheeks burned. What an absurd man! Here she sat all night, and most of the morning, brewing him teas and combining tinctures and shopping for him at the market so he'd be comfortable and pain-free after a ridiculous night knocking his head into other heads . . . and all he wanted was to be left alone.

Last night, she thought . . . when he saved her from the crowd and . . . so close . . . his breath on her cheek . . .

She scoffed inwardly.

She should have known. The only fool here was her. Sensing he wouldn't capitulate, she nodded once. Meeting his gaze asked too much. The way he kept his head down, it wouldn't have been worth it, anyway.

Britt grabbed her cloak and headed into Stenberg's marketplace with one dragul in her pocket, the other hidden in her hair, grateful to leave his irritating obsession with maintaining appearances behind.

Chapter Sixteen

HENRIK

He fell asleep.

Twice.

Whatever Kapurnickkian potion she slipped him did its work. The worst of his aches and pains dissolved, but took consciousness with it. He slept harder without her there, staring at him, bustling around, building herself into the fabric of his life with every ditty she hummed.

He couldn't afford the light she offered, because she would leave once her purpose here finalized. It would be so dim, then.

Hours after he growled Britt out of his house, remnants of his patchy attention and groggy mind pieced together. He carefully stood, stretched, drank as much water as he dared. He'd been a real bastid to Britt, and he still hadn't left his cottage.

He couldn't help it. Einar used to help him recover after the early fights, when the wounds were more gnarly because his skill hadn't been as strong, but this . . . care?

Never had someone bought soft foods, mixed up a potion, waited with fresh cool water, and watched with careful concern. That Kapurnickkian dragul keeper needed a stronger head on her shoulders. Whatever she sought at Stenberg, she wouldn't find it while making friends with and caring for everyone.

Too strange.

Too . . . much.

Care wasn't something he could bring himself to accept without understanding the steep price. Her unfettered benevolence created tendrils. Expectations. A draw.

He couldn't afford a draw.

The only caring lines he'd ever drawn were toward Einar and Selma. Einar was his brother-in-arms. The only one he could truly rely on, proven after years of dedication and survival together.

His search for Selma, an impossible non-entity, was purely selfish.

Henrik splashed cold water on his face a tenth time, allowing the sting to rouse him from the potion-induced stupor. The sleep had helped, which only put him in a more foul mood, because she'd been right. Britt had drugged him into it, though he was glad. The cool water ebbed the stinging, but not the dull *thud* of his swollen eye. Only time would do that. How he loathed the wild repercussions of proving himself in such a stupid way.

He couldn't take an assignment when he felt like this. Not that Oliver had assigned one. Henrik suppressed a curse when a rap on his door brought him to his senses. He spun, a towel in hand, to find Captain Oliver filling the doorway.

"Soldat."

Henrik stared.

Oliver had never visited his cottage.

"Ease off," Oliver commanded. Gingerly, Henrik patted his face dry. Oliver appeared as laden with stress as before, but not wildly so. His abrupt departure from Captain Arvid's ceremony itched under Henrik's skin, tainting the visit.

Henrik's voice was a rasp.

"Captain."

Oliver studied him. "I heard about last night."

"Oh?"

Wryly, he waved a hand toward Henrik's swollen face. "Few

Stenbergians aren't talking about it. Congratulations. I'm proud to cede the grappling title to you."

Automatically, he said, "Thank you, sir."

"Any updates on your jord shipment?" Oliver asked.

Shite.

He'd utterly forgotten about it.

"No, sir."

Oliver's gaze tapered. "You haven't located the twenty bags that went missing?"

With painstaking care, Henrik licked his lips and forced himself to admit, "No, sir." Excuses collected on his tongue. Captain Arvid's memorial. Britt. The draguls, and the grappling title. But he wouldn't betray them. Soldat's didn't receive the luxury.

"Twenty bags went missing under your care, soldat," Oliver growled, fire lighting his eyes. "I can't imagine *why* you wouldn't search further. Have you attempted anything?"

"I spoke with the ship captain, Ossian."

"What did he say?"

"He claims that two soldats took the jord and told him not to remove them from his inventory."

"Soldats?"

"Perhaps His Glory's, sir."

With irritation, Oliver muttered, "Obviously, Ossian didn't listen to them. Why?"

"Out of respect to me, I think."

Oliver grunted and showed little change in expression. The air brittled like stale toffee. "What do you make of Ossian's story?"

The sense of walking into a trap overcame Henrik as he said, "I trust Ossian."

Oliver scoffed. "He's a merchant that got caught stealing twenty bags of jord. You're a fool if you believe him. Fools don't become Second Captain."

Henrik fought visceral annoyance. Even with forced relationships, like ship captains, the soldats pretended to trust, but conducted studious testing of the relationship. Once it ended, all bonds disappeared.

Yet, he still trusted Ossian.

Oliver leaned forward. "Figure it out, soldat," he said with a soft undertone, "or your precarious position as Captain Arvid's replacement will stand on very fragile ground. There's more on the line than just jord."

Henrik wasn't entirely certain he cared. Harald's haunting words of, *you can have it,* followed him everywhere. He rubbed a hand over his forehead, gingerly avoiding his left eye. Why didn't this make sense? Because he'd been hit too many times? Or because *it didn't make sense.* What were twenty bags taken by His Glory's soldats set against a thousand?

What if he didn't want the position of Captain?

"Are the twenty bags required somewhere, Captain Oliver?" he asked.

"They're required," Oliver barked, "because His Glory says they're required. Understood?"

"Yes, sir."

"It shows an egregious lack of thoroughness that is embarrassing for all of us. Figure it out, soldat."

"Yes, sir."

Oliver went oddly silent, drawing Henrik's scattered attention. The Captain studied the table with a slightly tilted head, gaze narrowed. Henrik's stomach sank. What did Britt leave in plain sight? A moment of panic caught him in the belly. Had she left Denerfen?

No.

She'd never do that.

Before Henrik followed Oliver's gaze to assess, Oliver returned his focus to Henrik. He blinked twice, as if extricating from deeper thoughts, and quietly said, "I am disappointed in your lack of motivation for the Captain's slot, Henrik."

"Sir, I—"

Oliver lifted a hand. "You may not understand all that His

Glory has to offer. The respect of the position alone should compel any soldat to service, but if that isn't enough, allow me to extrapolate." He leaned closer, his eyes dangerously intent. "As I have mentioned before, if you are the Second Captain of His Glory's ranks, you would lack nothing, soldat. Nothing. Do you hear me?"

His words hung like honeyed syrup.

"You access *whatever* you want, no questions asked, all permissions given. Henrik, His Glory offers you all of Stenberg. All answers. All history. All *paperwork*."

Oliver straightened into his crisp, disapproving posture.

"Find the jord."

With that, he spun on his heel and left. Henrik, flabbergasted, fell silent.

All answers. All history. All paperwork.

What did Oliver know?

When Henrik spun, he saw what Oliver stared at. Nothing but small signs of feminine life. A bone comb for her hair, bits of cloth she made into a bed for Denerfen, and a half-eaten piece of fruit.

Not much.

But enough. He'd publicly taken Britt into Stenberg last night. Likely, Oliver heard the rumors. Having Oliver in his cottage, seeing her comb, felt like a deeper invasion.

Henrik reached for the envelope that Einar left behind, ripped it open, and dumped out a small piece of paper.

On assignment for a few days. Talk soon. Don't trust Oliver.

Chapter Seventeen

BRITT

Two awkward, cordial, strange days passed.

Henrik made himself scarce, mumbling something about *jord* and *search* and *Einar,* and they managed to carefully coexist without saying a word.

Tesserdress slept in Britt's pocket. Denerfen twirled around, flapping in intermittent bursts around the cottage. Tesserdress' Helandalenda potion drizzled down further with each application, and color leached from Tess' scales with each day that passed. She slept deeper, ate less, and played rarely.

Britt returned and borrowed census leaflets as needed. She dove into the Archives and other places on Stenberg. She sorted through any possible option, including those away from the Archives and Library. She haunted the wharf to listen at pubs, and attempted to speak to sailors to discern what ships returned when. Anything to find Malcolm, but to no end. The cleansing severely limited her options.

The trouble brewing in Henrik's gaze haunted her. From a distance and with the benefit of time, she more readily recognized that it hadn't been a bad mood that sent her away from his side.

It was something else.

Sadness?

Depression?

"Relief," she hissed to Denerfen from the depths of a pub near the wharf, but out of sight of the Quarter. "The man should have been relieved! He won five different matches. Was he? No."

She tossed a coin on top of the table and pushed to her feet. Like the others, this visit had been fruitless in her search for Malcolm. Thanks to the cleansing, no recent sailors stepped in to provide news from the world outside Stenberg. Rumor stated that His Glory planned to close the port for another week, if not more.

A seedy, restless crowd of men slid inside.

Time to go.

She'd spent all of this day searching for signs of Malcolm, utterly ignoring Selma. As she climbed off the stool where she sat, her mind returned to her greater exasperation: Henrik.

With a shake of her head, she forced herself to leave the pub, glaring at a man with a leer. Stepping into the sunshine stirred Tesserdress. The dragul wriggled in her pocket with a dark reminder of needed progress. Britt's stomach ached.

She *had* to find Malcolm.

Selma, too.

With exacting agony and a sense of hostile purpose, she forced herself to return to the Archives, but found little help there. She sorted through leaflets filed three months ago, but with a lost sense of momentum. Irritated that she wasted precious hours of Malcolm and Tesserdress' lives, Britt folded her arms on top of a table, pressed her forehead on top, and sighed.

How would—

A body sat next to her.

Britt startled from spirals of despair. Raquel, with her high brow, inquisitive eyes, and oddly subdued expression, sat close enough to touch. The droll expression on her neutral face sent Britt's hair on end.

Denerfen shuffled around Britt's neck, curling into a ball on the opposite side. To cover the unexpected shuffling, Britt ran her fingers through the strands near her ear. She smiled, though it felt painful.

"Ta, Raquel."

Raquel set three leaflets in front of Britt, spreading them wide. "I brought something I thought you might be interested in."

Their titles indicated they were from the same serial production, if not slightly different works. A beat of confusion passed before Britt understood.

She sucked in a breath.

CENSUS RECORD FROM STENBERG MAIN; NEW BIRTHS

Raquel spoke before Britt could betray her fear. The Sister of Stenberg faced ahead, her back straight, hands folded together in her lap.

"I hope those are helpful."

Britt's heart raced as she struggled to know what to say. These might be rather helpful, in fact. She could have sworn she had sorted through these years a day ago. Had someone removed them from the Archives while she searched?

"But—"

Raquel pushed off of the table.

"Have a good day."

The sound of her retreating footsteps rang in the silence. Britt stared at her, convinced a ghost imparted them. Blood rushed through her ears as she slowly peeled the leaflet open. Words filled the paper. Her glassy eyes roved page after page until one name snagged her attention.

All the air left her lungs.

Selma Anderberg.

BRITT STARED out at the sea that evening, arms locked over her chest.

How to tell him?

Henrik, she practiced slowly, *I . . . happened upon . . . three leaflets, each one corresponding with the birth year of people with similar surnames, Anderberg, and one of them is a baby named Erik born to one Selma Anderberg. I suspect your father is a man named Cristan Anderberg.*

No.

One didn't just *say* that.

Yet, how else? She couldn't extract the words from her brain. Also, how could she possibly explain Raquel handing these three exact leaflets over? Or the fact that Raquel ignored her as she left, leaflets shoved into her dress, as she must have assumed Britt would do? The sense that someone else controlled this unfolding set her on edge.

None of it made sense.

Clouds piled high in the distant horizon, crackling with energy. A distant purr of thunder swept closer, borne on a brisk breeze. Sailors in distant places rushed to secure drifting cargo ahead of the storm.

Henrik stepped inside the cottage after securing the shed closed with a rope. Britt jerked out of her thoughts, caught his eyes with a dazed expression, and blinked free. He froze, halfway through the door.

"Sorry. Did I startle you?" he asked.

The tentative cordiality threatened to break. She wished it would. A good fight would help both of them settle down.

She shook her head. "No. I mean, yes, you startled me, but . . . it's fine." Britt gained her feet and reached for the window panes. The irritating whine of gusting wind ceased when she shut them, leaving a void. The stillness resembled a tomb.

"Should blow out overnight, I hope," he said.

"Good to hear."

"Okay day in the Archives?"

"Yes."

He stood near the door, shifting his weight, his lips screwed into a tight bow on the side.

Britt set Denerfen on a nest of scrap material on the table. He curled up with a yawn and tucked his neck into a ball. By instinct, she set her hand inside her pocket, touching Tesserdress's scales. Two of them flaked away.

Despair threatened.

What more could she do on Stenberg?

Nothing.

She'd found Selma, too. Better than that, she had a surname, a husband, Cristan's name, and a previous address. How easy it would be to hand Henrik the leaflets, ignore the fact that Raquel gave them to her after they had *obviously* been hidden, and be done.

Nothing tied her to Stenberg . . . except her lessening hope to find Malcolm.

Dull as a shadow, Britt sat at the table, one hand on Tesserdress. The thought of leaving didn't inspire excitement either. She'd been here a week, but it felt like a lifetime. Her other hand withdrew the three leaflets.

"Stealing again?" he quipped. The chair scraped against dirt as he slid it out and lowered onto it. His wary gaze held questions, clearly afraid she'd pounce. She pushed the leaflets closer, flipping the top page open to the most recent leaflet. The one that gave *his* name, as well as his birth parents.

"It's worth it this time."

Clarity came too slowly. Henrik studied the words longer than they should have required. She forced herself to wait for him to discover it. These words painted a surreality. An answer. All the years of his childhood, his teenage toil, his adult life, funneled to this exact moment. A random spurt of time, wrested from the string of a normal day's events, borne on the cusp of a storm.

His breath caught.

He lifted a questioning, oddly still gaze.

She nodded.

Henrik chased the details a second time, a third. Sometime around the sixth and the seventh, it registered.

He breathed, "You found her."

With one shoulder slightly lifted, she nodded. "A piece of her," she amended. "I mean, them. All of you, I believe."

Henrik swallowed audibly.

Britt leaned against her chair, both hands in her lap, and allowed him space to think. Denerfen whistled as he exhaled in sleep. Henrik blinked, studied, stared, shook his head, and read the pages a twentieth time.

The edge of his thumb traced along the last name. Anderberg. "A woman who screamed that loud," he whispered, searching, ". . . a woman who screamed that loud wouldn't have . . . she wouldn't have wanted me to leave her. Right?"

His forthright demand, spoken in a whisper, stirred a welling of sorrow. Oh, sweet Henrik. The days of irritation melted free. She saw the lost expression in his eyes and wanted to cradle him close.

"No," she said softly. "No woman from a proud, militaristic society that idolizes men in your position, that screams when she's separated from her child despite the culture that surrounds the soldats, wanted you to leave. On the contrary. I can't imagine what horrors and terrors she experienced, releasing you."

He soaked that in.

"The soldats have your birth year wrong, I presume," she added. "It's different in the paperwork from what you told me."

He grunted, reviewing it. Off, but not by much. The soldats didn't celebrate birthdays, only the anniversary of their induction into the soldats, which they typically considered their fifth birthday even if it wasn't.

"How?" he rasped. He shook the paper, which undulated. Outside, lightning streaked by with a giant *snap*. The bulkhead crashed close, whipping with rain. Thunder announced its inevitable arrival.

Britt held his gaze.

"Luck."

If he doubted her, he gave no indication. Later, he might query with greater depth. For now, shock provided enough of a buffer to buy her time.

"Cristan," he whispered. "If this is my Selma, which it must be, then my father is named Cristan."

"The next step is to figure out where Selma lives right now," she added. "There's an address in that census, but it's anyone's guess if they still live there."

"Probably the mainland. If so, she's lost."

Britt tilted her head.

"Lost?"

"Islanders go to the mainland to die."

"What are you talking about?" she asked incredulously. "I've been there dozens of times, and it's lovely."

Henrik's brow lowered into confused lines.

"You're joking."

"Not at all. Have you never been there? Not once, in all your assignments?"

"No."

"Who delivers the goods to the mainland when you trade?" Her hair waterfalled off her shoulder as she tilted her head in curious inquisition. "You *do* trade with them, don't you?"

"I'm not sure. His Glory has the soldats deal mostly in the Isles."

"Hmmm . . ."

She attempted to understand that.

"Just because His Glory doesn't like the mainland," she said softly, "doesn't make it a bad place. There are brilliant people there, and the place is absolutely huge. You can easily get lost without meaning to. If she's there, we stand a chance of finding her. They keep a census, too. And I know people there. Besides, there's far more arcane, and that makes everything in life easier than here."

"We?"

His question, so calmly uttered, struck her. She couldn't conjure a response, because she hadn't realized she said it. Then, she realized how much she meant it. Of course, she had to find Malcolm before she could make more promises to Henrik.

But she didn't want to let this go.

Henrik tapped the folded leaflets. They stood in a small stack of fate in the middle of the table. "You're not calling it finished?" he asked. His neutrality vexed her.

"I'm not sure how to read you right now, Henrik," she admitted with a calculated hesitation. "Do you want to proceed on your own? Do you want my help?"

With difficulty, he asked, "Why would you *want* to help? You have other reasons for being here."

Britt drew in a curling, roiling breath that mimicked the gusts of wind outside. Steady. Long. Blasting, yet gentle. For several heartbeats, she searched within. Could she afford to help him?

Unlikely.

Unless . . . unless she took an equally great risk. Opened herself up for big help from an unexpected ally. Her desperation to find Malcolm and save the draguls surely rivaled Henrik's drive to find Selma.

"I want to see it through, Henrik, and find Selma for you. I'm a Helsing. Britt Helsing. And no Helsing backs down from an agreement. But my time is running out."

As expected, her declaration landed with the appropriate weight. Henrik's lips parted. His eyes widened.

"Helsing?"

She nodded.

Henrik reared back just enough to impart straight shock. "You're . . . the daughter of General Helsing?"

Another precise nod. "Niece, actually, but that's semantics."

"Norr's breath," he muttered.

She bit her bottom lip. Underplaying it hadn't softened the blow, unfortunately. After an interminable pause, Henrik leaned forward and rapped his knuckles on the table once.

"Make me a counter offer. I won't extend your bargain without extending mine. Thus far, I've given you access to the Archives, shelter, food, and privacy. What more would you require to accomplish why you're here?"

Relief washed through her. This whole time, they'd been fairly equal risk takers. Henrik revealing his longing to find Selma and Britt staying with a strange man while hiding her draguls. But if they wanted to really succeed, there would have to be trust.

How unlikely.

How bold an ask.

How futile the effort.

She licked her lips, locked in the internal debate, until she threw her metaphorical cards on the table. Tesserdress's life was at stake. She'd do anything to save her.

"It's my brother," she stated. "I'm trying to find my brother, Malcolm, and I don't know where else to look. I need your help."

Chapter Eighteen

HENRIK

A hint of insecurity existed in Britt's churning eyes as she offered him more information.

"Malcolm is a Major," she said, her heart in her eyes. Unease drove her to her feet, so she paced as she spoke. "When a messenger drake delivered a message from Narpurra saying that Stenberg was sailing to Narpurra to escalate a situation there, General Helsing sent Malcolm and a contingent of Kapurnickkian sailors. Something about existing agreements and charters and the mainland? I don't know."

Messenger drakes were arm-length dragons that delivered messages back and forth for many isles, but they favored Kapurnick. Unlike draguls, these drakes didn't have a bond, but they did form loyalty to a person.

How appropriate this strange twist of fate that would take his beloved Captain *and* her brother.

"Captain Arvid," he said.

She paused. "Sorry?"

He shook his head. "Continue."

With an elongated breath, she complied. "Okay. Well, there was a battle at Narpurra. Later reports said that soldats disguised themselves as sailors and infiltrated Narpurra island. A bloody, arcaneless battle followed."

Arcaneless. Only someone off Stenberg would signify that detail.

Hands wringing, she whispered, "Malcolm offered himself as a prisoner to exchange for four of his sailors. To spare their lives. The Stenberg sailors agreed. Those four returned to Kapurnick. One of them sent a messenger drake ahead of time, letting us know. I intercepted the drake, read the message, then sent it to General Helsing. Couldn't believe my luck, managing to head for Stenberg before news really arrived of what happened."

She squared her shoulders, chin high. "I left on the first ship that was departing before General Helsing had the full news."

"Ossian."

She nodded. Her firm-jawed ire trailed into exhaustion as she unclenched her hands and loosened her shoulders. "Malcolm means everything to me, Henrik. If Stenberg is holding him somewhere, I have to know." Quietly, she added, "More rests on his life than you think."

"And then you found me," Henrik concluded.

"Yes."

"Your brother is ranked quite high, but he must be younger than most Majors?"

"Yes. General Helsing runs the islands, with the help of two Undergenerals. Each Undergeneral has three Majors that work with them. My brother is the sixth Major. As such, he's in charge of maintaining relationships with jord traders outside of our main islands."

The Kapurnickkian isles held a different structure to their government with a ruling military commander acting as the overseer. On Stenberg, His Glory worked in capacity as both military and general leader. Kapurnickkian leadership had more leadership positions, but not by much. Considering how many other islands relied on jord, Kapurnick should have had more leaders to deal with the constant back-and-forth of trade negotiations.

"So you came all this way to find Malcolm?" he asked.

Britt bit her bottom lip. "Yes. Because of her."

She withdrew a hand from her pocket.

A tiny dragul curled in her palm, breathing thready and fast. The sloping, gentle features and lacking horn buds indicated a female. She tightened her coiled body, shivering, as if she'd taken a cold. If she hadn't looked so diminutive, he would have guessed her to be the same size as Denerfen. Color leached out of many of the scales, leaving her speckled with gray and notes of receding violet into lavender.

Tears swam in Britt's eyes. Her voice clotted. "Her name is Tesserdress. She's bonded with Malcolm. Before now, she has never been away from him for more than a few days."

"She's dying."

Britt nodded, her lips pressed. After a moment, she cleared her throat, blinking fast. The sorrow in her beautiful eyes cut through his chest. "It's more than Tesserdress. She's one of the only remaining females we have that can lay eggs."

A beat passed while that sank in.

Panic resulted.

Sheer, blind panic.

"If we lose the draguls, we lose jord." he whispered, stark. "Their manure is what allows us to grow food on Stenberg."

"Exactly," she whispered. "The isles reliant on jord would never recover their ability to produce food, and Kapurnick's economy would crash. Stenberg, who is most reliant on us, would have to turn to the mainland for soil. But His Glory wouldn't do that, and the Lordlady might not offer it." A haste born of passion elevated her tone. "Without draguls to produce jord, we lose all of our current structure. People will have to leave the islands to live elsewhere."

"The mainland," he hissed, then shivered.

Mournfully, she added, "Not only would the most beautiful race of dragons be swept away, but most of the isles couldn't sustain enough food to support our current populations. Kapurnick may be amicable with Narpurra at this moment, but there's no doubt Narpurra would happily betray us, rise to power when other islands fell weak, enslave many islanders, and eventually dominate. Over time, our numbers would dwindle and be so few . . ."

She trailed away.

Bloodthirsty and dramatic as the tale sounded, he couldn't fault her predictions. Narpurra. The power-hungry island that didn't rely on jord for trade, or life, would be the first to skip over what relatively little space existed between the islands and take over. The high mountains of Kapurnick hosted a plethora of military advantage, food, shelter, and strategy. They were a gem of a prize. Enough to sustain smaller populations without imports from the jord trade.

But Stenberg?

Catastrophic.

Without jord, Stenberg would have little sustenance. The mainland would have to export food, but Stenberg didn't have the resources to trade for all their bounty. Growing their own food left lean times, but created independence. Henrik leaned his knuckles onto the table with a hoarse breath.

"I know," she whispered hastily. "I know how bleak it is, but I couldn't tell you! I wasn't sure how much I could trust you. General Helsing has sworn us to silence and . . . if Narpurra or His Glory knew . . ."

Her barren whisper was as shocking and stark as anything he'd heard. Repercussions and ramifications wound out, putting him instantly into defensive and planning mode. For several minutes, they listened to the crash-bang of thunder. Rain descended with thundering applause.

"General Helsing *is* aware?" he asked.

"About the draguls?"

"And Malcolm."

She hedged a hesitant, "Well, yes. Malcolm left Tesserdress behind because it was supposed to be a quick skirmish and return, and it was too dangerous for her. Normally, he doesn't go on these raids, but Stenberg has been so difficult to work with the last year. He hoped to negotiate, to withdraw our jord contract if we must." With less energy, she admitted, "Tess and Malcolms bonding has never been easy or simple, and it's relatively new. Within the last year. He's still getting the hang of it. General Helsing knows that Tesserdress needs Malcolm."

He lifted his eyebrow.

"All of Kapurnick will know that Malcolm is gone by now," she said. "Taken prisoner by your people. Tesserdress is the youngest female we have, thus, is the most capable for new dragul eggs. When healthy, she could produce two per year."

"You have no other females?"

"We have some, but of varying age and health. Our numbers are desperately low after losing most of them in a plague not long ago. If we lose more, they won't be able to breed."

"This *also* means—"

"Less jord." She nodded. "Yes. That's also why Kapurnick has to be careful with this information, or else panic might follow. The dragul keepers, General Helsing, the Undergenerals, and the Majors know our predicament." Softly, she added, "And you."

Other issues existed. So few draguls meant the supply of jord was about to rapidly plummet, or already started. That explained the lessening numbers. Oliver would need to know, and soon. It nearly prompted Henrik to drop into a rapid-fire interview of Britt so he could gather details and build a more robust picture, but he held the temptation.

Could Oliver know?

If the captain found out, so would His Glory. What then? War? An attack? Save the dragul, but hold Kapurnick hostage to it?

Henrik delicately rubbed a hand over his face. He could see out of his left eye today, which was progress. He paced in front of the table. Questions later. First, they had bigger problems. Much, *much* bigger problems.

The need to keep Britt close had exponentially multiplied.

Working with her, gaining more information, would have to be a careful process. She'd taken a massive and calculated risk coming here to find Malcolm, and that female dragul didn't have long to live.

"I know you must feel pressure to tell your leadership," she butted into his rapidly forming plans with a hard tone, "but I'm begging you to wait until I'm on a ship toward whatever hellhole you're keeping Malcolm on. Clearly, he isn't *here*. At least, not that I've been able to find. I had hoped that he'd be here by the time we arrived. Narpurra's a similar distance . . ."

The *you're* in *you're keeping Malcolm* hit with a bitter twinge inside.

"We'll deal with the details of my leadership later," he said. "For now, we need to find your brother so you can save Tesserdress."

With a great deal more suspicion than he wanted to see, she asked, "You're willing to help?"

"None of us would benefit from her dying."

A flash of displeasure told him she didn't like the reasons, but she'd accept the outcome. Britt shrugged one shoulder in silent acceptance. She appeared stiffer than he'd ever seen. His mind raced to catch up, speeding past annoyance and into plans.

If she had just told him at the beginning . . . but the thought was pointless. How could she reveal a secret this explosive and dangerous to an unknown soldat? He couldn't fault her.

"If Malcolm was taken prisoner at Narpurra, they wouldn't register him on any official paperwork filed in the Archives," Henrik said. "At least, not yet."

"Got that," she muttered through gritted teeth.

"The island where they put him is a longer journey from Narpurra this time of year, with head winds and storms. They may have not returned, or were tasked elsewhere before you arrived."

All the color left her face.

"I hadn't thought of that."

Recalling Einar's conversation when Henrik had just returned, he continued. "They took Malcolm to the Unseen island. Einar offhandedly mentioned a prisoner that the soldats took there with that name."

"Where is the Unseen island?"

He gestured south east. "It's part of the Chain. Unless you've been there, the Unseen island remains hidden. The arcane that infuses the island hides it. You can't see it. Dodgy to approach, because of . . . arcane, mostly. Native arcane. Stenberg took over the island decades ago and drove out the locals, who placed ikons to protect it."

"So why is my brother there?" she screeched.

The female dragul—what was her name?—jerked awake with a pathetic little mewl. Britt instantly lay her fingertips over the dragul's wings in a soothing gesture. The dragul calmed, stirring restlessly.

"His Glory sends prisoners there because the ikons prevent escape, and we don't have to spare sailors watching them."

Her jaw dropped.

"How is that possible?"

Henrik rubbed his forearm and muttered, "You don't want to know."

Britt shrank against the chair. The Chain was a series of hundreds of islands extending from the southwestern island of Siloam all the way east, toward the mainland. Some of them were so close that islanders rowed between them within hours. Others required longer. Mapping them had proven an egregious, decades-long project. No archivist on any island wanted to commit to the idea. His Glory couldn't pull sailors away from their duties long enough to map the Chain out as a designated task, so the map fell into disrepair and disarray.

Also, most islanders didn't care about a map.

The cowed expression on Britt's face was the right one. At least she paid attention to geography, which some people in the Isles never bothered with.

"It's not impossible to find, if you can locate a ship captain who knows where it is. You have to have visited there before and escaped it. Most Stenberg captains know it because of their prisoner drops."

"Can you find it?"

"Yes."

Relieved, she nodded. Her other hand curled around Tesserdress. She hesitated, glancing at him, then delicately placed Tesserdress next to Denerfen on the blanket. A sheepish heat rose in her cheeks, as if she didn't want to explain how she'd managed to smuggle *two* draguls on to Stenberg.

He still couldn't fathom.

"I'll find a captain to take us," Henrik said.

"Right away?"

"I hope so. With the cleansing, plenty are stuck here, and growing antsy. Ossian might still be here, and he knows the island."

"What about the cleansing? His Glory closed—"

"Ossian owes me."

Her expression didn't ask for details, so he offered none. She wouldn't want the grisly story, anyway.

"How long does it take to get to the Unseen island?" she asked.

"Days, at least, depending on the weather and currents. I'll see what kind of ship we can manage. Ossian might know of a smaller, faster one." He nodded to the sickly dragul. "Will she make it?"

Britt put her hand over Tesserdress' scaled, lavender body. Her tail had coiled up toward her face, tucking her together like an amethyst loaf.

"She *has* to make it."

Henrik glanced outside, racing to absorb these new developments. A second dragul. Selma. Erik. Too much at the same time. He paused as he reached for the door. The slate sky brought an early night, with its rollicking thunder and heady wind gusts.

True sunset would creep in soon, heralding darkness. Good. He needed an escape and time to think.

"I need to talk to Ossian. I'm not sure when I'll be back."

Suspicion whipped into her eyes. Her lips pinched, cheeks tightened.

Exasperated, he said, "Do you want to leave right away, or not? I won't tell Oliver before we've saved the female. I promise."

Something in his visage must have mollified her, because her shoulders smoothed out. She nodded once, but didn't speak. Her hand hadn't moved from her protective shell over the dragul.

"If you don't trust me yet," he growled with more force than he intended, "at least trust that I have no interest in Stenberg collapsing because one of the last female draguls dies, all right?"

A flicker of reassurance dimmed her haughty gaze and assessment. With a tight nod, she turned to focus on her dragons. Denerfen watched Henrik from beneath hooded eyes as he slipped into the night and plunged into the storm.

WIND WHIPPED into Henrik's face, and rain sliced through the air like driving needles. He headed into the wind, slipping down alleys, and blending into a night as thick as ink. It provided a place to hide. To defeat this surreality and find steady ground.

Britt commanded his thoughts at first. So regal, yet concerned. Her hand protectively cupped over her dragul charges, her ferocity a sparkling force. Impressive that she'd kept Tesserdress a surprise this long. Small details aligned. The too-heavy wrist pouch, her protective hand always in or near her pocket, fluttering wings that didn't quite sound like Denerfen.

Selma intruded, overriding all the other conundrums. Captive Malcolm, dying draguls, and the shattering impact on the isles, could come later.

Selma.

His *mother*.

Against all odds, Britt found her. Henrik let his parents names sprint through his mind as he slipped into the Shadowlands, not so much searching as prowling. Thinking in the night.

Selma.

Cristan.

Erik.

Anderberg. Proof that he had, at one time, existed as a different person. If he hadn't become a soldat, who would he be? An Anderberg. Putting a name on it changed everything. He had heritage. History.

Parents.

Questions about his old life haunted him, as if he'd thrown open the box.

A cackle broke the night, issued from some poor soul sprawled along the edge of the road, half delirious with drink. Henrik ignored them, cutting a wide angle. He forced his thoughts away from Selma; he couldn't afford such a deep distraction.

To save the draguls, he'd forfeit his Second Captain spot. He knew this. Accepted it. Couldn't care less about what happened to the twenty bags of jord or what games Captain Oliver played.

Like Harald, Henrik hadn't wanted the promotion anyway.

Einar told him not to trust Captain Oliver, and Henrik trusted Einar more than anyone. Until he heard the information that Einar wanted to share, Henrik would let the question of jord rest. Though subtle, the decision *was* a rebellion.

He'd never rebelled before.

For now? He focused on the draguls. The gale whipped and the wind screamed as he hurried toward the ocean, Ossian bound.

It all sounded like Selma in his head.

Chapter Nineteen

BRITT

Henrik returned sometime in the night, clothes saturated, water streaming down his neck, and collapsed onto the floor beneath the table. He slept hard, woke up in the late morning, and sat at the table, staring at a cup of coffee.

His lack of information said everything.

Britt's sleep had been fitful and restless, but hope buoyed a weary heart. Malcolm! Prison island! If Henrik came through with a knowledgeable ship captain, she could be sailing that evening, Malcolm bound. A hopeful event.

Probably *too* hopeful, but she'd hedge her bets.

Tesserdress' life depended on it.

Henrik readjusted, propping his forearms on bent knees, as Britt administered the last of the Helandalenda potion to Tesserdress. She coaxed the final drop onto her fingertip, which Tesserdress, eyes closed, lapped at weakly with her forked tongue. Exhausted, Tess lay her head down.

"I couldn't find Ossian," Henrik said, shattering the still air. "Ossian must have left before the storm. Slipped out in the night, perhaps, when the port authority wasn't paying attention."

"Is it possible?"

"Yes. Particularly for a captain like Ossian. Later, if the port authority protests and says that Ossian broke the cleansing, he'll be able to blame it on the storm blowing them out of port, or him making a mistake. Regardless, I made some inquiries to find who *was* here."

She couldn't fathom what kind of *inquiries* he could make on such a dark and stormy night.

"Did you find anyone?"

He frowned. "Maybe."

"Who?"

"His name is Rhygard. I'm not positive he's reliable, but I know he's been to the Unseen island before."

"How do you know that?"

Darkly, he said, "He took me."

"Then what's next?"

Henrik regarded her, though his gaze appeared fathoms away. "We find Rhygard."

WITH HENRIK AT HER SIDE, Britt felt no fear as they ventured into a people-packed marketplace early the next morning. A gray sky lingered, but the thunder and lightning had passed. Rain-washed cobblestone smelled fragrant and fresh, driving all the sand from hand-drawn wagons back into the sea.

With slight pressure from Henrik's elbow, they veered left, between two market stalls cluttered with fish bone necklaces and baskets woven from the fibrous, purple fronds that decorated distant mountains. They grew shallow roots between thin rock crevices. Her curious fingers itched to palpate the bright yellow candles infused with ground up lava stone that, purportedly, had healing properties.

Yet no arcane.

Not a whiff of it.

Henrik paused at a back-roads intersection, wedged between rows of vendors. She had a feeling the sellers allowed him because they recognized him, and no fool would mess with a soldat on Stenberg homeland.

They wound through the back passageways. Henrik would pause, assess, gaze around, seeking more than simple goods.

No matter what degree of mutual purpose appeared between them in this last week, she couldn't forget that Henrik was a Stenberg soldat. Their tentacles wound deep. In a pinch, any soldat would opt toward their training and loyalty. He helped her to save his island, not to save her draguls.

She wouldn't bargain with the lives of all her dragons, her islands, or her own, on the hope that Henrik might shuck years of brainwashing and training to serve a different master. He made it clear that he supported her in order to preserve jord . . . and get more information.

Despite her heart tugging her closer to Henrik, she knew *exactly* where she stood: In between two very fragile worlds.

Henrik paused so quickly she collided into his broad back. Rubbing the sting out of her nose, she stepped away with a scowl.

"Rhygard," Henrik drawled. "How good it is to see you."

He directed the comment to a sotted man, sprawled on the ground. A miniature, squealing pig lay next to him, burrowed on its porky side near the man's waist. The stench of rotted food and wet refuse rose from the cobblestones. When Henrik's shadow fell across the porcine pair, the little piglet squealed, hopped to its tiny feet, and clattered off across the cobblestones.

Rhygard peered through slotted eyes and a sand-strewn face. "Soldat."

Henrik held out a hand. "On your feet. I need you and your crew. Immediately."

"I WANT TO HELP YOU," Rhygard whined, "but I can't! His Glory called a cleansing, and the port authority has stalled all ships. No one is supposed to sail."

At this news, Henrik's eyes tapered. Machinations whirled in his eyes, making Britt uneasy. Far be it from her to understand or predict what the inglorious His Glory might do, but based on Henrik's response, this wasn't good.

"I'll compensate you," Henrik countered.

Rhygard scoffed. "With what monies? They hold you on a tighter leash than us captains."

Henrik pressed his lips. His face became a mask that choked Rhygard's self-inflicted amusement off at the start. Rhygard dropped his gaze. "Right," he muttered. "Not in the mood."

"I need to get off this island and over to the Chain."

"Then I suggest you take it up with him."

Rhygard tipped his head toward His Glory's Temple, which lay somewhere embedded in rising and falling and sloping and tumbling streets. Henrik's scowl deepened.

"If I gain explicit permission, will you take us?"

Rhygard's shoulders pulled back, straightening his spine. Deepening interest appeared. "From who?"

"Oliver."

"How much are you offering?"

"How much do you want? I'll get it approved."

"Through who?" Rhygard spat back, one bulbous eye narrowed and wary. "Like we established, you ain't got monies."

"Oliver will pay. He distributes monies in our name when we require it."

The first sign of interest gleamed in Rhygard's deep gaze. He blinked, shuffling through questions, concerns. Finally, he breathed, "You approve it through Oliver and I'll take you. I have a crew of five."

"We need something fast."

"I'll take the Woebegone."

Henrik reared back. "That's a navy ship."

Rhygard grinned. "If Oliver says I can, then I can."

Henrik stared hard, and finally nodded once.

"It's done."

Chapter Twenty

HENRIK

Captain Oliver stood at his window, glaring out. His hands propped on his hips, legs spread shoulders width, and body drawn like a violin bow. A wrongly placed word and Oliver would snap.

What poor timing.

Henrik used his knuckles to gently rap on the door, his lungs tight as a cage. "Do you have a minute, sir?"

Oliver turned, glaring, then eased when he saw Henrik. In a two-second beat, Oliver scanned Henrik's face, still discolored, though not as swollen. His gaze darted over Henrik's shoulder, then back.

"Come in. Shut the door."

Henrik obeyed. Dust motes pranced and sounds of the marketplace below drifted through the canted window.

"His Glory was pleased to hear of your grappling tournament win." Oliver drilled his gaze into Henrik. "He sent his personal congratulations."

Curse his betraying pride, but Henrik couldn't help a moment of gratification. All these years, and His Glory had been the penultimate leader. Failings and faults notwithstanding, Henrik couldn't help the sense of relief and pride at doing something right.

No matter how brief.

The praise sank through him too quickly. Within seconds, it left a taste like barren ash in his mouth. He thought of Einar, and stuffed that aside.

"Thank you, sir. Tell His Glory it is most appreciated."

"Tell him yourself."

"Sir?"

"He wants to meet with you."

Henrik blinked, startled. "I'm sorry?"

"Despite not finding his missing bags of jord, His Glory has requested to personally speak with you in two days. You might notice," Oliver added with an irritated flare of his eyes, "that you've received no assignments since your return. His Glory wanted to grant you a reprieve of work after your reefer year, and a chance to recover from the grappling tournament."

His days had been far from relaxed as he attempted to find the missing jord, but he didn't mention that.

"Thank you, Captain."

Oliver relaxed a little. "All of this is a good sign of His Glory's goodwill toward you, Henrik. He hasn't asked for the same from Harald. There is nothing more important than this. Be here at first light in two days and you'll accompany me to His Glory's personal quarters in the Temple."

A fist squeezed Henrik's heart. To Henrik's knowledge, an invitation into His Glory's personal quarters had never been offered.

Oliver motioned with his hand. "Give me your jord updates, soldat. Surely, you spent the intervening time since our last meeting searching for their whereabouts. Where are the twenty bags?"

Henrik withheld a wince. Oliver wouldn't accept an excuse such as *recovering from the grappling tournament*, so he didn't offer it, though almost a full day passed with him sleeping. He changed tactics.

"I have unexpected news, sir, and then I'd be happy to recount my search."

"Explain."

"Information has come to me about a potential jord crisis."

Oliver's brow rose.

"Oh?"

"Details are sparse. I can't say much more than that. I'm working with my informant now, and only need a few weeks. And a ship. The Woebegone," he added. "I came to see if you could give me an assignment to figure this out before it becomes a problem."

But without knowing the details, he silently added.

Oliver, jaw grinding, stared at Henrik for a long time. He crossed one arm over his chest, the other framed his jaw.

"The Woebegone?"

"Yes, sir."

"And an assignment?"

Henrik forced the same confidence into his tone. "Yes, sir."

"You won't tell me anything more than that?"

"I can't, sir."

Fire flashed through Oliver' eyes, flowing free as quickly. He ran his tongue over his teeth. "You *can't*?" he repeated with utmost calm.

Carefully, Henrik shook his head.

Oliver quietly asked, "Update me on the twenty bags of jord, soldat."

Throat aching, he said, "I have no updates, sir."

"None?"

Henrik forced himself to keep Oliver's stare.

"No, sir."

"I see," he murmured with a silky fire that promised no good tidings. "Help me understand this, soldat. You are up for the position as Second Captain to His Glory, the second-highest honor a

Stenberg citizen could ask for. After a commendable year as a reefer, and breaking a grappling tournament record, you have a flawless slate. Your service is beyond exemplary. And you want me to assign you a task where I don't know the details, I have no idea what's at stake, and you still haven't found twenty missing bags of jord? This is not a complex task, soldat. You *find the jord*."

Henrik swallowed hard.

"Yes, sir."

Oliver braced both hands on his desk. "Does this *assignment* have anything to do with the new woman in your bed, soldat?"

A flash of rage shot through Henrik. He kept his expression impassive, though every tendon in his body tightened to the point of pain.

Norr's breath, he had to lie.

To his Captain.

"No, sir."

Oliver's lips curled into a snarl. "Sure it doesn't. Soldat, this is unacceptable. I reject your request for an assignment, and will let His Glory know that you have no update on the missing jord. Your appointment with him in two days' time will be very interesting. What a disappointment you have become."

Henrik schooled his jaw into paralysis.

"It's obvious to me," Oliver spat, "that you need something else to remind you of your place in this world. You will not take that assignment, as I have a different one for you. Your recovery and relaxation is officially over."

Henrik's stomach sank.

"Sir?"

"We have a missing child that needs to be found immediately. He's been gone for two days. His Glory has asked for a soldat to comb through the Shadowlands to see if he's being held there. His name is Chamsen, and he's eight years old. Blue eyes, brown hair, freckles on his cheeks. Wiry build. Last seen wearing short pants and a white shirt. He answers to Cham."

Henrik bit his tongue to stem the flood of questions. First, a child? Why couldn't the sailors handle it? Must be the child of a high-ranking island-owner or aristocrat in His Glory's pocket. Probably kidnapped, ransomed, or otherwise gone, for a variety of reasons.

Or something . . . *else*.

A test for Henrik, most likely, as they strove to promote him to second Captain. In all likelihood, the missing bags of jord might also be a test, though the elaborate nature of it was in question.

It wouldn't be unusual. Soldat leadership constantly put their soldats to rigorous testing. Obvious and oblique. Many soldats operated in between silent and rigid lines of expectations. They had unquestioning faith in each other, their leadership, and His Glory. Captain Oliver had promoted to First Captain because of his unswerving loyalty to the protection of Stenberg and their isles all of his life.

Unquestioning.

Yet, Oliver's steely eyes couldn't hide one thing: desperation.

"Why not the sailors?" Henrik asked.

"Does it matter?"

Decades of training battled within Henrik. Thoughts of draguls and Denerfen and Tesserdress occluded long-established thought patterns. The extinction of the dragul race would irrevocably change the isles forever.

He had to *tell* Oliver.

But he didn't, because instinct whispered a soft, *no*. The combination of Einar's letter, a higher sense of judgment, or a hunch about Oliver' strained nerves kept Henrik's lips shut. No soldat Captain had any reason to be this stressed over a missing child report or twenty bags of jord, even with pressure from His Glory. The soldats had long prided themselves on *not* being swayed by outside influences.

Henrik licked his lips. The space of silence in between his pause spoke readily enough. Not long enough for distrust, but Oliver wouldn't miss the hesitation. A good soldat never hesitated when issued a command.

"No, sir," Henrik said. "It doesn't matter. I'll find the child."

"Get to work. I don't want to hear from you until you've found Chamsen or a strong lead on the jord whereabouts or both. Do you understand?"

"Yes, sir."

"You have an assignment. Complete it as commanded or lose your rank."

Henrik's curling blood slowed, pooling to tingles at his fingertips. Oliver's threat echoed in the small room. *Lose your rank.*

Lose his rank?

In all his years, such had never been dangled in front of him. An insult as much as a threat, or perhaps unshadowed harassment.

Henrik said, "Yes, sir."

Oliver waved a dismissive hand.

EFFORTS TO FIND Einar resulted in nothing. He hadn't returned from his assignment. When Henrik returned to the cottage, he didn't illuminate the lanterns. He stood in the pulpy darkness, agitating his own fears.

Which revelation was worse? That the draguls teetered on a dangerous precipice that could sweep the isles into chaos, or that he might lose his rank?

"Henrik?"

He spun. Britt sat upright on the bed, peering at him. Moonlight limned her features, illuminating cheekbones and a high brow and lush lips that, for a wicked moment, he wanted to cover with his own.

If he buried her in a kiss, would she help him breathe?

He smothered those thoughts with a rise of heat in his cheeks. Now wasn't the time.

She tucked her feet beneath her, her weight propped on one arm. Her hair coiled in a tumbling waterfall down her right shoulder. Denerfen perched on her left with a sleepy yawn. He tottered from side to side, ready to plummet back to pillows and sheets. Tesserdress was a sleepy bundle on the pillow.

"Why were you gone so long?" she asked.

"I had to speak with Oliver, and I tried to find Einar. Agnes says he hasn't returned, but it took me awhile to track her down."

"Will he let you have the ship?" she breathed, her knees tucked beneath her nose. She straightened, like an eager child.

He shook his head. "No. He gave me an assignment."

Her outrage crashed her eyebrows and furrowed lines into her brow.

"What?"

"I have to do some reconnaissance tonight. Find a missing child."

"Missing child," she whispered. "How old?"

"Eight."

A compassionate murmur of, "That's awful," followed. She chewed on her bottom lip, body unwinding from the mattress. "But what about the draguls? Can someone else find the child?"

"Not without me telling Oliver about the draguls."

She slumped.

Henrik ran a hand through his hair. How to explain without sounding like a coward? He should have pressed Oliver harder, but he couldn't have said more without endangering Britt and the race of dragul's. There had been something . . . wrong . . . about Oliver' eyes and response. Something off about these tasks . . .

Henrik allowed himself to ask the question that haunted him the whole way home. Did Oliver already know about the draguls? Selma? He knew about Britt, to some small degree. But perhaps he knew everything.

He gave Henrik a chance to make things right.

Oliver had enough experience in the wide Isles—and had been the reefer once or twice before his promotion to First Captain—

that he'd be more than comfortable with draguls as a species. All the isles knew about draguls and their connection with jord.

Henrik sat on the edge of the bed near her. A mistake. His thoughts didn't clear with her so close. He couldn't escape the bittersweet smell of coffee grounds and sea spray. The light musk of a dragul, somewhat cloying, but aromatic. A cacophony of scents.

"Oliver is . . . distracted," he said.

Never had he taken an opportunity to speak so openly about his command to others outside the soldats. It was one thing to listen to Einar, who groused constantly about soldat leadership.

But to a Kapurnickkian?

He felt intrinsically aware of the tiny life which held the potential for so many others curled up on Britt's pillow and breathing with shallow, steady breaths. More scales had gone missing in the day, and one glittered on the linens.

"I need to finish this assignment," he said. "If I can locate the child tonight, there's a chance I can leverage it in the morning for a quick ride out."

"But—"

"It's my only option," he snapped. "I can't just abandon my life here, my responsibilities. Without . . ."

He trailed away, unable to articulate it. He couldn't save the dragul *and* betray his Captain. He couldn't. The loyalty was driven into him with lash marks and obedience.

Her expression hardened.

"Fine."

"In the morning," he said gently, "we'll come up with a new plan."

"This *is* the new plan!"

"Once Oliver has had time to think," he continued, desperate to make her see that he *was* fighting for her, "it'll be easier to convince him that we need the ship."

"You really believe that?"

"Yes."

Henrik shoved to his feet and pressed away before he did something he regretted, like shouting his frustration or telling her to leave him alone or covering those lips with his own or laying her flat on the mattress. Ravishing her the way he wanted would tie Britt more firmly to this gods-forsaken island in ways she might never extract.

Assignment, he reminded himself.

They were both here for an assignment, nothing more. The urge to protect her couldn't extend beyond Selma and draguls.

He left her glowering at his back.

Chapter Twenty One

BRITT

Unable to stand the hints of dawn dancing through Henrik's cozy cottage, the thought of *not* getting on a ship bound for Malcolm, or what it might mean if she couldn't get away to find her brother in time, Britt rose before full light.

Tesserdress grew weaker by the hour. She squeaked with protest whenever Denerfen moved too much. Aching muscles? A dragul-like fever? Or the breakdown of a sad heart?

"Hang in there." Britt stroked the delicate tip of Tesserdress' sweet nose. "I'll find you a ship, my darling."

Henrik understood the ramifications to Stenberg if Tesserdress wasn't reunited with Malcolm soon, but he didn't understand the ramifications to *her*. To dragul-kind. To Malcolm. Henrik may not have cared if it hadn't directly impacted his island. That meant saving Tesserdress lay firmly in her lap.

This time, she had a lot more information. Henrik told her where Malcolm would be, which was why she came in the first place. She could make this happen without his help. Britt Helsing wasn't about to rest her fate in the hands of a soldat. Henrik made his alliances clear last night.

Britt had her own.

She left a message, packed her bag, braided her hair, flipped a wide-brimmed hat on her head, and scooped the draguls into her palms. Tesserdress slept in Britt's left pocket, Denerfen on her right. Separating them wasn't ideal, but she had little recourse with Tess so uncomfortable.

Ten minutes later, under the persuasion of a bluebell sky, Britt waved to Old Man with a broad smile and grocery basket on her arm. With any luck, she appeared to be the picture of a Stenberg woman. Up with the burgeoning sunlight, grinning under a hat, and ready for her morning vittles.

Old Man lifted the gate for her to glide through, and lifted a steaming mug in a bleary-eyed greeting.

Market stalls stirred. Islanders groaned. A few vendors straggled out from beneath their tables, rubbing the heel of their hand into their eyes. Sunlight kissed the top of the bamboo market, waking the world with a buzzing energy. Britt passed all of them, basket empty.

She had a ship to find.

THE SHIP CLINGING to the edge of Stenberg wasn't sea worthy by a grand margin, but it *was* better than a skiff or row boat. Broad enough to fit a small crew, a below-deck area, and enough sails to make good time.

Britt shielded her eyes with a hand.

"How much?" she asked.

Captain Lars surveyed her, then smiled. Gold flecked his teeth. "Depends on what you're offering."

"Not *that*," she said coldly. "I can pay in silver."

The lecherous smile dropped.

"Eh?"

"Pure silver. I'll throw in Kapurnickkian potions, too."

Scoffing, he said, "I don't believe you."

She withdrew a vial from the pocket where Denerfen rode—and not very happily, at that. He nipped her thigh every now and then, in case she forgot his steep displeasure. Glimmering chunks of silver floated in the vial. A burned crest from the Guld Islands off of Kapurnick burned into the cork stopper.

Captain Lars' expression morphed. "Aye," he sang. "How very interesting." Lars propped a leg up on the side of his ship, folded his arms, and pressed them onto his knee. His tongue ran over his teeth as he surveyed her and the silver.

"You're running away?" he asked.

"No."

"Kapurnickkian?"

"Yes."

"Where are you going?"

"The Unseen island. Do you know it?"

His gaze tapered. She shuffled to the side, adjusting into his shadow. She could barely read his eyes around the glare haloing out. Undoubtedly, he stood on a higher position, right in front of the sun, on purpose.

"Unseen island? Makes this whole situation doubly interesting." His teeth tapped in deeper thought. "Who are you springing free from the Unseen island?"

"A friend."

"Why was he taken prisoner?"

"How do you know he was?"

Lars scoffed. "I'm not an idiot. Stenberg is the only place that goes near that island, what with the ikons. Captains are always dropping off prisoners."

With great irritation, she snapped, "I need to go immediately. Can you find it?"

His nose wrinkled. "Ability? Yes. Desire. None."

Britt ignored that. Anyone could be bought for a price.

"His Glory has called for a cleansing." Lars motioned toward the Temple with a flick of his wrist. "That makes leaving difficult. Not impossible, but it has to be worthy."

"I know."

His brow rose. "Course you know," he cried, "or else you wouldn't have come to me, love. No one comes to Lars unless they have to."

"You're not from Stenberg."

"I'm not."

"Where are you from?"

"Narpurra, but not the main island. Upprior."

Britt fought to keep her expression neutral. Yes, such swarthy hostility from an Uppriorian made sense. Lawless rebels, the lot of them. They declared their independence from Narpurra twenty years ago, and held no real governing body on their small spit of land except whatever mob boss had the most power at the moment. A real hotspot for the pirating type.

Which could *definitely* work in her favor.

His Glory couldn't hold his cleansing power to all islanders, but the port authority banished ships from the Stenberg port all the time. Failure to comply with His Glory's commands was a fast track to banishment. For islands that relied on exports and imports, troubled relationships with an island like Stenberg could be a real problem. Like Kapurnick, Stenberg held too much power.

"I desire to leave immediately," she said, because his damning silence had grown a bit too long. If he thought too much about it and the ramifications, he might renege. "I understand that tonight will be better for stealth, and leaving during the day is too much to ask."

"Demmed straight it is."

Exacting a promise from him was her goal. When it came to islanders, once given, a vow was fulfilled. All that many islanders owned was their self respect and a sandy beach. Even pirates from Upprior.

"Will you do it?"

His quizzical expression narrowed to slashes for eyes. "Tonight, you said?"

"When the port authority is asleep," she added, growing into the idea. "If he receives a present of his favorite brandy and has a reason to drink more heavily than usual, I think it would be easy enough to slip out of port."

"And when my ship is gone in the morning," he countered with a lecherous smile, "who is going to stop said port authority from exempting me next time? Can't afford to be banned from Stenberg."

"He'll be too drunk to notice."

"Will he?"

"I swear by it." She tipped her head back toward the main wharf, several minutes walk away. "You're out of the way. He might check once or twice, but the cleansing doesn't have much longer to go. There are so many boats here now . . ."

She shrugged.

Speculation gleamed. Leaving the island wasn't as dangerous as approaching during a cleansing, but still risky.

After a pregnant pause, Britt stepped away. She dripped with disdain.

"Forgive me, Captain Lars. I didn't consider you the fearful type, certainly not with your reputation. I'll be off to find a different ship."

She spun. For several hasty steps and desperate heartbeats, she thought he'd let her go.

A gruff call followed.

"Wait."

Britt steeled herself as she whirled around. The different vantage point cast him into greater visibility. He didn't appear as mangy and old from here. His timeworn voice and skin gave a sense of exhaustion. If she peeled away rough years of experience, he might not be much younger than General Helsing.

Lars tipped his head toward her hand.

"Two vials of silver and I'll take you tonight—if you swear the port authority will truly be drunk."

Britt pitched him the vial. He snatched it. "One now," she said, "and the second on delivery at the Unseen island. Vials three and four when you sail us to Kapurnick."

He leered, the silver vial vanishing.

"We are agreed."

She said in a voice of steel, "Before I return to the market to trade for brandy, which I'll make a present of to the port authority, I'm sending a note with the next mail frigate. My brother Pedr will know exactly where I'm going, your name and likeness, and my plans. If any harm comes to me during our voyage, you'll drown in the depths of the sea and your ship burned, under an ivory flag, and your bones fed to the sharks."

He had the presence of mind to pause. His head canted to the side.

"Ivory flag, you said?"

She nodded, an eyebrow cocked.

"That is . . ."

"The flag of Burning Beard, the pirate."

Captain Lars blanched. "You know him?"

"He's my brother."

"The one you're rescuing?"

"No. I have more than one, and I assure you that neither would take kindly to something happening to me. If you can get me to the Unseen island, then to Kapurnick, the reward will be *well* worth it."

His smile tightened with regret as he spat out, "I'll see you this evening."

THE URGE TO say to Henrik, "See? Doesn't have to be that hard to find a rebellious ship captain!" whisked her away from the wharf.

Bloody mess of a soldat.

Her ire fizzled as she left the wharf behind her, striding up the steep, cobblestone streets and toward the market, seeking a bottle of fine brandy. Denerfen stayed in her pocket for now. He'd be safer there while she worked through the marketplace. She'd have to pay for the liquor with her Stenberg healing potions, which made her stomach hurt thinking about it.

No matter.

It would be worth it.

Once near the Archives, she'd steer to the left and wind her way through the market, losing herself in the stalls for a few hours. At this point, there would be no returning to Henrik's cottage until after she saved Tesserdress, if at all, which is why she left a note. Her stomach tightened at the thought.

Of *course* she'd return.

Why wouldn't she?

Only a few dozen reasons, all of them trumped by the heavy feeling in her gut that told her she didn't want to leave. Not like this.

He left her little recourse.

The physical exertion warmed her, and the sparkling sunshine cut hope into her bleak outlook. Regardless of what Henrik chose last night—and how could she expect him to choose any differently?—she had a plan.

A way out.

The cost she offered Captain Lars was exorbitant, and they both knew it. General Helsing would pay the promised silver when they arrived at Kapurnick, but they'd have to dig from the deepest wells.

Later. She'd think of that later. There was no cost limit to spare Tesserdress' life, or the draguls. By extension, the greater and

Lesser Isles, as well as Malcolm's life. In comparison, four vials of silver wasn't much.

While cogitating over these things, a body strode up to her right side.

Another on her left.

She barely had time to look at one before the other grasped her arm, just above the elbow. His fingers squeezed to the point of pain. Her eyes jerked to the one on the right, holding her in a grip that pinched between thick fingers. The half-shaved head of a soldat, but not one she recognized from the Old Pub. She hadn't seen all of them, of course, but *this* one had no apparent familiarity, with his flared nose and thick jaw.

"Miss Helsing."

The man on the left, a soldat by his blank expression, cold eyes, and long hair braided on top, held her other arm. "With us," he demanded.

Breath in her throat, they steered her toward the Archives.

Chapter Twenty Two

HENRIK

Mud and sand caked the back of Henrik's arms the next morning as he climbed over a fence, dropped to the ground behind it, and peered through the crumbling stone. The young boy, Chamsen, raced for home. He'd extracted Chamsen from a kidnapper in Shantytown. The child abductor lay dead on the ground, left for the sailors or the sea birds to deal with.

Cham banged on the back door.

"Mor!" he cried. "Far!"

Henrik lay low, crouching out of sight, a knee pressed into soft soil. The affluent stone house, with painted-over flaws, bamboo roof shingles imported from other islands, brightly colored stone gardens, and signs of life all over the ground, belonged to a known acolyte of His Glory. A rich archivist named Ubba, admired for his knowledge of Stenberg history and law. Invaluable when His Glory had bright aspirations to dominate.

The door blew open. A woman with thick hair wrapped in a silk sleep turban stood on the other side. The boy, crusted with dirt and tears, threw himself into her legs. She cried out, clutched his thin arms, slumped against the door, and nearly fainted.

When Ubba appeared with equal parts astonishment, Henrik

backed away. The little boy wailed, burying himself in his mother's neck. Henrik couldn't bring himself to watch. As he turned to go, he caught Ubba studying the yard, scouring the fence, searching, searching.

Henrik vanished into the still-dark dawn hours. As he crept away, departing the affluent neighborhood through a complicated series of walled roads that made little sense, sunlight emerged in the distance.

Ahead, a shadowy figure stepped away from the wall, hands in pockets, a sense of lounging about him. Henrik recognized Einar right away. Einar didn't say a word as Henrik approached, but spun to fall into step behind him.

Wordless, Henrik slipped back a step. Accepting the silent communication, Einar took the lead.

THEY STOOD at the edge of a cliff that overlooked a bashing sea thirty strides below. Spray hastened toward them, then hissed a mocking retreat. The far corner of the Quarters lay at their backs. At the sailor's compound, a high and flapping orange flag whipped in the early-morning breeze. The presence of the flag kept the distant ships from coming into port during a cleansing, unless they were prepared to wait the cleansing out. Such a noisy spot would prevent eavesdroppers from the Quarter, and the sheer drop at their feet protected two-thirds of their surroundings.

"We need to talk," Einar said. His expression had clamped down. "About Oliver and Arvid and everything. There's about to be a rebellion—a big one. A group of soldats are leaving. We're breaking away. Before I give you details, I need to know where your loyalty lies."

The charged question didn't require further clarification, though it should have. The clues of the past several days lay out with an obvious array of issues. Increasing unrest between soldats. Captain Oliver's disrespect at Captain Arvid's tribute.

No *wonder*.

Henrik's response required no thought. "With you."

Though he'd never had his loyalty to Stenberg called on, after the charged discussion with Captain Oliver last night, he didn't care. All these years, and all this sacrifice, led to no trust. None. Something passed through Einar's eyes.

Quietly, he smiled.

"Really?"

"Did you doubt it?"

"Me? No. The others? Yes. They wanted to see how you reacted to the growing tension. Wanted to see if you'd support Captain Oliver blindly or not. You're Oliver's new recruit, remember? We had to be sure."

"They must be satisfied."

"They are."

"Why?"

"The fights. Not because you won," he added, "though that would help anyone build respect. The way you broke up the fights, protected Britt. Soldats listened to you, and you responded to Vilhelm's ridiculous arrogance. They said I could bring you in, but then I received an assignment. I just returned."

Henrik nodded once. "Good."

Einar huffed a laugh, looked away. The charged moment required both of them to take a pause. After a time, Einar said, "Arvid is leading a soldat rebellion. That's what I wanted to tell you."

A metaphorical stone slammed into Henrik's gut, robbing his breath. He jerked to the side, meeting Einar's sober gaze straight on.

"What?"

"Arvid is alive."

"But—"

Einar shook his head. "His death was staged, every bit of it.

He's alive on Narpurra, working with them as an ally to help us resist His Glory."

Henrik could barely comprehend the word *alive* in this context. In his mind, Arvid was gone. The pyre burned. The past sealed.

Einar continued. "Arvid convinced His Glory to give him the assignment to go to Narpurra, but Arvid had written ahead. The Narpurran government agreed to see Arvid alone. Once there in person, he made his request for help away from the sailors and Narpurra agreed. Readily. Except, the Kapurnickkians came to help Narpurra, which was unexpected. A battle did happen, which made it easier for Arvid to fake his death."

Grimacing, Einar shook his head. "A few sailors died because of the battle, and Arvid's struggling with that. But we have to accept some loss of life. He's still not sure how Kapurnick knew about the attack. Arvid thinks a different Narpurra leader sent out a drake to request reinforcement, but didn't have permission."

Blood drained from Henrik's head, making him dizzy. The whispered words sent him into a bloodless headache. Remembering Einar and the ten soldats who remained on the dock during Arvid's memorial ceremony cemented his deepening spiral.

"Why?" Henrik ground out.

"The whole rebellion idea started years ago. There's been building restlessness for a while, but it exploded right after you left for your reefer year. His Glory's demands turned relentless. Overnight, it seemed. His Glory commanded Arvid, Harald, and myself to take people from a Chain island and bring them back in order to enslave them."

"To do what?"

He shrugged. "We don't know. Something on Stenberg's eastern shore. We weren't informed. Regardless, His Glory had ordered other soldats to do it, and they did."

"Under Captain Oliver?"

Einar nodded, grave. "That's when we realized how dark it had become."

The taking of people to enslave them was a blatant rejection of a peace treaty signed decades ago. Narpurra was known to sidle around it, evading bold proof many times, but all other isles held to the agreement with willful regard.

Kapurnick, if they found out His Glory had begun to enslave people again, would cut off jord exports.

Einar scuffed his foot along the ground. "Arvid has an insider who says His Glory has plans and things in place, but hasn't told us exactly what they are yet."

"What did Arvid do?"

"Arvid refused. Oliver insisted Arvid find the enslaved and bring them back. It put a divide between them that spiraled into blatant unrest. Surely, you've noticed the division."

"Yes, but what about the enslaved?"

He shrugged. "We haven't been able to answer why or where they go."

Einar kicked at two black rocks. They careened over the edge, plummeting to the white spray below. If they hit the water, the swell of waves into the edges roared too loud to hear. Soothing, but agitated.

"Vilhelm is Oliver's new darling," Einar added. "The only reason Oliver hasn't put him up for Second Captain is because he's too new. It would have tipped the rebellion into full strength."

"Captain Oliver knows about the rebellion?"

"He suspects."

"Does he know about Arvid?"

Einar chewed on his bottom lip. "I don't believe so. The disrespect at Arvid's memorial could have been frustration at Arvid's refusals earlier. It could have been a deeper understanding. We're not sure."

Henrik chewed over the information, unable to stop his mind from reaching into the long impacts. If rebellions happened in the past—surely, they must have at some point—then history had forgotten them. Intentionally, he'd wager. They couldn't be the first unhappy group of forced workers. Enslaved workers, if one looked at it too closely.

Yet what did it mean? If His Glory lost half of his soldat force, would it really impact Stenberg?

Undeniably.

"You've joined this rebellion, Einar?"

"Of course."

"What do you want from it?"

"His Glory removed," he said instantly, "and freedom."

Henrik glanced at him from the corner of his eyes. Einar continued, impassioned now, with a burning fervor Henrik hadn't heard before.

"We want monies. We want compensation. We want the choice to take assignments or reject them. They dictate *everything*, Henrik. If we procreate, if our relationships legalize, whether we can keep our children. They're afraid of us. If they aren't, they will be. Should be."

The promise rang with authority. Bitterness.

They're afraid of us.

They will be.

These thoughts weren't new. Henrik entertained them before, in the quiet nights of his more rebellious stages. Before they brainwashed the fight out of him. Before he understood that the only way forward was to buy in, and thoughts could come later, when healing, rest, food, and shelter weren't the most precious commodities. But then healing, rest, food, and shelter were *always* the commodities.

"He sent me as a reefer," Henrik said quietly, "to keep me away from it. Oliver has known there's been growing discontent and he didn't want me to be part of it."

"Exactly."

The bastid.

"He might have suspected I'd been involved before you left. Oliver wanted *us* separated. He's had you pegged for years, Henrik, yet never asked if you wanted the promotion. The assumption is that you do whatever he says. It's wrong. I'm done. We are done. We want you to be part of us."

"How many are following Arvid?"

"Ten. Eleven including you."

So they *had* been watching him. Testing him. Trying to see if he'd reveal his true loyalties. This conversation aside, Henrik had no idea where he landed. Both in their eyes and his own.

Flooded by a sudden understanding, his attention snapped to Einar. "The Cleansing and the daily whippings are because of the soldats?"

Einar nodded, grim-faced. "Probably. In addition to whatever wickedness he's planning that we haven't been able to figure out. His Glory is baffling, Henrik, but he's not blind. Now that Arvid appears to be out of the picture, we're hoping it will cool His Glory's motivation to chase the rebellion."

The deep roots boggled his mind.

"Arvid's insider believes that His Glory knows there's growing unrest amongst soldats," Einar continued. "His Glory also knows that if he loses soldats, he'll lose just about everything, including sailors. We rebel, sailors will follow. The navy disintegrates, and so will His Glory's power. Without us, Henrik, he's nothing."

The casual confidence and certainty struck Henrik in the chest. "Sounds too good to be true," Henrik retorted. "You're overestimating the navy."

Einar shook his head. "I don't think so."

"And Narpurra?" Henrik folded his arms over his chest. "Whose idea was that?"

"Arvid. He's vouching."

Unease made Henrik restless. Riots in the soldat ranks stood against everything they were taught as boys.

"They ripped us from our families and made us into killing machines to work their will." Einar shook his head, a bitter edge heightening his voice. "They brought this on themselves. We want him and his acolytes gone. All of *it* and all of *them*."

The words reverberated.

All of them, gone.

All of it.

All of them.

That meant His Glory. Captain Oliver. The infrastructure they created. Probably even His Glory's personal soldats, so often complicit in the deepest betrayals. The Archives, Compendium. Where did this stop?

The firmness of Einar's voice spoke to the depth of expectation between them. He'd taken more than a calculated risk telling Henrik everything. Finally, Oliver' cryptic desperation made sense.

But why the assignment to rescue Chamsen? It had been relatively simple, and hardly proved his worth. Henrik hadn't shown motivation to discover the jord question. Winning the grappling tournament proved his physicality, but the lack of unraveling the jord mystery left him a weak candidate. Captain Oliver could promote Vilhelm, but it would ensure the rebellion unfolded.

"Narpurra?" Henrik countered hotly, because the point required a second attempt at discussion. "*Why* Narpurra? They're wild and unpredictable."

"Who else?"

"Kapurnick!"

Einar scoffed. "Don't be a fool, Henrik. Just because you're fond of a Kapurnickkian woman doesn't mean their political structure would help us with a rebellion. They have their own problems, and Arvid says they're almost destitute."

The wind evaporated from Henrik's lungs.

Einar chuckled, slapped his shoulder. "I saw the dragul during the fights. She does pretty well, acting local, but she's not *that* good. I sense there's quite a story brewing there. Agnes is dying to learn the truth."

He owed Einar a lot more information. The space between him and Britt was layered, and at some point, he'd share each one with Einar. For now, Henrik forwent explanation of Captain Oliver's current state of mind, Britt, and the draguls, to say, "Britt needs to leave immediately. She has a . . . family emergency, for lack of a better word. She needs to go to the Unseen island in the Chain. I can explain it all later, but not right now."

Einar raised a querulous eyebrow.

"That fast?"

Henrik cut his disbelief short. "I need to find a ship that'll take us immediately and without being detected."

"Are you sending her, or are you going with her?"

"I don't know."

The thought of sending Britt alone was a coward's betrayal. Repugnant. And yet . . . what obligation did he have? She was a wily woman that made it onto Stenberg on her own, despite being on a ship packed with jord and dozens of wild sailors. Plus, she found Selma in the Archives while navigating hints of his soldat world.

Did she need him?

Did he need her?

He clenched his fingers, not liking that train of thought. No matter where it branched, the endings felt wrong. Horrific. Archaic, even. Sending her on a ship willing to break the cleansing interdict and risk being an enemy to Stenberg wasn't ideal. Those rangy types would sooner rape her and ditch her body overboard than help, unless the exorbitant cost made it worth the risk.

But if he left Einar and the other soldats at such a delicate time in this rebellion . . . with Captain Oliver breathing down his neck and distrustful . . .

A cold shudder skimmed Henrik's spine as he sank deeper into his thoughts. Hadn't Britt foretold this? When they first spoke, she mentioned His Glory forcing people onto ships, stealing jord, scuttling ships.

For a long time, Einar and Henrik listened to the breaking waves. After too long watching the sunrise bloom overhead, and wondering what Britt would think of this situation, Einar clapped a hand on Henrik's shoulder and squeezed.

"Don't be a bastid, Henrik. Go with her."

"Captain Oliver already threatened to take my rank if I didn't complete a last-minute mission last night. I did, but now I have to complete some paperwork and find the missing jord. He's already fuming."

Einar growled, "He threatened your rank?"

Henrik nodded.

"His Glory is watching," Einar spat. "That's why. Oliver is under pressure, too."

"I see it."

With a shake of his head, Einar set aside his rage. "Let's just say that if you're not on Stenberg for the next week or two, Oliver won't notice. If he does? It won't matter. Nothing will be the same. We've got your back."

Einar's hand slipped away from Henrik's shoulder. The quiet promise of underground distraction wasn't as concerning as it should have been. Henrik's lack of concern felt like an answer to where his loyalty lay.

"What do you have planned?" he asked.

"A statement," Einar said. "Although Arvid is supposedly dead, we're not, and Oliver still has a problem on his hand. It's a reminder that we're not to be underestimated, but we promised Arvid we wouldn't go full bore without him."

Henrik's breath swirled in his lungs. That solved it. He'd go with Britt and suffer whatever consequences remained. Captain Oliver could deal with His Glory. "If I go with Britt," Henrik said, "I give up everything here."

Einar nodded. "It's worth it."

Chapter Twenty Three

BRITT

ritt knew better than to fight two soldats with determined stares in a teeming marketplace. A crowd circled the whipping stock and growing fervor guaranteed she'd create more problems. Her heart raced, worried for Denerfen and Tesserdress. Two soldats, and no Henrik in sight.

This couldn't be good.

Her stomach twisted when they whisked her inside—no change of shoes, no veil—and through the Archives. The irate steam in the Matron's eyes as they passed would have set every leaflet in the place on fire, but her compressed lips betrayed no sound. Two other Sisters of Stenberg watched in various stages of bewilderment and shock as the soldats marched by, carrying Britt between them.

On the second floor, they peeled to the right, away from the shelves she'd perused. A door, ensconced in a back corner, awaited. The soldat on the right tossed it open. They pitched her inside. She caught herself before slamming into the sharp corner of a table, veering away from Tesserdress taking the impact just in time.

Cerulean sky and brilliant sunshine spilled from a high window cut into sealstone walls. It silhouetted a broad-shouldered man.

Hungry chants from bloodthirsty Stenbergians rang below. A deep voice drawled as she straightened, shoving hair out of her face.

"Britt, is it?"

The low voice was unfamiliar and tense. The man spun. His close-cropped hair and clean-shaven face indicated Stenbergian leadership. The raw force radiating from his powerful arms indicated a soldat. He didn't need to say his name.

Britt elevated her chin.

"Ta."

A flicker of his lips might have been a smile, but looked more like a grimace. "Miss Helsing, you may call me Captain Oliver."

CAPTAIN OLIVER HAD MORE fright and tempest built into his scowl than His Glory. Comparatively, one looked like a ghoul, and the other a goblin. She couldn't decide which belonged where. Oliver's deepening disregard and haughty irritation made for a more nefarious foe. His Glory had been far too curious, though it must all be an illusion.

The way Oliver regarded her made it obvious that fear was every bit as powerful as curiosity. She had the presence of mind to be grateful that the draguls remained in her pockets. Denerfen couldn't bite the back of her neck and give her away, though hoping he remained quiet seemed a stretch.

A palpable vainglory in Oliver's stare set her teeth on edge. With a tilt of his head, he commanded her to sit. She folded her arms over her chest and refused. Surprise halted his momentum. She couldn't help but remember her first night in Henrik's cottage when Henrik had done the same.

"You don't want to sit?" he asked.

"Not if you tell me to."

"You understand that I have brought you here to speak with me?"

"Yes."

"Do you refuse to speak with me?"

"No. I refuse to be alone in this room with you and comply with your commands. I am not one of your soldats. If you want to speak with me, you may do so out there, in the Archives, with the Sisters of Stenberg to witness. Acting like a brute and forcing me into the Archives isn't going to win my cooperation."

A glacial smile curved his lips. Oliver regarded her for a full ten seconds before he said, in a much louder voice, "Oh, the tempestuous future of the dying draguls! Fading, one at a time, and putting the lives of all at risk. How are your Kapurnickkian leaders—"

She silenced him with a hiss.

He ceased, triumph glazing his stone-cold stare. The tight fist of dread gripped her heart. She swallowed rising hysteria. Her tone was too controlled when she muttered, "Fine. I'll speak with you."

Her arms hung at her side while Oliver closed the door, angling himself inside the confined space. He didn't attempt to close the gap, but she didn't like the desperation hidden in those eyes.

"Britt Helsing, am I right?"

Hearing her full name from a Stenberg soldat commander set her senses awhirl. He smiled with too much of his teeth when she refused to answer.

"A pleasure, as you said," he continued. "There's always been rumors about General Helsing's daughter—niece, is it?—but a lack of noteworthy accomplishment has failed to propel your name any farther from mediocrity."

She curtsied.

He chuckled tonelessly. Oliver clasped a folded paper. Tucked inside were smaller, thinner leaflets. Very *familiar* leaflets. The same that Raquel had given to her days ago containing Selma's name.

Had Raquel given her copies?

"By the look on your face, I don't think I need to ask if you recognize these papers, Britt Helsing."

She fought a yawn. "I've never seen them before."

He flashed a smile, as if flattering her. "I'm not interested in wasting time or speaking to a Kapurnickkian spy. Certainly, this is not a debate. I know you have these same leaflets in your possession. Copies, in case you wondered."

She almost choked. "Spy?" she cried.

"What else might we call you?"

"A tourist!"

"Let's not be offensive."

Her hands balled into fists at her side. She loathed that his flickering gaze noted her frustration, and he repeatedly used her full name.

"Britt Helsing, I have a deal for you. I know why you're here on Stenberg. Information regarding the terrible state of the draguls has long reached His Glory's ears. He knows the dire straits they're in. He knows your brother is imprisoned on the Unseen island." Oliver waved his arm in a half circle around his head. "His Glory orchestrated all of it."

A creeping flush heated her from toes to cheeks. His Glory thought a lot about himself, but this was something else entirely.

"Why do you think the Sister of Stenberg gave you the paperwork Henrik sought?" he continued. "Why do you think you've been unmolested on our island? Given free reign in the Archives?"

The chilly grip extended all the way to her heart. Wrapping, squeezing, tightening. The clammy hold plunged through her chest with radiating panic. She couldn't move. Barely managed a thought beyond, *all of it was a lie.*

Oliver considered her, little more than distantly interested. He had the power in this situation, and he knew it. Like everything else on Stenberg, this conversation was no accident. She had stepped right into his choking arms.

When he readjusted his stance, he engaged his thighs, as if bracing for a blow. She longed to provide one, right in his midsection. The resulting wheeze would be gratifying, if it did not end her life.

"Despite me counseling His Glory to use your presence for control over the draguls, and thus, our own fate, His Glory has chosen something else."

Oliver's jaw ticked, as if such an admission pained him. Britt couldn't trust anything he said was real.

"A bargain," he concluded. "An exchange, if you will. We will let you and your dragul go if you provide us with information. Nothing big," he clarified with a musing voice. "Just . . . tidbits."

Britt kept her hands away from her pockets by sheer willpower. The only bargaining chip she had *was* the draguls. Thus far, he'd given no indication he knew about Tesserdress, only that she had one dragul. If they had all the information, Stenberg wouldn't want Tesserdress to die, but that didn't mean they needed Britt alive. Though, if she survived this, General Helsing might kill her.

"Tidbits about what, Captain Oliver?"

"Your sweet tone doesn't fool me, but a commendable attempt. You've been staying with Henrik all this time, have you not? Looking for your imprisoned brother, I presume."

Gathering ice spiraled from her heavy-beating heart and into her veins. It crackled all the way down her chest, past her knotted stomach, and into the curved arches of her feet.

"Henrik?"

"Our most commendable soldat, though up-and-comers are proving as talented, if youthful. I've been preparing him to assume a Captain's position for the last several years. One can't be a soldat Captain without at least one reefer year under the belt," he added, as if such should have been obvious. "Growing . . . unrest . . . among the soldats deemed it prudent to send Henrik away for a year. Let him see the islands, the context of jord shipments, and away from such . . . irritating ideas."

Britt fought not to get lost in the details. *Unrest amongst the soldats?* What a cad. He was grooming Henrik to be a leader, removing him from joining his fellow soldats in a bid for freedom, probably.

She understood all too well.

"All I hear you saying is that you don't have control of your soldats," she replied with a judgmental lift of her brow.

He failed to care. "Flatter yourself brave with mincing words if you wish, Miss Helsing, but I couldn't care less about what you *think* is happening. Tell me about Henrik. Answer all my questions about our soldat and you'll find your way onto a ship to find your brother and spare your dragul."

"If I don't?"

Oliver perked up. He motioned outside with a sweep of his hand, "How convenient that it's a cleansing, is it not? There's no one lined up for today's whip as of yet, which would be unfortunate for such a large crowd. His Glory has ordered us to rid the vermin and scum from the island in order to make it clean for His Glory's very presence. To prepare for greatness and the bodies of our enemies beneath our feet. To expunge evil and reveal our depth of gratitude to Norr, in his demanding and powerful wisdom. Only the chance to rid Stenberg of *your* presence permits me to stand in these hallowed archive halls today, you see. Cleansing, and all that."

A prescient *thud, thud, thud* and the crackle of roving whips snapped outside. No accident. This room, with the open window, was on the side of the Archives that overlooked the street where the whipping post stood.

Her stomach bottomed out.

Whips.

Of course.

The blood that stained the streets would be flowing again soon, only this time it might be hers. His Glory purged anyone that didn't agree with his strange and sometimes rabid dictates. Could she afford to fall into the ranks of Stenberg disobedience?

Betray Henrik and walk.

Seal her lips and endure.

A phantom whip bit through her shoulders with searing teeth. If Stenberg whipped her, it would do more than filet her skin and potentially hurt her draguls. The aggression would incite a war. If General Helsing didn't immediately retaliate, Pedr would. Her pirate brother would avenge her with arcane fire on Stenberg. He certainly held the power of destruction in sheer arcane prowess and knowledge. Burning Beard's torrential and wrathful rage would descend.

It didn't have to be that way.

If she answered the questions, she was already prepared to depart. Draguls safe, bag on her back. She'd escape to Malcolm without sneaking away, imparting the silver, setting her life into the hands of a pirate, or hoping Malcolm was where Henrik believed.

But . . .

. . . Henrik.

His tortured eyes and living grief about Selma. The memories he whispered with softness in his voice. Such a tender touch for a wildly powerful man. He was so much more, and he didn't know that. The beautiful world awaited.

He didn't know *that*, either.

Why would Oliver want information on Henrik? Her mind roved fast, skimming over the strange divide between soldats during the grappling match. The tension in the air. Oliver briefly touched on a possible insurrection, but it must be deeper.

She wrapped her lips around her answer.

"No."

His brow lifted, as if bored.

"No?"

She shook her head. "Deal with your soldat problems on your own, Oliver. You won't hear a word about Henrik from me."

He blinked so sluggishly that it appeared he'd fallen asleep standing. When his eyes opened again, fire consumed him. He might have expected resistance, or back-and-forth banter over what she received in exchange, but this was a man clearly unused to open rebellion.

She hoped he choked on it.

With hostility so suppressed it sounded like silk, he murmured, "Do you realize the ramifications?"

Britt squared her shoulders and glared.

"Beyond my sailor peeling the skin off your back with his whip, of course." His upper lip curled in a feral smile. "Not to mention you rotting on a ship until we take you to the Unseen island for you to die. Will your dragul waste away without you?"

An uplifting of hope buoyed her.

He spoke only of Denerfen. He didn't speak of the dire straits the draguls were in back at home, and believed she sought Malcolm because he was a prisoner, not because of Tesserdress' weakness.

The realization spun the power back to her.

"Scary threats," she said with equal chill and disdain. "Now, let me tell you what *I* know. I know that your island will be out of control if the soldats rebel. I know you're their leader, and would probably be held responsible. You're desperate, and desperate men make stupid decisions. I know that the moment that whip touches my back, Kapurnick will declare war. Hellfire and wrath will descend from all corners of the sea." She tilted her chin up. "Whip me. I *dare* you."

His expression, poised somewhere between curiosity and loathing, remained marbled glass.

"As you wish."

He thudded on the door with the back of his boot. It cracked open, revealing the two soldats. When Oliver spoke, he addressed the soldat on his right.

"Prepare a letter for Kapurnick. Tell General Helsing that it's regrettable that Miss Helsing snuck onto our shores, attempted to glean information as a spy, and planned to return to the Kapur-nickkian isles with said information. Per our laws, she will be treated accordingly, and their islands will have no recourse for war. Such is the fault of the spy who embedded herself within our land."

She didn't have time for her outraged gasp. The soldats seized her, dragged her out of the room by her arms and her hair. Agony tore through her scalp, prickling down her neck in hot needles of pain. Panic instilled deep in her belly, a relentless, fighting force all its own.

She released it.

Her shrill shouts couldn't cover his authoritative command.

"Take her away!" His voice rang through the Archives as the soldats whisked her from the room. No amount of protest removed his words. "Put her on the whipping block for removing sacred records from the Archives, violating the cleansing, spying on His Glory and the soldat subordinates. Fifty lashings."

FEAR BECAME a molten thing inside her.

She kicked, shrieked, elbowed, to no avail. They held tight, her arms wrenched to the side and behind. Their hands dug into her flesh, making her fingertips tingle, her wrists ache. Only the draguls kept her from thrashing into pieces. None of the Sisters of Stenberg slowed their progress as the soldats shoved her outside.

Sultry air swarmed her, rife with sparkling sunshine. The gath-ered crowd had swollen to greater proportions. Thirty. Forty. Fifty? Didn't matter. Too many, and their lust for pain lay thick in the air.

Denerfen went wild in her pocket, but the general roar of the crowd outside was too loud to distinguish his cries. Britt tripped over her feet, slashed her toe open on a rock, and bit back a cry of fear as the crowd parted. That hateful wooden structure appeared, flecked with blood, gore, bits of bone and shredded whip.

The whipping post.

A sailor stood nearby, bullwhip in hand. Five different thongs curved from the handle to the ground. Embedded stones skidded along the edges. How perfect that the whipping block was positioned exactly across the road from the Archives, considered one of the greatest treasures in His Glory's famed arsenal.

The bloody bastid.

Fear bled to sheer panic. A whimper escaped her in a shaky breath. Fifty lashes? She'd never survive. One of the soldats chuckled, a dull, roaring thing. His breath smelled foul, like rancid bean paste.

"Change your mind?"

Words and breath failed her. Britt couldn't conjure up a *no* any more than she could look away. The whip handler had meaty forearms, scars on his wrists, and a wide belly. He avoided her eyes. His gaze tilted to clouds as the soldats yanked her across the bloodstained cobblestone road.

The crowd roared, stamping. Hands clapped. Shouts echoed. Bets called back and forth, and the tinkle of coins exchanged.

Ye gods.

What filthy animals lived here?

Curses streamed off her tongue as she renewed her determination to break free. If this war would start, if His Glory would impose such a heinous situation, she wouldn't go down without hurting one of them, at least.

One of the soldats cuffed her on the temple with an open palm. Her ears rang. The hit knocked her senseless for a moment, dulling the racing thoughts. The sharp edge of fear blunted. They shoved her against the post.

The sailor reached for the ropes to bind her. Bits of dried blood and skin ground into her dress. The pulse slowed in her ears as she realized there was no way out. She bit back a retch.

"Wait!" she pleaded to the sailor. "Let me remove my dress. It's . . . my mother's. It's . . . special."

The whip handler hesitated, nodded once.

The soldats took delight in ripping the dress from her body. The fabric tore in half, peeling to the side. Jeers, catcalling, and whistling rippled through the crowd. Frantic, she stumbled out, thankfully clad in her underdress. One soldat painfully gripped her arm while the dress bunched on the blood-clotted ground.

"Stay back!" she screamed at the dress. "Don't you—"

The soldats slammed Britt against the whipping post, smashing her nose. Struck dumb a second time, she had no breath to protest. Welling pain rose from the injury. Tears smarted her eyes from the impact. Terror over the anticipation of that giant bullwhip slicing through her muscles distracted her from the pain.

The whip handler kicked the dress off to the side and tied her wrists to the board.

"Sorry," he hissed, then cranked the rope so hard the rough fibers dug into her skin. She let out another wasted cry. Thoroughly secured, sailors formed a circle to keep the crowd clear. A savage chant ballooned behind Britt, rippling.

How many amassed to watch? A hundred? More? The cool breeze danced across her almost-bare back, where the soldats had torn through her underdress with their hideous fists. Her skin puckered from exposure. She panted so fast the world spun. Britt pressed her forehead to the whipping board and braced for the thudding, tearing havoc to start. At least the draguls were in her discarded dress.

They're not getting the whip, she chanted in her mind. *They're not getting the whip.*

Quiet descended.

A body stepped close, with the dull *thud thud thud* of heavy boots. A hard chest pressed too close to her spine, invading her space, grinding against her hips. A hot voice whispered in her ear.

"You don't have to do this, Britt."

Oliver.

The pig.

He trailed one finger down her shoulder, swirling and spiraling in circles that led to her elbow. She shuddered at his foul touch. Blooming filth must follow in his wake, like liquid black tattoos, marking her.

"You need only answer a few questions."

She spat on his cheek. The spittle gathered just below his eye. "To the locker with you, pig-face bastid," she hissed.

His lips twitched. He turned, shouted, "Beat the skin off of her back!" and strode away. Ravenous, bloodthirsty Stenberg islanders cheered, and she loathed every one of them. Britt's fingers wrapped around the top of the board. She bent her knees, pressed her forehead to the top, and clenched.

A hush rolled free, roaring in her ears. A loosed tiger. A wild thing.

After an interminable pause, the crack of the bullwhip split the silence and searing heat sliced across her back. The shock was worse. The raw violence and aggravation stole her thoughts. At first, it startled her more than it ached.

The second lash followed.

A cry raced free. Pain sprouted, sparking along a thin line of skin, then disappeared. Heat dripped down her skin as she ground her molars together, choking on a sob. A third slammed into her ribs, creating a dumb confusion and numb disbelief, as if her body couldn't keep up with what happened.

Reality joined the hellfire bane of the fourth stroke, alerting every tingling, terrified sense. Her nails dug into the wood. Splinters cut through her fingertips, but she felt nothing. Nothing except magma seething in bubbling wounds. The coppery taste of blood in her mouth from biting her tongue. The smell of sweat from sheer panic.

The fifth stroke brought ravaging fire.

Tempest.

Agony.

Agony.

Agony.

Chapter Twenty Four

HENRIK

E inar strode alongside Henrik as they wound through the Quarters. Weight floated off Henrik's chest as they left the seaspray, and their conversation, far behind. He had time to think about what to say to Britt.

The decision had been made, but how would it lay out?

Einar spoke in a musing way, as if he didn't plan to overhaul the entire thread and structure of Stenberg society, when he asked, "Where are you headed?"

To Captain Oliver, he almost said, but did it matter now?

Not at all.

"I . . . don't know," he admitted.

"Agnes wanted me to meet her at the market. Come with me and we'll figure out a plan to get you a ship."

Henrik sent him a sidelong glance. "No assignment following the heels of your last?"

"There is one."

"Are these Captain Oliver given assignments?"

Einar's lips twitched with hints of a smile, and they left the final answer at that. "Agnes really likes Britt, by the way," he added after a general pause.

"Yeah?"

"A lot."

"Agnes is nice."

Einar hooted, then gave a sly grin. "Not always."

Unable to help it, Henrik laughed.

They strolled through the subdued streets, absorbed in separate thoughts. The tang of the morning built with warming sunshine, heating the cobblestones and thickening the air from the stormy aftermath. Unbearable humidity would soon descend.

A commotion near the Archives drew Henrik's attention. He lifted his head to find a swelling crowd congregated around the whipping block. Einar rolled his eyes, shaking his head.

"Stupid cleansing. Can you—"

Einar broke off.

His words shuttered.

Henrik stopped, clued in by Einar's tightening body language. He spun to follow Einar's gaze. A familiar head of sandy blonde hair topped the whipping block. The bullwhip slammed with a distant thud, jerking the lean body tied by the wrists to the top.

Was that . . .

No.

"Shite," Einar hissed.

Blood roared through Henrik's ears, racing through his veins. He didn't realize he'd taken off until Einar joined at this side, arms pumping. They skidded over the slick cobblestones, leaping barrels, sprinting toward the whipping post side by side. They approached the packed crowd.

"Move!" Einar bellowed.

Henrik bent his head, angled his shoulder down, and rammed his body into the teeming mass. He blew past onlookers, shoving them aside, spraying them left and right. Screams of protests cut short. He heard nothing.

Nothing but another *crack*.

Henrik spilled out of the gathered crowd and locked in on final confirmation.

Britt.

Her broken, bruised, and ripped skin didn't hide her limp profile. The gentle curve of her shoulders, lashed to a mangled, gory mess. A team of sailors appeared behind the whipping block as he shoved into the circle. They shouted at him to go away. He couldn't hear anything but his own panting. The whip handler, thongs ready behind him, let another strike fly. Britt's body spasmed, her head lolled.

Henrik's weight shifted, leaning on calm calculation. Instinct graced the moment, taking over. He slipped into soldat.

Into flow.

Into *exactly* what he knew best.

Henrik threw himself into the path of the whip, interrupting it mid-lash. His weight landed on the whip handler, sending them both to cobblestones. Henrik rolled off his back, bounced to his feet. He grasped the handler's wrist, wrung it. A crack of bone and an ear splitting scream resulted.

Einar appeared at Henrik's side. He flung the whip to the side, away from an approaching sailor. Harald emerged from the crowd, grasped it, flicked his wrist into motion. The whip stopped an attacking sailor around the ankle. With a jerk and a scream, the sailor toppled.

Einar vanished behind Henrik. Harald advanced out of the crowd.

Henrik charged for Britt.

Two of His Glory's soldat's appeared on either side of Britt. Henrik threw himself into the space between them, slamming into one from the side. They toppled together as three more sailors swelled out of the fleeing crowd.

Timmer, appearing at the front of the crowd, laughed maniacally as he flung a fist into the eye of His Glory's closest soldat. Brass knuckles gleamed from his hand.

Blood sprayed.

The waiting crowd dispersed in a storm of panic. Einar shouted commands. More sailors rushed forward, then scuttled away as Einar emerged. Henrik plowed into the second advancing soldat, who tripped over his feet, fell back, slammed his head to the ground. He slackened, eyes closed.

The edge of red disappeared as Henrik hustled to Britt's side. Blood coated her underdress and pants. Blood saturated her dress, discarded off to the side. He crouched at her side with a purl of deepest fear.

"Britt?" he whispered.

He touched her cheek.

She moaned, a shuddering, weepy thing. Sensing eyes on his back, Henrik glanced over his shoulder. Captain Oliver leaned his palms against the windowsill of the second floor in the Archives, staring out. A promise of vengeance filled his eyes.

Henrik pointed at him. "You and me!" he shouted. "This has just begun."

Captain Oliver scowled.

Henrik returned to Britt.

B lessed mermaids.

The pain eased.

A dull roar throbbed through her ears, similar to swimming too far underwater, or a fever dream, or the bang of drums after too much mead.

Norr, that bastid. The sea god didn't grant her the mercy of passing out. Not entirely. Not yet. He must truly loathe her, forcing her to dance along consciousness. Awake enough for spasms and burning. The time in between each lashing had stretched into eternities.

Did the whip handler prolong it on purpose?

Had time warped?

All occurred in a tunnel. Somehow, she braced her body for another thrashing. If she released the board grinding into her palms, she'd lose her tenuous grip on life. What was it now? Twenty?

Eighty?

A roar broke the blur of noise. Thuds. Shrieks of pain. Rampant horror, and a strange, humming quiet. Britt attempted to open her eyes, but she lacked the ability to control her body.

Where was Denerfen?

Tesserdress?

Nothing happened. Had Oliver returned? A rough whisper interrupted her wild thoughts. "Britt?"

No noise came from her lips, though her mind formed the question.

Henrik?

"Hang in there," he crooned. "I'm cutting you down. Can you stand?"

She moaned.

"I'll stand for you."

A sharp, cool metal grazed her wrist, then the pressure of the right rope released. She dropped, but an arm caught her. Pain lanced through her, bringing a wash of darkness with it. Britt sobbed. An unnatural, juddering moan unleashed from deep inside.

"Gods." Henrik spat. "No matter where I touch you, this is going to hurt. I'm sorry, Britt. I'm sorry. One more."

She tried fruitlessly to form his name. A distant tunnel floated forward. The chasm of black reverberated his voice. The second rope disappeared.

She crumbled.

He caught her.

"Gods, Britt."

An excruciating slice of pain tripled through her back, starting where his arm wrapped low on her waist.

"Where are they? The draguls."

"Dress," she gasped, barely audible. "Dress. Please."

"I'll get them."

Tears jarred out of her eyes, though she couldn't see. Black rimmed from the edges, encroaching forward. The final tie to life broke with a crack.

Finally.

Norr blessed her with the black.

Into the abyss, she fell.

JOSTLING.

Creaking.

Muffled voices.

Bright sunshine.

Searing, hot, scorching.

Rabid pain.

Agony's sister, Misery.

Britt's chest pressed against someone. A shoulder? Arms wrapped her thighs, holding tight. The open air was a horrid kiss against her flayed back. Each movement sent spasms over her ribs.

Gulls cawed.

Ocean roared.

Firm wood sounded beneath boots.

Sand.

Salty spray.

Another familiar, scratchy voice.

"Looks like she's early."

B ritt lay on her stomach, hair tucked into a rough knot Henrik managed to tie while the hastily-found ship escaped through choppy waters.

Light fell through a round porthole, illuminating a storage room. He'd created a makeshift cot from low, freshwater barrels and a rare slab of lumber. Britt lay on top of her dress, which was spread over burlap bags to soften the edges. Bloody rags and a box lay on the floor in-between his feet. Clean rags stirred from a pile with an outraged cry.

Norr's breath.

He'd almost forgotten the draguls.

Henrik lifted a scrap of fabric. Denerfen reared his neck, snarling. He recoiled, probably from the astringent scent of a cleansing potion.

"Easy," Henrik murmured. "She's safe now."

Denerfen's front legs lifted, wings splayed, as he stood on his hind legs to sniff. He immediately sought and found Britt. Henrik leaned down, palm flat.

"Climb on."

Denerfen paused with deepest distrust, gave a little squawk, and strolled on top with his teeth bared. Henrik lifted the dragul to her shoulder. Slash marks curled near Denerfen's usual spot on her right side. The left remained miraculously unscarred.

With a low coo, Denerfen butted his head against Britt's chin and curled up. He cried, a piteous whine, and nudged her earlobe with a nibble. Henrik resisted the urge to call him off. A dragul and their bonded were a special knot. He'd not stand in the way.

Nestled amidst the other scraps lay Tesserdress. Whatever jostling and terrors they experienced this morning hadn't served her. A broad bald patch flaked off her neck in a shower of glittering scales. She stirred, but didn't open her eyes. He replaced the fabric over her, then plucked another piece and covered Denerfen, as well.

The captain had been nice enough, but Henrik wouldn't take chances.

Never again.

He ran the tip of his thumb along his bottom lip as he studied Britt's flayed back. Each welt brought the wash of rage all over again. Angry, cardinal slashes. Bruises. They'd flayed her, but he'd seen worse. The sailor with the whip hadn't driven all that hard. If Henrik was correct, he'd executed as light a touch as possible. The thong with the glass shards had been removed, or else she would have been churned meat.

He felt no guilt over breaking the bastid's wrist.

A gentle rap came on the door, drawing Henrik from seething ruminations. He cleared his throat, extracting from the livid thoughts, and crossed the room. Denerfen hissed from beneath the fabric.

The captain stood outside, a cup in hand. He lifted it. "Broth. It's warm, but not hot. There's a Kapurnickkian healing potion in it. She'll know it. Might ask for them, too. Better if we start it now."

Henrik accepted. "Thanks."

The captain hesitated. "It's the Tollybryck potion. So rare I've never seen it. Can't imagine where she stole it, but good thing, too. Heals really fast, you know. Got arcane in it. In case she asks, I pulled it from her bag."

Henrik executed his most perturbed stare, winning the trepidation he hoped for. The captain's hands flew in the air.

"All good, my man! I was looking for healing potions, that's it. She said she had some potions as part of our deal. Kapurnickkian's always have them, you know. Especially the dragul ones. I didn't take nothing else. You can check."

His stubborn chin and undeviating relenting would have to be enough. Henrik hated being at his mercy, but admitted a grudging respect. With His Glory's cleansing edict, the orange flag high, and blood on the cobblestones, only a madman or a fool would defy the orders to leave. *This* madman had willingly defied His Glory in broad daylight.

"What's your name?" Henrik asked.

"Lars."

"Why'd you help?"

"Got me reasons." Lars sent a nervous glance over Henrik's shoulder. "Is she going to live?"

"Yes."

Lars breathed a loud expiration, cheeks puffed. "If you think she won't make it, let me know. We'll take her to the closest island and dump her there."

Henrik growled.

"What did you say?"

Lars held up both hands. "She might be pretty, but she's not worth Burning Beard's wrath! He's the only reason I agreed to take her before you lot showed up."

"Burning Beard?"

"She came to me this morning, looking for passage to the Unseen island. I agreed." A hand went to Lars' pocket. "She promised to pay four vials of silver. Gave me the first one in advance, too. That's more than I'd make in a year with typical runs. Anyway, if she dies on my boat, I'm dead. If she dies on an island, let the devil pay *them* his visit."

Lars disappeared.

Musing, Henrik returned to her side. He sniffed the broth, not surprised to scent a certain . . . undertone. Vanilla? Stenberg islanders teased the Kapurnickkian isles for their obsession with tinctures and potions, but rumor had it that they had a true talent.

Arcane, some said.

His Glory did not endure the arcane. Most arcane existed on chain islands in the Lesser Isles. The Greater Isles bothered with the strangeness and unpredictable nature of the arcane if it benefited them, but not often.

While Henrik lowered to his makeshift chair, Britt's fingers twitched. Then her wrists. Her eyes fluttered, accompanied by low moans and a feeble lick of her lips. A glazed facade peered at him, blinking several times.

"Henrik?"

"It's me."

Panic brightened her eyes. "Denerfen!"

The dragul nipped her ear with gentle lips. She shuddered, pulled her head back to see him, and winced. Slowly, her eyes encompassed the room. She didn't move her torso. Henrik gave her the space to take it in.

When she closed her eyes, he said, "We're on a ship. Well, a boat, though the captain thinks enough of himself that it might as well be a ship."

"Ship," she murmured.

The haggard way her brow lowered, and she grimaced, made it clear that recollections patched together. He kept speaking, if only to anticipate her questions and spare her the agony.

"Tesserdress is also right next to you. She's not in great shape, but she wasn't hurt, that I can see. Neither was Denerfen. He's upset with me because I wouldn't let him near you until just now. There was . . . too much blood."

"Thank you." After a few breaths, she rasped, "In my bag, there are potions."

"Lars is ahead of you. Can you drink?"

Grimaces, and collecting tears, crossed her expression as she wiggled close enough to the side of the makeshift bed to bring the mug to her lips. She sipped slowly, then slurped, and finally drank. He withdrew when she gulped so hard he could hear it.

"Easy."

"No." She shook her head, then winced. "I need to drink it all. It'll . . . it'll help. Who gave it to you?"

"Lars."

"Again," she insisted, but with little vigor.

He complied. She finished to the final drop. Her cheek lowered again.

"Thank you."

Don't thank me, he wanted to say.

She spiraled into sleep. Denerfen inhaled her breath, then slowly lowered his neck to the top of her back. His gentle exhale wheeled over her wounds. A shimmer plumed from it and settled on top.

Henrik rested his head in his hands and settled in to wait.

LARS CHECKED on her at midnight.

"Gotta make sure the lass is breathing!" he hissed. "We're passing the final safe passage islands before we head to the chain, and I won't risk her dying on my ship! Not to mention landing on some arcane-infested island I know nothing about. I'll risk the wrath of His Glory, but not Burning Beard. I won't!"

Henrik allowed Lars one confirmation of Britt's steady breath. Lars came no closer than the doorway, but held a lamp close enough to see. Once satisfied, Henrik sent him away for the night. After he left, Henrik gently administered what little salve Lars had available and covered her back with a wet sheet, rigging it around boxes so it barely draped her terrifyingly alive skin.

The quiet creak of the boat sliced through the night. True to his word, Lars pressed as hard as the winds allowed, with full sail. The sense of racing across the top of the sea like a skiff kept Henrik's worst fears subdued.

Captain Oliver would follow. Fortunately, Henrik knew exactly what to expect at the Unseen island.

He could only hope Malcolm had survived.

SOMETIME IN THE middle of the night, Tesserdress awoke. Henrik carefully scooped her into his hand, and set her near Denerfen. She calmed when her head rested on Britt's shoulder.

Exhausted from his rescue mission the previous night, Henrik fell to a restless sleep on the floor. The steady rocking woke him before daybreak, when light bled into the sky and through the window. Britt remained on her stomach, but faced the other way. Henrik rubbed a hand over his eyes.

He must be imagining things.

In the night, Denerfen scooted onto her back, his head stretched out. A spiral of bruises and welts and scars lay beneath him, but not open wounds. Sealed wounds. Not scabs either, but closed skin.

Denerfen readjusted his neck, breathing toward a particularly deep, jagged strike that slashed shoulder to shoulder. In this muted light, the glimmering exhalations continued, rocked by a slight quiver that wasn't heat or cold.

Something.

The skin underneath Denerfen had healed. The rest remained a raw, ragged mess, shiny from the salve, though certainly repairing faster than expected. Henrik studied the angry welts near the dragul. She'd be sore and tired and in pain, but the open wounds didn't bubble with pus. No hideous streaks appeared overnight. Her risk of dying from a stale wound would cut in half if she wasn't gaping wide open, scabs cracking with every movement and bleeding. The tips of his fingers pressed into the scars along his neck.

He remembered well.

Henrik lowered to the ground, pressed his back to her makeshift cot, and closed his eyes. He sank to sleep again before the worst thoughts consumed him. Before he remembered the soldats surrounding her. The ropes on her wrist. The thongs biting her back. Her utter lack of sound.

His vigil continued.

LARS WAS A CUR OF A MAN, but not nefarious. His unnatural fear of Burning Beard kept him from being an issue.

"That's the last of the Tollybryck." Lars jabbed a dramatic and pudgy finger at the mug he passed through the doorway on their third day. "She'll be less sleepy."

A hint of relief flitted through Henrik. Silence commanded the agony of the past three days. Her lack of movement, of deep breathing. Even the draguls didn't stir much, except Denerfen. He woke up with roaring hunger, ate ravenously, and disappeared into the same sleepy torpor and gleaming breath.

"She's healing fast, isn't she?" Henrik queried.

"Yep. It's no mistake, but the Kapurnickkian potion," Lars said with some pride, as if he had anything to do with it. "Arcane, for sure. Potions *and* a bonded dragul?" He whistled. "She has the ultimate mixture. Lucky lass. Anything else you need?" Lars glanced into the room. "Clean rags or water?"

Henrik shook his head. "No. Thank you."

"You haven't left the room, except for a minute or two here and there. Beautiful day, up top. You need fresh air?"

Henrik couldn't decide whether Lars wanted a chance to sit alone with a half-naked Britt—which positively would never happen—or if the old man was lonely. He chattered every opportunity he had, which wasn't many. Henrik wouldn't risk waking her.

"I'm fine," Henrik said, though he couldn't help adding, "How's the sea today?"

Lars cut a hand through the air with a smile. "Sliding on glass. Wind is good, and the sails are full. Confident we have another day, maybe two, before we hit the Chain. Navigation after that'll be rough, but she'll be all closed up."

"Then?"

Lars shrugged. "Who knows? Navigating around the Chain ain't easy. Could be fast, might be slow."

Henrik thought of Tesserdress. "Fast as you can," he reiterated.

Lars rolled his eyes, muttering to himself as he departed. His uneven walk thunked up the hatch stairs, more waddle than stride. Henrik watched him go. He hoped Britt would wake up in time. He didn't want to take the draguls and search for Malcolm without her, but he would.

He owed her.

That much, and more.

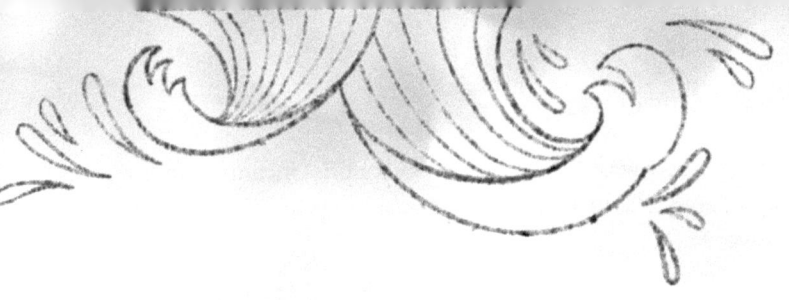

Chapter Twenty Seven

BRITT

The smell of the ocean roused her.

It swirled her nostrils with a reassuring fragrance, heightening the tang of draguls and their sickly-sweet breath. A strange taste lay on her tongue, distantly familiar, and lingered with a friendly burn.

Britt's eyes opened, locking onto a wooden wall. Light bled from a round window, spilling with loose tendrils into a close space. Something scratchy beneath her, and an uncomfortable pain in her breast, made her wriggle her shoulders. Discomfort lanced from shoulder to rib cage.

Ouch.

Memory didn't dally. The bullwhip. The Archives. Soldats and pain and fear for her draguls. Little else recalled with it, except hazy snatches of a dream-like state, filled with Henrik's voice, Denerfen's comforting nibble, and agony so intense she felt faint at the recollection.

Swamping emotions followed it. Only the gentle up-and-down pitch of a boat drew her into the moment. Clearly, she lay in a boat. Warped wooden boards testified to an old one, cluttered and complaining.

She lifted her head. Pain rippled down her sides with the

effort, but it wasn't unbearable. Sore. Stiff. Uncomfortable, but not agonizing. She turned her head. A cry of protest resulted from her lower back.

Denerfen.

He yawned, jaws split wide, and sighed. She smiled weakly, relieved to find him alive. He harrumphed, but wriggled closer like a tired puppy.

On the other side of the room, Henrik slumped against the wall, chin on his chest. Folded arms locked over his torso. His head bobbed. His tousled hair and wrinkled clothes were a mess. The distinct smell of antiseptic tinged the air. At the foot of her bed lay rags stained with old blood.

Denerfen, strolling around her side and over an arm, nudged her ear in a cat-like head butt. She hazarded a glance at her wounds, but couldn't twist far enough. With a wary test, she wiggled her shoulders and her arms. Prickles spiraled around, but she gritted her teeth through it. The pristine misery of the open air on her wounds had been worse. This felt less . . . flayed. More . . . tight.

With an eye on Henrik, Britt swallowed the frog in her throat instead of clearing it. "Did you heal me, Den?" Her raspy whisper caught on itself.

Denerfen leaned forward to head butt her again, but toppled onto her wrinkled dress. Giggling, she reached for him, but halted halfway there. Pain sprouted along her spine until she stopped. He gave a squawk and a flutter of wings.

"Where is Tess?"

Denerfen whirled, motioning to Henrik with a nose. Britt frowned.

"She's with Henrik?"

A little wooden box perched near Henrik's lap drew her attention. It held a weary-looking Tesserdress in a pile of clean fabric scraps, freshly tousled.

Tears burned Britt's eyes. Any doubt over her decision to defy Oliver burned away. She'd done the right thing for a soldat who had broken her away, cared for her and her draguls, spirited them to a ship, and off of Stenberg.

A growly voice asked, "Tears?" a moment before a thumb swiped one off of her cheek. Henrik's sleepy and concerned gaze asked a deeper question. He gently set Tesserdress next to Britt and knelt at her side.

She lifted her arm. He made a move to stop her, "Britt, don't —" but she paused.

"It's tolerable."

Her palm rested on his warm forearm. The heavy touch drew his gaze. He studied her fingers, not seeming to see, before he met her eyes without a word of protest. He brushed a tendril of hair out of her eyes.

"How are you?"

She couldn't fathom what she looked like after how many days on this bed, and cracked a smile. "I feel like death."

He didn't return the levity. Britt squeezed his wrist, endeared by the broiling storm in his shadowed eyes.

"I'm fine, Henrik."

"You're mangled," he growled. "You're beaten bloody, half to death, with welts and bruises and—"

He broke off. His voice shook, forearms flexed as he drew in a deep breath, held it, and intentionally released in a slow tide. It contained his fury, but only just.

"They whipped you, Britt."

Unable to help herself, she traced her fingers along the edge of his jaw. His nose twitched under her touch. A hidden recoil. A protective impulse to prevent what he felt, and bottle it up tight. She removed her touch.

"That won't break me, Henrik."

The sentiment didn't calm him. "What happened? Why did Oliver whip you?"

"Can I sit up? I'm thirsty. My stomach hurts from laying on it. I want to drink something, but I'll throw it up like this."

As he stood to help, she halted, boldly aware of her half naked state. His wry reply carried a hint of laughter.

"After four days of taking care of you just like this, don't tell me you're getting shy?"

Heat brightened her cheeks with a reassuring sign of improvement. Britt bit back a witty retort and conceded with a nod.

With greatest respect, he helped her sit, draping a light sheet over her shoulders for her to hold onto. She gripped the edges of the sheet in her hands, breath held against the movement. Pain ripped across her back in driving slashes that made her nauseous. Her stomach roiled, erasing hints of hunger. She had to sit very still before her whirling head calmed.

When it settled, she looked straight into his eyes.

"Better."

He didn't believe her. His lacking smile heightened her concerns. The lashes might be on her body, but the scars would endure on his heart. A silent understanding swept the air between them, loaded with an implication she could barely touch. His indignation and fire were all for her.

A tap on the door startled Henrik out of the brief, silent interchange. With a scowl, he whirled around, crossed the room, barely opened it.

A gruff voice asked, "She dead?"

"She's awake and speaking. You can't see her, though."

"Don't get your unders in a twist," the man replied. "As long as she's alive, I don't care. We passed the first islands in this part of the Chain."

Henrik's defensive tone lightened.

"Oh?"

"There's a storm coming. I give it a day, maybe two, until we find the Unseen island. Could be rough, might be fine."

Britt reached to the side, finding Tesserdress. Scales flecked off her back as Britt stroked her too-knobby spine. Without further Helandalenda potion, her decline accelerated.

"That long?" Henrik asked.

"Yep."

Departing feet followed. "Hey!" Henrik called. "Can you bring biscuits and water?"

Another grumble replied. Henrik's hand remained on the doorknob after he closed it. He turned to Britt, appearing momentarily amused.

"That is Lars."

"I remember him," she said with a wry smile. "He's as delightful as I remember."

"He's something."

Henrik returned to her side, then motioned for her to lean forward until he could peer at her wounds with narrowed scrutiny.

"How are they?" she asked.

Moving slowly, he reached forward, palpated the skin. The pressure didn't hurt, but sent the hair on the back of her neck on end. Everything felt achy and sensitive, particularly the warmth of his touch, his flowing, ribbony breath.

"The wounds are closed," he said with a sense of wonderment. "Lars rooted through your bag, brought Kapurnickkian potions. Tried to convince me that he wasn't trying to steal from you." A hint of greater levity lingered in his tone as he continued his perusal. "So bruised," he murmured, as if describing the edge of a miracle.

His palm pressed onto the sensitive place at the back of her neck, where her shoulders joined. The powerful radiation of his heat banished the aches and pains in the area.

"No fevers."

"Thank Burning Beard for that," she said.

"Yes, let's thank him, *and* let's talk about Burning Beard. Lars is beyond terrified of him. How did you induce such fear in a salty old sea captain? He natters on about the pirate all day long. Said that you claimed Burning Beard as your brother."

Henrik settled on a stool across from her, his boots hung on a rung along the bottom. He had braided his topknot of hair, which shone from a recent washing. The comical sight of him attempting to fold his strong body and long legs onto the flat stool nearly made her laugh, but it would have thoroughly ached. Her ribs stung with any small breath.

"How did I induce fear about Burning Beard, you mean?"

"Do you know the pirate?" he asked.

"Yes, definitely."

"Lars believes that if you died, Burning Beard would descend and kill him. Seems to think that the man is a pirate, fish, and angel of death. Lars is stomping around, muttering about a drake named Drake and sails on fire."

Britt pressed her lips together to withhold a smile, but couldn't help it. With amusement, she burst out, "Surely, you've heard of Burning Beard!"

"Who hasn't?"

"Most sailors fear him."

Henrik rolled his eyes.

"And with good reason," she added, chidingly. "It would be a terrifying thing to see a man light his beard on fire and take over your cargo. Anyway, I met Lars earlier, to arrange a ship passage to Malcolm." She shrugged. "I may have told him then that the wrath of Burning Beard would descend if he tried anything funny with me."

Henrik's tongue ran over his teeth as he considered that. "*Would* Burning Beard descend with wrath and fire?"

"Yes, eventually."

"How?"

"We have ways of communicating," she said vaguely. "Besides, a little fear never hurts anyone."

Deadpan, he asked, "He's truly your brother?"

Britt straightened. "Of course! His name is Pedr, and he *is* rather protective. Though, I don't see him as much as I would like."

Before he could inquire deeper, another rap came on the door. Henrik held up a finger, cracked the door as little as possible, and blocked the opening with his body. A few quick words were exchanged, and Lars left.

Her weak, "Thank you," went unnoticed.

Henrik firmly closed the door again, bearing a tin plate of crumbled biscuits and a mug of water. She sipped, grateful for the liquid down her throat, and accepted the dry biscuit. She nibbled the end and prayed her stomach wouldn't rebel.

Henrik settled, hands on his thighs, with a pointed stare. He opened his mouth, surveyed her face, and closed it again. With a sigh, he said, "Eventually, I'm going to ask you what happened, but not right now. Your color is already pale, and you look exhausted."

With relief, she nodded.

"Thank you."

Henrik motioned to the biscuit. With a firm tone, he commanded, "Eat the whole thing. I had him bring salt pork for Denerfen, which he's all but inhaled without chewing. I've been able to coax a little into the other one," he nodded toward Tesserdress, "but she hasn't taken much."

Britt's cavernous heart, so desperate for relief from the pain, and to understand the horrible things that happened, brimmed full with his care. It was one thing for him to minister to her with such ready hands.

But her draguls?

Henrik *was* the man she protected, and the confirmation felt as dizzying as sitting up again. When she set the half-eaten biscuit on the plate and declared, "Enough, thank you," he gestured to the bed.

Reluctant to return to her stomach, she hesitated.

He paused. "Will it hurt?"

"I think so," she admitted.

"Would you lean on me?"

With her heart in her throat, she asked, "You mean it?"

"Yes."

Although tempted to refuse him, exhaustion flooded her. She

nodded. Gingerly, he sat next to her, arranging himself until a pile of makeshift pillows filled his lap. A tilt of his head commanded her to lay down, so she carefully lowered until her head and shoulder lay on his thighs. Several minute adjustments later, she found a comfortable position, and exhaled her tension with relief. His masculine, salty smell blanketed her as he shuffled tendrils of hair off her cheeks, smoothing them behind her ear.

"Sleep," he whispered.

She obeyed.

LARS MONITORED Britt out of the corner of his eye.

He kept a careful and steady distance as she stood at the side of his boat, overlooking the sea spray. Henrik stood protectively at her back, one hand planted on knotted ropes leading to a high mast, the other hand on the gunwales, locking her inside his hold. Any closer and his chest would collide with her shoulders.

After days in that awful, tight room, fresh air danced over her cheeks. It felt almost as good as Henrik washing her hair that morning. His strong fingertips in her scalp, massaging soap into the greasy and bloody strands, had been the purest form of pleasure. She basked in the memory, luxuriating in the drying strands around her neck.

A loose linen dress fluttered around her bare knees, a gift from Lars, who had an extra from a former passenger. It hung a little wide across the shoulders, but sufficed. Her legs trembled a little with the effort to stand, but gained strength. With her wounds fully closed, the worst of the sensitivity had passed. Her greatest discomfort came with movement. Standing left residual aches instead of active agony, like echoes of a voice. Her appetite restored, too, though Lars had little food to offer.

Denerfen's wings shivered as he spread them wide, tasting the air with his tongue. She stepped away from the railing, because Denerfen had tumbled off her shoulder more than once in the past. The heady winds would be difficult for him to navigate if he plummeted off the ship. Tesserdress slept below, her body limp despite semi-regular breaths.

Meanwhile, Lars still studied Britt like a mouse watching a cat. "Lars," she drawled, "I'm not going to attack you."

"Might not," he snapped, "but you'll sick that hellspawn brother on me, won't you?"

He tightened his arms over his chest and scowled more deeply. She rolled her lips together, but managed not to laugh.

"You have been of greatest help," she said. "I owe you my life. I wouldn't send Burning Beard after you with what you've done and all the resources you've provided. Thank you."

His head tipped as he considered, losing the refined insecurity. With his head held higher, Lars strode toward the prow.

"Should arrive in a few hours," he shouted over his shoulder. "Better be prepared, soldat."

Britt turned her head up to face Henrik, who gave no reaction to the announcement. As she healed the physical remnants of that hellish day on Stenberg, Henrik withdrew to greater extent. They hadn't yet spoken about it, and distance provided some clarity.

"Why are you so quiet today?" she asked.

"Thinking."

"About?"

He offered no elaboration. Too entranced by the fresh air and sea spray to pry into closed warrens, she closed her eyes, inhaling deep. Denerfen continued to sniff the air. Henrik lowered his head until he spoke directly into her ear.

"Will you tell me why Oliver ordered you whipped?"

The question instantly weakened her.

Blessed mermaids, how could she tell him the truth? What would he say? A possibility existed where Henrik called her a liar. Would he believe that his own Captain, a man whom he appeared to respect, had betrayed him?

Not to mention the effect his warm whisper had against the shell of her ear. Britt ignored the butterflies beneath her ribs.

"First, will you tell me how you found me?" she asked. "It will put puzzle pieces together."

His scorned look returned. "I had been speaking with Einar and followed him to the market. I saw the crowd. The whip handler was," he swallowed hard, "mid-strike."

She glanced over her shoulder, soaking in his dangerous tone, snapping eyes, thickened words. A soldat like Henrik didn't wear such fury without meaning it. He wouldn't have shown such tender care or righteous indignation for just anybody.

Time to trust him.

Again.

"What did you do?" she asked.

"Broke the bastid's wrist."

"The whip handler?"

He nodded, not a hint of remorse in his face. "Would have snapped his neck, but His Glory's soldats converged to intercept. Two came up behind you, I dealt with them. Sailors came out of the crowd, so Einar and Harald handled them. And . . ." Surprise softened his tone. "Timmer."

"Timmer?"

He ran his bottom lip through his teeth. "Timmer," he repeated, as if he hadn't worked that detail out himself. "I don't know how they knew or what happened after that, except I grabbed you. Einar carefully gathered your dress and he led me through the crowd. From what I could tell, other soldats fought with the sailors. Timmer and Harald kept them from following us. I need to speak with Einar and confirm it, because I focused mostly on you."

"The other soldats helped the sailors?" she choked out. "You're . . . you're kidding."

Grim faced, he shook his head. "No. It was soldat against soldat. Ugly, if you ask me."

"You were fighting each other."

"Yes."

"Has that happened before?"

"Not that I'm aware of. In light of new information I received from Einar in the minutes before, it's not as surprising as it could be."

"A rebellion?"

His eyes jerked to hers. "You know?"

"Not much."

He rubbed a hand over his face, like a man at the end of his tether. "There's more. So much more to the story, in fact. Einar revealed . . . a lot. But it's not as important as you telling me how those bastids got their hands on you and strapped you to that board. I want to know every person involved."

It gave her the courage to draw breath and say, "Oliver."

His head didn't whip around. His eyes didn't fill with outrage. He stared beyond sea, sky, and ship.

"I figured," he whispered. "But I'd hoped . . ."

Britt softened.

"You knew?"

"Saw him." He breathed a ragged exhale. "Staring out the Archives window, watching the whole thing."

With flagging courage, she rushed to explain. "I was walking and two soldats grabbed me, one on each arm." She paused, struggling to take the memories out of her mind and put them into her voice.

He reached over, set his hand on top of hers.

His gentle urging, devoid of judgment or retaliation, gave her another surge of courage. She explained the room, Oliver's accusation, the questions she refused to answer. As she relayed her decision, she held her shoulders a little straighter.

"We may have only known each other a few weeks, but I couldn't do that to you," she said quietly.

For a long time, Henrik said nothing. He gripped her hand and stared into a stormy ocean. It matched the battle warring in his eyes. Frothy gray clouds split the distant western horizon. Waves formed white caves, like dollops of frosting.

Henrik put a hand under her jaw, lifting her face until she stared into his eyes. Softly, he whispered, "Thank you."

Her heart trapped in her throat as Henrik studied her lips. She held still, afraid to shatter the accelerating moment. As if drawn by an invisible string, she leaned closer. Her hands pressed to his chest, fingers straightening over a slamming heart.

He wrapped a hand low on her waist.

"Britt—"

A peal broke overhead. The scream cut like an eagle, but sounded dense, guttural, lofty. A shadow cut across the boat, soaring over the waves.

Lars shouted, scattering the moment.

"The devil bring you!" he cried. "You brought that bastid right to us, lass. I knew you'd be trouble, cursed woman! Demmed Drake." Lars shook a fist at the creature scraping the sky. "Get away from here!"

Britt's breath caught as she stared overhead. A magnificent creature soared above the masts, spiraling through ropes and sails. The peaked cry repeated, a strange mixture of a low-toned growl and a sea eagles' pitch.

A drake.

No, *Pedr's* drake. He was the only person fool enough to tame one away from its nest on Kapurnick and keep it as a pet.

"Henrik," she breathed, "do you have a string?"

"A string?"

"Quickly! A string? A ribbon? Anything?"

"Yes," he muttered, "I regularly carry ribbons on my person."

With a cry, she fumbled with her dress, rippled a button free, then held out her hand. "Give me your knife."

"What?"

"The one you keep on you! Hurry."

The drake spread wide and wild wings, tipping either direction, cutting into direct currents and back out again. He lowered, always closer.

"Drake!" she shouted. "Drake, here!"

The dragon stopped mid screech. She shouted a chant, a lyrical, moving, lilting, soaring ditty that would have sounded bawdy and perfect in a tavern, but was wildly out of place here. The drake circled in tighter spirals as he descended. The shadow cast deeper, faster, wider.

Lars abandoned the prow and plunged below deck.

"What are you doing?" Henrik hissed.

She grabbed the handle of his knife, chopped a lock of hair, and wound it around the button. As the arm-sized dragon plunged, she shoved her hand into the air with a grunt. Tears sprinkled out of her eyes from the wrenching movement along her back.

Drake whooshed by, snatching the button and hair off her palm with his giant talons, and disappeared with another screech. Heart in her throat, she watched Drake wing away, heading northwest.

"That," she whispered, "is Drake, my brother's messenger drake." A wide smile stretched across her face. "Buttons and hair are our special signal. He used to leave buttons on my pillow when he returned home from trips and was searching for me. He'll recognize my hair. He's on the way to help! Do you understand? Henrik, we have a chance!"

Chapter Twenty Eight

HENRIK

I t took two hours for Britt to convince Lars that death hadn't descended, nor was Drake's appearance a sign that they should abandon their plan at the Unseen island. The dragon left without any harm to the ship, and Burning Beards signature bright yellow-and-pink flames didn't flare from a ship on the horizon.

"Cursed bird," Lars spat as he raced back up the stairs, casting a wary gaze around. "Not even that, is it? A bloody dragon."

Britt kept her amusement to herself. Henrik had too much in his head to badger her for details over a drake that she knew on a first name basis. No one else bothered to name messenger drakes.

Instead, Henrik stewed over the ramifications of her story.

Oliver.

That bastid. He wouldn't be the first soldat whose position of authority created a superiority complex and the idea that control belonged to him, but it didn't soften the blow.

Which led Henrik to think of Einar, who hastily shoved Henrik and Britt onto the boat, then waved them away, promising to deal with the massacre at the whipping post, the port authority, and Oliver.

"Plans already in place," he cried with a fevered stare and

maniacal grin. "You just kicked it off a few days early. See you soon!"

Einar's answer frightened Henrik more than the question.

What a perfect ignition for the soldat rebellion.

These ruminations churned as the wind carried them toward the mirage-like Unseen island on wide waters. Sapphire waves swamped the world, crashing into the prow with a spray of sparkling drops. The closer they moved toward the Unseen island, the farther Henrik fell into certainty that Oliver would follow.

Immediately.

He'd lost both prizes, Henrik and Britt, and had to make it up to His Glory, among other things. Henrik attacking a sailor and interrupting a punishment sanctioned by a soldat Captain was a bold refusal of authority *and* promotion.

A slight chance existed that Einar and the soldat rebellion would keep Oliver busy enough not to follow, but Henrik doubted it.

Einar's unruly passion drifted downwind to Henrik. He allowed his frustration to burn high and bright, fed by quiet, suppressed, seething indignation. Memories of years of abuse stirred, grew. Henrik didn't stop or hold back.

A light touch on his arm drew his attention away, reducing the metaphorical flames to char. Britt stared up at him with unfettered curiosity and a hint of uncertainty.

"Henrik?"

He shook his head. "Sorry. Just . . . thinking."

"Everything all right?"

No, he thought. "Yeah," he said. "Fine."

As his thoughts cleared, Lars shouted from the back of the boat.

"*Land-el!*"

Britt, scouring the horizon, frowned. Lars slammed his hand into a tapestry of bells that rang, pealing with tinny delight through the air. The storm swept them fast across the sea, chasing them.

"I don't see any land," she said.

"That's because you don't have an ikon."

"An ikon?"

"It's native arcane to the island. The Unseen island has special runes that the original occupants painted everywhere to protect it. It's why you can't see the land. The ikon, if you have one, over-powers the arcane and allows you to see."

"Are the natives still there with Stenberg's prisoners?"

His soft response hid great emotion.

"No."

Lars barked a reply from behind her. "The original inhabitants used a special black tar to paint the ikons. It comes from the island." His giant nose wrinkled, as if he smelled a horrible stench. "Legends say there's a bog beneath the sand that keeps the flora and fauna of the Unseen island healthy, and it's simmering. Ready to disintegrate."

"Dense place," Henrik murmured.

"It's not a legend either," Lars snapped, as if they'd challenged him. He glared from a few steps away. "It's the truth. There's arcane in those ikons. Angry power, too. The natives put special ikons out to stop Stenberg, but it didn't work."

"When will I see it?" Britt asked.

"You won't see it," Lars grumbled as he turned away, but didn't leave. "Not until our hull bumps into the shore. Even then, you'll only see a few paces ahead. The rest'll look like water."

"Is it . . safe?"

Lars hooted. "Safe? You think His Glory would put prisoners on a safe island? No, it's not safe! Nothing about the Unseen island is safe. Safe!" He spat, then cackled. The sound grated Henrik's nerves.

"Once you cross the ikons, there's no leaving," Lars added, shoving aside the lid of a barrel and reaching within. "That's when you start to see."

Britt glanced at Henrik.

He nodded.

She paled.

"You have to have been on the island and escaped in order to see it again," Lars added. He gestured to his left forearm, flexing the rolling muscles. An ebony slash across the middle of it, with one dot on either side, rippled.

"Is that an ikon?"

He nodded.

"Does it carry arcane?"

"Not really, but it allowed me to leave the island. The Follorat islanders lived on the island before Stenberg decided they wanted it. Decades ago, His Glory drove, starved, and forced the original natives away. They did everything they could to protect their island, but it's no use when His Glory descends. Not even ikons could save them."

Regret burned deep in Henrik's gut, though the responsibility wasn't his. The soldats long before him wreaked that havoc, but he couldn't help a sense of ownership. Domination of chain islands wasn't a new story. Kapurnick, Narpurra, Stenberg, Siloam. The four greater island powers had a long and storied history of dominance and control. Long ago, Caledon was an equal player in the power struggle, before their main volcano erupted and exploded their land to rubble.

"The ikons are sensitive," Lars shouted over a gust of wind. He coiled a thick rope around his forearm. "If you touch them, bad things happen."

Britt held her whipping hair out of her face.

"Like what?"

"Black sludge," Lars immediately countered. "It'll suck you in and trap your legs and suffocate you with tar. You'll feel your flesh boiling as you slide below. Not to mention the vittra." He shuddered.

Britt seemed more curious than afraid, but she had reason to fear. If there was anything to be said about the Chain, then diversity was it. Arcane, natives, islands, environments, they varied from island to island. One never knew what they'd encounter, sometimes on perfectly predictable islands that hadn't changed in years.

"The vittra is a legend." Henrik set a gentle hand on the small of her back, his fingertips barely gracing the skin. "As far as anyone can tell. Tall tales told by prisoners drawn mad by the jungle fumes, I think, but Lars isn't wrong about the ikons. Leave them alone."

She put a hand on his arm. He turned it over, revealing the same slash and two dots that Lars had shown. A vague tattoo, hardly noteworthy. Her fingers scrolled along the edges.

"When did you receive this?" she asked.

"Years ago."

"How?"

Henrik shook his head, lips a thin line.

Lars appeared with a heavy thud of feet. "We're going in. Prepare yourself."

Henrik gripped Britt above the elbows, drawing her closer to the hatch in the floor. "Go below," he commanded. "I'll head inland, look for Malcolm. You stay with Tesserdress and Denerfen and I'll bring Malcolm to you. We have to find a specific ikon first—"

"No."

"Britt—"

"My brother is there, and I need to take Tesserdress to him now. There isn't time to waste if we want to save her."

"Insane," he countered. "You can't handle the exertion."

Stubbornness backlit her eyes.

"Watch me."

He half-expected her to rip his hand from her arm and shove him off the side. Instead, she covered his hand with one of her own, and the affectionate touch stole his breath. "It'll be fine, Henrik. You'll protect me."

Those words encompassed more than he deserved. Disbelieving, he could only stare. Of all the ways to disarm him . . . After what she endured, what right did he have to refuse?

"What if your wounds open?"

"They won't."

"You're exhausted."

"I'm stronger! You've made me sleep too much. Besides, Denerfen and the Tollybryck potion did most of the work. Sure, I'm sore, but not weak. I can do this. If you don't," she added, "I'll follow you by myself."

"Not if I lock you in the brig."

Her brow dropped into a fierce glare. Her slashed eyes and tightly folded arms promised an explosive response.

"You lock me in this ship," she growled, "and Pedr *will* show up in a blaze of fury. My draguls are at stake, Henrik. No lock, no ship, no sea will stop me."

With a ragged sigh, Henrik scowled. He felt worse leaving her on the ship by herself than taking her with him, in some regards.

"Fine," he snapped, "but you stay with me at all times. This island is trouble. Big trouble. Ancient arcane at work, and it *is* angry. It would rather kill you than host you, so do not venture away from me. You understand?"

Britt nodded once. "I hear you. I'll stay close, but how will I get off the island?"

With grim resolve, he motioned to his arm. "We'll get you one of these."

"What about Denerfen and Tesserdress?"

"They'll be fine. Far as I know, the restrictive arcane doesn't apply to animals. The Follorat people let them come and go."

Lars changed the rigging, slowing the mainsail. The boat went from skimming the top of the sea to chugging in a silent, steady rhythm. The *splash, splash* of waves bashed the bow. Lars moved intentionally, but without panic. Every passing second made his glower more pronounced, as if he sailed into the very devil's maw.

Ahead lay water. Splashing, churning ocean, speckled with white caps and blasted by the wind.

"*Land-el!*" Lars cried again. Nimble as a young man, he leaped from his post at the helm. Wood scraping sand preceded a jarring stop. After tossing a rope overboard, Lars disappeared off the side.

Britt stared out, regal in the lowering light.

"You're sure?" Henrik asked.

She nodded.

His soft hand propelled her to the side of the boat. "Come. The sooner we find Malcolm, the better. As soon as we can leave, we leave. I suspect that Oliver will have chased after us right away, if he's not already here. I don't want you involved. Understood?"

Britt cast her gaze to the empty northwest horizon and nodded.

Chapter Twenty Nine

BRITT

She splashed into thigh-deep water, though nothing was visible to her but waves and a strip of sand.

The sandbar lingered a few paces ahead, covered by the same liquid blue waves that claimed the horizon. Odd, to see a long wedge of sand, to know the boat docked at it, but view mostly waves. The strange dichotomy made her brain hurt. She'd seen underwater sand bars and reefs, but never a lone strip smack dab in the middle of the sea.

Henrik joined at her side, disembarking after her. Lars waded ahead. He stepped as if normal, but the mirage of waves hit his knees without splashing. Water slid back and forth, unbothered by the arcane illusion. The surreality made it stranger still. Like the bizarre haze that overcame her dreams after Pedr smoked red leaves from Uppa island.

Britt asked Henrik, "You're sure this is where Malcolm is?"

Henrik nodded, though she couldn't fathom how he knew anything for certain these days. All might be a lie. Even if it was, this was the only information they had. She couldn't waste more time in Stenberg, and this gave them a rare chance of saving Tesserdress.

"Yes."

"Then let's go."

As she sloshed ahead, Henrik brought up the back. Both draguls hid safely in her pockets with several squeaking protests from Denerfen. He peered out, head poking out with hissing displeasure.

Britt stepped slowly both for her sake, and Tesserdress'. Frothing waves left her ankles wet as she stepped on the sand. With each placement of her foot, an equal measure of compact beach revealed ahead. As she glanced over her shoulder, no illusion hid the boat, the horizon, the disappearing sky as night eked closer.

She kept her attention forward, watching as Lars used a sledgehammer to drive a spike into the sand. A thick rope lay on the ground beneath him, looped around the spike. She exhaled noisily, and with relief knowing dry land existed nearby.

Real, but not quite.

Once Lars finished, he strode up the beach again. Silence accompanied them on the sloping path. Thirty steps away from the sea, the khaki sand turned white. Pristine. Flecks of umber nestled in the crests and swells.

"Careful," Lars hissed as she narrowly avoided a weed with a spiked purple flower bobbing at the end. "Don't step on any of the plants. They all have ikons."

"All of them?"

"Look at the leaves."

She knelt. Her wet skirt clung to her ankles, and sand clotted her toes and shins. Under the sprouting leaves beneath the spiky flower ball shone a scribbled, ebony design. Marks slashed together, no visible alphabet. Not a word in the isles language, but infinitely the darkest black. Fathoms of depth lay in it.

"The bog underneath it all, remember?" Lars grimaced. "Touches everything."

"Fascinating," she whispered.

Henrik stood at her side when she climbed to her feet again. His gaze darted from tree, to beach, to tree, and back.

"Walk a little farther, just behind me," he instructed. "Lars is right about the plants. Avoid touching anything but open ground."

"What would happen if I stepped on a plant by accident?"

"It would probably bite you."

Her voice pitched higher. "Bite me?"

He didn't deem that question with an answer, but she gazed more curiously at each plant as she passed.

"The barbs of those flowers have poison," Lars said. "Other weeds, too. The ikons cause it. You'll die within ten minutes of the bite. And yes, the plants *do* bite. Except for the vines." He shook a finger overhead. "They strangle."

She trailed behind Henrik, marveling over the strange advancement of the beach. She could see everything behind her, but only waves ahead as they traversed. Weeds became more abundant, slowing each step. Lars occasionally tottered from one foot to the next, avoiding greenery.

They maneuvered close to a foggy, indistinct darkness. It curled out of and around the waves, wafting like coy smoke near the sea.

Henrik tugged her to a stop. His intent gaze held a note of warning. "If you don't go in, you can still leave the island without an ikon."

"I'm going."

"Know that when you proceed, you'll have to receive an ikon in order to escape. That makes a hasty exit rather difficult, unless we've already found and received the appropriate ikon. Which we will keep an eye out for."

Lars nodded confirmation.

Understanding the source of Henrik's anxiety, her lips rounded into an O. "I see," she murmured. "If Oliver finds us and I don't have an ikon . . ."

"Exactly."

"How does one acquire this exit ikon?"

"You do it by finding a specific ikon on a tree. You touch it, say,

Great Follorat spirits of the island, I honor your ikons, your power, and your history. I ask for safe passage off your beaches, and the arcane does the rest."

"That's not so bad."

He scoffed. "When you know where the ikon is."

She lifted an eyebrow. "Do you?"

"I knew it last time."

"Will you know it this time?"

"It moves," Lars called, with the infuriating confidence of someone that knew everything and couldn't fathom why no one else did. "The bloody ikon moves. Look, haven't you been on the sea before?"

She ignored him, though the urge to smack him didn't die easily. Before she could ask Henrik a question, Lars butted in.

"The ikons prevent people from leaving, but not going in. You can go in all you want, but you have to find the right ikon to leave. Could take days, weeks. There are more trees than you can comprehend, and the ikons make everything an illusion. Looks small, does it?" He scoffed. "The island is as big as Stenberg."

Terrifying.

"I accept the terms," she said.

With a resigned sigh, Henrik ushered her forward a step.

Henrik kept a hand on her waist, slowing her, as her next step brought a wall of verdant foliage to the forefront. All at once, the sea disappeared. What had once been water immediately transformed into a raw jungle.

Britt paused, arrested by the stunning sight.

Where the endless ocean once stood, a towering rainforest loomed. Stumpy, thick trees, with trunks as big around as her arms could hug. Branches sprouting at poky intervals. The jungle grew with stalwart union, clawing higher in visceral competition. Conjoined leaves, shoved upright from round, thick trunks, created a suffocating, dim ceiling. The sun inched toward the horizon, where hints of vague pink and jetted crimson slivered between each giant leaf.

Broad leaves dominated the fauna, thick as leather hides. The bottle green tones ran to midnight black, except for when the sun rippled along the interior. A dazzling trail of plush emerald resulted.

Lush flowers trailed around the trunks in winding spurts, decorating the dark wood with bright brilliance.

Sound exploded at the same moment. Distant insects, a vague cry that might have been a bird, or a monkey. Restless grinding and shifting leaves filled her ears. Her eyes watered with an assault of smells. Decay, foliage, perfumes.

"It's . . ."

Lovely didn't quite describe it. If a jungle could have teeth, this one would bite. The urge to hold a weapon and plunge forward at the same time trickled through her, as if something ancient and hungry beckoned.

Lars side swept a glance at Henrik.

"You entering?"

"Yes."

With a crack of his neck, and a flex of his left arm, Lars said, "Me too. Ain't no going back after this, lass."

She lifted her chin.

Lars plunged ahead. Henrik clasped his fingers around hers and followed, forcing her to trail behind him. The heat of his hand provided a reassuring balm.

Sand gave way to a firmer texture beneath her bare feet. A type of crumbly soil, intermixed with churning black. Her knees trembled, but not from weakness. The oppressive weight of humidity pressed upon her chest with relentless force. At eye-level, they passed a painted mark. Tarry slashes, decorated by swirls, ovals, and interconnected stripes, filled a tree trunk.

Ikons, he'd called them.

A haunted, frightening sensation filled her from toes to nape with each glance at a different ikon. They passed many. At least every other tree, if not more. Plenty of islands tried to prevent foreigners by using powerful wards, but they generally targeted natural issues. Unexpected rip currents, tide shifts, dangerous beaches, poisonous coral for fish.

A permeating smell hung in the forest. Boggy, like burning peat. The stench added to the general malaise in the air. How had Malcolm endured this place?

They inched around a corner. Lars stood off to the side, studying a collection of bleached white bones. His booted toe turned them over, revealing half of a skull crushed to smithereens. Her stomach roiled.

Malcolm?

Henrik's grip on her hand tightened.

"Months-old bones. Probably from the vittra," Lars declared. "She crushes her prey. See the head? Caved in. Might have been that ikon, if not the vittra."

With a tip of his head, he motioned to the tree. A black ikon, so deeply dark it almost appeared blue, filled a palms-width on the middle of the tree trunk. Vines and flora grew around it, instead of over the top, as if even nature itself was repelled by the latent arcane power.

"She?" Britt asked.

"The vittra," Lars breathed, so quiet she almost missed it. "There were many of them, all women. They've been slowly killed off. They left most of these ikons behind. Their power remains. The only vittra left is bitter that Stenberg took their land, and she commands all the arcane the other vittras left behind. Seething and angry doesn't do her justice. Legends say vittras can read minds, memories, intent."

Lars kicked sand over the bones, more uneasy with each passing moment. "This poor bloke must have touched the ikon and wound up dead."

His scoff teemed with brittle annoyance. Britt curled her fingers into her palm. The draw of the inky texture would have lured her closer, had Lars not warned her.

"How does the vittra kill her enemies?" she asked, striving for a nonchalant tone, and failing. "A club? Does she have hands?"

"Well, she's a dark spirit, isn't she?" Lars cried. "Does whatever she wants. The natives used to call them Legion, but with the others gone, call her whatever you like. She rises from the ground in a black cloud. Gives off a permeating smell that'll knock you senseless, then she clubs you in the head with a weapon made from the bones of those she killed in the past."

"Sounds terrifying."

"There's no words for a vittra," he growled. After a thoughtful silence, he added, "Except cold. Legends say she'll numb your teeth with her frost."

She cast an eye to Henrik. "What do *you* think?"

Henrik stood within reach, one leg braced ahead of the other. His neck swiveled here and there. Assessments and careful calculations filled his gaze as he gave a noncommittal half-shrug. She almost doubted he had listened at all.

"There's bad arcane here, for certain," he said, "but I never saw a vittra. Some islanders believe the vittra are the bloodless spirits of natives that Stenberg killed to take the jungle."

The sound of his voice, as stalwart as ever, lent great comfort despite the dark undertones. Better than the purring background noise of the unsettled jungle.

"What do you think, Lars?" she inquired with deepening curiosity around Lars's moral compass.

"If someone drove me out of my boat, I'd haunt the bastid until they died, then I'd wallop them in the afterlife. No one parts me from sweet Birgitta."

She staved off a laugh. Birgitta must be Lars' ship. His violent promise ran a little *too* bright.

"Listen, this is when things get thick and difficult to see," Henrik said. "We need weapons before we advance."

Tesserdress wriggled, shifting her dress. Britt put a hand on her pocket to soothe her. Lars extended a giant machete, tapped Henrik on the side of the arm with the dull side of the blade, and said, "Better you than me."

Henrik accepted it with a murmured thanks. A gleam entered

his assessing stare as he studied it. He grabbed Britt's hand and pressed it to his back. "Don't let go of my shirt. If you need to slow down, let me know. I'll match your pace, but plan to move steadily. Don't make unnecessary noises. If you need to speak, tug twice on my shirt."

He lifted his gaze over the top of her head. Lars must have given some indication of approval, because Henrik turned back to her.

"Ready?"

Britt nodded.

Lars did the same.

They strode into the jungle together.

Chapter Thirty

HENRIK

Britt gripped Henrik's shirt, tugging on his shoulders in a reassuring way. Thank Norr, the woman finally listened.

As they advanced into the jungle, a trove of old experiences rose to Henrik's mind. Remembrances he'd rather not deal with. He stuffed the recollections of overwhelming arcane, a shipload of prisoners, stumbling around for the right ikon, and almost probing the wrong one several times, into the gut-deep box.

His first time on the Unseen island had been part of his early soldat days, before he proved himself into the ranks. Without succeeding, he might have been shunted off to the Navy to be a gods-forsaken sailor. Another shudder wracked him at the thought.

Henrik kept the machete tight in his left hand. A natural trail broke through and around the intense vegetation. Such thickness existed on no other island. Ikons sprinkled most visible surfaces, and others lingered in hidden crevices. The unwieldy ebony, unnatural in its depths, drew the eye.

Perhaps that was the point of his arm ikon. An aid for what to avoid. Though unlikely that all three of them would make it off this island unscathed—no one left the Unseen island without some sort of injury—he'd be damned if it was Britt or one of the draguls. After what she accepted to protect him from Oliver, he owed her Malcolm.

And everything.

Henrik slipped easily into that space where he embodied awareness. Instinct guided. He honed into smell, sounds. The silence in which Lars and Britt trod was a welcome boon. They made it easier to turn on his soldat's senses. For the first time in his life, all the training culminated in something that mattered.

As they advanced into the morass, vines gained new life. They tightened around trunks, slithered over branches, plunged into inky earth. Movement never ceased, whether vines wriggled up a tree, twirled in place, or shot through the air, knotting branches together. The world spun while he walked underneath an arch. Steady ground against mobile vines created a weird sensation of standing still while moving. He floated across the shifting sea, in a way.

Over an hour into their traverse, Britt tugged twice. She'd released his shirt and had both hands in her pockets. The right pocket swayed, bucking up and down in a violent fit.

He frowned, whispered, "What's wrong?"

"I . . I don't know," she cried quietly. "She's panicking."

"Tesserdress?"

Britt nodded. Worry changed her eyes. Instead of snapping glass, filled with amused irony and implication, they were a smoky sea. Lightning and thunder in a bottle.

Strange mewling and squeaking sounds emitted from her pocket. He'd never heard them before. Denerfen issued his fair share of odd noises, but nothing like these. Like a miniature pig about to die.

Unnerving.

"Silence that infernal thing," Lars hissed. "You'll call the vittra! She feeds on pain and weakness, you daft idiots."

Britt ignored him.

Henrik didn't.

The vittra was a real enough legend, though he couldn't be certain the lone one remained, or that she was truly alone. Other soldats told tales. Soldats he trusted not to embellish, the way sailors loved to expound.

He'd glimpsed no sign of a vittra on his visits here, but he'd been obscenely paranoid about every step, ikon, and trail. It brought him out of here alive. One soldat didn't make it. Those thoughts returned to the gut box.

Henrik turned his attention overhead when the rustling noises increased. The vines tightened around a tree, grinding into the wood with scraping moans. Ground moss and bark drifted from above.

The escalating tension between the dragul and the heightened vines brought Malcolm to the forefront of Henrik's mind. Henrik knew little about Malcolm, except his position as a high-ranking member of the Kapurnickkian military. Dragul bonded. A man of action, presumably. Courageous, too, if he took the place of four others. If he was still alive, he wouldn't be happy to see a soldat, nor quick to reveal himself.

And if he wasn't?

Henrik shuddered.

Every now and then, being a soldat forced him into a place of required trust. In the past, he had to lean on islanders. On untrained people, unzealous, without obligation to compel their work. He didn't like it, but situations required it more often than expected. A gamble of the highest sort.

Today, the same gamble would be necessary.

He calmly stated, "Malcolm? We're here for you."

Britt's shoulders pulled back. Her head snapped to his. He held up a quieting hand. With painstaking care, Lars set a foot on clean ground and slowly spun to watch behind them. Henrik never thought he'd be grateful for Lars' presence, but he was.

A flutter of movement, different from the methodical tightening of the vines, drew Henrik's eye. Might have been a bird. The chirp of invisible avians rang so distantly they might be an arcane-inspired illusion. A few rare species were reputed to live here, though he hadn't seen them in his infrequent and quick visits.

Sailors, more often than soldats, brought the nefarious criminals here to work out their own life. Most didn't survive more than a week. Few knew about the roving ikons, the latent arcane. Every now and then, a criminal escaped. Stenberg drowned them if discovered again.

"My name is Henrik."

Another fluttering from the trees, like a man dodging from one space to the next. A movement not native to the vines, for it moved too fast.

"Britt is with me."

A cry issued from Britt's skirt.

"Tesserdress, as well. Britt and the draguls are here under their own independence."

Henrik leaned to the side, allowing a brief glimpse of Britt at his back. As quickly as he moved, he returned to protect her from the front. He kept a wary ear out for the periphery and hoped Lars truly did watch their back.

A footstep.

Cracking twig.

"I'm a soldat," Henrik continued, louder now. "There's another man. Lars. A captain. He brought us in his boat, and at a great risk for his own life. I know Stenberg brought you here, but I mean you no harm."

"Tess!" Britt cried. "Stop. No, Tess!"

Tesserdress sprang out of her pocket, nearly crashing to the forest floor with a giant screech. Britt lurched forward, scrambling to keep the flailing dragul in her hands. Britt barely managed to stop Tess from plummeting to the ground and snapping her delicate wings. Scales bloomed through the air in a shimmering dust.

A body stepped out of a tangle of thick forest with a hoarse question.

"Tesserdress?"

Britt wheeled around, mouth agape. Henrik braced himself, machete up. A man stood there, wrapped in tattered clothes, bedraggled, too thin, familiar eyes bright.

The dragul screamed.

Chapter Thirty One

BRITT

B ritt trembled long after reuniting with Malcolm. He held her hand and spoke at a rate that only a Helsing could achieve. Henrik didn't struggle to keep up, based on his cool hauteur, but Lars stared with a lost expression as Malcolm rambled.

"You're fine?" Britt repeated. He'd promised as much already, but she couldn't believe it. Even with him standing before her.

"Fine." Malcolm rolled his eyes and drew out the vowels. "I'm *fine,* Britt. As you can see."

She shook her head.

Blessed mermaids.

The plan *worked.*

"The Unseen island is not so much a prison," Malcolm continued, squeezing Britt's hand, "as a survival game. There's not a lot of fresh water, and what little I harvest barely keeps me alive. When I arrived, it was me and two others, though I didn't see them right away. The first attacked me the night the soldats dropped me into the ocean."

"Attacked?" Britt gaped.

"I dispatched him," he said, as if discussing the weather, "and prepared for the second. I could tell there was another one, but didn't know where or when he'd descend. Eventually, I found him. He tried to be friendly and work together, which I was willing to do. As I suspected, he used the opportunity to commit the layout of my camp to memory. Later in the night, he attempted to slit my throat."

"Attempted?"

He scoffed.

She didn't ask more questions.

Grisly death and barbarity was nothing new. General Helsing and life in the Isles didn't favor those with weak stomachs or loose moral codes, but imagining Malcolm surviving while waiting for Pedr or Britt to arrive made her throat tighten.

Malcolm's silvery eyes were like a fox. His full face, gaunt. His once-pleasant, teasing smile had turned to stone and exhaustion. He looked as if he hadn't eaten in weeks. The amount of food wouldn't have mattered. Separated from his dragul, he would suffer the same wasting despair and physical change.

Without dragul breath mingling with his . . .

She shuddered the thought away. She didn't have to think about that anymore. The alleviation of stress and worry on Tesserdress' behalf was a palpable thing, but their issues were far from over. Back in Malcolm's clutches, the dragul would be safe. Sort of. She wouldn't be actively dying, anyway, which was a definite improvement. Already, the color of Tesserdress' scales improved from bleached ivory to hints of lavender.

Now, they had to return to Kapurnick.

Tesserdress' scales still littered the air like falling flakes, sluffing whenever Malcolm moved too quickly. Soon, the molting would stop, the withdrawal would reverse, and Tesserdress would gain her appetite. As long as she ate, she'd gain form and health again. For Malcolm, the process might take longer.

Malcolm sent an acerbic stare over her shoulder, right to Henrik, then to Lars. "Who're you two?" he asked, teeth half bared in blatant challenge. The thought that he would fight Henrik in this state was laughable.

To Henrik's credit, he neither postured, nor tensed. He waited, but didn't tear his eyes off of Malcolm. She couldn't help but wonder if Malcolm heard Henrik's introduction earlier, before he revealed himself. Was he playing dumb now?

"This is Lars, our ship captain, and Henrik." Britt surreptitiously stepped between them. "Henrik is my friend, and he came as a protection for me. Lars defied a cleansing edict on Stenberg to sail for here. There's more going on than you think." More firmly, she commanded, "Back down."

Warily, Malcolm muttered, "Fine." His concern swiveled to Tesserdress as he touched her with the tips of his fingers. "How is she?"

"Not good, but now she'll make it."

Malcolm stopped, tilted his head toward his dragul, and breathed gently on her. Tesserdress, coiled on his shoulder, answered with a relieved coo. Malcolm's gaunt, pale features when they first arrived alleviated a little, and Tesserdress' improving energy was nothing short of astonishing.

With moderate safety assured, Britt plaited her hair and brought Denerfen out of her pocket. He perched on her shoulder and observed. His tail swished across her back in a pleasant cadence, legs perched daintily beneath him.

Henrik peered over his shoulder. "Let's find the ikon and head back to the ship. Something doesn't feel right. This island is too quiet."

At his observation, Britt heard nothing but silence. The noises that welcomed them into the jungle had dispersed. The blanket of calm felt like the precursor to an attack. Ignoring Henrik, Malcolm studied Britt with greater scrutiny than before.

"How are you?"

Malcolm moved to put a hand on her shoulder, but she stepped back.

"Don't."

His expression hardened, if possible. "What's wrong?"

"Nothing we haven't taken care of."

"Britt—"

"Pedr is coming from the northwest," she blurted out. "He should be here soon. At least, I think. If he's not in the harbor already, he's close."

His expression darkened. "The northwest? But . . . why would . . ." He stopped, frowning. "Right. Of course. Only Pedr. How do you know?"

"Drake flew by. I sent a lock of hair with a button."

Malcolm let out a long breath, ran a hand through his hair. "Thank the sea for small miracles. We can get Tesserdress home." With a carefully neutral tone and a sharp eye, he asked, "I suppose General Helsing didn't send you?"

Britt pressed her lips.

Malcolm cursed under his breath.

"I'm in for it when we return, I know." She rolled her eyes. "But it was worth it. The moment I heard the news, I sent a drake to summon Pedr and hopped on a ship for Stenberg. Anyway, I'll explain it all later."

"Too bloody calm," Lars hissed, whipping from side to side. "Can we get a move on it? The demmed vittra's going to descend if we don't get out of here!"

Malcolm straightened, gaze cast overhead. As the glow reduced outside the canopy, it came to nothing here. Daylight ebbed into darkness with the slow pulse of leeching life. "We have to go to my camp first," Malcolm said.

"No returning for anything." Henrik stepped forward. "We don't have time. We need to find the ikon and leave now."

A flash of irritation cut through Malcolm's profound and obvious relief at reuniting with Britt and Tess, who coiled near his neck, wings flapping. Malcolm clasped Tesserdress with one hand, not trusting her to hold herself into position.

"I already know where to find the ikon. I've kept track of it. It's at my camp. The vittra isn't on this part of the island. She's been howling and hunting on the other side for days. You approached at the exact right spot. Usually, ships draw her close, but she's unlikely to have seen you yet."

Lars relaxed marginally, but his eyes didn't stop darting.

Henrik tilted his head. "Why did you follow the ikon?"

"Because of Pedr," Malcolm insisted. "I knew he'd come, if Britt couldn't. But," he added, glaring at her, "I had a feeling *she* would show up first."

"You have that much faith in your siblings?" Henrik asked.

The disgust on Malcolm's face didn't earn Henrik any loyalty. "Don't insult us." He turned to Britt with a gentler tone. "Follow me. We'll have you touch the ikon, and then we can go. I've already got the sign." He flashed his left forearm, revealing the mark. "I've been following it, just in case."

Malcolm spun, Britt still in his grasp, and cut into the forest. "I figured you or Pedr would eventually find me," he continued with muted whispers. "I didn't know how long it would take. I've been moving my camp based on the ikons, avoiding the vittra by sheer luck, most nights. I think she can sense my good intentions."

"How?" Lars asked.

Malcolm shrugged. "Not sure what else I've seen or sensed, but as long as I move, it's been tolerable. Loyalty to the safety ikon is the best strategy, so I follow it."

"Safety ikon?"

"The exit ikon, safety ikon. I don't know what it's called. Whenever I'm near it, though, the animals stay away. I've taken to calling it that."

A flood of questions occupied her, but she forced them back for the obvious prudence of survival. Later, on Pedr's boat, they'd hash out all these details.

"Ten minutes," Malcolm whisper-shouted over his shoulder, already moving again. "We're almost there, and it's not far from the north beach. If Pedr's approaching from the northwest, we can find him through one of my established foot trails. They're easier than hacking through this. Lars, you go first. Take this trail up ahead. Britt, you follow. Henrik and I will catch up. No, Britt. Don't argue with me. Do it. Now."

W hen Major Helsing wasn't separated from his arcane-bound dragul, hacking away at jungle bushes, and scrounging food from a hostile environment, Henrik had the idea that Malcolm was a brute of a man, with broad shoulders and a hard glare. As the relative of a famed Kapurnickkian General, softness wouldn't be in his makeup.

All in all, Malcolm wasn't that far lost. Remnants of baser physical strength lingered in his thick neck and stout arms, but he'd clearly been diminishing on the island. Whether as the result of separation from his dragul, sheer starvation and stress, or a combination of both, it would take a while for Malcolm to recover.

Henrik didn't hate him, but he wasn't about to admit that. Malcolm had all the overtures of a solid older brother, which made Henrik more inclined to like him. Anyone that protected Britt earned his favor, but Henrik and Malcolm were hardly cordial yet.

While Lars and Britt worked their way ahead, Malcolm's tense glare locked on Henrik's face.

"So, my sister found a soldat to help her."

A drawling question laced the words, tinged with a sense of

disbelief and exasperation. Henrik could relate. Britt stirred up equal parts disbelief and exasperation within the same breath.

"It's a long story."

"I plan to hear it."

Henrik nodded. "Fine. I'm open to whatever questions you have, but the situation is complicated and we don't have time. This is not the place for hashing it out."

"Catch me up on the basics, so I know what's going on. Soldats are paranoid, but you're a step beyond a regular soldat if you're willing to deal with my sister to release me, and I want to know what we're facing."

"Fair."

"You know about the draguls, obviously."

"I do."

"Does your Captain know?"

"He knows something, I don't know how much."

"Were you commanded to this mission?"

"No."

Interest illuminated Malcolm's expression as he murmured, "Fascinating," in a tone exactly like his sister. He tipped his head toward a snoozing Tesserdress, draped over his shoulder like a wet towel.

"She's why you're here, isn't she?"

Henrik didn't answer.

With a hidden scoff, Malcolm continued, "Any soldat worth their weight in jord would understand the importance of saving Tesserdress, assuming my sister told you about Tesserdress and my bonding and our need for her eggs?"

Henrik nodded once.

"Then something big happened to Britt. My sister wouldn't discuss the draguls with a soldat unless forced."

Henrik leaned into the sense that Malcolm spiraled toward something, though a visceral reaction to the word *forced* made his gut clench.

He remained quiet.

"If you're here helping me clear the island, that means you're at least invested in returning Tesserdress and Denerfen to Kapurnick, but I can't imagine what your plans will be beyond that. Any soldat would be honored to turn a weakness such as ours to His Glory. I imagine the payout would be worth it."

Henrik licked his lips, irritated at the immediate leap to material gain, though he couldn't fault the logic. He would have thought the same. Before his reefer year, he might have even sought it. If he turned in that dragul, he could ask for almost anything.

Henrik shoved that aside. Selma didn't matter right now, because he owed Britt more than a distracted attention.

"Your question about my motivation is understandable and fair," Henrik said, "My motivation isn't for my own island. Not anymore. Nor is the explanatory story mine to tell," he hastily added, with a quick glance at the trail where Britt and Lars continued behind them. Britt looked intrigued by the adventure, but Lars was reluctant.

Very reluctant.

Malcolm used the silence to add pressure. Henrik cast about for the right words, found no better replacement, and finally said, "I owe Britt. A lot."

Malcolm's eyes widened for a full three seconds. His gaze flickered over Henrik, as if he must resort to visible measures for understanding, while he sidestepped down the path. He managed a halting reply before returning his attention to the trail.

"Oh?"

"Let's not harp on it," Henrik growled. "My goal on this island is to safely deliver Tesserdress to you, and help all of you return to Kapurnick. After that, we'll re-evaluate. For now, your sister has my loyalty."

The words rippled.

Your sister has my loyalty.

Treason.

A soldat had no loyalty except to His Glory. But what if His

Glory betrayed *them*? Why didn't the relationship work in reverse? The profound cracks in his life's foundation that formed when he saw Britt on the whipping post deepened. They sank low and wide.

"To that end," Henrik continued before a barrage of questions could muck up their time and distract his original purpose, "Captain Oliver will be here soon, if he isn't already. He seeks me. There's no doubt. It's a matter of time before he arrives or gives chase to our ship as we leave."

"What's your plan?"

"Depends. Is Pedr who he says he is?"

If the switch in topic surprised Malcolm, he gave no indication. "Yes. He marauds under the pirate name Burning Beard."

"He truly is?"

Amused, Malcolm said, "Yes. Didn't Britt tell you?"

"Yes."

"You didn't believe her?"

He sighed. "It seemed . . . extraordinary."

Malcolm snorted. "That's Pedr. He defies belief."

"Pedr can take you to Kapurnick?"

Malcolm nodded.

"Good. Then my plan is to stay here. Britt will go with you. I trust you to see her home. It'll be better if I'm not with you to draw Captain Oliver and other soldats into your path."

"This will fulfill what you owe her?"

"That's up to her."

Malcolm's hands opened and closed in loose fists. Jaw tensing and loosening in sync with his fingers, he said, "Okay. There really is more, isn't there?"

Henrik sighed, rubbing a hand over his eyes. "More than you'll want to hear. The moment you and Britt have the ikon that allows you to depart, leave. I'll draw Oliver away."

"Fine, but what if Oliver doesn't come?"

Henrik laughed.

Oh, if only.

"He'll come."

Malcolm shrugged. "I'll keep Britt with me. No doubt she'll be grateful to head home and protect Denerfen and Tesserdress."

"She won't like it," Henrik warned.

The older brother emerged. Rigidity tightened through Malcolm's tawny muscles, highlighted by so much starvation and time. "What is she to you?" he demanded.

Henrik shook his head, ran a hand through his hair. "To the locker if I know. It's safe to say there's no one quite like your sister, and I have no idea how to read her. We were . . . bound by a mutual agreement. She's free to go. With luck, this will recompense some of what I owe her."

Malcolm eyed him with profound disdain, his upper lip curled. "Must be worse than I imagined. Regardless, it doesn't matter. I'll get her to Pedr's boat and leave. She'll go."

"Are you willing to exploit her love for the draguls to make her leave? Because I will, if you won't."

Malcolm grinned. "We might be more alike than I thought, soldat. Don't worry about it. My sister is under my care. Good luck against Oliver. You're going to need it."

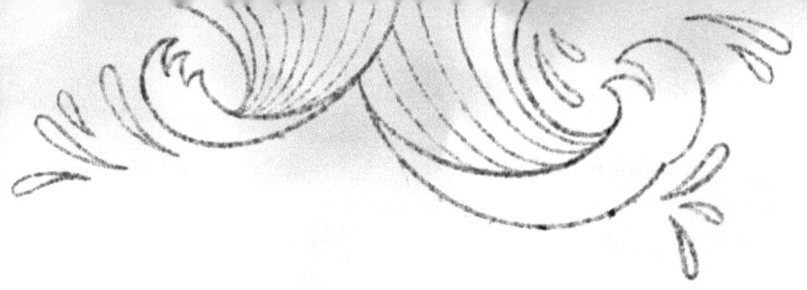

Chapter Thirty Three

BRITT

Malcolm and Henrik took their sweet time.

Britt ground her teeth as she inched her way along the darkening jungle floor. "I don't like this," she sang. "I don't like it."

Wisely, Lars walked behind her, preventing her departure. She couldn't skirt around him, or her shoulder might brush an ikon. The thin footpath required them to walk single-file, avoiding ikons with every paranoid step. As night descended, the ikons glowed a brilliant lime green.

Lars claimed that every ikon resulted in some horrific fate, which made them all the more terrifying. Some ikons recurred frequently, but new ones popped up often.

Malcolm and Henrik's low registers had faded after only a few steps. The plush jungle made her think of the inside of a pillow. Stuff and fluff everywhere, warping the way sound registered. She moved cautiously until, what felt like hours later, Malcolm and Henrik reappeared.

With only a nod between them, Malcolm delicately slipped past, then Lars, with the ease of someone used to this jungle navigation. He scraped the edge of her waist as he slid by, activating a quick tug of pain across a still-sensitive scar. She sucked in a breath through her teeth. He didn't notice.

"Let's go," he commanded with all the annoying self-right-eousness of the older brother she deeply loved. "We're not far from the camp. We'll take my trail to the beach after you touch the ikon."

Britt attempted a glimpse at Henrik, but Lars stood in her way. She caught only Henrik's profile in the light of an ikon. He studied the jungle.

Did he avoid her attention on purpose?

The sense that *something* else occurred overcame her.

Malcolm's silent tour of the interior was wildly unvarying and underwhelming. Continuing marbled flower petals, pungent fragrance, vague noise, rampant ikons. While the jungle seemed to constantly speak, she couldn't make out individual voices. Everything close had silenced, the rest came from distant reaches.

Animals, insects, or powers?

Did the ikons scream?

Or did they sing?

Malcolm grabbed her elbow and spirited her away from a dropping vine, which grazed her elbow as it fell. The unexpected movement inspired a flow of magma-like heat across her scarred back. She bit the inside of her cheek to withhold a cry, and earned a concerned glower from Henrik that she registered only by dim ikon light.

Malcolm glanced at the vine, then Britt, one eyebrow lifted in silent warning. An ikon swirled along the vine near her eyes, like an elaborate, tiny mandala had been stamped into the virescent leaves every handspan. The heat probably burned it into the fibrous plant. She tucked loose strands of hair behind her ear. The failing braid melted around Denerfen, hiding him.

"We're here," Malcolm said.

Ahead lay a small area cleared from thickest brush, with less size than the state dining room table General Helsing often used. A delicate mat of woven fronds, stacked on piles of rocks, hovered above the thick, black ground. The crumbled dirt had a sheen like ravens' feathers. Little wonder that Malcolm had chosen this spot to camp. Despite the nighttime density, ikons glowed from a near-ceiling of vines all over the trees, the leaves. She could easily make out Henrik's expression several paces away.

Malcolm paused at the base of a tree. He crouched, one hand protectively cradling Tesserdress as he lowered, and pointed to an ikon embedded in the fibrous trunk.

"This ikon is the one I keep following and seeking. The one that I call the safety ikon. You called it the exit ikon?"

Henrik shrugged his response. A slice of visible trunk revealed a slash of white and two dots on either side, silvery-lime in appearance, stamped on the thick bark beneath. The exact same symbol on their forearms. This was white, not green or black.

Lars muttered, "The man's brilliant."

Henrik frowned. "Too easy."

"How did you keep track of that tiny thing?" Britt cried.

"Not much else to do, except search and wait. Besides, once you know what you're looking for, it makes it easier. The vines, you see? They won't touch the ikons. Plus, it only moves every so often. I think it's somehow connected to the vittra and her movements, but I'm not sure. After awhile in here, you start to . . . get a feel for it. It's almost like the arcane respects those who respect it. Time has passed and I haven't harmed anything, so . . . I think the arcane helped me. Anyway, I realized that the ikon power isn't bad. It's not even mean or vindictive. It's . . ."

" . . . watchful," Lars said.

Malcolm nodded.

Britt kept her doubts to herself. Such a simmering arcane was likely waiting for something very specific. Revenge, perhaps. Revenge on Stenberg, to the point. Like Henrik, uneasiness stirred within. Indeed, this felt too simple.

Henrik's machete still poised in front of him as he spun on his heels, surveying the small space.

"Britt," Henrik commanded with the quiet of a moving predator, "touch the ikon with the five fingers of the arm where you want the mark. Say, *Great Follorat spirits of the island, I honor your ikons, your power, and your history. I ask for safe passage off your beaches.*"

"What would happen if I don't say it right?" she asked.

Lars uttered something that sounded significantly like, *and then the vittra eats you, you bastid,* but she couldn't be sure.

Henrik leveled an irritated glare his way.

"It's more about intent than exactness," Malcolm muttered. "But that's really close."

Britt dropped to her knees, but a gleaming sword at her throat stopped her words.

"RISE," a gravelly voice said. "Slowly."

Britt clenched her teeth.

Oliver.

The sword guided Britt from her knees and onto her feet. She moved a heartbeat at a time, captured by the hot metal pressed into the base of her throat. The edge of it shivered, threatening to bite into the sloshing blood just beneath the surface.

Denerfen hissed and ducked beneath her hair. She resisted the urge to snatch him off her shoulder, afraid that Oliver would slice her neck open if she moved unexpectedly.

She glanced up.

Oliver stared at her, sword arm extended in a firm and sure threat. Very little remained in his eyes but sheer desperation, and how well she knew that panic. This was a man teetering at the edge.

"Up," he sang. "Up, up, little Kapurnickkian. The big, bad soldats have things to settle and lives to steal. What a handsome little dragul you have there."

Henrik, Lars, and Malcolm stood out of view behind her. Shuffling feet surrounded them, moving slow, but fluid. Soldats flowed into a half circle behind Oliver, deftly avoiding ikons in the way of highly trained warriors. She counted at least four in her view, recognizing none. They had a slightly different appearance, but she couldn't peg it exactly.

An ambush.

Of course.

"Your fight is with me," Henrik said, his voice taut with fury. "Let her and the dragul go."

"Don't think I will," Oliver said.

Britt kept a wary eye on his hand, poised to flick a wrist and end her life in the length of time it took her to bleed out. But if she leaned back and—

"Don't even think about it," Oliver ground out.

He shoved her. Britt's spine slammed into the tree. Her head crashed onto a branch, jarring her teeth. Pain rattled all the way down her toes, screaming from welts and bruises. She stifled a moan as the resulting agony ricocheted through her head. Her back arched, shrieking in protest all the way down. A cry choked her. Denerfen, with a squeal, dug into her neck to stop himself from falling.

"Better," Oliver said.

Vines crawled across her chest, securing her. She tried to swim out of the daze. Did the vines move of their own accord, or did a soldat yank them around her torso and squeeze the breath out of her lungs?

"Stay put," Oliver commanded, swinging his sword away from her neck and pointing it to Henrik, Lars, and Malcolm. "All of you."

The splashing lights coalesced back into blurry figures, then limelight bodies. Oliver had pinned her to the tree with the safety ikon, and with uncanny timing. Seconds before she might have had the island working in her favor . . .

"This is between you and me, Oliver," Henrik growled.

"Sure."

The vines tightened. She gasped.

"My plan stands," Oliver said.

A cool brush of teeth came along her spine. "Denerfen," she whispered, "no."

The vines doubled down. Agony ripped across her back. The hot squeeze of blood dribbled onto her clothes as tender wounds sprang open. Her stomach muscles clenched, but didn't alleviate the strain. If Denerfen or Tesserdress had still been in her skirts, they'd be ground to a pulp.

Her hazy vision cleared, sharpening into an ugly picture. Henrik, his face contorted into a barely controlled snarl, stood in front of Lars and Malcolm with his shoulders puffed up, arms clenched, legs braced. Soldats in similar defensive states circled his back. Lars faced them with shaking knees and saucer-sized eyes. Beads of sweat rolled down his neck.

Malcolm kept an assessing stare on Oliver, unusually cool and aloof, though his hand hovered at his side. She hadn't seen any weapons on him, but he must hide something. Tesserdress was nowhere in sight.

"Last chance, Oliver. Britt has nothing to do with this," Henrik said. "Let her go."

Her name on his lips had an oddly powerful magic. The snarl in his voice stirred something deep within.

"I think she does, Henrik." Oliver held his hauteur like a pro. "In fact, I know that she does . . . because she's somehow earned *your* loyalty. She's not the only one who you've been fool enough to care about."

A grunt, and a suppressed shout, sounded from the other side of her tree. A man stumbled forward, falling flat to the mat of woven fronds that Malcolm created. By whatever miracle no ikons were triggered, Britt couldn't fathom. The man moaned, face turned to the side, eyes closed.

Einar.

But not the Einar she knew.

Swollen left eye, split lip. Blood dried on a tattered shirt. He breathed in an uneven, ragged way. Broken rib, probably. The one eye visible and without swelling was glazed and drawn. Rich black earth coated his distorted face. He didn't make a sound, but grimaces tore across his face, contorting every breath. After a wave of pain, he controlled his expression for a few seconds.

Henrik's only visible reaction was his bobbing throat. He didn't spare Einar another glance. Oliver smiled, frigid as the netherworld where the harpies lived and breathed frost, torturing the souls of those found wanting.

"Let's talk, Henrik."

"I'll talk," he immediately countered, "when they go free. Britt, Einar, Lars, and Malcolm."

"No."

Henrik spread two hands, seemingly unconcerned. "It's my price."

Oliver ruminated. Between the blood leaking from her reopened wounds, the pain with every staggering heartbeat, and the ever-tightening vines threatening to grind her into dust, Britt struggled to draw a breath.

She opened her mouth to shout, but a vine wrapped over her teeth. Someone she couldn't see controlled the jungle ropes. She choked, nearly gagging from the pressure, wrought mute. Her tender, barely-healed wounds grated beneath the rough-textured bark. Heat poured over her.

Henrik kept a trained gaze on Oliver, but it felt as if he stared right at her. In the distance, a familiar, high-pitched scream loosened. Malcolm's eyes shot to hers in silent question. She nodded once, almost imperceptible.

Drake.

Pedr had arrived.

Her hair stood up on end as she formed a plan. Little wonder that Oliver had followed all this way, but his speed in finding them was remarkable. Had they docked on a different part of the island? Based on what little information Henrik gave about his previous visits to the Unseen island, she presumed that these soldats also had the exit ikon already.

Oliver created a rather advantageous and strategic situation. With Einar in tow, he could rid himself of leaders in the soldat resistance and control the narrative over what happened. Henrik and Einar would be slain, thrown into the ocean as shark chum, and Stenberg would forget them. Henrik might never know the truth about Selma.

Britt wouldn't have it.

None of it.

"How about I kill them first," Oliver offered, "and then you talk?"

Malcolm advanced a step. Henrik twirled the machete once in bold invitation, legs braced. "What you saw at the whipping post is a meager promise of the fight I will bring to this jungle, Oliver. You will not walk out of here."

Boredom, instead of careful calculation, crossed Oliver's expression. With a long-suffering tone, he said, "I'll release the girl."

"Lars, too.'

With a scowl, he said, "Who is he? Kill him!"

Two soldats moved to comply, but Henrik swung his machete into the closest tree trunk. The touch cut an ikon in half . . . or it should have. The clang of metal bouncing free reverberated with painful ululations.

The ground turned to sludge around the tree, slowing one of the rushing soldats. Tar clung to his ankles, pulling him to his knees. He shouted, but the tenacious substance had a fastidious hold, tripping him.

Oliver hesitated.

Henrik brought the machete closer to the next ikon, deftly avoiding the filth by stepping to the side of a forming oval. That ikon's power only went so far.

"Shall we dance, Oliver?" Henrik murmured. "Your time on Stenberg is working against you, Captain, and you chose a poor battle ground. I know this island, and her ikons, better than you. Will you risk it?"

Oliver scowled. "Fine. I'll release the girl and the captain, but Major Helsing and Einar stay."

"Agreed," Malcolm said.

A sword slammed into the tree from her left, severing her bonds. Instant release rushed through Britt. She dropped to her knees, hacking a cough. Blood trickled down her back, seeping through the shirt. Under better illumination, blood must gleam on the smooth trunk. Denerfen fluttered with pitiful squeaks. She reached back, clamping a hand on him a second before his bite.

"No," she whispered, pulling him free.

In this state, she wouldn't survive even the smallest emergence.

A soldat strode toward her. She threw out a hand, pressed the ikon at the bottom of the trunk, and whispered, "Spirits of the island, I honor your . . . your power. Your history. Grant me passage off this beach."

The words were all wrong. The cadence didn't match what Henrik said, but her thoughts raced too fast to recall it perfectly. With any luck, the arcane *did* have a heart. Searing pain slashed her arm, slapping a tarry mark with two sharp dots on either side. She swallowed the throb, which was pitiful compared to the agony awakening across her back.

Thank you, she silently whispered.

The soldat jerked her off her feet, reactivating the agony. Pure hatred carried her venom. "You bastid!" she shouted, slamming a heel into his shin. "Let me go!"

He released her with a grunt. Britt threw herself across the open space, into Malcolm's arms. An inferno raged, blooming across previously-healed wounds, but she ignored it.

"Don't do this!" she cried.

He put his right hand on her back, tensed when he felt the welling blood. "It's fine, Britt," he said, too loud. "It's fine. We'll work it out."

Between their bodies, his left hand gave her Tesserdress. Britt accepted her, grateful beyond words that the dragul remained silent. Passed out? Terrified?

"Your back," Malcolm hissed in her ear, without the dulcet sweetness meant to buy them time. She pushed Tess into her pocket.

"Go," Henrik commanded in a barely-controlled tone she'd never heard before. "Get out of here. I mean it, Britt. Get on that boat and leave."

The same soldat as before ripped her away. "Your chance to escape ends in five seconds!" he bellowed.

Britt stumbled, barely catching herself, until Lars grabbed an arm and hauled her up. She cried out against the wrenching pain, unable to help it. "Go, you foolish chit," Lars cried. "To Birgitta!"

Britt veered toward a trail heading north that they hadn't ventured yet. Presumably, the path to the north beach that Malcolm spoke about, where she'd find Pedr. She gazed over her shoulder as Lars hurried her along.

Henrik stood back there. His steely eyes met hers, solid and unswerving and glittering with furor. She'd never seen such hatred, such malefaction. For several heartbeats, she had no idea who that soldat was. The time for revenge had come, perhaps both for the island and for Henrik.

Lars swept Britt into the trees, snapping at her when she nearly trod on an ikon.

"Watch it!"

She risked a final glance. Henrik glared her out of sight, willing her not to return.

Well.

He would be one angry soldat when he realized her plan, indeed.

"TELL ME YOU TOUCHED THE IKON," Lars hissed under his breath as they scurried around an impossible number of ikon-laden vegetation. "Tell me we'll make it out of here!"

"I did."

"Finally! Some stroke of luck."

The growth was eccentrically tight around this trail, but Malcolm had created a more defined trail than expected. She pressed on, Lars swearing at her back, Tesserdress heavy in her pocket. Denerfen wriggled in her hands, but she gave no freedom.

"I'm telling you," he growled. "These Stenbergian—"

Britt slid to a stop.

"Quiet!"

He obeyed, mouth snapping shut so fast it would have been comical under different circumstances. Through the blending forest noise, she could just make the unnatural sound out again.

Drake.

"Keep going!"

Britt ignored the ikons and raced down the trail. Leaves sliced her face, her neck, the back of her hands, her forearms. Streaking blood smeared her clothes and pungent, nauseating fragrances filled the air, jarred loose as she rampaged through the forest.

"The ikons!" Lars shrieked. "You're activating them!"

"We'll have to deal with it," she shouted. "We must go!" After a few panting breaths, she demanded, "Tell me about them."

"What?" Lars shouted.

"The ikons!"

"What about them?"

"What happens if I touch them?"

"Anything!"

She skidded to a stop. A held hand prevented Lars from speaking as she gazed around a slightly-more open area. Thick trunks with skinny, straight branches, and fewer vines. Ikons glowed here as much as Malcolm's camp. She paused, arrested at the sight. Though she'd seen them imprinted on the leaves minutes ago, she hadn't comprehended their sheer number.

Thousands.

No, hundreds of thousands.

One ikon, in particular, drew her gaze, if for nothing else but the sheer size of it. As long as her forearm, and as wide. Her breath calmed as she approached. The smooth design drew her, with a swirling, oily appearance. So flat and shiny against the grainy bark of the tree. Stunning, with the tones of deepest emerald that ran through it, spiraling into the darkest sea.

She lifted a finger to touch it, utterly entranced.

Was it as smooth as it appeared?

A hard palm landed on her shoulder, shooting new spirals of pain into her bones. The spikes jolted her out of the swirl of curiosity with a gasp.

"They draw you in, imbecile!"

Lars jerked her away, and the hazy spell broke. Britt winced, sucked in a breath. Tears collected in her eyes. Lars paused. He eyed her bloody dress, his hand, her shoulder, and jerked away. Apology lined his twisted expression.

"S-sorry, Miss. I—I didn't realize. All the blood."

"It's fine." She swallowed hard, shaken. "Thank you for stopping me. I didn't . . . know. They're so . . ."

"Fascinating?"

Sheepish, she nodded.

"They'll fascinate you to death." He pointed to the ikon she almost touched. "Especially that one."

"What does it mean?"

"That one calls the vittra. See how the lines form a half circle, like the sun? Others jut out, reaching higher? Then on the bottom, arrows pointing down? It's the vittra."

With a shiver, she hurried through two trees. Somewhere ahead, waves crashed. "Why would someone call the vittra?"

"Why would someone live here?" he countered. "There's no logical reason for any of the Chain Islands, is there? The arcane makes everything strange."

She called over her shoulder, "How many different ikons are there?"

"Twenty seven."

"What do they do?"

"I'm not telling you!" he shouted. He clumsily dodged a hanging vine, swerved around a low-lying branch. "Don't waste your breath on stupid questions."

"Just tell me!"

"They call tar from the earth! They summon the vittra. They send poison in the air, and darts into your eyes, and pungent aromas that'll cause hallucinations. The ikons do whatever the Follorat islanders and vittras commanded them to do! Now stop wasting our time. We need to find the beach and escape. We're lucky nothing has stopped us thus far. Don't press it!"

Distracted by another peal from overhead, Britt said nothing. Fifteen seconds later, they spilled onto a beach. In the near distance, Burning Beard's ship awaited, sails awash with flames like glittering rose gems in the night.

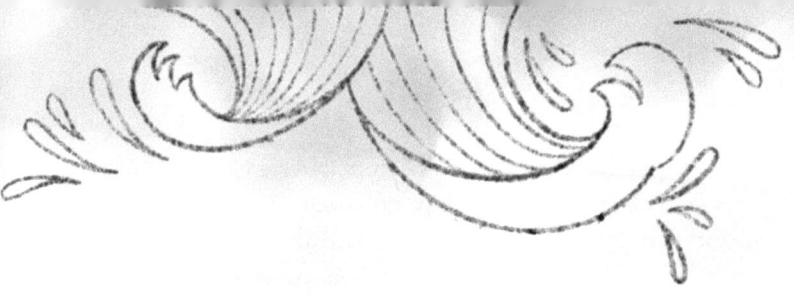

Chapter Thirty Four

HENRIK

Six soldats, plus Oliver. Einar in the middle, which was no advantage. One soldat had just extricated from the tarry ground with burns on his skin, but otherwise not injured enough to discount. Henrik was surrounded on all sides, except his back, where he had no coverage except Malcolm. Nothing overhead to use as leverage, either.

Henrik tightened his grip on the machete. Besides the machete, he had only a hand knife. No smaller backup knives hidden in his boot. He'd been a fool, thinking himself safe on Stenberg, when a good soldat was always prepared. Lars could have outfitted him further before they left the ship.

Instead, Henrik let Britt's safety distract him.

Curse himself a bastid.

Malcolm would be an asset, but not much. Soldat warfare was a brutal art that most islanders didn't bother to learn, but the Helsing siblings had surprised him thus far. These soldats were His Glory's personal soldats. Six of the ten had been peeled away for this excursion, which meant a great deal more than made sense.

Did Captain Oliver attempt to quell a rebellion?

Or something else?

Henrik had faced worse odds before, but he had other soldats on his side at the time. Certainly none poised against him. Lars and Britt vanished into the chaparral, leaving a rippling tension. A distant part of his mind couldn't believe she'd left without arguing about it, but she had draguls to save.

Malcolm's camp lay in tatters, with Einar on the woven mat. Bodies and seething rage occupied what little open space existed. Captain Oliver nodded toward Henrik's right hand.

"Drop the machete, Henrik. We're discussing."

"No."

"Drop it or Einar dies."

Henrik clenched his jaw. Training screamed at him from distant recesses. The urging not to care. *Your life first, others second. You'll never save a situation if you're dead. It's the calculations of war, and not personal.*

Another false imprint of the soldats.

War *was* personal to those with the burden of fighting. Perhaps His Glory, impassive in his stone castle, could command such emotional distance. With Einar half dead, and Britt potentially running to her demise, the entire operation had *personal* underwriting every ticking minute. Einar would call him shite if he gave into Captain Oliver's demands. More than likely, Einar acted weaker than he was.

Henrik hoped.

He could only fight two soldats at once, not six. Which was Captain Oliver's goal, of course. Overwhelm him into submission, like a good soldat.

Malcolm said nothing, but remained tense as a panther, his focus darting from Oliver, back to Henrik, and then to the soldats in turn. They stood stolid as walls, arms at their sides, deepest disregard written in their expressions. He looked to Einar, as if debating. Einar's upper lip twitched up twice. Silent soldat speak to *hold*.

Henrik played the gamble.

He said nothing.

The hard stare between him and Captain Oliver turned into an expression of surprise on Captain Oliver's part.

"Really?" he queried. "You refuse a command to my face and with Einar on the line?"

"Gladly."

"A first for you. Color me surprised."

Henrik paused, feeling out the air. It had been a test, but not the kind he expected. Nothing had changed. The vines tightened, and loosened. They moved, as always. Yet a hum existed that hadn't before.

A . . . percussion.

Out of the corner of his eye, he saw Malcolm glance down.

"I could have passed this off as insubordination, Henrik," Oliver continued. "I planned to tell His Glory that you had a fit of lunacy, interrupting a Norr-given punishment of the girl. You were roped into the greater good of Stenberg, saving the dragul, and all, and His Glory might have allowed you forgiveness. Now it's a blatant rebellion. I can't help you out of this. Better to kill you."

"Really?" Henrik countered, tilting his head toward the closest soldat. "You brought six of His Glory's personal henchmen on the off-chance I was on a peacemaking mission and didn't have time to explain myself?"

Oliver smiled, but it struggled. Two of the soldats at his side rocked on their feet, a mask of bored agitation in place.

"We all have things we want, Henrik."

"Yes, and what do you want, Oliver?" Dropping the *Captain* rang the air like a drum. "Why would you come here to murder two of your most talented soldats when you know that other soldats will rebel? Already have, in fact. There must be something in our deaths for you."

The percussion intensified into a thrumming *woop, woop, woop.* Malcolm slipped back half a step, legs braced. He hissed some-thing, but Henrik couldn't make it out. They had to buy time so these wildly gesticulating vines could reveal whether the *real* problem was on the way.

Had Lars and Britt triggered an ikon?

A long pause burdened the air. Vines burst through the leaves, swirling in a frenetic dance. Malcolm, head tipped back, inched another step to the side. A soldat slammed a hand into Malcolm's shoulder, shoving him to the ground. Malcolm careened to the rich earth, limp as a noodle for a man completely on edge, and rolled once. No protest crossed his lips.

When he stopped, the shimmer of an iridescent symbol shone from the trunk, just within reach. Henrik couldn't make out which one. Sweat rolled off Oliver's forehead, dripping onto his shirt. Meanwhile, the soldats shuffled, focus locked on the twisting vines, which strangled with greater fervor.

The low *woop, woop, woop,* became thunder.

Oliver's lips pinched into a frown brimming with hatred. "This is over, Henrik. You're done. You gave up everything by your outright rebellion."

The surge of loathing Henrik felt expanded into a wide chasm. The soldats did whatever their leadership asked. Blind faith. Lifetime servitude. Murder. Destruction. Darkness. Their leaders didn't give the same.

"Is this service, Oliver?" he snapped. "His Glory uses children as weapons. He enslaves them, rips them from their families, demands utmost obedience, or else?"

A pained grimace contorted Oliver's expression so quickly, Henrik might have imagined it. Henrik held his gaze, if only to keep Oliver's attention off of Einar, whose hand had slipped off his chest. The tip of his middle finger discreetly drew in the ground, like a twitch.

Henrik didn't dare look directly at it.

Not yet.

The vibrating vines hummed in a steady chorus, highlighting the approaching storm. Tighten, twist, flap, grind. Flowers flailed in wheeling circles. The burgeoning hum escalated to a steady, high-pitched whine. Two soldats glanced at the ground, brows wrinkling as ebony mist crept upward.

Einar's finger moved more frantically now.

Oliver's upper lip curled over his teeth. "You see," he drawled, "it's a bit different than you think."

"Oh?"

"His Glory didn't care about you, but I did. I advocated for you. Sent you on the reefer year to complete the final requirement so you could step into the next Captain position when it opened. I *fought* for you!"

"You commanded me!" he shouted in return. "You drove my bones to dust. You ripped away my freedom. You took her from me."

"I gave Selma to you!" Oliver thundered. "I gave those papers to the Sister of Stenberg so you could find your birth mother and be done with it. You were supposed to find her, realize she was gone to the mainland for her foolish display, and focus on completing the final jord recovery."

"I'm not talking about Selma," Henrik growled.

Understanding brightened Oliver's eyes.

"Shite, Henrik!" he shouted. "You've ruined everything and brought this on yourself. Why did you have to *care*?"

Oliver's rising ire cost him a morsel of control. Fraying control. The on-edge man had turned to near wild desperation, and that's when Henrik understood. These six soldats didn't come to help Oliver, they came to spy for His Glory. To ensure that Einar and Henrik didn't make it out alive and to confirm Oliver's allegiance to the Stenberg tyrant. Oliver had no way out except to destroy Henrik, Einar, and Malcolm. Effectively eliminating three different threats against His Glory and proving his worth.

Brutal, heartless leader.

His Glory, the voice of Norr, should have guided, governed, and cared. Instead, he held innocent lives at stake against men who had given everything they were, could be, and had ever been, to his service.

Henrik twirled the machete around his wrist. It sang as it spiraled. He caught it at the top, crouching.

"You're supposed to return with my head?"

"And your balls," Oliver snarled.

Henrik ducked his head and laughed, he couldn't help it. His half-closed eyes looked right at Einar's hand, masking the glance. A word formed in the black bracken. He couldn't quite make it out.

But then . . .

Yes.

He knew it immediately.

Together.

The growing cacophony drew Oliver's eyes higher. Screams, pirouetting into shrieks, sliding back to earsplitting screams again, shattered the world. Wind breezed by, swirling air, fallen petals, putrid stink. The powerful stench made his eyes water.

"If you want my balls," Henrik declared over the rising noise, "take them from my dead body. Here's the real grappling tournament. You and me, Oliver. One champion to another."

A hellebore smile crossed Oliver's lips. "You have six soldats and me to contend with." Oliver withdrew his sword. "Not even our beloved grappling champion can hold his own against six of his equals."

Henrik braced himself. Einar hadn't moved, almost obscured by the creeping black fog that formed a circle around the soldats. Malcolm had eased onto his hands and knees, next to the trunk where he'd been so easily tossed. His hand inched closer to the ikon.

Henrik crouched, machete at the ready. He beckoned for the first soldat with a wave of his hand. He bellowed, "Together!"

Einar leaped to his feet.

Malcolm slapped the ikon.

A scream descended.

Chapter Thirty Five

BRITT

"Bloody stars," Lars whispered. "I'm not going out there."

The ocean crashed, swirling up the beach in pockets of white foam. Moonlight tipped iridescent light on the world, shimmering in the tufts of the waves. Darkness and starshine widened over an island far more sprawling than she first imagined.

Britt waved a giant frond back and forth, screaming until her voice hurt. Overhead, Drake flew, his shadow cutting across the glittering white sand in an ominous, moonlit shade. Burning Beard's beacon turned, heading their way.

Britt almost collapsed with relief.

"He saw us!" she cried. "Pedr is on the way."

"Pedr?" Lars sputtered when she whipped around, accidentally smacking his face with the giant, clover-shaped frond. The fibrous material reminded her of leather. He punched it away, glowering.

"My brother! I told you."

"Burning Beard?"

"Yes!" she snapped, heading for the forest. "His name is Pedr."

Lars paled further.

"You weren't kidding? He's really your . . . your . . ."

"Make your choice, Lars. Do you want to face Burning Beard or nine soldats in the jungle?"

"The soldats!"

"Stop it!" she snapped. "Do you really think Pedr is going to harm you when you're here working beside me? So help me, Lars, if you don't pull it together and do what I say, I'll tell Pedr that you captured me and brought me here. Keep waving that frond!"

Gulping, Lars raised an arm and frantically waved. "Fine! I'll draw his attention. But if I die because of Burning Beard, I'll spend the entirety of my afterlife making you miserable."

"Agreed."

"Sets fire to everything," Lars muttered darkly, arms waving. "Burns ships, people, animals!"

"He does not," she muttered, then added, "well, the animals anyway. Keep waving, all right? I'll be back."

"How are we supposed to know if he sees us?" he shouted after her.

"You'll know!"

She scrambled through the underbrush, seeking a specific leaf. The sprawling, giant leaves from earlier couldn't be found here, but she didn't dare venture farther inside. Yet. She'd escaped the haunting jungle and had no desire to, as Lars put it, tempt fate.

She would.

Didn't *want* to.

A cry escaped her as she found the desired leaf, large enough to wrap her waist like a skirt. At the same moment, fire illuminated the horizon. The billowing sails that announced Burning Beard sprang to greater life, torching with instant and encompassing flames. It appeared the entire thing would go up in smoke. Arcane, all of it. Mostly an illusion, though he'd lost many sails in the past when he hadn't paid attention.

Lars shrieked as she hurried back to his side.

"That's it!" he screeched. "We're doomed! He'll scuttle his ship right into the island and set the whole thing ablaze—just because he likes it! They say he feeds on destruction and the screams of the dying. Without it, Burning Beard turns to smoke!"

Britt rolled her eyes so hard it almost hurt, but a vine grabbed her ankle, distracting her scathing report.

She fell with a thud.

Her chest hitting the ground sprayed sand, shoving granules into her nose with a painful push. She struggled for air, her ribs paralyzed, as Denerfen squealed. The vine wrapped her ankle and yanked.

She skidded across the sand, the prickling granules raking her stomach as she gasped. A brilliant, lime green ikon blazed on the vine around her ankle. Hasty attempts to see it brought recognition. The leaves that spiraled from it were the same she'd just taken.

Blessed mermaids, but she'd inadvertently activated one.

Desperate, she dug her fingers into the passing sand grains, seeking purchase. Grasping for anything, Britt whipped around, but it was no use. Sand flew by, filling her skirts, her sleeves, thickening the air in her lungs. It collected in her open wounds like fire. She coughed, wheezing, as the darkening forest approached yet again.

A firm *thud* sounded as something slammed into the ground ahead of her and cerulean sparks sprayed. They shattered in a spritz, arresting her momentum. She stopped. Britt blinked once, twice, unable to see through cloying sapphire and gray smoke. The sizzling vine retracted with a hiss, the burned end withdrawing and curling and coiling as it slithered into the jungle. The rest lay limp around her ankle, cut off.

"Blessed mermaids," she whispered.

When another vine snaked toward her, a second explosion sounded from the sea. A moment after the explosion, fuchsia sparks slammed to the ground in a spray in front of her. They ignited in a fountain that formed the face of a charging dragon, sculpted out of moving, mauve flames, and consumed the approaching vine. It retreated with a hiss.

"Pedr," she whispered.

Britt whipped around, knees in the sand. Other spiraling dragons shot out of the ship, racing to the island, consuming vines that whipped free. The screeches and shrieks of the foliage as they retracted and wheeled away, chased by the consuming monsters, rang in her ears.

With a laugh, she shoved out of the sand, ducked a slow vine, and returned to Lars. A rowboat lowered from the side of the fiery ship closest to them. Pained tears clotted her eyes. Seeing it, Lars gripped tufts of hair in his hands, nearly pulling it out.

"Shite!" Lars cried, "He's coming!"

She dropped to her knees, spread the leaf, and bent it on two sides. The fibrous material snapped, breaking into thirds. She left it creased, spun it, and did the same until it formed a rudimentary box.

Archaic, but enough.

The empty boat that launched from the ship skipped forward, sliding over the waves with giant oars and no oarsmen.

"Oh sea gods!" he cried, glimpsing the boat skipping toward them over the top of the water. "We're doomed!"

"Pull it together!" she hissed.

She yanked Lars off the sand and pointed to the leaf.

"I'm putting my two draguls on this leaf. They will not stray off because they'll obey my command to stay. The moment that rowboat lands on the beach, you take the draguls to Pedr's ship. Tell him that I put them in your care before returning for Malcolm and Henrik. Do *not drop my draguls*. Do you hear me?"

Lars' fear peaked.

"Going back?"

"You think I'm staying here?" she cried. "You're mad."

With gentle haste, she extracted Tesserdress from her pocket. The poor dragul was worse for wear, pressured by the strain of withdrawal on an already weakened body and the trauma of getting dragged through the sand. The boon of Malcolm's presence rendered only a little energy, but the hasty separation wrought a terrible toll. Tesserdress's wings drooped. She offered no protest. Without Malcolm, she'd die before dawn.

Britt wrestled tears. "Hang in there, Tess."

The approaching skiff closed in with every second, bridging the distance with unerring speed. Arcane born, as was everything Pedr did. A dark breeze swept by, carrying the scent of bog and peat and wet leaves on the wind. Her eyes watered at the fetid smell. Britt yanked the knife from Lars's belt.

"I'll take that."

"Hey! You can't leave me here with . . . with him . . . unarmed!"

"If you're watching over my draguls, then you've never been safer."

"A bloody lie! No one is safe with Burning Beard."

Was it true?

Mostly.

Pedr certainly wouldn't hurt the draguls. He'd wait until Britt returned to take any drastic action against a man that she left *with* the draguls. She hoped.

With Pedr, one never knew.

"Lars, I promise you a bigger reward than my first offer if you return those draguls safely to Pedr, all right?"

He mollified only slightly, wrenching his focus off the approaching boat only to check on Tesserdress. He recognized his lifeline, at least. Britt pried Denerfen off her shoulders. He stood on her palm, wings wide, head cocked. His adorable, glittering eyes regarded her with steep suspicion.

"Load it up, Denerfen. All the venom you can manage."

Denerfen blew steam. A torrent of confusion appeared in his wide, beautiful eyes, brilliant as the moon.

"All of it, if you can."

He whimpered, wings lowering.

She pressed him against her cheek.

"Trust me?"

His reluctance was a darling trait, the sweet dragul who

loved her so deeply. Of course, the moment she needed him to bite her, he acted as if he wouldn't. But he would. She trusted him. Denerfen huffed, breath billowing in and out of his nostrils, wings spread, as she set him on her neck and braced herself. After a hesitation, the telltale brush of teeth scraped her neck.

Denerfen squeaked.

He bit.

The loaded venom sliced into her skin like an ice dagger. It drove deep, twirling. She shuddered as his teeth withdrew. Carefully, she lifted him off, settled the weakened dragul next to Tesserdress, and said, "You are in charge of Tess, Denerfen. Don't leave this box until you find Pedr. You can take comfort in him. If you leave her side . . ."

The reluctant dragul curled up around Tesserdress, imparting heat, with a surly, weary glare aimed at Britt. A stern finger and a command to stay put brought a resentful bellow of sooty air her way. Denerfen put his head over the top of Tesserdress's body and closed his eyes. Imparting that much venom, combined with this hellacious night, exhausted them both.

She asked too much.

Lars cried out.

"Shite, girl! You're disappearing."

The dragul venom spiraled through her blood, whizzing with a strength and purpose she'd never felt before. She waited until Lars and the draguls were safely on board. When the rowboat burst through the breaking waves, Britt raced into the jungle.

SHE CHARGED THROUGH TREES.

The ikons' fervent green light radiated in an overwhelming array. She didn't have time to waste with sheer awe at their glittering forms because the invisibility would buy her twenty minutes, if luck was on her side. She needed every moment.

With a glance to her left, she slapped the closest ikon and sprinted faster.

The race to Henrik and Malcolm felt like she stepped into a tunnel of leaves, bushes and brambles. Instead of heeding a trail, avoiding the glowing runes, she touched everything she could. Her fingers razed leaves. Her shoulders hurtled through branches, rustling each individual leaf and branch. Her feet trod on gleaming roots. She smacked trunks, branches, flowers, whatever she found.

When the vittra ikon loomed ahead, she slammed her palm on it, and sped by. The soldats wanted to fight?

She'd bring the fight to them.

Roars chased her. Trees collapsed. Branches seized. Seams appeared in the ground. The island turned to instant upheaval as the arcane came to life all at once. She darted through the growth, unseen, thus avoiding most dangers.

Monsters hurled their bodies out of hidden crevices as she darted past, but they couldn't find her. A glimpse over her shoulder revealed smoky wraiths, gathering from the ground, dissipating in confusion. Pearlescent teeth snapped from flowers. Vines sought their prey, ready to strangle. Giant boulders elevated from the ground, but found no head to smash. Puffs of rancid air hissed from the tree trunks, but she held her breath and hurried by.

Denerfen's venom continued falling down her back, not yet fully integrated. It would return her to Henrik and Malcolm, but not to the beach. At some point, she'd emerge from the venom in the jungle. A terrible plan, but better than surrender or abandonment.

Selma left Henrik, but Britt would not.

She'd fight.

Britt skidded to a stop at a swirling gray miasma of fog, exactly where the soldats should have been. She stopped, reaching for it. The clouds were so thick they floated in her palm, dissipating only when she made a fist. Liquid squelched from the sides, leaking silver between her fingers.

When she attempted to push through, it repelled her. Thrusting her shoulder against it, she bounced off, collapsing to her back. She shouted, paralyzed with the pain.

Blessed mermaids!

Such agony.

The throb washed through her in waves, prickling and awful. Blood leaked freely again, oozing along her sides. Several seconds passed while she gritted her teeth, screaming into the night.

Slowly, the misery retreated. She shoved to her feet, dizzy. What little moonlight had guided her disappeared. The vague sensation of something closing in swept the island, and the building wind didn't help.

"Oh, no you don't," she growled. "I'm getting *in* there."

Behind her, the ground quaked. Trees dropped, searching for the fool that pressed upon them. Giant, club-like appendages swung low, finding nothing to hit. No one to blame. Rampant destruction, awaiting.

She ran the circle of fog, thumping every ikon within her sight, studying the broiling gray mass, until a hint of breakage along the bottom caught her gaze. At the last second, she dodged a falling limb from overhead and skittered through the seam and into the cloud. The open wounds along her back bled in earnest, but Denerfen's coursing venom numbed the worst of the pain.

Hope curtailed the rest.

Dirt turned to sludge beneath her feet, bubbling like a cauldron. Stench drifted from the top of the wretched stuff. Steam issued between burps of hot ground. She splashed into an ankle-deep puddle, and then shin-deep. As she waded through, seeking a path through the murk, a shrieking sound swept above. Incandescent wings shimmered, like something foul loosed from hell.

Another break in the cloud.

Britt let out a cry.

An opening out of the fog! She threw herself into it before it disappeared in the spreading smoke. A shrieking singsong whistled in her ears as she emerged to the other side.

Chaos reigned.

The soldats had separated into two groups. Malcolm and Einar stood together, back-to-back, spinning between four soldats. Two other soldats, and Captain Oliver, cut Henrik off from their help. Her jaw dropped.

Einar?

Upright?

But . . . he'd been . . . half dead.

An act, then. He'd feigned weakness while he still had strength. Watching him whirl, twirl, and dodge blows gave new meaning to the word *berserk*.

It was real.

Einar proved it.

The return of a painfully high-pitched scream grated Britt's ears. Tar water bubbled from the interior of the circle with broiling steam that turned the air to a sickly sauna. The gray fog created a barrier. Helpful, as the island fell apart outside of it. The monsters that chased her out there hadn't crossed the fog.

A small wind funnel whipped in a frenzy, skipping from soldat to soldat, as if it couldn't decide where to land. Horrific caterwauling accompanied the whirlpool's movements. The storm-like surge hopped, jumped, stirred, distracted. A terrifying face appeared now and then. An old hag with oily skin, black hair like jungle vines, bleached, soulless eyes and a gaping maw. The number of soldats seemed to confuse her.

Ah.

The vittra.

Britt forced herself to ignore that force of nature for a presently bigger problem. Malcolm and Einar were still upright, but appeared to be weakening as they battled the four soldats. It wasn't going well. Britt sprinted across the muddy space, never so grateful to be invisible. The vittra moved unexpectedly into her path, forcing Britt to dodge right through the tornado or run into a soldat. She chose the vittra.

A terrible whirling sensation whipped through her, sliding like needles across her rebroken skin. The agony revitalized. For three eternal, horrific seconds, her soul seemed too slippery for her body. The vittra's storm might wipe away all known memories, or take her mind.

She felt the rending all the way to heart flesh.

It stopped.

Britt's momentum carried her through the arresting funnel and out the other side. The vittra's howls increased as she whipped around, empty eyes searching, searching, but unable to *see* Britt. As Britt swirled to a stop, she halted before a burly soldat. He towered above Malcolm, sword in both hands, ready to chop her brother in half.

She slammed her foot against his knee, kicking it inward. A sickening *crack* split the air. The soldat toppled and fell into the brackish, surging waters.

As that soldat fell, another closest to her spun in a different direction. Taking advantage of his lapse in focus, Britt rammed an elbow into his kidney, uppercut her hand to his chin, and jumped on his back as he slumped into the water. He went down, smacking his head on something hard. The waters splashed.

Einar blinked.

"What the—"

Malcolm roared. "Britt, no!"

Behind Einar, a third soldat advanced with a fist headed for Einar's face. Einar, barely dodging the blow, attempted to grab the soldat and pull him over his shoulder. In the strange waters, his balance failed. The soldat knocked Einar into the heated swamp rising past their knees and grabbed Einar by the throat. Malcolm contended with the fourth soldat, shouting commands for Britt to leave.

The whirling wind scuttled over, greedily slurping up the unconscious soldat. The wheeling, brazen song turned into a cackle. The smell of copper filled the air as the soldat, obliterated to smithereens, was consumed up by the vicious wind. The roving whirlpool became a twirling bloodbath of bones, flesh, and body parts.

Britt vomited to the side.

"Where are you?" Malcolm demanded. "Britt?"

She wiped her mouth with the back of her wrist and ignored him.

Grabbing a knife that floated to the surface of the tarry water, Britt spun, slammed the weapon into Einar's attacker right below the ribs, angled into his lungs. The soldat screamed, then gurgled. He fell to his knees as she wrenched the blade out, shoved him onto his side, and stabbed him through the heart.

Blood bubbled into the briny water. The vittra, gleeful, swept closer. Britt dodged away at the last second, turning her back to the spray of gore that resulted.

"Shite, Britt!" Malcolm shouted. "What are you thinking? Get out of here! The vittra will take you next."

Einar struggled to his feet. "What is going on?"

"My sister!"

The fever coursing through Britt began to slow. The lowering effects removed the full heat of the swamp as her cooling blood began to swirl. A sign she'd reached the halfway mark already. Only ten minutes of venom left.

Warmth swirled around her legs. The brackish water was getting hotter, thicker. No longer did it resemble heated seawater with black spots, but . . .

. . . thickening tar.

Malcolm shoved an elbow into the face of the fourth soldat, while Einar supported him from behind. That brought the attention of one of the soldats clashing with Henrik. Leaving Malcolm to finish that soldat, Einar lunged for the other, peeling his focus away from Henrik. Einar and Malcolm cleared the way for Henrik and Oliver to square off without the other soldats in the wings.

Silver light glowed from outside the broiling clouds, enclosing them inside. The building power of her heating blood deepened. Never had she felt such fire. Like her inner core liquified. As if every particle of her body cried out for more venom, then trembled when she couldn't provide.

Oh, no.

This wouldn't be good.

Einar abandoned the last injured soldat to the vittra, and turned his attention to Henrik. Oliver and Henrik stood against each other, weaponless, snarling with equal parts loathing. They shouted, circling.

Malcolm surged forward. One of his sleeves had been utterly ripped off. He panted, blood spilling from a wound on his shoulder, and another under his arm. Einar held out his hand, preventing Malcolm from advancing toward Henrik.

"No," he whispered. "This is Henrik's fight."

Malcolm, watching for only a moment, whirled around. Hoarse, he called, "Britt?"

Hand trembling, she touched his arm.

"Malcolm. Something is . . . wrong. The venom should last . . . longer."

He spun. Her teeth rattled. The vanishing venom swept her power away. Her legs locked, trembling. Shudders wracked her body from heel to shoulder. Bubbles broiled from the middle of the mud pool, exactly like her blood.

Malcolm scrambled to catch her invisible form as she collapsed.

Chapter Thirty Six

HENRIK

Waist-deep sludge gurgled around Henrik's stomach. He attempted to hold his arms above the fetid, burning waste as the vittra swirled off to the side, keening and watchful. The vicious old hag seemed genuinely interested in their spar. When her giant nostrils appeared in the whirlwind, they sniffed a draught of air that stirred up more currents.

Intrigued, or simply waiting.

The acrid water sloshed against a scrape along his back, stinging and horrendous. A fitting tribute to Britt's wounds, inflicted by his own Captain. He lunged for an attack, but Oliver sloshed away in deft avoidance. Desperation created greater speed than Henrik expected.

"You wanted to find Selma, you fool," Oliver snapped. "Why did you search?"

"You knew Selma?"

Oliver scowled. "I knew all the soldat mothers."

"How?"

"We watched you! We watch all potential soldat recruits. We know their strengths and weaknesses. We strive to serve His Glory from the very beginning. And Selma was a problem."

The words rippled in Henrik's mind. *Was a problem.* He didn't have the strength to ask why, but Oliver, clearly on a roll, continued with merciless regard.

"Selma never wanted to give you up, though you were the most promising of the cohort. You and Einar." He jerked a head back, his lips twisted in a sneer. "Son of a maid in your household."

Maid.

Your household.

"Einar and I arrived together?"

"Yes!" he cried. "You never left each other. You, the strongest of all of them, were the one I was convinced would be the one to follow in my shoes. You who showed such promise. How, Henrik? How did you go astray?"

The final word issued as a lost question. At this critical juncture, Oliver fell prey to his own frustration. He leaned into emotion, seeking the source of his own failure. He thought Henrik was the perfect *soldat*, like the son he couldn't raise on his own. He had plans for Henrik to create some sort of enduring legacy . . .

But Henrik's curiosity mucked up Oliver's plan. Instead of knuckling down and not asking questions like a good *soldat*, the year as a reefer created suspicions around Stenberg, His Glory's dealings, and other islands. Henrik developed relationships. A definitive no-no for *soldats*. Einar, for one. The captains he sailed with, for another.

Then the final one.

Britt.

To Oliver and his unerring hunger for control, the islanders in Henrik's life posed nothing but threats.

Oliver lunged, but Henrik splashed away, too lost in thought to do more than evade. Try as he might, he couldn't keep his insecurities, his queries, from streaming past.

"His Glory knew!" Oliver shouted. "His Glory knew you sought your mother in the Archives. Knew that the girl he met was associated with you. We knew it all along. We watched you from the moment you returned up until the whipping block. You were meant to rise up as His Glory's Second Captain. Of course he would vet you! You fool. You didn't even find the twenty bags of jord!"

"Where were they?"

"Not far!" Oliver cried. "They were a test of your thoroughness, and you failed. You distracted yourself with a woman and threw away everything."

"The child?" Henrik countered. "You had me find him to distract me."

"Yes," Oliver snarled. "So we could get to your ridiculous woman and demand what she knew. As a result, His Glory knows that he cannot trust you, and he's sent me to dispatch you. You bloody fool," he finished quietly.

"This ends now," Henrik ground out.

Oliver beckoned with a surly clasp of his hands.

"All six soldats are gone, Oliver," Henrik panted, circling him. The water lapped at his waist. Wails screamed behind him. "You've lost six of His Glory's personal guards. If you somehow manage to kill Einar, myself, and Malcolm, you'll never survive if you return. That's eight soldats you'll have to explain, and eight soldats His Glory will have lost. I'm sure that'll help him sleep, with the mainland stirring up problems and the other soldats ready to rebel."

Oliver attacked.

The water slowed him, allowing Henrik space to move. Instead of fighting the fluid, he eased into it, ducking and slipping away. Scalding drops spotted his cheeks. He wiped them off with a forearm, but they were replaced as Oliver frothed closer.

The heat billowed and radiated around the vittra, uncomfortably warm, but inescapable. The ground began to slip away beneath their feet. Trees canted, falling toward the spongy hole where the world sank. The gray fog tightened as it circled, moving slow, and then fast. The ikons gleamed, torrid green waypoints in the night.

Oliver scrambled to attack again, but Henrik moved too quickly. The water worked against them. Fog spiraled and a funnel formed, sucking and lowering. Oliver clutched a handful of Henrik's shirt, yanked him close. Henrik slammed his forearm into Oliver's elbow, forcing his hand to break grip.

They slipped away in the liquid. Henrik caught hold of Oliver's shirt, but Oliver twisted free with a sputter. Oliver grasped for Henrik again, roiling in and out of the water. A deluge of molten liquid poured over Henrik as Oliver shoved him under the water. He ducked the advance, surfacing before his former Captain, but was unable to get a grip and drown him.

In the distance, Einar and Malcolm stood off to the side, edging away from a forming whirlpool. Ground collapsed away from Henrik's feet. Oliver, popping out of the water a few steps away, hurried to the side. The vittra cackled, her hollow amusement ringing like bells. The sound felt like an ice blanket on scorched skin.

Was it acid swishing around his legs? Was it heat? Everything hurt as he clung to the side of the spiraling, whirling pool and into the draggled waters. Oliver, teeth clenched, launched himself across the forming whirlpool. He slammed into Henrik, taking them backward into the water.

Henrik struggled, hot liquid slipping between his lips. The foul taste expanded between his teeth. He slapped, lunged, kicked, flailed, but Oliver had an uncanny strength that legend remembered him for. They grappled in the superheated sludge.

A root appeared under Henrik's feet. He used it as leverage, shoved away in a burgeoning slide, and burst into the open air. Sludge drained out of his nose as he gasped. The top of Oliver's head bobbed to the surface. Henrik lunged for Oliver, though the attempt was weak. His hand grasped Oliver's throat, but the filthy swamp made his skin too wet. Oliver escaped with a shout and a shove.

Dirt crumbled, giving way to a spinning, sludgy heart. The collapsing middle of a black tunnel. Of hellspawn.

Down.

Down into a forming, spinning hole.

It whirled like a hurricane, collapsing all around it. Henrik angled toward the edge as the ground vanished. The vittra screeched. Her lanky black hair hung over skeletal arms and shoulders, swaying in the whirling maelstrom. As the ground crumbled, succumbing to the whirlpool, another root sprang free from the ground. Henrik lunged for it, gripping a knobby center, and held fast.

Oliver, flailing for purchase, held the edge of a boulder, head barely above the whirlpool skimming by. The maw had no end, the hungry devil. The vittra's howl rang above, ready to claim and consume their flesh. Old bones whipped past, drudged from the sand. The natives killed by Stenberg soldats, most likely.

How apropos.

Oliver, face blanched with a stroke of sudden terror, dove. He gripped Henrik's ankle, wrenching them down. Henrik clung to the roots with mucky hands. Attempts to kick Oliver off failed.

The vittra descended.

Henrik gritted his teeth, shouting as he wrapped his hand so tightly around the root that it cut into his palm. Oozing blood, as warm as the foul waters, compromised his hold. Through squinted eyes, he cast a look overhead.

Where was Britt?

The draguls?

Einar?

If they survived, it would be worth it. Einar would carry the soldats forward to something better. Britt would have saved her draguls, her brother. Henrik could go down with Oliver, and wasn't that right as well? If there was a life after this, he hoped to find Selma there.

One hand dropped. He looked down. Oliver, terrorized, screamed. His pale face lost all color, bleaching to white. A hiss broke through the ghoulish currents, whispering.

Henrik looked up, face-to-face with the vittra.

You.

A bony finger pointed at Henrik's heart.

I see you.

The spinning gray web blurred to nothing as the vittra's skinny finger hovered over his chest. A cracked fingernail, split down the middle and caked with tar, trembled. Her empty eyes had a life of their own.

"What do you want?" he asked. A whisper, but it roared amidst the blasts. They were in a cocoon as he dangled, perched above a cauldron of death, Oliver clutching greedily for purchase.

Peace.

"Can I give it?"

She paused, aged face canting. After an interminable time, she hissed, *Not you. You are not they. I see in your mind that you are not one of them. You cannot pay for the blood.*

The vittra plunged. She rushed through Henrik and toward Oliver, her swampy, icy spirit a welcome rush compared to the broiling heat. Quick as she whipped through, it ended. The vittra sped to Oliver.

A wordless scream wrenched from Oliver's lips as the vittra grabbed his clothing and tore him away. Henrik's legs swung over the whirlpool as Oliver's weight disappeared. The vittra plunged them into the abyss. Oliver's screams cut off all at once.

Henrik, relieved of his burden, grasped for another root. The gray, spinning walls abated. He hauled himself higher, thinking of Britt. Selma. His strength flagged, the heat was too great. As he struggled for another root, his grip failed. He fell.

A hand caught him.

A second.

A third.

He dangled over the open, spiraling chasm sweeping away sand and earth. Sea water poured in from somewhere, whipping to a frenzy of steam and cooling heat. The hands hauled him up.

He climbed.

Flailed.

Thrashed.

Each step brought him a little closer to the high ledge, closer to a new future. Like a final baptism, he burst out of the spiraling vortex and onto solid earth.

Chapter Thirty Seven

BRITT

The world passed in a strange dream.

Heat, then cold, breathed icy winter down her skin. It crackled all the way into her fingers and toes with shivery exhales. She sought warmth inside. Deep in her gut, her soul. None arrived. The glacial flow bathed her, and she shivered. The reopened wounds provided a painful anchor outside the hellish, freezing death. She could not succumb while everything throbbed with such totality.

Her own blood burned, burned, burned.

Twisting. Gutting. Wrenching.

The torrential cold returned.

Too frozen.

Much, much too frozen.

Tremors sprinted up and down her torso. They shook the small bones in her fingers, her wrists. She felt like a bag of bones, wielded in an ancient ceremony. Her teeth clacked. Blood and warmth leached from her skin. Another plunge into arctic waters. Too weak to protest, she endured. There was no fighting against this.

Except . . . something appeared.

What were those graying apparitions?

The hair on the back of her neck stood on edge as her body jostled. Her distant voice wanted to cry out in pain, but she couldn't. Nothing existed in her throat. No external manifestation of the thickening interior. Arms clutched her. Her body elevated, shifting. The muscles protested.

All became a blur.

Deeper, the cold fever sprouted. Like roots, seeking the hidden recesses and darkness, where the pain didn't exist.

Deeper.

Darker.

Deeper.

The venom dissipated. Something else beckoned. A quiet place, where the jostling didn't hurt. A quiet place, where still waters lay like dappled pewter. A quiet place, with no disturbing waves. A quiet place without the whisper of sound.

Deeper.

Into the quiet place, she sank.

Chapter Thirty Eight

HENRIK

Einar, a shade away from death, hauled Henrik onto the sand with both hands. Malcolm, with only one arm and teeth gritted, pulled him farther from the ledge. Henrik dropped to the inky earth, breathing deep.

The island shredded itself. Sand collapsed. Trees toppled. Branches hurtling by threatened to slice open his cheek. The three of them scrambled away from the widening whirlpool lip, twice as big as before. All wind slipped into its center as the ground drew to a single point of collapse where Oliver and the vittra had disappeared.

Over the shrieking wind, Henrik shouted, "We need to get to the beach!"

Einar gestured to the side. "We need to take her!"

Henrik's stomach sank.

"Her?"

Einar grimaced. "Britt."

Malcolm and Einar tripped toward a tree away from the whirlpool, one without signs of uprooting. He caught a glimpse of two ankles and the realization made his blood run cold.

"Shite!" he shouted. "What was she thinking?"

Malcolm stumbled behind them, a distinctly greenish hue

around the edge of his cheeks. One arm lay mangled at his side, white chunks of bone sliding out of the edge of perforated skin. He held it close, but bits of dark earth and blood sprinkled it. The glaze in his wide eyes spoke to shock, but at least he stayed upright.

Henrik put a hand on his uninjured shoulder. "Can you run?"

Malcolm grimaced, nodded.

Henrik ran a hand up Britt's invisible leg and to her shoulders. Her body shook with dangerous intensity. He scooped her into his arms. Her ice-cold skin, but feverish head, permeated the slime thickening his clothes.

How much venom had Denerfen injected?

Einar stood at Malcolm's uninjured side, an arm around his waist. His already swollen eye had doubled in both size and bruising. He'd be lucky to keep the eye. Malcolm cradled the broken arm to his chest, wrapped his other arm around Einar's shoulders, and gritted his teeth.

They plunged into the tearing jungle, which clawed at them with whipping vines, soaring branches. Ikons melted off the trees, their lime, metallic gleam descending down the trunk and forming metallic pools at the bottom. The trail wasn't hard to follow. A path of destruction led away from the whirlpool, all of it fomented by ikons. Had Britt activated each one on her way back to the fight?

Foolish woman.

Brave, too.

He braced himself against the wind, gratified that he could see her knees. Her thighs appeared a hint at a time, and a filthy, tattered dress. No blood thus far. They pressed on, into the dark night. As they hurried away from the vittra's lessening funnel, the wind ebbed. Hints of an opening in the trees lurked ahead.

Ever ahead.

Henrik dodged a flying tree branch. Malcolm shouted as Einar whipped the two of them to the side, narrowly avoiding a dropping tangle of vines. A warm squelch of something drew Henrik's attention down.

Blood.

It coated his arms, and Britt's dress. Her waist and elbows appeared. Crimson smeared all of it. The whip wounds seeped over his arms again. He'd never shake the horror of seeing it a second time—and all to save *his* life. Not in a thousand lifetimes.

"Shite," he muttered.

Henrik pressed harder, moving too fast to know if she breathed. Einar and Malcolm staggered to keep pace. Malcolm, shouting directions, guided them through the worst of the windy torrents and onto the beach.

Henrik skidded to a stop.

A pitch black sky swilled overhead, spiraling into a single, horrifically dark point behind them. No lightning or thunder accompanied the unnatural funnel, which pointed at the island and grew higher. Moonlight stained flying bones. Trees. Branches. Vines. Everything wheeled through the air, higher. The noxious tar odor had faded, and so had the worst of the wind, but they weren't safe yet.

Above it all, the vittra screamed.

"Bloody idiots!" a voice shouted. "I'm over here!" Lars raced toward them, cutting through sand. A terrified expression distorted his white face. "Get out of there! The vittra is destroying all of it."

Not far into the ocean bobbed a rowboat. The small vessel slipped around the beach, steered by no one. On the ship farther into the bay, a man with a brilliant, bright red beard and hair to match stood with one leg propped up.

"Pedr," Malcolm breathed. He fainted.

Lars sprinted over, slowing. He paused, looked at Malcolm, Einar, Henrik, the visible half of Britt, and swore under his breath.

"Get to the rowboat! I'll carry the Major. Can you make it?" Lars asked Einar.

Einar nodded through a grimace, one arm clutching his ribs.

Lars picked Malcolm up and darted away, lithe as a rabbit for a man his age. Einar stumbled in the sand, but stayed upright. At the rowboat, he collapsed.

Henrik stepped into the rocking rowboat with Britt in his arms. Blood trickled down his elbow, dripping as he carefully lowered. The rowboat jarred off the sand and into the water, pulled by unknown arcane. Waves slammed into the little hull, but the rowboat splashed quickly through with impressive adeptness.

Britt tight in his arms, Henrik watched the swirling cloud consume the island. Britt had overwhelmed the arcane, likely, by activating so many ikons at the same time. From farther away, the full measure of the Unseen island sprawled left and right. It was a U-shaped place, thick with jungle, white beaches, and the sinister growl of ancient rage. The destruction widened. Steam hissed. Waves clashed. Trees vanished into waves. Frenzies, the sailors would have called them.

A righteous sea storm.

Hovering above it all, the horrific, cinereal cloud localized over the top. The vittra's distant, drawn-out keening sang amidst the whistles and swirls of the storm.

From the ship, Britt's brother Pedr laughed and laughed.

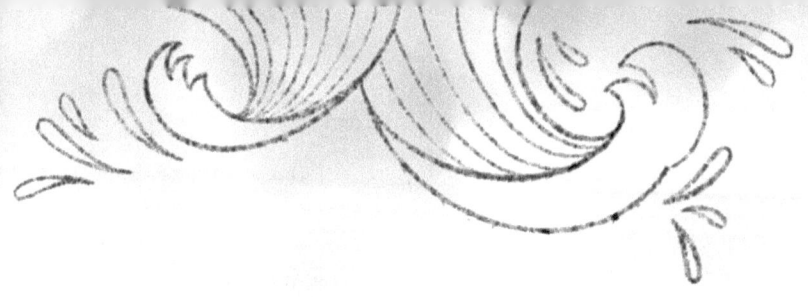

Chapter Thirty Nine

BRITT

T he petals of oblivion peeled away like an awakening
flower. Britt watched them disappear from shades of
ebony to murky gray. The lightening layers washed with
color. Dappled yellow, then gentlest umber.

Within the changing landscape, she sensed noise. A creaking,
restless groan. Her body tipped slightly to the left, and then the
right. The subtle motion was at once familiar, and most welcome.

A ship.

Smells surrounded her. They were . . . soothing. Pine. Brine.

Pedr.

Asleep, she thought. *I've been asleep.*

The brush of a tail whispered over her collarbone. It swept
across her neck and roused her from the plumbless depths. With
it, came an understanding of terrible and corporeal agony.

She *hurt.*

Everywhere.

The misery spared no portion of her body as she slid into
awareness. Raw and unremitting anguish. Forced to look away or
die, she turned her attention to her fingertips. They rubbed a soft
linen sheet, set atop a mattress. Feather ends poked her fingertips
from the mattress, prickling, yet velvety.

A groan wrenched from her throat. The deep hum resonated into her ribs in an undeniable sign of life. Memories stirred, but she fought to keep those at bay. She wanted to rest in this moment, not comprehend the overwhelming agonies. The moment she awoke, there would be no returning to calm. No peace existed for the angry pain.

"She's waking up."

At that voice, her eyes instantly flew open.

Sunshine poured into a room lined with wood. She lay near a wall, banners of sun falling on her clothes, staring into the anxious and calm eyes of a man she knew hardly at all, but better than anyone else.

Henrik.

A hint of a smile appeared on his full lips, decorated with relief, surrounded by the beginnings of a stubbled beard she wanted to touch. She'd seen so little relief in him before. He brushed a lock of hair out of her eyes, tucking it behind her ears. The tender gesture was at odds with the turmoil in his wrinkled lips.

"Britt?"

She blinked several times before recalling everything available to her memory. The whirling branches. The building storm. A vittra, screeching herself out of the confines of hell to roar into the present. Blank spots existed, though.

What of Oliver?

The soldats?

"Malcolm?" she whispered.

Henrik tilted his head back. "On the other cot." He winced. "He had a rather nasty arm break, and then all that horrid tar and paste got inside. Turns out, Lars isn't a bad doctor, and Pedr is a whiz with arcane, so all signs point to Malcolm's recovery. Eventually," he tacked on.

She licked dry lips, processing that.

"Tess?"

"Hasn't left Malcolm's side. I didn't know she was such a

vivid purple."

A hint of a smile surfaced.

"She's vivid purple in some spots," he amended, "though most has changed to a dark lavender. The bald spots are healing, too. Her scales have almost totally regrown."

Britt frowned. How long had she been asleep for Tesserdress to change so utterly? He anticipated her question.

"One week."

"But—"

"You had an infection."

Ah. That explained the rampant exhaustion and weakness. Carefully, she pressed her hand to her cool cheek.

"Den—"

Before she could get his full name out, her dragul head butted the underside of her jaw. She chuckled, brought a hand up. The movement caused a ripple of familiar pain down her back. She grimaced.

"It hurts?" Henrik asked.

Though tempted to lie—it would be a wasted effort, she never could hide her emotions from her face—she nodded.

"The wounds reopened. They might be in even worse shape than before, with all the swamp and tar."

"I can tell," she croaked. He brought a mug of water up to her mouth. Carefully, he helped her sip. A strange flavor tinted the water, tasting lightly of cardamom.

"Pedr put something in it. Told me to have you drink it up whenever you wake up. There's not much left."

Quizzically, she asked, "Have I awoken already?"

"Several times."

"I don't remember."

He smiled. "I know."

Reluctantly, she accepted the rest. Pedr would be the one to obey without question. He knew what to do, particularly with arcane and potions. She'd always trusted her older brother, but never more than today.

Henrik tipped her a surly glare. "You owe us a *lot* of explanations."

She smiled. "I know. First, tell me what happened. I want to know everything."

Henrik reached for her hand, enclosing it in both of his. Though calloused and tough, his grip was warm and gentle. She enjoyed the heat flowing into her fingers.

"Not yet."

"But—"

"Later." He shook his head. "It'll take you a bit to heal up, since we can't do the Tollybryck potion again. Pedr gave you his only supply. The whole story will take a while to explain, and you still aren't remembering much. We also want to hear yours," he added with a stern scowl. "Besides, we need Malcolm awake too. He's been in and out as much as you."

"Fair."

He added a soft, "I'm not going anywhere."

Blessed relief flowed through her, and so did something warm. Tingles rushed from her stomach out, prickling along her arms with reassurance. It left her feeling lightheaded. She floated above the clouds instead of rocking on the boat. Ah. The potion.

Of their own accord, her eyes drifted shut. Heavy treads entered the room, then Pedr's booming voice, made small in a restful whisper.

"She drank it?"

"All of it," Henrik said.

"Good. She'll sleep for a fair bit again, but she needs it if that back is to heal." His voice became more distant as Britt floated higher, ever higher. "We're on course for Calsica, as Einar has requested. I've slowed the currents around us, so the trip should take us two weeks. Which will give Einar, Malcolm, and Britt all the time they need to heal. Meanwhile, you can get a hold of your other soldats through Drake."

A WEEK LATER, Malcolm and Britt stood in Pedr's quarters. Einar and Henrik remained without, staring at the sea, discussing the burgeoning soldat rebellion and what to tell Captain Arvid when they saw him next.

Sparkling sunshine cut through Pedr's glass windows. They filled nearly every wall, except one. Few of the windows had curtains to provide privacy. As Pedr normally sailed alone, with only his arcane to aid him, he rarely had reason to require it.

The brilliant wooden cabin was a conglomeration of mahogany, cherry, and pine, all acquired from the mainland. The boards gleamed. Arcane kept it pristine, well cared for, despite the hammering sea. A lovely landscape awaited outside, with fluffy white clouds and endless water.

Pedr interrupted the calm scene. "I'd like to take a whip to you myself, Britt, after pulling a stunt like that on the Unseen island, with arcane as wild and vicious as I've ever known."

His threatening glower punctuated his violent words. For a moment, Britt considered the possibility that he *would* take a whip to her. She brushed it off. Pedr acted tough, but he had a kitten's heart.

"I know."

Malcolm sat across from her, his eyes slotted and burning with a frustrated fire. His arm, bandaged with fresh white linen and tied around one shoulder, was a bulky mess. "What were you thinking?" he hissed. "Activating every ikon? Calling the vittra?"

"*You* called the vittra too!"

"As part of a greater plan."

Coolly, she said, "I had a greater plan too. And it saved your life. And Tesserdress," she added, matching his tone. "Did you forget about her?"

Malcolm turned away.

Pedr tipped his head toward her in a slight concession, but the fire hadn't receded from his eyes. He leaned his hips against a desk, his palms propped behind him. The stance sprawled his shoulders wide, allowing Denerfen to lounge. Her dragul adored Pedr.

"Oliver might be missing," Pedr mused, tilting his head toward Denerfen to respond to a headbutt, "and fittingly so at the vittra's hands, but that doesn't mean that my anger about your whipping is appeased."

Her brow rose. "Missing?"

Darkly, Pedr said, "There's more to the arcane of that island and the vittra than you want to know."

"He might not be dead?"

Pedr shrugged.

"Pedr—"

He held up a hand, and she silenced. His eyes gleamed when he promised in a low purr, "In order to be sure, I'd have to speak with the Arcanist of Land, and Jordaire's a real bastid. The bastid knows the Follorat islanders' old arcane very well, though. I'm not asking him. For now, Oliver is not our problem. You won't distract me, Britt. After what Oliver did to you, I'm not done with Stenberg. Nothing you say is going to change my mind. If you made any friends there, I suggest you tell them to leave."

"Leave Stenberg alone," she snapped. "The islanders there are innocent."

He scoffed.

"If you want someone to punish, then punish His Glory."

Pedr folded his arms across his chest. "Don't think I don't have plans in motion already. That arcane-avoidant fool has more than just Burning Beard coming his way."

Reluctantly, Malcolm said through clenched teeth, "Shall we point out the dervish in the room? Henrik came through for us, as I never expected a soldat to do."

Pedr grinned. "Interesting, isn't he?"

Malcolm muttered incoherently.

"He's had a tough time of it," Pedr observed, quietly. "Dreams at night, you know. He's restless. Quiet. I think pitching his Captain to the vittra had a bigger effect on him than he'll admit."

In her head, Britt agreed. Not that Henrik made it easy to know, with his impassive expressions and offsetting smiles. He was social enough to stave off sheer isolation, but betrayed little depth in conversation.

Reluctantly, Henrik had filled her in on the events with Oliver, the vittra, the judgment the arcane old hag brought, and the words she whispered. *You are not one of them. You cannot pay for the blood.* Whether it meant he wasn't a soldat, a Stenbergian, or something else, they debated often.

Malcolm watched Britt closely.

"Protective, too." Pedr braced a hand around his chin, gaze tapering on Britt. "*Rather* protective. Does he have a reason to be?"

She straightened, but didn't know how to address such a question. Weeks had passed since the Unseen island and the vittra's wrath, but her wounds required more time to fully heal. Pedr had closed more than one spot with stitches. They tugged at her, annoyingly insistent. He'd remove them tomorrow.

"We're . . . friends," she said.

Pedr laughed outright. "General Helsing is going to hear about this mess with His Glory and Oliver and Henrik, I presume?" he asked, and she was glad to change the subject. He stared hard at Malcolm, and his question was too aloof to be innocent.

Britt held up two hands. "I'm not telling her."

"Not me!" Malcolm cried.

Pedr shrugged. "Too bad, little brother. Auntie dearest is your problem. Forgive me. I meant to call her General Helsing."

Ten years their senior, and with no parents to guide the three of them, Pedr had always ruled more like a father than a brother. General Helsing, their hostile old aunt, had provided physical necessities and structure, but little else.

Malcolm scowled, unwilling to press Pedr's authority.

"Fine."

"You have to talk to her, anyway," Pedr pointed out. "Won't Major Helsing have to give a report on his captivity?"

Malcolm's glare glittered beneath hooded lashes. Pedr laughed, the full-bodied sound rippling through the room. He set a large, gentle hand on Malcolm's good shoulder.

"Congratulations on the promotion, surviving a battle, imprisonment, and a vittra. With war on the inevitable horizon, the soldats falling to pieces, and an open rebellion on Stenberg, sounds like you have an illustrious career ahead. With any luck, you'll rule better than General Helsing and boot her out of power for the rest of our sakes."

Pedr turned to Britt. His brow rose. "Are you finally going to accept my offer and live on the seas with me? You can bring your dragul. I wouldn't mind Denerfen living on my ship. Might be safer for him, anyway, with the hellfire that's about to descend. You can join me in the Westlands."

Her teeth sank into her bottom lip. What a siren call. *The Westlands.* A secretive, mysterious place, where sailors departed to explore and never returned. He always chased the Westlands.

Only Pedr.

Rumors whispered of protective, dark arcane and ice mountains and pillared forests and an unending stretch of caves below hardened rock that never ceased its oddities. Only Burning Beard had ever returned, thus cementing his reputation.

"Is that where you came from?" she asked.

He only smiled.

"You don't know how tempting it is," she drawled, "but, no. I can't. Not yet."

Pedr betrayed no surprise. He stacked his hands behind his back and leaned on them, his curious gaze fixed on her.

"You know the offer is always open?"

She nodded.

"What next for you then, Britt?" Malcolm asked.

Outside of Pedr's cabin, the rest of Burning Beard's ship unfolded. From his personal berth, Pedr had a full view of everything: main mast, sails, deck, bow sprint. Down below, Henrik leaned on the railing, hair tousled by the wind.

"I have a woman named Selma to find," she said with growing resolution. "And apparently, she's on the mainland."

Chapter Forty

HENRIK

Water slapped the hull of the rowboat.

It squeaked around, sloshing, splashing. The cool droplets were a welcome antithesis to the heat of the day. Henrik navigated the vessel with two oars, grateful to tug, pull, work. It soothed the building angst, created by nightmares of hot tar that woke him in the middle of the night. When his dreams jerked him awake, Britt's hand always held his in silent comfort. Her touch soothed enough to fall back asleep.

"Don't worry about my ship," Pedr had said as Henrik lowered into the rowboat ten minutes prior. Britt stood next to Pedr, Denerfen perched on a shoulder. "They can't see us. Also, don't worry about finding us. Just row out from the island. I'll pull you to me."

Henrik didn't bother asking how. Arcane teemed and sploshed off this boat, which was both infused, sealed, and brimming with it. He didn't have a single idea how Pedr managed to tug and pull ocean currents or what it meant. Knew only that he didn't dare touch anything. He was learning that, with Pedr, one never knew.

So Henrik rowed, grateful for the rigorous workload easing his pent-up agitation that two weeks on the sea built.

Twenty minutes later, the rowboat hit bottom on the edge of

Calsica, the lawless island home for pirates just outside main Stenberg. Somewhere out here, ship captain Ossian should await. Henrik stabilized the rowboat, but needn't have bothered. One body, then a smaller, more slender second body, stole out of the shadows and to the prow. Hoods pulled over their heads, they settled inside the rowboat next to each other.

Timmer.

Agnes.

Two others appeared, one at a time. Then two more. A second rowboat, manned by Lars, pulled up to Henrik's side. Eleven bodies entered the skiffs.

"Everyone here?" Henrik whispered.

Timmer affirmed with a nod. "Hungry, tired, cold, but here. We've been hiding since Oliver ambushed Einar and took him away. The rebellion we planned paused until we knew what happened. We barely escaped Stenberg. Without Agnes, we'd be fish chum."

Henrik absorbed that with a nod. Amongst the waiting faces lurked Harald, too. The others Henrik couldn't see, not yet. A miracle they'd all managed to survive. The two skiffs rowed back.

Vanished.

No one said a word as they worked toward Burning Beard's ship, which appeared like a mirage as they drew closer. Pedr stood near the wheel, one leg propped on a stand, wind in his ginger hair as he stared out. Britt waited at the railing. As they approached, she threw a long netted rope overboard.

Henrik gripped it, held tight. Agnes stood, grasped the rope, and tore up the ladder with surprising speed. Timmer, following close behind, slapped Henrik on the shoulder and began after her.

Two large hands appeared at the top of the ship, grasped Agnes under the arm, and hauled her the rest of the way. She cried with relief, throwing herself into Einar's awaiting arms and disappearing from sight.

Within an hour of arrival, Burning Beard's ship dissipated quietly into the night.

WHILE THE OTHER soldats that followed Captain Arvid reunited with Einar, who had fully recovered and wouldn't release Agnes, Henrik stole along the ship and up to the helm. Pedr awaited.

Pedr sent him a sidelong glance. "Narpurra?"

"Narpurra. The other soldats will join Arvid. Timmer left a message with the remaining soldats alerting them to the circumstances surrounding the deaths of Captain Oliver and the other soldats. He told them first to give them a chance to find their way to Narpurra and join, if they want. Eventually, word will get through the ranks. Supposedly, Arvid has an inside person on the island that works close to His Glory. "

"Think his Royal Turd already knows?"

Henrik's lips twitched. "His Glory might know something is wrong with Oliver, but I doubt he'll understand the particulars. We don't have many drakes."

Pedr snorted. "He knows. Just needs it confirmed."

Henrik shrugged. The world tended to view His Glory as a deity; the literal son of the sea god. Henrik had growing doubts.

Pedr reached out to a line, touched it. Swirls of green light sped from his fingertips and higher, zipping through the twisting strand that ended at the sail. The sails moved. Pedr touched another knot of ropes. Amethyst zipped past, into the tops, and more shifting occurred.

"But *you* are not going to Narpurra," Pedr stated, and there was no question.

"Not me."

"To the mainland?"

Henrik hesitated, jaw tight. His thoughts swirled around Britt, Selma, Erik, his father, and all the ghosts that Oliver stirred up. The mainland hid answers. Possibly his mother. The daunting thought of going there was not fun. Neither was the vast, floating chasm of freedom.

Freedom.

The word didn't make sense. What was he supposed to do with it? What now? He didn't understand, so Henrik latched onto the one thing that made sense.

"Britt is determined to find Selma, so wherever your sister is going, that's where you'll find me."

Epilogue

PEDR

The tang of the sea spray hit Pedr like a slap. He closed his eyes, relished it. The thick air swirled like mist through his lungs, a soothing balm as steady as the slap of water against the hull. It would rain soon.

Welcome back to Kapurnick, he thought.

When he opened his eyes again, he regarded Malcolm, Britt, and Henrik's retreating forms. They'd already docked the rowboat at the pier and approached the main island. Kapurnick's jagged black-teeth mountains, gauzy drapes of greenery, and sparkling beaches awaited. He thought he remembered the sand between his toes.

He banished the recollection. No need to torture himself with what he couldn't have. Besides, it's not like Britt walked toward anything that he wanted . . .

. . . or so he tried to convince himself.

Their aunt awaited, and she was the last person he'd want to see.

A sharp pang shot through his left wrist. He glanced down, found he gripped the wheel with white knuckles, and released it. Shite, but it was embarrassing how stressed out Kapurnick made him.

Rain began to dot his shoulders. From behind him, Einar drawled, "So . . . you're not going ashore."

Einar leaned against the side of the ship with his arms folded over his chest. Pedr sent him a glare. The elongated tone meant Einar hadn't asked a question, but tested a statement of fact. Pedr liked Einar, but it wouldn't take much prodding and answer-seeking to change that.

Somewhere in the background, a gentle shuffle and churn of movement meant Agnes prepared to go to shore. Eventually. Britt, because she had a good head on her shoulders, wanted to test their aunt's general disposition first.

Rabid dowager of a woman, General Helsing.

"Aren't you from here?" Einar asked. Einar knew that answer already, so Pedr didn't bother confirming it.

Pedr shoved away from the wheel, striding toward the front of the ship. He reached down, tapped three different boards in a shanty-like ditty with the tips of his fingers. Lights illuminated the woodwork beneath his feet with each tap, fading as quickly as it appeared. A cranking, groaning sound moved below, followed by the clank of metal on metal.

Then a splash.

Kapurnickkian waters weren't as shallow as Narpurra, but Pedr still didn't want to tie up at the pier. Technically, his boat could never be truly grounded. The arcane backed him out of the most impossible situations, which meant he could moor at the harbor instead of in the bay, but no reason to draw attention to his powers.

Particularly with Einar on deck.

Amused, Einar glanced over the side of the ship, where the anchor currently sank. There were a lot of strange things about his ship, if one looked close enough. When one commanded the arcane, one didn't require logic.

"The ship to Narpurra," Einar continued, as if they had a rousing conversation, "won't leave in the upcoming storm. The other soldats are disappointed, but they're excited to get there."

The soldats Pedr had escorted off of Calsica and over to Kapurnick emptied the moment he stopped the ship. They'd already clambered aboard another one, ready for Narpurra. His two rowboats returned, empty. The ship vanished in the settling ocean fog.

Thrumming rain danced on his deck, splashing a lovely staccato. It would deluge soon, which meant he could refill some of his fresh water supply. Pedr slapped two boards and a rope. The crank of opening holes followed. The rainwater would sluice down the slightly-slanted decks and into the collection holes, which meant one less thing he'd have to ask of the old steelback General Helsing.

"You know," Einar mused, contemplative, "no one believes in Arcanists anymore, and isn't that a shame? Strange how the four most powerful wielders of the arcane could just . . . vanish into folklore."

Pedr straightened. A definitive undertone existed in Einar's words. The former-soldat had a wise eye and a keen understanding of situations, regardless of what context he knew. Troublesome.

Thankfully, Pedr's saving grace came in the form of a light voice.

"Einar?"

Einar's attention immediately snapped to Agnes. She appeared at the bottom of the ladder leading to the forecastle with a broad smile. Her dress, as emerald as the Kapurnickian waters that Pedr's once-home island was so known for, sashayed to Einar's side. Perhaps *floated* was the right term. Agnes moved like air. Soft. Flowy. Constantly shifting.

Einar slipped an arm around her waist and hooked her into his side with a low growl. She giggled and the sound made Pedr sick. He turned away, his stomach in knots. The wash of emotions that followed was a swamp. Jealousy. Rage. Resentment. Longing. Desire.

Mila, he thought.

Nope.

No.

Not . . . he couldn't . . . that was . . .

Pedr turned toward the stern, filling his mind with waterborne obligations. He needed to activate the arcane to lower the sails, check their food rations, and try not to look at the black mountains he longed to climb.

But he couldn't.

That foul old curse that tied him to his ship . . .

No matter how hard he tried, Pedr couldn't block the sound of Agnes dancing with Einar in the rain. The rain pounded relentlessly, soaking them through. Pedr couldn't retreat to his berth fast enough. He couldn't wait to break this curse.

And break it, he would.

The Queens and the Kings

THE ISLES SERIES BOOK 2

We have an *epic* tale waiting for you in the next book!

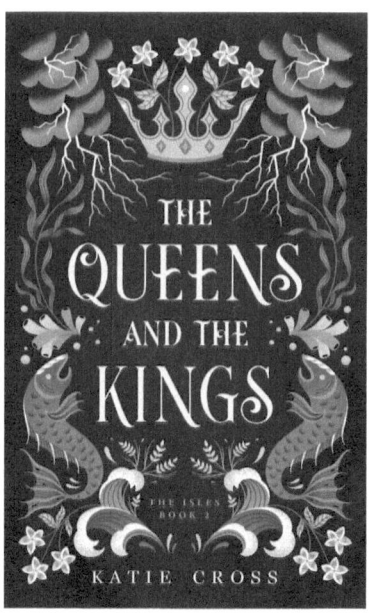

You can purchase your copy at www.katiecrossbooks.com or online retailers everywhere.

Yours in magic,

Katie Cross

About the Author

Katie Cross is ALL ABOUT writing epic magic and wild places. Creating new fantasy worlds is her jam.

When she's not hiking or chasing her two littles through the Montana mountains, you can find her curled up reading a book or arguing with her husband over the best kind of sushi.

Visit her at www.katiecrossbooks.com for free short stories, extra savings on all her books (and some you can't buy on the retailers), and so much more.